CPSIA information can be obtained at www.ICGtesting.com
Printed in the USA
BVOW040915070313

314963BV00001B/1/P

9 781619 210639

Praise for Barbara Elsborg's *Worlds Apart*

"This love triangle that morphs into mutual polyamory has numerous hooks, not the least of which is the playful tone, quotes from Teddy Roosevelt, and interesting sex sandwich situations including all orifices. A satisfying conclusion lays all fears to rest."

~ *Library Journal*

"*Worlds Apart* was funny, and charming, and even heart wrenching at times. The plot development was fantastic, and the characters were so intriguingly wonderful. I highly recommend *Worlds Apart* to someone looking to take the leap into the world of Menage a trois."

~ *Sizzling Hot Book Reviews*

"I don't want to give away too much, but if you enjoy MMF or like MFM and have never read any MMF, this is a way to get your feet wet so to speak. The sex scenes sizzle and had this reviewer panting a few times."

~ *Guilty Pleasures Book Reviews*

"All the main characters (and the minor ones) are wonderful, fully developed people, who will have the reader, laughing, crying and hoping for an HEA... This is an absolutely wonderful book. A definite keeper."

~ *Love Romances and More*

Look for these titles by

Barbara Elsborg

Now Available:

Cowboys Down

Worlds Apart

Worlds Apart

Barbara Elsborg

Samhain Publishing, Ltd.
11821 Mason Montgomery Road, 4B
Cincinnati, OH 45249
www.samhainpublishing.com

Worlds Apart

Print ISBN: 978-1-61921-063-9
Digital ISBN: 978-1-60928-830-3

Editing by Sue Ellen Gower
Cover by Angela Waters

First Samhain Publishing, Ltd. electronic publication: May 2012
First Samhain Publishing, Ltd. print publication: April 2013

Chapter One

Taylor stared at the two smiling faces on his computer screen. His parents looked tanned, fit and healthy. So they should, having spent the last five years living in an up-market golfing retirement community in Spain. Taylor didn't begrudge them their happiness. They'd waited long enough before they'd reached out for it, and a part of him wished they'd done it sooner.

"Stop scowling," said his mother.

Bloody Skype. Taylor rearranged his features into a smile.

She harrumphed. "Now you look like a chimpanzee. And you need your hair cut."

Taylor glowered. "I don't have time to do this."

"We don't ask for much, Taylor," his father snapped.

A splash of guilt wrapped its tentacles around his heart. "I don't *want* to do it." *Shit.* That sounded more like a whine than an authoritative refusal.

"I don't see what the issue is," said his father. "It's just until we sell. A few months at the most. The estate agent reckons we'll get a much better price if the house is tidied up a little and lived in."

"I already have a place to live," Taylor said through gritted teeth.

"But I thought you were staying temporarily with a friend," his mother oh-so-bloody-helpfully pointed out.

Taylor glanced at the bedroom door. His current *friend* was crying in her bathroom because he wasn't making an effort in their relationship. Taylor wasn't sure two weeks qualified as a relationship. He'd only moved in with her because he had to vacate his flat.

"We wouldn't have asked if you'd still been living in London, but now that you're back in Leeds, you're on the doorstep," his mother said.

"It isn't just the tidying up," said his father. "The remaining contents of the house need to be dealt with. Take some photos and email them. I'll send a list of what we want to keep, either to send out

here or put in storage. The rest can go to auction, be given to charity, or if there's anything *you* want to keep..."

"There's still stuff you want after all this time?" Taylor regretted the question even before he saw the shadow cross their faces. There was one thing they'd want until the day they died, though it wasn't in the house. *Christ, he hoped not.*

"Probably not, but we'd still like you to check," said his father.

"Why can't *you* come back and sort things out?" Taylor asked, though he already knew the answer.

"Because the deal on this cruise is too good to miss. A hundred days at sea? It will be fantastic. We're getting a huge discount and your father's looking forward to lecturing again."

And *that* wasn't the answer.

It had taken them a long time before they could bring themselves to leave Sutton Hall, and five years away from the place before they could bear to sell it. It wouldn't kill him to help them, and it would solve the immediate problem in the bathroom who was no doubt practicing weeping without smudging her mascara.

"You don't need to worry about the garden. We have someone dealing with that. What *is* that noise?" his father asked. "Is there a cat in pain?"

The crying had grown louder. Taylor picked up his laptop and moved to the kitchen.

"Goodness, I thought we were at sea already," his mother said with a laugh after he put the laptop on the table.

"You can run ICU from the hall just as easily, can't you?" his father asked.

Taylor glanced at the boxes piled up against two walls of the small kitchen, floor to ceiling. Since he tended to meet his clients on neutral ground, he could run his private investigations company from anywhere. Until this call from his parents, he'd been planning to decamp into a hotel.

His mother sighed. "If we knew you were there looking after the house and taking care of everything, it would lift such a weight from our shoulders."

And pile it on mine. His mother had gone for the jugular—guilt. Responsibility, duty, care—the words might not have been spoken, but Taylor knew when he was beaten.

"All right," he said in as grudging a voice as he could muster.

"Fantastic." His father looked at his mother and smiled before the pair turned to face him. "Thank you, Taylor."

His mother waved. "Thank you, sweetheart."

"Niall's the name of the chap doing the garden," his father said. "He's been working in lieu of rent. Gas, electricity and water's on. We'll be in touch when we get back."

They cut the connection before Taylor could ask what the hell *that* meant. Not the getting in touch but the—

"Tay...lor," hiccupped a feeble voice.

He turned to see Sophie standing in the doorway. Taylor noticed that despite her professed devastation, she'd changed into the new red underwear she'd spent thirty minutes admiring last night. It probably cost a fortune and was little more than three small triangles that barely covered— *Shit.* He felt a surge of lust and mentally slapped his cock down. She might be crying, but she was also scheming.

Red-eyed and sniffing, Sophie stepped toward him. "We need to talk."

Four words guaranteed to strike terror into most guys' hearts, but not Taylor's, because frankly, he didn't give a fuck. He'd had enough of sitting on her couch being forced to watch cookery programs when there was never anything to eat in the fridge, enough of waiting to use the bathroom while she plucked and polished and pouted, enough of her brushing her hair exactly one hundred times before she came to bed. Heaven forbid he interrupted her, or she started again, claiming he'd made her lose count. He was surprised she could count that far. The sex had been pretty good, but there were plenty more women out there. Anyway, he'd fulfilled his guilt quota for today in agreeing to help his parents.

"Please," Sophie said.

"There's nothing else to say." Taylor closed his laptop, put it in the nearest box and carried it to the door.

"But I love you," she whispered.

Christ. Two weeks and she thought she loved him? She didn't even know him.

In the fifteen minutes it took to call a cab and carry all his possessions down to the foyer of Sophie's apartment building, she shot through the five stages of grief.

"You don't mean it. You're just trying to teach me a lesson."

"You fucking, selfish, wanking, arsehole bastard of a..." Taylor

didn't think he'd heard her swear before and his interest piqued. He stared at her expectantly, but she ran out of cuss words and moved on to bargaining.

"If you stay, I'll let you watch football on TV."

"If you don't stay, I'll kill myself."

The hopeful look he shot her didn't go down well. Taylor should have known she couldn't take the joke.

"Fine, fuck off then and I hope you rot in hell."

Of course he would, but he planned on having a good time before that happened. Her final comment was the point on which he'd hoped to leave, but as he glanced around and picked up the last of his things, she started at the beginning again.

"So what would you like for dinner? Shall we go out?"

Taylor sighed. With his job, he ought to be better at getting people to see sense, but the problem was in this instance, he wasn't being paid for it and he just didn't care. He didn't do involved, he didn't do emotion. It made life simpler. He took her key from the bunch in his pocket—coincidence it was next to the one for Sutton Hall?—and pressed it into her hand.

"Thanks for everything," he said, and walked out.

"Fuck off," she screamed. "I never want to see you again, you...dick brain."

She probably had that right. The door slammed behind him.

The taxi waited at the curb and the driver gave him a hand to load his stuff. It filled the trunk, the backseat and front passenger seat. Taylor told the driver to follow him, gave him the address in case, and carried the last couple of boxes to his BMW in the underground parking.

It had been a mistake to stay with Sophie. Usually, Taylor never went out with the same woman for more than a couple of dates, and that was only if he hadn't gotten into her pants on the first. He'd never moved in with a woman before. He could see why now. Sophie had caught him at a low spot. Taylor had needed to vacate his apartment, but the one he'd hoped to make his home had been unexpectedly taken off the market. He put most of his stuff into storage and only brought what he needed. The couple of nights he'd intended to stay with Sophie drifted to two weeks, mostly because he'd had a lot happening with work and he was too busy to sort out an alternative. Really, the request from his parents couldn't have come at a better time.

Except the idea of living at Sutton Hall filled him with as much dread as the word commitment. Maybe more.

The taxi followed him along the A65 to Ilkley. On the way, Taylor rang his personal assistant.

"Hi, Taylor, had you not noticed it's Saturday?" Emma asked.

"God, is it?" He smiled. "I've moved out of Sophie's and I'm moving into my parents' house in Ilkley. For the time being, I'm going to run ICU from there."

"Oh great. So I don't have to work from the two square inches of Sophie's kitchen table anymore. Do I get four square inches at your parents'?"

"There's a room we can use as an office."

Emma's heavy sigh told him she wasn't happy.

"What?" he asked.

"That's a lot farther for me to travel."

Taylor sucked in his cheeks. "So start half an hour later."

Emma sighed again. "Okay. What's the address?"

"Sutton Hall, Thorpe Lane. It's on the Middleton side of town."

"See you Monday."

Taylor pressed the button to end the call. He'd worried Emma might not want to come so far out of Leeds. Half an hour was a small price to pay. He then called Jonas, his friend and sole operative.

"Hi, what's up?" Jonas asked.

When Taylor told him, Jonas laughed. "About time you dumped Sophie. Bird from hell, that one. I'll see you on Tuesday. I'm in court on Monday."

"Plead guilty."

"Very funny."

Taylor ended the call. Jonas was giving evidence in an insurance swindle case in London. A guy had set fire to his premises and Jonas had taped him admitting it. Taylor turned right at the lights, drove down the hill to cross the river where he'd played as a boy and up a steeper hill until the sharp turn onto Thorpe Lane. He took a meandering path down the rutted lane, trying to avoid the worst of the potholes. Some of them looked big enough to swallow his car.

By the time he pulled in through the weatherworn gateposts, his heart was banging in his chest. He glanced at the giant stone acorns

that topped the posts and remembered how, as a kid, he'd imagined huge squirrels salivating over them. The rusty gates were still attached—just—and Taylor continued up the drive, his hands tightening on the wheel. He'd spent eighteen years of his life here before he'd left to go to university, and in the seven years his parents had continued to live here, he'd only returned for brief visits. Since they left for Spain five years ago, he hadn't been near the place.

He drove along the avenue of trees fronted by overgrown rhododendron bushes, and when the house came into view, his heart clenched. Taylor loved and hated Sutton Hall in equal measure. He'd lived here for fourteen happy years and then four hellish ones. He never thought he'd call this place home again.

Taylor pulled up on the sweep of gravel in front of the stone steps and the taxi stopped behind him.

"Quite a place," said the driver as he lifted Taylor's boxes out of the cab.

Constructed well over a hundred years ago from gray Yorkshire stone, Sutton Hall was a three-story, seven-bedroom monster with a turret, crenellated battlements, and a higgledy-piggledy roofline that would make an architect cringe. Taylor swept his gaze over the house. The windows were dirty, the paint cracking and the drainpipe next to the drawing room hung loose. *Oh fuck.* It looked old, tired and miserable, which was about how Taylor felt.

He paid the driver and walked up the steps to the front door. Once the taxi left, Taylor let himself in. He braced for the smell of mildew and old age, and instead inhaled the faint tang of freshly baked bread. He shook his head. Had to be his imagination recalling his mother's baking. He'd always come home from school to fresh baked biscuits or carrot cake or scones. Until he was fourteen, anyway.

Taylor took in the shabby carpet, grimy mirror and the few dust-covered items of furniture, and sighed. His attention was drawn to the only splash of color, a vase of bright yellow and white flowers that sat on a table at the foot of the flowing staircase. Fake flowers that had somehow avoided dust bunnies.

His phone rang and Taylor pulled it out of his pocket. "ICU Investigations, Taylor Sutton speaking."

He tucked the phone between his head and shoulder while he carried his boxes and bags into the hall from outside.

"Do you follow people?" asked the male caller.

"Yes," Taylor said, wishing for a change it was someone looking for

buried treasure or some old book on fly fishing.

"I need you to track my wife."

"What do you want to know about her?"

"If she's cheating on me."

How good would it feel, just for once, to be surprised by the answer to that question too? Was the world full of cheating partners? Taylor might have the morals of an alley cat, but he didn't sleep with two women at the same time. Well, not unless it was actually *at* the same time.

"And what are you going to do with the information once you have it?" Taylor put another box down in the hall.

"If she's screwing someone, I'll fucking kill the bitch."

Taylor went as cold as if he'd stepped into a snowstorm. "I'm not the guy for you." He ended the call.

Usually husbands *thought* that unattractive sentiment rather than vocalized it, but although Taylor wanted the work, he wouldn't take the chance of a partner resorting to violence after he'd received the surveillance report. Bad enough that people were hurt emotionally by what Taylor did without him making it worse. He shrugged. Maybe he wasn't the heartless bastard most thought him to be. He remembered Sophie and the others, and his smile faded. Yes he was. He didn't know why he behaved so badly with women. There was no way he'd ever get married if he didn't manage more than a couple of dates with the same one. Whenever he thought he was getting close to someone, and there'd been a couple he'd really liked, he fucked it up.

With all his bags inside and the door closed, Taylor sighed. He walked over to look at the flowers on the hall table and absentmindedly picked up the telephone next to them. He frowned when he heard the dial tone. What the hell were his parents thinking? Hadn't they cancelled the line rental? And where was that smell coming from?

Taylor put the phone down and stared at the flowers. Then he bent and sniffed them. *Christ, they're real.*

He heard someone pounding down the stairs and turned. A guy who looked the same age as him skidded to a halt at the bottom and held out his hand.

"Taylor." The man almost exhaled his name.

Taylor stared into unusual green eyes, took in the wide smile and eager expression, and uncharacteristically found himself lost for words. The guy was the same height as him, slim and very good

looking. He had untidy dirty-blond hair, sharp cheekbones and smooth skin. His white linen shirt hanging loose over faded jeans matched Taylor's attire, except Taylor's shirt was tucked in.

"Your parents did tell you I'm working on the garden?"

His father's parting words echoed in Taylor's head. "Yes."*Oh Christ, and living here.* He searched for the name and found it. "Niall."

Taylor found his hand being energetically shaken. Niall looked at him expectantly, his face and body tense as though he was waiting for something to happen. Taylor had no idea what.

He employed his usual technique of silence and eventually Niall sagged.

"How long have you been living here?" Taylor asked. He wondered if his parents had even met this guy.

"Six months."

Which was coincidentally how long Taylor had been back in Yorkshire.

"Want a hand with your things? A drink? Some lunch?" Niall asked.

"The boxes can wait until I've had a look around. Lunch would be great. Then you can explain how you come to be living in my parents' house."

Niall nodded and headed for the kitchen. Taylor turned the other way and pushed open the door to the drawing room. Everything was the same as when his parents had lived there and yet everything was different. Without them, the couches looked old and lonely and the fireplace unwelcoming. Even so, it didn't look as though the place had been empty for five years. Maybe Niall had worked on the house as well as the garden.

As Taylor moved from room to room, he forced himself to think about the happy times, when he and his father had set up a racing track that ran down the stairs and around the dining room. They'd persuaded his mother to leave it up for weeks and she'd vacuumed around it. The real Christmas tree smothered with homemade decorations had always stood in the hall, filling the air with the scent of pine, while an artificial one with more refined decorations graced the drawing room. But there had been no tree of either sort after Taylor's fourteenth birthday.

The orangery, used for formal meals, was not the light, airy room he remembered. It was so full of plants and flowers it was hard to spot

the furniture. The foliage had run riot, giant ferns competing for space with a banana plant and citrus trees. How the hell had they survived? Where did they get their water?

Taylor glanced into the breakfast room and was surprised to see a desk and chair in there. His father must have converted it into a study, and Taylor saw it would be perfect for his office. He'd just need another smaller desk for his PA. As soon as he'd sorted the house out, he'd start looking for an office in Leeds. Since he'd moved up from London, it had been easier to run ICU from his apartment, but he needed a break between work and leisure. Taylor ignored the kitchen where he could hear Niall clattering and went upstairs. It felt...wrong having some stranger in the house, as if it were Niall's house and not Taylor's.

His parents' bedroom looked untouched as did his. Everything in the Spanish villa was new. Taylor liked it, liked the idea of a fresh start for them, but he recalled being surprised how little they'd taken to Spain from the UK. It was as though once his parents had decided to move, they wanted all links severed. Taylor closed the door of his room, sat on the bed and took out his phone to call them. No answer. *What a fucking surprise.* Taylor was annoyed he hadn't registered his father's comment more clearly. What the hell were his parents thinking letting this guy live here?

With no sign of any other bedroom being occupied, Taylor headed toward the stairs leading to the third floor. Before he stepped onto them, he turned and went back down. He might not want the guy in the house, but he had no right to invade his privacy.

When he walked into the kitchen, Niall turned and smiled. The light in his face made the breath catch in Taylor's throat. He was a really good-looking guy. Taylor swallowed hard and let his gaze fall to the old wooden table where he'd eaten so many meals. What looked like freshly baked bread sat next to a dish of butter. There was a plate of sliced tomatoes sprinkled with basil leaves and topped with wedges of torn mozzarella, a bowl of crisp, mixed lettuce, a dish of hummus and another dip he didn't recognize, and a wooden board holding cheddar, Brie and Stilton cheese. It looked delicious and Taylor was unaccountably annoyed. This was *his* house—well, his parents' house—not the bloody gardener's.

He slumped at the table and grabbed a plate.

"What would you like to drink?" Niall asked. "I have beer, wine, champ—"

"Water," Taylor snapped, though he could have murdered a beer.

And champagne? What was that about?

Niall filled two glasses and sat opposite.

"I assume my parents told you I was coming," Taylor said in a gruff voice. "They want me to tidy things up before the house is sold. So I'll be living here for the foreseeable future." He was about to add that he could deal with the garden as well as the house and that Niall could leave, but the words died in his throat because firstly, he had zero interest in gardening and secondly, he realized what his parents had done. They knew how hard this would be, coming back here. Having someone else in the house would help dispel the ghosts.

"The lettuce, basil and tomatoes come from the garden," Niall said. "I can show you—"

"I remember where it is." Taylor knew he was being rude, but something about this guy made him...uncomfortable, on edge, nervous. "How did you come to be living here?"

"I'm a friend of your parents. I was helping with the garden before they moved to Spain and they asked me to keep an eye on everything. When I had to leave the place where I was living, they let me move in here."

Taylor swallowed a forkful of tomato and mozzarella and restrained his sigh of pleasure. Proper buffalo mozzarella, not the cheap stuff. And the bread—he could eat the whole loaf. "How come they've never mentioned you?"

"I asked them not to tell anyone. I'm...hiding." Niall dropped his gaze.

Taylor's fork froze on the way to his mouth. *What the hell?* "From the police? Have you committed a crime?"

"No and no. It's a family thing." Niall's fingers tightened around his fork. "I won't intrude on your life. I'll keep myself to myself on the top floor. When I'm not in the garden, I'm reading, so don't worry that I'll be playing hard rock in the attic. I'm no Robin Trower."

The fact that Niall knew of Robin Trower sent him up in Taylor's estimation and a smile slipped across his lips. "Me neither. Do you play the guitar?"

"I used to."

"Like riding a bike," Taylor said and was rewarded with another smile.

By the time they'd analyzed Trower's talent, discussed his channeling of Hendrix's bluesy style, and debated which album was

his best, Taylor had begun to relax. He liked Niall. His droll sense of humor made him laugh and the fact that Niall had secrets too somehow made Taylor feel more comfortable. They could have their own lives and yet share one together. Taylor hadn't lived with anyone since he left home, but the more he thought about it, the better it felt to have someone with him in this house.

After Niall helped haul his boxes either into the office or up to Taylor's room, Taylor felt as though they'd been friends for years. They'd settled into an easy camaraderie.

"Want to come and look at the garden?" Niall asked.

Taylor followed him out of the back door. Sutton Hall sat on about an acre, much of it trees, but beyond the stretch of lawn at the rear was a walled garden. Niall had been cutting the grass, that was clear, the neat lines from the mower pointing to the wall and the door in the middle. Taylor's heart hammered as they walked over the lawn. Niall was chattering about plants, but Taylor wasn't listening, he was remembering. He'd loved this enclosed garden. It wasn't a secret place but he'd always pretended it was. Taylor had thought this was where he'd find his sister, but he hadn't.

Niall opened the door in the wall and Taylor followed him, wiping his sweaty palms on his pants. It was hard to be here again. Niall was quiet now as Taylor walked around, taking in the walls smothered in trailing ivy and climbing roses, the greenhouse and neat vegetable plot, the little orchard, the beds of flowers—such a riot of color they looked like firework displays, and then the burst of wilderness at the back—and the tree house. *Fuck it. Still here?* He turned to face the hall and gaped. *And what the hell is that?*

"A hot tub." Niall answered his unasked question.

"My parents had a hot tub? Why not put it next to the house?"

"Privacy?"

Taylor winced. He wasn't going to follow that train of thought. "Does it still work?"

"No. I could probably fix it."

"Yeah, why not. It'd be a selling point." Taylor turned in a circle and came to a stop facing Niall. "It looks just the same as it did when I was a child. How did you manage that?"

"It was overgrown, that's all. Why redesign something that was already perfect?"

Perfect. Taylor was torn between wishing the walled garden was

different and rejoicing it was the same.

"Have you always worked on gardens?" Taylor asked.

"In one way or another. Did you play in here as a boy?"

"Sometimes." Taylor slammed his shield in place and strode back toward the house.

Too soon. Too fast. Too much. Niall's heart wrenched as he watched Taylor storm off. From the moment Niall had failed to see recognition in Taylor's eyes, disappointment had seeped through him until his spark had almost gone out. He shivered. He'd been so sure Taylor would remember. Now he had to pull back and tread more carefully.

Chapter Two

Don't look desperate.

Roo tried to arrange her features into something other than desperate and smiled at the middle-aged woman sitting behind the desk. Dorothy's mouth fell open as her gaze swept over what Roo was wearing.

"I'm perfect for this job," Roo said in an attempt to distract her. "I could do it with—"

Don't blurt out your life history.

Roo pressed her lips firmly together.

And stop tapping your bloody foot.

She curled her toes inside her shoes under her padded footwear.

"I'm not sure this one's for you," said Dorothy.

Please.

Dorothy peered at Roo over her glasses and Roo was reminded of the way her old headmaster used to look at her, that *I'm very disappointed in you* stare, just before he gave her detention.

"They require someone with experience." Dorothy closed the folder.

Don't beg.

"Please," burst from Roo's lips. "I'm desperate. I've been for forty-seven interviews in the last three weeks and no one's even asked me back for a second. Not even Burger King. This job is perfect for me."

"That's what you said about all of them."

"Yes, but this one is...perfectly perfect. I've got loads of experience in all sorts of relevant areas. I'm always finding stuff that's lost. Only the other day I spotted an earring under my bed that's been missing for weeks." Oh, that didn't make her sound good. Better not mention what else she found under there.

"In my last job, it was me who discovered someone had been taking rude pictures on the photocopier." Because the idiot had left a

copy behind. Roo felt decidedly wary about using it after that, knowing a guy had pressed his cock and balls against the glass. She'd suggested an identity parade to the IT guy, but he didn't think it was funny, which made Roo suspect he was the culprit.

"I'm halfway to being a detective already. This job would be exactly right for me." Her foot was back tapping ten to the dozen.

Dorothy narrowed her eyes and Roo stopped tapping.

"ICU requires an office assistant, not a private detective."

"Yes, totally perfect for me. I might not currently look like an office assistant, but I'm great at assisting. I live for assisting. I can assist in an office, on the street, in a restaurant. Anywhere, really. I'm always assisting old ladies across the road whether they want to go over or not." She let out a strangled laugh.

Shut up, shut up, shut up.

"I don't think this is for you. They want someone discreet, efficient and organized." Dorothy looked at Roo's headgear and raised one eyebrow.

Which is not me, darn it. But Theodore Roosevelt, Roo's namesake, had said, "*Whenever you're asked if you can do a job, tell them 'Certainly I can' and then get busy and find out how to do it.*"

"Under this," Roo gestured to her costume, "lies a paragon of efficiency."

Dorothy stared at her. "Someone with integrity, who's courteous, flexible and not prone to panic."

Shit. "I never panic."

"Someone not dressed as a—"

"I was offered fifty pounds cash to wander around like this. I couldn't afford to turn it down."

Dorothy gave her the sort of look that suggested she should have thought about it harder. Roo played her sympathy card and wobbled her bottom lip. "If I don't find a job this week, I'm going to be thrown out of my bedsit. If I'm homeless, I stand no chance of finding work." She tried to squeeze out a tear and failed, though she wasn't lying. Homelessness had never been closer.

The employment agency clerk appeared unmoved by Roo's amateur dramatics. Roo wondered if throwing herself on the desk would work. She checked the surface. Coffee cup, pens, phone—she'd probably break something. With her luck, it would be her arm.

Give in gracefully. Not easy considering what she was wearing.

Roo stood and the chair came with her. She wrenched it off her butt and plastered a half smile on her face. "Thanks anyway. I'll come again tomorrow to see if you have anything else." Just as she'd done daily for the last three weeks.

She'd reached the door before Dorothy called, "I'll add you to the list. Two thirty. Here's the address. Don't let me down."

Roo waddled back to take the slip of paper before the woman could change her mind. "Thank you, thank—" *Once is enough.*

Yippee. She eased through the glass door of the agency, trying not to crush her costume and as she headed down the street, did a little skip and clicked her heels together at the side.

Roo's exuberance faded when she read the details. ICU, Sutton Hall, Thorpe Lane, Ilkley. *Oh God.* She'd assumed the interview would be in Leeds. She had no time to return her costume or the pedometer Ken Nazir had forced on her, and then go home and change. In any case, she needed the money for doing this for an entire day. Roo furrowed her brow. Ken hadn't specified *where* she had to advertise his restaurant. On a train seemed as good a place as any. She might even be able to persuade him to fork out for the ticket.

Roo handed out leaflets as she headed for the station. Easier to wear the costume than carry it. She'd take it off before she went in, hide it and no one would be any the wiser.

Taylor watched on the computer screen in his office as another interviewee for the position as his PA walked into the drawing room of Sutton Hall. Taylor cringed. A middle-aged guy wearing a shiny suit was never going to be right.

"He might as well leave now," Taylor said.

At his side, Niall sighed. "Could have a sick wife, three teenage kids to support and be shit-hot on the computer."

"He looks wrong."

Niall's jaw twitched. "You mean he doesn't have legs to his armpits, huge breasts and no morals?"

"I definitely wouldn't want him then." Taylor shuddered. "Man boobs? Arrggh."

Niall snorted. "Is he the last?"

"One more." Taylor checked his watch. "But she's late, so she's out."

Since Taylor had returned to Sutton Hall a month ago, he'd lost three PAs. Emma had decided it was too far to commute and neither of his next two choices had lasted more than a week. He'd never had this problem in London.

Taylor hadn't thought he'd want to stay this long at Sutton Hall. The plan had been a couple of weeks to clear the place and then move into a modern apartment in Leeds, but he was too busy with work to even look for an office let alone a place to live. Niall made living at the Hall so easy. A meal on the table in the evening. Company when he needed it. Silence when he didn't. The only issue was Niall himself. What the hell had happened that he needed to stay hidden away? Taylor still hadn't wormed the truth out of him, which didn't say much for his skills as a PI. The guy intrigued him in more ways than one, which was probably why Taylor hadn't pushed.

He glanced at Niall, who was staring out of the window. *Christ, he's good looking.* Niall turned as though he sensed Taylor's gaze, and Taylor looked back at the monitor. When Niall had offered to help him pick the next office assistant, Taylor agreed because he needed to stop looking for beauty and go for brains. Since he also needed Niall's help in Leeds tonight, and it was almost impossible to persuade him to leave the house at all, let alone twice in one day, Taylor had reluctantly agreed to do the interviews here rather than in some anonymous hotel.

The recruitment agency had whittled down the applicants for the position of personal assistant to five, and then squeezed in one more a couple of hours ago. The five who'd turned up sat in complete silence. The three men were in suits, the women in skirts and fitted blouses. Very fitted in the case of the blonde. Taylor ran his tongue over his lip as he stared at the swell of her—

"Not the right basis on which to choose an assistant," Niall said.

Taylor bristled. Sometimes he thought the bloody guy could read his mind. "How do you—?"

"Because all of your previous PAs have had legs to their armpits, large breasts and wore beautiful shoes. Think about the men instead."

Yeah right. Taylor had only included guys in the list because he didn't want to get accused of sexual prejudice, but he preferred a woman for the job, someone easy on the eye, who'd make him coffee and do what he asked because they fancied him. Not that he'd written *that* on the job spec.

"Leave them sitting there until one of them shows some initiative," Niall said.

Actually Taylor didn't want someone with too much initiative. A message on the door had invited them in, told them where to go and they'd all followed the instructions. Maybe he should have left a pot of coffee with a *Drink this* sign. If there'd been another note telling them to walk out the back door and roll on the lawn, would they have done that? Although Taylor wanted someone who did as they were told, he didn't want a sheep.

Ten minutes ticked slowly by.

"I give in," Niall said. "They're all idiots."

Taylor laughed. "I'm intrigued now. How long are they going to sit there?"

"I suspect until they drop dead."

Five more minutes before Taylor heard Niall exhale in frustration, and then the door of the living room flew open and a chicken burst in.

"What the fuck?" Taylor gasped.

"Hi, everyone," the chicken said in a perky voice. "Thank goodness I'm not too late. I had difficulty getting across the road." She laughed and then sighed when no one else joined in. They sat staring at her in mute shock.

"Damn. Maybe I *am* too late. Have you all been in for your interview and you're waiting to see who's been chosen?"

Mumbles of "No" came from the zombies. Taylor was riveted to the screen. The chicken pulled back the hood of her costume to reveal a woman in her mid-twenties with short, untidy dark hair, bright eyes and a dazzling smile. He sat up straighter and felt Niall tense. She ran her fingers through her hair. It made no difference. It still looked a mess.

"I bet you're all wondering if you missed an instruction for the interview, aren't you? Wear an outrageous costume and not a suit. Don't worry. You didn't. I'm stuck in this one. The zipper won't budge. I've just spent ten minutes wrestling with it. Would someone give me a hand?"

Taylor glanced at Niall. His attention was fixed on the screen, his mouth a thin line. He wished the guy would lighten up. Niall rarely laughed these days. He had when Taylor first arrived, he always seemed to be chuckling, but now it was rare to see a smile on his face. Instead, when Taylor caught him unaware, Niall's look was one of

nervous anticipation, his eyes holding hints of promise and fear. It felt to Taylor as though Niall was waiting for something. Presumably his worries about this family issue were growing worse. Taylor had kept asking him about it, hoping he could help, but Niall always clammed up.

The man in the shiny suit stood to assist with the chicken's zipper. The woman wriggled out of the back of the yellow-and-white costume, and tossed it behind the couch. Taylor took in her rumpled, red V-necked T-shirt, pert breasts, the miniscule blue skirt, her long, long legs and then lurched to a halt on the huge brown chicken feet. He sniggered.

She offered her hand to the man. "Thanks so much. You're an expert chicken skinner. Good thing you're not a pleasant peasant, and I'm not a pheasant and need plucking. Try saying that fast. Okay. You're a pleasant pheasant—*arrgh*—maybe not. I'm Roo. You are?"

Taylor watched her shake hands and introduce herself to the others.

"So no one's been interviewed yet?" she asked. "And you've not seen anyone? Why are we waiting?"

"Didn't you read the message on the door? It told us to wait in here," said the woman with the book.

Roo sat and then almost immediately jumped up again. "Maybe something's happened to the person interviewing us. He might have choked on a bone or been bitten by a snake or maybe he slipped with a knife and he's bleeding to death on the kitchen floor."

Taylor let out a choked laugh.

"You're being ridiculous," said the other woman.

Roo sat down. "Hey, this is a private investigation company we're interviewing for. Who knows what's happened. Maybe this is to test our powers of observation and our ability to think on our feet. Could be the guy's been murdered." She stood.

"What are you going to do?" Niall asked. "She's the only one who's shown any initiative, but she's a nutcase."

"I like nuts."

Roo was about to go look for a murder victim when the door opened and a tall, slim guy with tousled blond hair stepped into the room.

He looked around. "Sorry to keep you all waiting."

Drool alert! Roo swallowed hard. Every inch of this guy was jaw-droppingly, mouth-wateringly, pants-wettingly gorgeous and she couldn't even see every inch of him. *Don't look at his crotch.* Ice-green eyes, chiseled cheek bones and those lips—*oh shit*—lips that were saying something and she'd flipping well missed it. *Damn.*

One of the women walked out of the room with the subject of Roo's nighttime fantasies for weeks to come, and Roo sighed with relief that he'd not been speaking to her. She settled into a corner of a couch and winced when she registered she was still wearing the chicken feet. Roo kicked them off along with her shoes, curled up with her feet tucked under her and closed her eyes. *Think calm, sensible thoughts.*

He had a lovely, bitable butt.

Shit.

What had Dorothy said they were looking for?

Someone who was discreet, efficient and organized.

Roo never betrayed a confidence. She liked to think she was organized. She made loads of lists. She even had lists of lists. But the word efficient worried her. Roo might make lists but then she lost them. She tended not to think in a linear way, which meant she was easily distracted. It really didn't take much to sidetrack her—an unusual crack in the pavement that might suddenly open to swallow her, an overflowing litter bin that could contain a rotting skull. Even thinking about being distracted, distracted her. Roo gave herself a mental smack upside the head.

Concentrate.

They wanted someone courteous—she always said please and thank you in a polite voice. Well, unless people were rude, and then she said it sarcastically.

Someone flexible—she could wrap her legs around her neck if she was lying on the bed, and she could stand with her palms flat on the floor without bending her knees. Roo grinned. She knew that wasn't what was meant, but now she'd seen Mr. Gorgeous, the thought of demonstrating her flexibility appealed.

Someone with integrity. Well, she tried to be honest but sometimes it was better to tell fibs. Kindness above everything else because love comes before the truth. Not that she'd ever been in *proper* love. She thought she had. Lots of times. But if the guy didn't love her back, then he wasn't right for her and so she couldn't have loved him. Any of them.

Probably.

Still hurt though.

Concentrate.

Someone not prone to panic. Yes, well, that could be a problem. The words Roo and panic went together like bread and Marmite. Not that she liked Marmite. Okay, going together like bread and butter was better, though butter was bad for you and she didn't often eat it. Though she did like it and always picked it if there was a choice between that and some low-fat spread.

Concentrate! What was I thinking about?

Panic.

Well, it didn't take much to throw her into confusion. She'd been told by numerous teachers and...other people she didn't want to think about ever again, that she had an overactive imagination. Roo wasn't so sure about that. Wasn't that the whole point of having an imagination? You want it to be overactive to make sure you don't do anything dangerous. Surely she wasn't the only one concerned about what would happen if an alien spaceship landed in your garden, or if vampires really existed, or if that big dog walking toward you was a werewolf. Play dead or run? Roo had decided she'd climb a tree.

She snuggled deeper into the cushion. She was tired. The chicken costume weighed a ton and her feet ached. She'd had to walk from Ilkley station, down a gentle slope and then up the equivalent of Kilimanjaro before she reached Thorpe Lane. From there it was a hop, skip and a series of jumps over pot holes for at least another half a mile before she'd found the gates to Sutton Hall. It lay at the end of a long, rutted drive and was surrounded by woods. The place looked really old, a bit like the Munster's House, come to think of it.

Roo might as well have turned round at that point. There was no way she could get here every morning without getting up at the butt crack of dawn. A bus into Leeds and then a train to Ilkley—the cost would cripple her, let alone the time it would take, and then there was the long slog from the station. In any case, Roo had to face the fact that the chance of getting this job was miniscule. But she never gave up on anything without a fight.

As Teddy Roosevelt said, "*Believe you can and you're halfway there.*"

Chapter Three

When Roo opened her eyes, the room was empty. Where was everyone? She wiped her mouth to check for drool and sat up. Had she snored, said something embarrassing in her sleep or—*Oh God*—farted? Roo had no idea whether she did any of those, but she always worried she might, and one of them or all of them could be the reason no boyfriend had ever hung around.

She stood and pulled at the hem of her skirt to straighten the material and drag down a few nonexistent inches. "*Do what you can, with what you have, where you are.*" *Thanks, Teddy!* Except if she tugged the skirt too far down, it showed a bare patch across her midriff. *Oh damn.*

This was as far from her interview outfit as she could get, but then she'd imagined spending the day as a chicken and had dressed to stay cool. She ought to extract her shoes from the binding of the chicken feet, but it had taken so long to get the damn things to stay in place without them twisting backward every time she took a step, that Roo was tempted to remain barefoot. But then that didn't look—

"Ms. Smith?"

Roo spun round. The guy with blond hair stood by the door. He was tall, had to be at least six-three. The late-afternoon sun illuminated him from behind and dazzled her, and it rather looked as if he had shimmering wings. She tilted her head to one side to check. No, oh that was disappointing.

He tilted his head to meet her gaze. "If you'd like to come this way."

Roo straightened. She'd come this way and that way, in fact any way he wanted. *Bad girl.* How could a guy as attractive as him fail to be great in bed? But then maybe he was crap in bed and the good looks were to compensate. That might be true of all good-looking guys. It had been in Roo's experience. Not that she was very experienced. He stumbled slightly and Roo gulped. Good thing he couldn't read her mind. Good thing no one could. They'd be very confused.

Too late now to retrieve her shoes, she padded barefoot after the angel down a hallway lined with oil paintings. *Oh boy, are those eyes following me?* Roo suppressed a giggle at the thought of the actual eyeballs jumping off the painted faces and running after her. And why did people look so odd in old paintings? The guys in particular. Like they had a pole stuck up their butt. They never smiled. Roo liked people to smile, which was probably one of the reasons she'd been prepared to dress as a chicken. Life was too short to be sad for long.

She hadn't realized she'd stopped to stare at a picture of a yacht in rough seas until she heard a quiet cough and turned to see her escort gesturing toward an open door. Roo hurried to catch up, and as she stepped into the room, she stubbed her toe on the raised threshold and fell headlong. A weird yelp burst from her throat and Roo thrust out her hands, but didn't collide with the wooden floor rushing to meet her. Arms caught her, hauled her upright and steadied her.

"Wow," Roo gasped. "Good catch. Thank you, Ang...el."

She'd tried and failed to stop the word slipping out.

He let her go so fast, Roo almost fell again. She lifted her head and looked across the desk at...ah well, this had to be Lucifer. Dark hair, piercing black eyes, lashes longer than they had any right to be—in other words longer than hers—oh, and a wicked smile. *My God, the two of them look like bookends.* And Roo quite fancied being the book.

Very bad girl.

Very, very bad girl.

Very— Oh stop it.

Not that she was going to get the job, but if she did, she'd be far too busy daydreaming about these two to get any work done.

"Please take a seat," said Satan.

The only seat Roo could see was the one next to him behind the desk so she walked over and sat. His eyes opened wider. *Dear Lord, they really are black.* And she'd kill for his eyelashes. Well, not kill obviously, but—

"That chair," he said, pointing behind her.

Her cheeks on fire, Roo slunk over to a leather chair turned so its back was to a small desk. How the hell had she missed that?

"I'm Taylor Sutton," said Beelzebub. "ICU is my company. This is Niall McCarthy. He's here to make sure no one trips up on the way in."

Roo laughed and relaxed a little. "Roo Smith. Pleased to meet you." She jumped up to shake their hands. The heat of Niall's hand

sent tingles racing down her arm. Taylor's hand felt cool in comparison, but he let go of her as if he'd touched a live wire. Roo returned to her seat, fighting off the urge to run, though she wasn't sure if she wanted to run into their arms or out of the door.

"What's Roo short for?" Niall asked. "Ruth?"

Roo shook her head. *Darn it, why did he have to ask that?*

"Ruby?" Niall asked.

"No."

Niall frowned. "Rosalind? Rowena? Rona?"

"No." Well, at least they hadn't assumed she had a mother called Kanga and a friend called Pooh. At least not yet.

"Rumplestiltskin?" Taylor asked.

Roo laughed and then squirmed. "Roosevelt."

Both men gaped at her.

She tightened her mouth. She wasn't going blurt out the sad details of her unfortunate birth and misadventurous childhood. Unless pressed. *Oh God, all right.* As she opened her mouth, a phone rang and saved her. And them.

"Yes?" Taylor snapped.

With that tone, Roo was surprised he had any clients. He really needed someone with a gentle voice to ease the distressing facts out of those desperate enough to hire a private detective. Someone like her. She practiced a few telephone yeses in her head. *Yes? Yeeeesss? Yep? Yip? Yurp?Yarp?*

"You should have been here yesterday," Taylor barked.

Roo glanced around the room to stop herself staring at Niall. It was shabby, cluttered and old fashioned. There were piles of papers stacked on the floor alongside a towering heap of books. The shelves above were largely empty. Taylor's desk was a huge wooden thing with a computer monitor and a laptop on one side, dirty coffee cups the other. *I'd love a coffee. And something to eat.* The last thing she'd eaten had been a slice of bread that morning. As if on cue, her stomach rumbled loudly. Roo coughed to disguise the sound, but when she caught Niall's gaze, he was staring at her. She swallowed hard.

"That's not good enough," Taylor shouted.

Roo jumped and diverted her gaze from both of them. All she could see through the window were trees, and she wondered if there was a garden. Roo had always wanted a garden, though she knew

nothing about flowers. She debated getting up to have a look, but decided it might be rude and stayed where she was.

Eventually the mobile was slammed down with such force, Roo let out a squeak. So much for not panicking.

"Sorry about that," Taylor said, and smiled at her.

His face crinkled, his cheeks developed dimples and she caught a glimpse of perfect white teeth. Roo almost melted, but not quite. Something about the smile didn't look genuine, as if he'd practiced in front of the mirror until it was perfect, except it looked too perfect. A smile to get him into women's pants. She let her gaze drop from his mouth. *Oh fuck.* His lovely neck. His Adam's apple went up and down. Roo waited for it to move again.

A throat being cleared brought her back to reality and she straightened.

"Why do you want this job?" Taylor asked.

She tried to look discreet, efficient and organized. The flexible could wait.

"Because I'm discreet, efficient and organized." *What else? Oh yes.* "I'm courteous, I'm integri...integrou...I have integrity and I'm not prone to panic." She smiled and then let the smile slip. "Well, not unless there's cause to panic, for instance if I was in the middle of a field and looked up and saw a swarm of pterodactyls—is the collective noun for pterodactyls a swarm?" She shook her head and continued. "Or if I was tied to train tracks and a train was coming, or if I was buried up to my neck in sand and the tide was rising. I might panic then. Panic has its place. The adrenaline spurt can be very useful, particularly if you meet a velociraptor." Her foot began to tap.

The men exchanged glances.

Drat, did I just say what I think I did?

"How flexible are you?" Taylor asked.

Was that a smirk? "Very." Roo went for her sultry stare and kept her arms and legs where they were, fighting the urge to show how she could press her thumb back to her wrist. The legs around the neck could definitely wait. "I can start immediately and work whatever hours you like." *All night would be appealing.*

Taylor coughed. "Let's try again without you repeating the job spec back to me. Why do you want this job?"

Oh bugger. "I need it. Desperately." Roo tensed. "No, forget I said desperately. I don't want to sound desperate. But I am desperate. I'm

prepared to do anything. Almost. Well, anything legal. Maybe illegal if you really wanted me to. Though I'd have to think hard about that." *Shut up. Now.* "I thought working for a detective agency might be...interesting." Her voice faded to a mumble and she slid down on the leather chair.

"Most of the time it's boring." Taylor tapped a pen on his desk like a woodpecker and Roo found her foot keeping time. "I need someone to do the filing, answer the phones, deal with correspondence, book appointments."

"I can do that." Roo tried to radiate efficiency, stopped tapping and sat up straighter. "And if you don't mind me saying so, your telephone manner could do with some work. You're a bit brusque. The people who call need help, not someone barking at them."

Taylor stared at her openmouthed. *Ah, too much information.*

"Why did you arrive dressed as a chicken?" Niall asked, not a hint of amusement on his face.

She flopped like an old tulip. This was hopeless. "I'm advertising Kenplucky Fried Chicken. Just for the day. As a favor for a friend." Actually, Ken Nazir wasn't exactly a friend, but Roo thought it might sound better. Then she straightened again. "How do you know I was dressed as a chicken? Did you have a camera spying on us? Is that legal? Did I dribble? Did I fa— Oh God." She put her head in her hands.

Taylor laughed. Roo glanced up.

"Why did you leave your last job?" He clicked on his keyboard. "Childers Advertising? In London? Why did you come up to Leeds?"

Roo's heart clenched at the thought of Tom—her boss, her friend, her lover—except he'd been a crap boss who'd stolen her ideas and pretended they were his, he'd never been her friend, and although he'd fucked her, he'd never made love to her. She saw that at the end when she should have seen it at the start. There was a difference between lust and love, and Roo had to stop thinking every guy who wanted to fuck her also loved her, because they didn't. And she had to stop falling in love with every guy she invited into her bed, plus these two who she'd only just met.

Bugger, he's waiting for an answer. She had the made-up excuse for why she'd left Childers ready in her head. She'd repeated it so many times, she ought to sound convincing by now, but when she opened her mouth the truth came out.

"My boss was a lying, cheating scumbag who ought to be

castrated with a spoon, and I wanted to get as far away from him as I possibly could before I was tempted to raid the cutlery drawer."

Shit. Roo slapped her hand over her mouth. Where was a slip in the space-time continuum when she needed one?

"Thanks for coming. We'll be in touch," Taylor said.

That's a no, then. She didn't blame them. She wouldn't give herself the job. Roo pushed herself up, thought about shaking hands and decided not to. She gave a little nod. "Thank you for seeing me. I appreciate it. Oh, and I really would try not to yell at clients on the phone."

"It was the window cleaner," Taylor said.

Oh, course it was. "Ah, sorry. Though—no, sorry."

No point in saying he was more likely to get clean windows if he was pleasant. Roo closed the door quietly behind her, started to leave and then tiptoed back to press her ear to the wood. Had she really blown it spectacularly? Did they like her just a little bit? The door opened and she almost fell into the room. Niall was holding the handle. He raised his eyebrows.

"Showing how resourceful I can be," Roo said and strode off purposefully.

"Other way."

Her shoulders fell and she reversed direction.

Niall closed the door on Roo and removed the smile from his face before he turned to look at Taylor because he knew what the guy was going to say.

"Oh Christ, I have to have her," Taylor said. "Roosevelt? What were her parents thinking?"

"What are *you* thinking? She couldn't organize herself out of a paper bag."

"I know, but she'd have fun trying and I'd have even more fun watching her."

Niall exhaled. "Yeah, for about five minutes before she drove you insane. That was a woman who'd drive from New York to Miami via Los Angeles."

Taylor laughed, but the glint in his eye told Niall that Taylor had already made up his mind. Niall felt desperate that Taylor *didn't* hire her. He felt he was just getting somewhere with Taylor, and Roo was a

distraction neither of them needed. He'd had the horrible sensation that Roo had seen something she shouldn't when she'd looked at him. The fact that he'd let that happen alarmed him.

"You asked me to sit in on the interviews to give my opinion, and my advice is don't choose her. You'll be repeating the mistakes you made with the other three."

Taylor's face hardened and Niall's heart sank. "And what mistakes would those be?"

Careful. "You told me you never fucked the help—your golden rule—but you were close to it with—"

"No, I wasn't. I admit I'd thought about it with Francine, but that was all."

"So why put temptation in your way again?"

It wasn't just that Roo would be a distraction. Part of Niall's reason for arguing was that he didn't want Roo to get hurt. She was like a burst of sunshine on a cloudy day. Hard to remember when he'd last thought that about any female. In another life, Niall would have pursued Roo, he'd felt that spark between them, but he verged on success with Taylor and wasn't going to give that up. Once upon a time, Taylor had made the sun shine in Niall's life, and Niall still hoped it would happen again.

"She's cute," Taylor said and headed over to the window.

Yes, she is. "Such a good reason to give someone a job."

Taylor frowned. "She'll cheer me up if I'm having a crap day."

That hit Niall like a dagger. Hadn't *he* been doing that for the last month?

"She didn't come by car?" Taylor asked.

A bright white-and-yellow chicken was making its way down the drive, but not in a straight line. Roo zigzagged. Taylor sighed.

"Evidently not," Niall said. "Well, that settles it. She lives in Pudsey. How could she get here?"

"She can use the train or bus, and then walk—maybe she has someone who'll give her a lift." He turned to face Niall. "Why are you so down on her?"

"She's...trouble." *Because you'll want her and not me.*

"She's funny and cute and sexy."

Niall clenched his fists behind his back. "You said *this* time you wanted someone who was going to stay. Noticed a pattern here? You go

for the young and pretty ones and they leave."

Taylor glared. "Well, they didn't leave because of me."

"Didn't they?"

His glare hardened. "No." He slumped back behind his desk. "Who do you think I should choose then?"

"Phil."

Taylor rolled his eyes. "He had sweaty hands and stank of aftershave."

"He has a wife and three teenagers to support."

"Yes, how did you guess that? Sometimes I think you're bloody psychic. I'm not a social worker. The job's beneath him. He won't stay and I'll be back where I started."

"Ben?" Niall tried.

"Arrogant little shit."

Niall raised his eyebrows and Taylor squirmed."Yeah, he did remind me of me, but I need someone yesterday and he has to give a month's notice. Roo could start tomorrow."

"What about Lucy? She seemed bright and keen. And she's available immediately."

Taylor rolled his eyes. "A degree in economics from Cambridge? I want someone to do as I tell them, not someone trying to tell me what to do." He gave a deep sigh. "How about Steven? He's already a PA. He's young and enthusiastic."

And gay. Had Taylor noticed? That why he'd put him last?

"And gay," Taylor added.

"Is that a problem?" Niall asked.

If Taylor said yes, Niall thought he might as well give up right now. One long month of being so near and yet so far had left Niall in a state of painful frustration.

"No, that's not a problem," Taylor said. "The problem is that he wants to be a detective, not work in the office. I already have Jonas out in the field. It's someone to sort all this out that I need." He gestured to the room.

None of the three PAs had made much of a dent in Taylor's mess, just made a mess in his head from what Niall could tell. Taylor might deny it, but he'd lusted after Emma, then Francine followed by Nina. Of course, they had to go. Niall had made sure of that.

Taylor sighed. "I want Roo—Roosevelt, oh Christ." He laughed.

"You should choose Phil."

Niall could perhaps have persuaded Taylor to choose Phil, but he didn't have the surplus energy today. Plus a tiny, tiny part of him wondered if Roo could do some feminine magic and make Niall's world turn again. Might she be the spark he'd been waiting for? Or just more trouble?

"I *should* choose Phil, but I'm not going to. I want Roo. If she's useless, I'll get rid of her."

Taylor checked his screen for her mobile number, turned his speaker on and punched numbers.

"Yaruuup?" Roo said.

Taylor snorted.

Roo cleared her throat. "Yes?"

"Eight thirty to five thirty. Other hours when needed. Start tomorrow. A month's trial."

Her squeal was very loud.

Chapter Four

By the time Roo reached Kenplucky Fried Chicken, it was six thirty. A noisy children's party had overwhelmed the restaurant and her arrival was greeted by screams of delight. She felt a desperate need to escape from the costume, but the kids clamored around her, tugging at her wings.

"Do the chicken dance," one of the little monsters shouted.

"Chicken dance, chicken dance." The call was taken up by the other kids and Roo heard the serving staff sniggering.

Oh damn. Roo winged it and launched into an impromptu strutting walk, did a few jumps and pecked at the remains of the meals on the tables which made one little girl cry. *Oops.* She felt a hand at her neck and then the chill of ice cubes slithering down her back inside the costume. As the ice made its way toward her bum, she wriggled and jerked and raced around in the confined space like a—ah, a headless chicken. Roo saw Barry, one of the staff, backing away, smirking. *Bastard.* The kids thought it was all part of the act and were creased up laughing—except for the one still crying. Roo eyed the door marked private and burst through it into Ken Nazir's office.

She closed it, leaned back against it and then arched forward as the ice found a way out and dropped to the ground. Ken looked over his desk and frowned.

"Laying ice cubes?"

Roo sighed. "Eggs are too expensive."

"I expected you back an hour ago."

"I kept going until I'd handed out all the leaflets." Every passenger on the train from Ilkley to Leeds had been given one. It had earned her a telling off from the conductor though he'd taken one too. The handout offered fifteen percent off meals including drinks if produced at time of ordering.

"Don't think that means I'll pay you more."

As if. "Can you give me a hand with the zipper?" Roo asked.

She sighed with relief when the costume was off and sat to untangle her shoes from the Velcro straps of the chicken feet.

"They're dirty," he said.

"I've walked miles." Roo unclipped the pedometer from the inside of her waistband and put it on the desk.

He picked it up and raised one bushy eyebrow. Roo hoped he couldn't tell that she'd spent an hour of the day on a train, but she *had* walked up and down the carriages. He counted out five ten-pound notes and handed them to her along with her backpack.

"Thank you," Roo said, and fought off the urge to cry, "Mine, Mine" and run away cackling manically.

"Depending on how many people come in with the leaflet, I might want you to have another go."

"Fine."

Roo had no intention of dressing up in that costume ever again, but she'd learned not to count her chickens. *Ha, ha.* Tomorrow the Prince of Darkness who ran the detective firm might decide he didn't need her to assist with anything after all.

Even so, Roo bounced most of the way back to her bedsit. *I've got a job. I've got a job. I've got a job.* She was still bubbling when she reached her building but took a deep breath before she unlocked the front door of the three-story house.

Roo occupied a small basement dungeon complete with bed of nails and Chinese water torture—a perpetually dripping tap—while her landlord had the flat directly above. Since she owed him a month's rent, Roo needed to avoid him. She crept in silently and thought about telling Taylor she'd be good at this sort of thing until she slammed to a halt halfway down the stairs and barely managed to stifle her yelp.

All her things were piled up outside her room—clothes, books, bed linen, pillows. *Bloody hell. That's not good.* The door was ajar, music coming from inside, and Roo peeked in to see her landlord slapping paint on the wall. An insipid magnolia already covered most of the primrose yellow daubed on by Roo. She would have liked to believe Mr. Aziz was finally getting round to dealing with the outbreak of mold. It had been rising faster than her overdraft and given her yellow paint application a look of a Jackson Pollock. But Roo had long suspected he wanted to rent out her place to a relative and had been waiting for the opportunity to throw her out.

Not paying her rent on time was reason enough.

She fingered the fifty pounds in her pocket. It wouldn't change his mind. He'd snatch it and still throw her out. She'd had enough of this place anyway. The bed was really uncomfortable and the dripping tap drove her crazy. This was supposed to be a temporary stop, and she'd lived here since she arrived in the city.

Roo crouched down and quietly sifted through her heaped up possessions. There was no room for books, or her lovely vase rescued from a Dumpster, or the posters of half-naked men she'd fastened over the black speckles on the walls. She stuffed the suitcase until it was bulging, forced a couple of cans of food into her straining rucksack, and wore her coat even though it was too hot for it. Because she had no free hand to carry her pillow, Roo wedged it under the coat. After one final check of what she'd left behind, she waved a reluctant goodbye to her bed cover—if she put that where she'd stuffed the pillow, she'd look as though she were giving birth to an elephant—and walked up the stairs out into the night.

When she reached the pavement, Roo plastered a smile on her face. Okay, she had nowhere to live, but she had a job, clothes, a small amount of credit on her mobile phone, two cans of SpaghettiOs, and she looked pregnant but she wasn't. Life could be worse.

But not by a lot.

Her smile faded as reality over her situation hit home. Roo had moved to Leeds from London three months ago and didn't yet have any friends she knew well enough to stay with. She could probably find a budget hotel, but it would eat her money. She needed a cheap, temporary solution until her first pay check from ICU. Maybe her only paycheck if things didn't work out.

"When you're at the end of your rope, tie a knot and hold on," Roosevelt had said, and suddenly a bright light blinded her. Well, not really, but it was a road-to-Damascus moment and Roo *always* paid attention to those. She turned and headed for the retail park just off the city ring road, dragging her wonky-wheeled case behind her.

Outside the Asda-Walmart superstore, Roo wedged everything under a shopping cart and rode the moving walkway to household goods, trying to stop the pillow from sliding down. She found a two-person tent for the amazing sum of twelve pounds, a foam mat that would at least keep her off the ground, a sleeping bag and a battery-powered lantern. Water was the only other thing she thought she'd need and she put a large bottle in the cart. As she paid at the checkout, she wondered how the hell she was going to carry everything.

"Long to go?" The cashier nodded at Roo's swollen belly.

"Could drop out any minute," Roo said and then laughed at the expression of horror on the woman's face.

"Remind me again why I have to do this," Niall said.

"Because I asked nicely." Taylor spotted a gap, glanced in the mirror to check there was no one behind and braked. "And you need a night out." He looked over his shoulder and neatly reversed his black BMW into a tight space between two cars. "You've never come into Leeds with me." He switched off the engine. "Plus we tossed. You lost. You get the girl." Though they were both wired up just in case.

Niall climbed out and glared at him across the roof of the car. "A two-headed coin?"

Taylor laughed. "You should have checked. Stop scowling, you're not going to attract anyone with a face like that."

A blatant lie. Niall wouldn't find it hard to pick up a woman—or a man. Yet as far as Taylor knew, Niall had never had a guest of either sex in the house and had never stayed out overnight. Since Taylor arrived a month ago, he'd levered Niall out of his top-floor room and away from his beloved garden to face the real world on only four occasions. All of them short trips to the pub in Ilkley. Even the groceries were delivered.

"Remember how to flirt?" Taylor asked as they headed toward The Lite.

Niall snorted.

"Oh yeah, that's going to work. A disdainful snort. You probably only need to stand there, but want to try out some pick-up lines? Do you even have any?"

"How about—Do you have a map? I keep getting lost in your eyes."

"Christ, maybe you shouldn't say anything. Dumb and handsome works."

A rare smile flittered across Niall's face. "Ever kissed an elephant between its ears?"

"What?" Taylor frowned.

Niall pulled out his pockets. "Want to?"

"If I see you do that, I'll kick you in the balls."

Niall pushed his pockets back in.

"Try something less cheesy," Taylor said.

"Do you know how to use a whip?"

Taylor groaned. "You're going to get your face slapped."

"There are two hundred and sixty-five bones in your body," Niall said. "I'd like to make it two hundred and sixty-six."

"I'm really sorry I asked." But he sniggered.

Niall stepped in front of him so he had to stop walking. Niall bent his mouth to Taylor's ear and whispered, "Come home with me right now. I'm going to fuck you until you scream."

The sensation of Niall's warm breath washing against his cheek made his cock perk up and Taylor jerked away. *What the hell?*

"Think that will work?" Niall smirked.

He knows the effect that had on me. Shit.

"Don't try it on the bouncer," Taylor blurted.

Niall stepped aside and gave one of his rare proper smiles. Taylor had the uncomfortable sensation they were playing some sort of game and he didn't know the rules. He started walking again.

"Don't worry." Niall caught up. "If it's me she goes for and wants to be seduced, I'll seduce her. You'll get your evidence."

Taylor faltered. "You do know that you don't actually have to *do* anything? I mean apart from talk to her. A kiss is okay, but nothing more. I'd lose my license." *And why don't I want Niall to kiss her?*

"I think I'd worked that out."

They stopped at the entrance, and Taylor pulled Niall to one side before paying. "Better turn the recorders on. We'll buy a drink and then stand as close as we can to the group. Apparently there are four in the party and she's the only one wearing a red dress."

When they went through the second set of doors, they walked into a wall of sound. The pounding music was accompanied by multicolored flashing lights that flew around the walls, floor and ceiling.

"Wow," Niall said. "It looks like the place is full of psychedelic fireflies released after a rainbow's splintered."

Taylor turned to stare at him. "What?"

"Nothing," Niall mumbled.

"You'll need to be really close to her or the recorder won't pick up anything," Taylor said.

Niall nodded and they headed for the bar. Taylor looked around for Sherry Bennett. She and her husband had been on the point of divorce when her uncle had left her a pot of money and Sherry suddenly decided she'd like to give the marriage one last shot. Taylor felt sorry for Phil Bennett. He hadn't asked for the divorce and hoped his wife still loved him, but he didn't know if the halt in the proceedings had come about because she wanted to stop him getting half of her inheritance. "The crazy thing is," he'd said to Taylor, "I don't want her money. I want her."

Hence the honey trap. Not a job Taylor much liked, but tonight he was killing a few birds with one stone. He was earning easy money, he'd maneuvered Niall out of the house, which had to be good for him, and there was a strong possibility once they'd obtained the evidence that the pair of them would get laid, assuming Niall was up for it. Though not by Sherry Bennett. Taylor wasn't that much of a bastard. Except, the getting laid bit wasn't sitting easy on his stomach and Taylor didn't know why.

He bought two Coronas, winced at the extortionate cost, and handed one to Niall.

Niall leaned back against the bar and downed half the bottle. "She's on my left."

Taylor stayed facing the other way.

"Ah, and heading over here," Niall added.

Taylor turned and watched as four women in short, tight dresses negotiated a path to the bar. Sherry was as pretty as her photograph. They all looked slightly tipsy, staggering on high heels and giggling as they bumped against each other. And Taylor fancied none of them. *God, am I ill?* The image of a chicken filled his head, Roo's cheeky face emerging from the costume, and he sighed. Maybe he shouldn't have given her the job.

Niall put his bottle down and stepped into Sherry's line of sight. Taylor could almost see her melt under the intensity of the guy's gaze. She didn't even look at Taylor but fluttered toward Niall like a woman to chocolate, and stood staring into his eyes as if she'd been hypnotized.

Niall tipped his head to one side and smiled. "Please don't say no and break my heart."

Four female jaws collectively dropped. One male jaw almost did. *Christ, he's smooth. And that smile? Why didn't he do it more often?*

"Dance?" Niall held out his hand.

Sherry didn't even hesitate. Taylor watched them move into the middle of the floor and then edged closer to listen to her friends and record their comments.

"Bloody hell, he's fucking gorgeous."

"How come she pulled first—again?"

"It's not fair. She's just greedy."

"Would you have turned *that* down? Christ, I bet he's hung like a donkey."

Taylor stifled a laugh.

"It was Sherry's round as well."

"Might as well say goodbye to that. God, look at the way she's draped herself all over him."

"Lucky cow."

As Taylor pretended to talk on his mobile, he took pictures of Niall and Sherry dancing. A muscle in Taylor's cheek twitched when Niall skillfully avoided the kiss aimed at his lips.

Sherry had one hand on Niall's butt, the other up the back of his shirt. Niall had his arms around her but his hands weren't moving. Sherry had pressed her face into his chest. In a way, this wasn't a fair test. Taylor wondered if there were any women in the whole of Leeds who could resist Niall.

Or any men.

It wasn't that strange, was it, to have a physical reaction to a good-looking guy? One good-looking guy in particular?

Oh Christ. I'm still going for self-denial?

Niall was sexy as hell without even trying. Didn't mean anything was going to happen. Taylor stuck his hand in his pocket and wrestled with his cock.

He frowned as Niall walked back to the bar with Sherry. Niall was scratching his chin, the sign that Taylor should help him bail because he'd gotten what they needed. *Fuck that.* In one dance? He'd done it in one fucking dance?

Sherry had her arm looped through Niall's and he glared at Taylor. In a fit of perverse jealousy—only in that Niall had done the job so easily—Taylor turned and strode to the exit. Though once he was outside, he realized he'd have to wait. He could hardly strand Niall in Leeds, especially if the guy ended up needing help to get away from whoever it was he hid from.

Taylor paced back and forth in front of the club. What had happened to his plan for them to get laid? He wasn't going to pay again to go inside. Taylor supposed they could go to one of the city center bars and find a couple of women, but the thought that Niall might be the one who got lucky and not him, made Taylor's gut ache. That had never happened in London. If Taylor went out with his mates, he was always the one the women fancied. Unless he was with Jonas. Women *really* liked him. Bloody animal magnetism.

Apart from the fact that Taylor was confused as hell, his self-confidence had taken a knock tonight. That was all that was wrong. He just needed to get laid and everything would be fine again. Roo was the answer to his troubles. Not that he had troubles. Niall was right. She was going to be a useless PA. But Taylor fancied her. The thought of Roo pressing her breasts against his chest, wrapping her legs around his waist filled his head and his cock. The rule about fucking the help didn't count because she wouldn't last. *Yep, Roo's the one to break my dry spell.*

Ten minutes passed before Niall staggered out looking white as snow and Taylor caught his arm in concern.

"You okay?"

Niall had only had one beer. Even if he'd had more after Taylor deserted him, it wasn't possible to get drunk so quickly. He'd once seen Niall consume a bottle of wine and there had been no reaction like this.

"Need...to go back," Niall gasped.

Taylor put his arm around him and helped him to the car. "Are you sick?"

"Be...okay."

Pale as Niall looked, Taylor could feel the heat of his skin through his shirt. The guy was burning up.

"Shit, why didn't you say you were ill?"

Taylor aimed his remote at the car and opened the passenger door.

"Did you have another drink? Maybe someone slipped something in it."

"Why didn't you stick...to our arrangement? I about scratched...the stubble off my chin."

Taylor got in the driver's seat and started the engine.

"Why didn't you?" Niall asked.

Taylor turned to him and snapped, "Because you made it look so fucking easy."

Niall clipped his seat belt in place and turned his face to the window.

Taylor took a deep breath and pulled out into the road. "Sorry, I'm a bloody idiot."

"Okay."

Taylor drove in silence until he reached the A65, then spoke, "Want to play what you got?"

Niall took the recorder from his pocket. A few moments later Sherry's voice came out quite clear.

"What's your name?"

"Niall."

"I'm Sherry. God, you're gorgeous. You local?"

"No."

"Not got an apartment nearby we can use then?"

"For what, sweetheart?"

Sherry laughed. "What do you think?"

"Something on TV tonight you want to watch?"

She laughed louder. "We could record ourselves and put it on the TV except you'd have to destroy the copy."

"Why's that?"

"I'm married, though not for much longer."

"Poisoning him?"

She giggled. "Divorcing him, soon as I've spent my money. Now, where are you staying? Is it very far away?"

"Not very far. I just need to tell my mate I'm leaving."

Niall switched off the machine. "Okay?"

"Perfect."

"Sorry I messed up your plans."

Taylor glanced left. Niall was staring at him.

"So you should be." Taylor tugged his mobile from his pocket and tossed it to Niall. "Call Phil Bennett and play that when I tell you."

The sound of a phone ringing out filled the car.

"Phil? It's Taylor."

"Oh."

Taylor frowned. "You did ask me to call tonight."

"Yes, I know. I just...go on, then. Tell me. Is it bad?"

"Yeah, it is. Listen." Taylor nodded to Niall and he played the conversation.

When it finished there was silence.

"You okay?" Taylor asked.

"Yes. Thanks." The guy gave a short laugh. "At least I know. I'll send you a check."

"You want the tape?"

"No. It's enough that I know."

Taylor ended the call. "I wonder if he wishes he'd never asked me to do this? I believed him when he said he didn't care about the money. If she spends it, she still might be made to pay him half the inheritance when they divorce." He gave a short laugh. "Love. It's such a pile of shit. What's the point? Losing your head in some temporary insanity? Wasting weeks, months, years of your life only to finish fucked up in one way or another?"

Niall glared at him. "That's not true. There are plenty of happy relationships."

"Research shows one in four marriages only continue because those involved can't find a better alternative."

"So three out of four are happy. Your parents are still together, aren't they?"

"Yes, but—"

"And they're happy?"

"Yes, but—"

"There is no but, Taylor. Love makes the world a better place. The pleasure it brings outweighs the sad times when things go wrong. Better to look for love and never find it than give up on it."

Taylor gave him an incredulous stare before he turned his attention back to the road. "You think it's okay to waste your life searching for something that doesn't exist? Looking for some soul mate who'll *complete* you?" He laughed. "Have you not noticed what I do for a living? What puts me in a bad temper? What makes me not trust anyone? I deal daily with the results of people believing in love. I see men and women hurt by cheating and lying partners, leaving wrecked lives and broken hearts all around."

"You're ignoring all those who're blissfully happy. They're off your radar but they're there, living ordinary lives but happy to come home to someone, looking forward to sharing their day, talking about their successes and failures, making plans for things to do together."

Taylor pulled up at a traffic light. "Maybe they are, but it's not me. Maybe one day when I find the one, but not yet. Some poet said that love is the sexual excitement of the young, the habit of the middle-aged and the mutual dependence of the old." He grinned. "I'm staying in the first stage as long as I can. In lust, not love. It has all the benefits and none of the disadvantages."

Niall sighed. "And someone else said that only little boys and old men sneer at love."

"Yeah, well, I'm still a little boy at heart." He revved the engine and Niall *tsked.*

"So have you ever been in love?" Taylor asked.

"Yes."

Taylor glanced across at him. "What happened?"

"Nothing happened. I'm still in love. I will be until the day I die."

Taylor shook his head in disbelief. "Is that why you won't come out with me? Why you stay holed up in the attic? Why you're hiding? You love someone you can't have? Forget her. Move on."

"No," Niall said in a quiet voice. "I can't do that."

Chapter Five

Roo was exhausted by the time she'd hauled her life out of Ilkley. After the long slog up the hill and along Thorpe Lane, she was shuffling like an old lady. Fortunately, it was a dark night with the moon hiding behind thick clouds and no streetlamps along the unpaved road, so unless they had werewolf vision, no one could see her. Unfortunately, rolling her case in and out of unexpected potholes was jolting every muscle in her body. Her feet ached, her arms ached—even her teeth ached.

She snuck in through the open gates of Sutton Hall, turned right and went straight through the rhododendron bushes and into the woods. She needed to stay well away from the house and far enough from the drive that the tent wouldn't be seen. When Roo couldn't make out the shadow of the house, she thought it was safe to assume she wasn't visible either. On the down side, she could hardly see where she was going.

What she needed was a clearing, a spot with enough space to put up the tent, preferably with hot-and-cold running water, a mini bar, a convenient...convenience but no animals, no small or large bugs and definitely no human-ingesting aliens within spitting distance. Not that Roo ever spat. Unless she swallowed a fly. Or if spit killed aliens. Though she wouldn't know until—

A rustling noise froze Roo's brain and body, except for her heart, which beat loud enough to betray her presence to anything in the vicinity. When no ten-foot-tall, stumbling monster emerged from the woods, she frantically gulped air. *Make a note: Don't hold breath when scared.* Lowering her case and numerous bags to the ground, she fumbled inside one of them until she found the lantern. When Roo flicked the switch nothing happened. *Oh darn it.*

Roo knew there were batteries inside because the label said so, but maybe one of those little plastic strips protected the terminals. If she moved back toward the drive, out of the dense part of the wood, she might be able to see better, but if the lantern didn't work, she might never get back to where she'd left her things. She imagined

herself doomed to spend eternity roaming the woods looking for her tent. She'd be the stuff of local legends.

Or not.

Tipping the lantern upside down, Roo carefully slid the cover off the batteries and felt inside. *Yep, there it is.* Roo yanked at the strip, and the batteries flicked up and out past her scrabbling fingers.

"Shhhit."

It took several minutes of tentative fumbling through leaves and dirt, imagining she was uncovering a vampire's resting place and that any moment a hand might emerge and drag her down, before she found both batteries. And another curse-ridden couple of minutes before she managed to insert them the right way round, but the moment she had light, Roo sighed with relief. Though it made the woods look creepy. It reminded her of that childhood game, grandmother's footsteps, where someone stood with their back to their friends as they crept toward them. If the person turned and saw them move, they had to return to the start. Roo had the uncomfortable feeling that if she turned her back on the trees, they'd creep nearer and keep coming. She'd be wrapped in their branches and— *Stop it.*

Roo spun in a circle and swung the lantern. "Saw you," she whispered.

Oh God, if a twig cracks now, I'll freak out big time.

Setting the lantern on her case, she removed her unborn child in a joyous, pain-free delivery and wrapped it in her coat so it didn't get dirty. When she opened the packaging on the tent, she winced. Roo had been hoping for one that with a single twist popped up ready to crawl into. She crouched by the light to read the three pages of instructions.

The next hour was one Roo suspected would live with her forever. She'd struggled to put the poles together, then to fathom out where to put them in the football-pitch-sized piece of fabric, and then how to take them apart when she realized she'd got the wrong ones linked. She'd knocked off the heel of her shoe hammering pegs into unyielding ground, but finally the damn thing was up, a gray sweep of nylon that looked like a mini spaceship, except it had a distinct un-aerodynamic sag on the left hand side. Roo was too tired to rectify it.

She unzipped the entrance and dragged all her things inside, along with the light, then zipped herself in. Amazing how a thin layer of material could make her feel much safer. It was actually quite cozy, and if it hadn't been for the lack of facilities, she could have lived there

for ages. Though probably not if it rained.

Or if it was cold.

Or windy.

Or if it snowed.

Her phone showed it was two in the morning and she groaned. Still, on the bright side, she was only a few minutes' walk from work. No need to get up early. She took a swig of water, brushed her teeth—*oh yes, I* do *spit*—then unzipped the tent and emptied her mouth before she stripped to her underwear. She unrolled the foam mat, which immediately rolled back up. Roo glared at it, stripped the wrapping off the sleeping bag and then climbed into it, flattening the mat as she stretched out, hoping it wasn't going to roll up again and make her a sandwich filling.

The last thing Roo did before she snuggled her head into her pillow was to set the alarm on her phone—8:15—and switch off the light.

Damn, I need to pee.

As Taylor pulled into the drive of Sutton House, Niall lifted his head from where it had been resting against the window.

"You okay?" Taylor asked.

"Better. Sorry. I think maybe you're right. Something was slipped into my drink."

Niall twisted suddenly to look out of the window past Taylor.

Taylor glanced right. "You see something?"

"A light."

Taylor braked.

Niall turned to stare through the back window. "No, I must have been mistaken."

"When I was a kid, I used to see—" Taylor's mind went blank. *What the fuck had I been going to say?*

"See what?" Niall whispered.

"Dunno." Taylor pulled up outside the front door instead of taking the car round to the garage.

He waited for Niall to get out and then locked it. Taylor felt unsettled, anxiety nibbling at his gut. There was a dull pain in his

chest, and his ribs ached as though some memory was trying to break free. *I'm...disappointed, but I don't know why.*

Niall followed him into the house and locked the door.

"See you in the morning," Taylor said.

Misery swamped him as he trudged up the stairs. Niall was the one not well, so why did *he* feel so bad? Because he'd hoped to be in bed with a woman? Taylor closed the door of his room and leaned back against it. When had he last fucked anyone?

Sophie. A month ago.

Taylor released a bark of laughter as he dropped onto the bed and flopped on his back. Had it really been a month? *Fuck it.* That was unheard of. A month since he moved into Sutton Hall and a month since he'd gotten laid. He frowned. *This damn house.*

He'd been through three PAs in this past month too. Taylor sat up. *Oh fuck. Had* they left because of him? Maybe Niall was right. Could they have lied about the lottery, finding Jesus? Had Emma really found it too far to commute? He hadn't harassed them, had he? Chills skittered down his spine. Maybe they just hadn't fancied him. Taylor gulped.

Was his lack of pulling power simply a logistics issue? Because he didn't go out as much as he had in London, he'd reduced his odds of success? Leeds had plenty of places to troll for willing women, but it seemed as if Taylor's plans to go out either faded as the day wore on, or if he did manage to escape from Sutton Hall, he struck out.

This bloody house.

And to make matters worse, when he *did* go out *and* manage to drag Niall with him, Niall was the one who could have scored.

For the first time since he was a teenager, Taylor's confidence in his ability to attract women was wavering. He'd agreed Niall should be the one to approach Sherry, but her three friends had been standing right next to Taylor and ignored him. He lifted his arm and sniffed. Fine.

Yet whilst Taylor wanted women to find him attractive, part of him was only too aware that he hadn't really wanted to interest any of the three with Sherry. Though he'd let Niall think he'd spoiled the evening by needing to come back here, Taylor hadn't been bothered. He didn't know if he was seeing sense for the first time in his life or sliding into depression. One thing was for certain, he was confused.

Maybe it had taken a month of no sex to make him appreciate

one- and two-night stands brought pain along with pleasure. Was Niall right? Was there someone out there for him to love? Could someone love him? More to the point, did he deserve to be loved? Since that day, sixteen years ago, when his ten-year-old sister had disappeared into thin air and Taylor's life and that of his parents' had changed forever, he'd grown up feeling as though there was something missing inside him.

His parents were still together, in spite of everything. Many marriages wouldn't have withstood the strain, and despite his moaning to Niall, Taylor knew some people found love. His parents weren't happy for a long time, but they were now. Well, as happy as they could be. They smiled when they Skyped him. Which reminded Taylor, he'd still not responded to their latest email. He'd photographed the furniture and paintings and bits and pieces as they'd asked. They'd not yet said they wanted to keep anything, but reading between the lines, Taylor had sensed the implication that he hadn't found something they wanted him to.

There was only one place he hadn't checked.

Maybe two.

Taylor rolled off the bed and moved over to the window to draw the curtain. His hand froze on the material. Niall stood with his back toward him in the middle of the lawn, staring down toward the walled garden. Had he heard something? Seen something? Niall shrugged his shirt from his shoulders and kicked off his shoes. When he stepped out of his chinos and boxers, Taylor watched mesmerized.

What the fuck is he doing?

Taking his clothes off, you idiot.

Taylor's pulse rocketed, blood rushing through his veins to fill his cock. *Oh Christ. What the—?* He'd never seen Niall without a shirt. Now he stared at broad shoulders tapering to a narrow waist and a perfect tight butt. *Oh fuck, I'm staring at his butt?* Then Taylor's attention was drawn to a tattoo that ran down Niall's back, crossing from his left shoulder to curve over his right hip and run down his leg. He'd caught a glimpse of it at Niall's neck and been intrigued, but he was surprised how big it was. *It turns me on.* Taylor swallowed hard and rubbed the heel of his palm over the stiff outline of his shaft. *What the hell's the matter with me?* He let out a strangled laugh. *Who I am trying to fool?*

"Turn around, Niall," he whispered.

The moon slid from behind a cloud and Niall stood bathed in light as if he were some perfect statue newly unveiled but already entwined

by ivy. Niall couldn't have heard him, but he turned. The tattoo continued down to his ankle and spread over his foot. But Taylor's gaze was inexorably drawn higher to the flat plane of the guy's stomach and a cock that rose long and thick and— *Oh fuck. What am I doing?*

Taylor wrapped his fingers around the bulge in his chinos and squeezed. Did Niall suspect, guess, want him to watch? Taylor couldn't bring himself to look Niall in the face. Niall *had* to hope Taylor would see him or he wouldn't be standing naked in the middle of the lawn. Unless this was some bizarre religious celebration and Niall assumed Taylor was fast asleep in bed.

That wasn't impossible. Taylor knew very little about Niall. Because he hadn't wanted his own skeletons uncovered, it had been easy to leave Niall's where they lay, so when Taylor pushed and got nowhere, he'd let it drop. If Niall wanted to confide in him, he'd do so. That was how Taylor felt. He didn't know if his parents had told Niall about his sister, but regardless of whether they had or not, Taylor didn't want to talk about Stephanie.

Now Taylor wished he knew what Niall was thinking, but then he didn't know how he felt himself. He looked down at his hand, squeezing and stroking around his zipper. *Ah damn it, yes I do.* The idea of rubbing himself over Niall's hot, silky skin, the thought of pushing his cock into the guy's warm, wet mouth, shoving his whole length into his tight asshole made Taylor's butt cheeks clench and he shuddered. *Where the hell did that come from?*

Fuck, fuck, fuck. Stop looking. But he couldn't.

He'd known the moment he set eyes on Niall that the guy was trouble. If he'd had any sense, he'd have asked him to leave. Taylor stepped away from this sort of temptation. Maybe this was why he treated women as he did, never contemplating a long-term relationship, because he suspected ultimately, he wouldn't be satisfied. Taylor released a shaky breath.

Taylor liked women, he liked sucking their breasts, playing with their clits, fucking them hard and fast, slow and gentle. He liked to fuck them in the ass too, though he didn't find many who'd let him. Taylor liked what women did to him, the feel of soft, gentle fingers playing, but he'd always wondered what it would be like with a guy. And he'd wondered that more than was healthy since he'd moved back to Sutton Hall.

Sometimes Niall eyeballed him when he didn't think Taylor was

watching, and Taylor saw an expression on his face that forced him to leave the room. Need, longing—who the hell knew what it was? But it made Taylor's cock stir. And he'd seen Niall's stir too and the way Niall tried to hide that from him. They'd been tiptoeing around each other for weeks.

Taylor took the step forward to stand in the center of the window and he looked straight at Niall. *Maybe he won't see me.* Taylor would take it as a sign. Niall lifted his head and stared back at him. No smile. No frown. Only some intangible sense of need.

Almost before he registered he was doing it, Taylor finished unbuttoning his shirt. He let it fall from his shoulders and his hands moved to the button on his chinos. He yanked pants and boxers down together and kicked off his shoes. Before thinking too hard stopped him in his tracks, Taylor walked out of his room and headed down the stairs.

What the hell are you doing?

What the hell do you think?

Turn round.

Keep going.

The internal conversation continued until his feet carried him out of the back door. Taylor was filled with a mixture of relief and concern to see Niall still stood in the middle of the lawn, his seductive, terrifying cock sliding in his hand. Taylor's heart surged into his throat as he padded across the damp grass and came to a halt in front of Niall.

"You seem to be standing naked in the middle of the lawn," Taylor said. "Waiting for something? A bus? A lunar eclipse? Coven of witches to dance with?" He took a deep breath. "Me?"

Niall stared at him. "What do you think?"

Taylor glanced up into the sky, his pulse racing. "Should be any minute now. Look out for broomsticks."

Niall laughed and the sound wrapped around Taylor like a warm blanket. He could count on the fingers of one hand the number of times he'd heard Niall really laugh. Taylor watched as Niall continued to stroke his cock, his fingers dragging the foreskin over the crest then sliding down to caress his balls with his thumb before pulling up again. Taylor wanted those fingers on *his* cock, wanted to feel what it was like to be touched by a man. And that tattoo...a tree? A vine? Something very intricate, but it was hard to make out in the dim light.

Taylor knew, though he didn't know how, that Niall wasn't going to make the first move, and perversely felt annoyed. *I came to you,* he wanted to shout, but instead took a deep breath. Fuck it, this was just sex. What did it matter who started it? Hadn't Niall done that when he'd stood there in full view and stripped? Taylor swallowed hard and then reached out to wrap shaking fingers over Niall's where they held his cock. Niall's tremulous sigh made Taylor's balls tighten. Then their hands began to work together, fingers entwined as they grasped and squeezed the steel-hard shaft.

And again, though he didn't understand why, Taylor knew Niall wouldn't touch him, that he had to bring Niall's hand to his cock. Taylor wanted it there, wanted to feel Niall's fingers caress him. Niall's breathing was noisy in the still of the night, his stuttered breaths punctuating Taylor's every move. *Do it. Do it.* When Taylor pulled Niall's other hand to his groin, Niall's breathing grew noisier still. They stood maybe a foot apart, playing with each other's dicks, guided by each other's hands, fingers slipping and sliding, cocks preening and crying silent tears of delight. Taylor couldn't look Niall in the face.

"I've dreamed of this," Niall whispered.

Am I *dreaming?*

The strangeness and familiarity of touching another man's cock, like his and yet not like his at all, buzzed in Taylor's head where pressure grew as synapses snapped to link neurons. Explosion loomed lower down. Their hands moved faster, fingers tightened and their breathing became more ragged.

"Oh fuck," Taylor panted.

Taylor's hands were slippery with precome as he raced toward orgasm. He'd have been ashamed of coming so fast with a woman, but suspected Niall was as close as him. Taylor's balls drew up to cup the base of his cock, white light flared in his head and he closed his eyes. *Yes, yes, yes.* His toes curled as he spurted into his hand and into Niall's. Taylor sucked in a breath with each wrenching spasm, pleasure racing through his veins. Then Niall was coming, releasing warm, liquid silk onto Taylor's fingers as he gasped into the night air, and somehow that moment was just as good.

As Taylor opened his eyes, he saw silver light shimmering just over Niall's shoulders. For a moment, the light seemed solid enough for Taylor to touch and then it disappeared. *What the hell?* He blinked. Had to be some weird refraction of moonlight or alternatively a head rush brought on by an orgasm-fried brain.

Oh Christ. An orgasm-fried brain. What have I done? He lifted his head to look into Niall's eyes and saw everything he didn't want to see. Pleasure. Desire. Expectation. Reality checked in. He stood naked in the middle of the lawn, jacking off with a guy. How could he have been so stupid? *I am* not *fucking gay.* Burning with embarrassment, he pulled free and walked away, come dripping from his hands until he stooped to wipe it on the grass. He'd gone no more than ten yards before he turned and stalked back.

"That's never going to happen again," Taylor snapped. "I like women."

"I ask nothing of you," Niall said.

Taylor scanned Niall's face, but it was now empty of expression. He turned and walked back to the house. *Mistake, mistake, mistake,* said his brain.

No it wasn't, said his cock.

Chapter Six

Roo's expectation that waking at 8:15 a.m. would give her time to get up, get ready and get to work had been a touch unrealistic, she thought as she took the chewing gum out of her mouth and used it to attach her heel to her shoe. She squirted paste on her toothbrush, sucked on it, fastened her blouse and slipped on her shoes at the same time. *Brilliant multitasking!* Then unzipped the tent and climbed out to pull on her skirt while she brushed a bit more vigorously. Roo threw the toothbrush back inside, and zipped the tent again. Then unzipped it to grab her purse. Zipped and unzipped it to get the water bottle so she could refill it. Roo wasted another minute staring at her spaceship trying to think if she'd remembered everything before she headed for the road.

In daylight she could see she wasn't far from civilization. Roo bulldozed her way through the rhododendrons to reach the drive and brushed bits of foliage from her hips. Then she ran.

After a couple of yards, the heel fell off her shoe and she lurched to a halt. She went back to grab the wayward plastic cube, slipped it in her purse and set off again on an awkward lope.

Sleeping in the tent hadn't been too bad, probably because she was so exhausted. The can of SpaghettiOs hadn't appealed for breakfast, so she hoped Taylor was the sort of boss who provided donuts and pastries and freshly brewed coffee—and a shower. Though she needed to empty her bladder before she drank anything, and running wasn't helping that requirement.

A motor bike roared up behind her and Roo squealed. *Darn it, stop panicking.* The guy—or maybe woman—in black leathers didn't stop until they pulled up in front of the main entrance. Roo lollopped up the drive. By the time she reached the house, the biker had gone inside. No sign on the door on this occasion to tell her to walk in, so Roo pulled on the rusty metal rod that hung vertically on the left side of the door and heard a clangy echo inside.

Then she jigged on the spot. *I need to pee. Why didn't I go in the woods?* She should have changed her shoes, but her only other pair of

smart shoes were high heels and she couldn't run in those. Roo really wanted to make a good first impression when she wasn't dressed as a chicken. She pulled on the rod again. And again. *Hurry up. Hurry up.*

It seemed hours before Taylor opened the door. "You should have—"

"Sorry." Roo burst past him and rushed inside. She dashed through the entrance hall and careened in a lopsided gait down the corridor toward the office where she'd been interviewed. Commonsense told her the bathroom would be down here somewhere. She flung open a door—*Oh Christ, a jungle?*—and slammed it again. The next revealed the kitchen and a bemused Niall stared at her. Roo was too desperate to drool.

"Bathroom?"she gasped.

"Next on the right."

Roo grunted her thanks, sighed when she found the Holy Grail, and locked herself in.

By the time she'd washed her hands and checked her face in the mirror to make sure she'd not come out in measles overnight, she'd calmed down, but what she saw in the mirror over her shoulder made her excited again. *A shower.* She'd have to be very quick, but since the shower in her bedsit produced hot water for only ninety-three seconds, Roo was used to washing at speed.

She whipped off her clothes and stood under twenty three seconds of arctic torture before the warmth kicked it. There was even shampoo and conditioner. Roo couldn't resist. She should have. The top came off the shampoo when she upended it over her head and the entire bottle of viscous green liquid dripped down her face. *Shit.*

The towel was minute but Roo managed and after briskly rubbing her hair, she finger combed it and emerged from the bathroom to find Niall in the hallway, leaning against the kitchen door. *He's lovely.* Even though he wasn't smiling, Roo fancied him. She didn't usually go for blonds, but she liked his disheveled hair and the guarded look on his face as though he was determined to hide his feelings. It made him feel genuine, unlike Taylor with his perfect smile.

"Thank you. Sorry," she mumbled. "Desperate. No, not desperate. Oh drat, yes, I was." Desperate for the loo. Desperate for the job. Desperate to kiss you. *Don't say anything else just in case brain slips up and tells mouth to speak.* Roo was pretty sure her face was bright red. It felt hot enough to fry an egg.

"Desperate for a shower?"

His gaze slide from her damp hair to her face.

"Strange...itching," Roo muttered. *Damn that sounds even worse.*

"You've picked up a friend on your travels." Niall pointed to her shoulder. "Going to freak out?"

Roo looked at where he was pointing and smiled. "Oh, a spider. No, I don't mind spiders, but I can't cope with worms or earwigs. Come on outside, little fella. Which way?"

Niall opened a door at the end of the corridor and Roo stepped out on to a paved area with a lawn beyond. She picked up the spider's thread and let it dangle over a windowsill. When the spider settled and Roo was unattached, she went back inside. Roo didn't even step on an ant if she could help it. All life had a purpose, even wasps. Though she wasn't too sure about Tom, her ex-boss. Or snakes.

Taylor came strolling up the hallway, followed by the biker, a tall, muscular guy with dark, straggly hair that brushed his shoulders. *Wow, is this where all the good-looking guys in the country have been hiding?* Roo couldn't help but notice the swiftness with which Niall disappeared. She'd been hoping he'd offer her coffee.

"Couldn't you stop running?" Taylor asked. "Straight through the house and out the back?" He gaped at her hair. "You usually shower when you use the bathroom?"

"Yes," Roo mumbled. "Sorry. I like to be completely clean after I've used the loo." *Shut up.* "Not that I really *needed* the shower. It's just a strange habit of mine. Dates back to diapers. No, forget I said that." *Shut up, you twit.* Both guys stared at her with their mouths open. "I had to save a spider. Not a tarantula or anything, just a—"

Taylor made a slashing motion across his throat and gestured to the guy behind him. "Roo meet Jonas. Jonas, this is Roo, our new PA. Jonas is an investigator like me so you're working for him too, taking messages, making appointments, typing up his illegible notes."

"Pleased to meet you." Roo shook Jonas's hand.

Wow, firm grip and big anthracite eyes. He pulled her forward slightly and his nose twitched. *Is he sniffing me?*

"Back at you," he said and let her go.

"Come into the office." Taylor gestured for Roo to go ahead and she tried not to limp.

"What happened to your heel?" Taylor asked.

Well, he was a detective. Of course he'd notice.

"It fell off. I tried to stick it on but it came off again on the way here."

"Maybe the glue wasn't strong enough. What did you use?" Jonas asked.

"Um..." Roo mumbled.

"Let me have a look and see if I can fix it," Jonas said.

Roo sat on the chair in front of the small desk and took off her shoe. When she pulled the heel out of her purse, she tried to peel off the gum, but of course the damn stuff was solid now. Jonas took the heel from her hand.

"You trod in—oh." He laughed. "Wrong end. I've never seen anyone try that before."

Taylor sat behind his desk. "What?"

"Sticking a heel on with chewing gum. I'll just be a minute. There's something in my bike tool kit I can use."

Jonas slipped out and Taylor stared at her, tapping his pencil on the desk. Roo tried to look efficient, organized and keen, and tried really hard not to tap her foot in time to Taylor's taps.

"Your blouse is fastened up wrong," he said.

Oh shit. Roo fumbled with the buttons.

"Right. No need to wait for Jonas. He knows how I operate. I'll run through what we do. The calls you'll get will be to do with surveillance, intelligence gathering, serving of court papers, tracing people who've skipped owing money, investigating insurance claims, checking alibis for court cases, tracing missing people in adoption scenarios and acting as a go-between. Stuff like that."

Roo wondered if she was supposed to take notes because she'd forgotten most of that already. Taylor looked across at her and she tried to think of an intelligent question. *When do we break for coffee? How long do I get for lunch? When will I get paid?*

"When do we br—what do you do most of?" she asked. *Wow, that was close.*

"Observing people in connection with false accident or sickness claims, and matrimonial work—checking assets and following husbands and wives who suspect each other of cheating."

"Right."

"We work for private individuals, companies, solicitors, councils, government departments, insurance companies, banks and we do

subcontract work for other companies like ours."

Roo nodded. He could have been talking gibberish.

"If I'm not here to answer the phone, all I need you to do is take a message. If it's an enquiry about a job, I'll contact the caller later. You got that?"

Roo nodded. It was the safest thing to do.

"When I've accepted a job, I need you to start a file, using the client's name, summarizing the instructions they've given. Name, date, contact details and what the job is. There'll be an estimate of cost to sort out and I'll show you how to do that. Everything has to go in that file. Every detail, no matter how insignificant it might seem. If we get written correspondence, it has to be scanned in, but we keep the physical copies too. Okay?"

Roo nodded. Her head was going to fall off in a minute.

"Photos are printed out on that machine. Back up everything."

"Right."

Jonas came in with her shoe and handed it to her, heel attached, then leaned against the window.

"Thank you." Roo slipped it on her foot.

"One thing that will save me some time is if you ask a couple of questions of the caller to determine whether it's a case I'd want," Taylor said.

Oh for a pencil.

"If you get a call from someone who suspects their partner of cheating, ask them if they have kids or if they run a business together. If the answer to either one of those is yes, then they don't need my services. The relationship has already broken down and it will never be right again."

Roo frowned. "But—"

"No buts. Their lives are wrecked and they'd be paying me to confirm it."

"But it could be that by the time they want to hire you, they're ready to face the truth and you'd be denying them that chance. I don't see what's wrong in helping them to do that."

She glanced at Jonas, hoping to see him agree but his face was blank.

Taylor leaned across his desk. "And that's what I do for people who don't have kids and don't work together."

Roo gulped. "But—" Taylor glared, but she carried on. "Maybe their partner *isn't* having an affair."

Jonas laughed. "You know the chances of that being true?"

"They don't get as far as phoning a company like ours until they have evidence they can't ignore," Taylor said. "Once the dynamics of their relationship have changed, everything they once trusted is open for re-examination. It's all over, they just don't yet know it."

"That's...sad," Roo whispered.

"That's life," Taylor said. "You can't be emotional about this. If you care, you can't do the job."

She swallowed hard. "I don't think you *can* do a job without caring. I mean if you discover someone's been unfaithful, don't you at least feel sorry for the innocent one?"

"No." Taylor shook his head. "No such thing as the innocent one. There's any number of explanations as to why relationships break down. If a guy's cheating on his wife, could be he has good reason to. Maybe she makes his life a living hell. Maybe she won't have sex with him. Maybe she nags at him all the time or says *but* a lot. Or could be he's an arrogant sod who wants his dinner on the table at seven every night, then his comfort fuck *and* his attractive secretary on the desk each lunchtime. So long as there are no kids involved and the couple doesn't work together, *and* the client doesn't sound like a raging lunatic, I'll probably take the case."

Roo frowned. "But—"

"That's enough. I'm not paying you to question my business decisions." Taylor got to his feet and beckoned Jonas to come with him. *He's going already?* He hadn't even shown her what computer programs he used.

"I—"

"Shut up," Taylor snapped. "Sit there, take messages, tidy up and don't throw anything away. Even a chicken could do that. I'll be back after lunch."

He walked out after Jonas and slammed the door so hard, Roo flinched.

"What bit you on the butt this morning?" she muttered.

Well, she'd dealt with surly bosses before and coped. Roo looked around the room and wondered where to start. Maybe tidying would give her a better idea of what Taylor did. She picked up a box to lift onto the desk, the bottom fell out and papers cascaded onto the floor.

"Shit."

"Even a chicken?" Jonas laughed.

"Don't ask." Taylor was so annoyed with himself he could barely speak.

"I'll meet you there." Jonas headed for his bike.

Taylor breathed a sigh of relief once he was driving away from Sutton Hall. Everything had gone wrong from the moment he'd opened the door to Roo. He groaned. No point blaming her for the fact that he'd spent a sleepless night trying to figure out what the hell he'd done on the lawn with Niall.

He knew what he'd *done*, he just wasn't sure *why* he'd done it. What was he supposed to say this morning? *Nice wank. Let's do it again sometime.*

Not going to happen.

So he'd tried to pretend it hadn't happened in the first place.

Impossible.

Flirting with Roo would have gone some way to helping him get his head straight, but instead she'd annoyed him so much he'd wanted to sack her. Actually, make that yank her into his arms and shut her up with a kiss. Instead, he'd shouted at her and she now thought he was an asshole. He was.

Taylor pulled onto the road toward Harrogate, Jonas accelerating away in the distance. What the hell was it about Roo? Even as his cock was unfurling in his boxers, he'd told her to shut up. He was an idiot. Roo was the perfect chance to prove to himself and to Niall that he was into women. Maybe it was time to break the rule about fucking the help. Maybe *not* doing it had been the reason he'd lost his three PAs. The thought cheered Taylor. When he got back, he'd suggest taking Roo out to dinner to welcome her to the company. Nothing wrong in following up lust at first sight.

Niall heard the door slam, felt it in his bones and shuddered. Was he the cause of Taylor's bad temper? Niall dropped onto the red cushion in the corner of the attic room, closed his eyes and released a deep sigh. This morning, when he'd gone downstairs, Taylor had acted

as though nothing had happened last night, though not hard to miss the guy had gone out of his way to avoid him. No accidental brushing allowed. Niall sighed again. The ladder he'd dared to approach and then struggled to climb had turned into a slide and Niall had slithered to the bottom of the board to end up back where he started.

Maybe not quite. Taylor *did* want him, but fought the attraction. Though it wasn't enough that Taylor was attracted, not enough to spill into each other's hands, not enough if they eventually fucked each other. Body and soul, Niall wanted his love. More than wanted—needed, had to have it. It was as essential to him as the air he breathed.

Shivers trickled the length of his tattoo. Time was running out. Niall had to accept that love might not come from Taylor and that the sacrifice Niall made had been for nothing. He shook his head and opened his eyes. Not for nothing. He didn't regret these weeks spent with Taylor, even if it hadn't been the time of joy he'd wished for. One truth remained—Niall would love him until the day he died, because everything that was wrong about Taylor was Niall's fault.

Now Roo was downstairs and in theory another rival, though Niall was considering revising his strategy. For the first time, this was a woman he actually liked, and judging by Taylor's yells and the slamming of the door, maybe one that Taylor didn't know how to handle. Her reaction to the spider had pleased Niall more than he could say. Roo was impossible to predict and that was refreshing. Did he have the energy to pursue her too? Should he?

Perhaps he had no choice. There was little point repeating past mistakes. Time to try something different.

Roo had just finished arranging all Taylor's books on the shelves when the phone rang.

She picked it up, blew out a breath and said, "Good morning. ICU Investigations."

A strangled sob was the response and Roo's heart clenched.

"My name's Roo," she said. "What's yours?"

"Alice," a woman whispered.

"How can I help you?" Roo whispered back.

"I think my husband's cheating on me."

"What makes you think that?"

Roo gulped as water poured through the flood gates. Receipts for hotel rooms, late nights at the office, an unfamiliar scent, leaving the room to answer a call on his mobile. And after Alice had detailed all that, she went through it again, making excuses. Her husband was covering for a colleague over the hotel room, he had a huge deal he was brokering—hence the late nights, the scent was some trigger-happy sales woman in a department store, and he hadn't wanted to disturb her TV program by taking a call in the room.

"Do you think he's cheating?" Alice asked.

Roo swallowed hard. "Do you? Deep down is that what you think?"

"Yes."

"Then he probably is."

"No, no." More wailing. "I need to know for sure. Will you follow him?"

"Do you have kids?" Roo asked.

"No."

"You don't work together?"

"No."

"Give me your details and I'll ask my boss when he comes back. Is there a number he can call or do you want to call back this afternoon?"

Roo picked up a sheet of paper and wrote everything down.

Niall came into the room while she was still speaking. He mimed drinking a cup of coffee and Roo wanted to kiss him. Well, she would have wanted to kiss him whether he was miming that or not, but she nodded her thanks. He leaned against the doorframe watching her.

"Have you actually asked him directly if he's cheating on you?" Roo posed the question more to prove she was actually talking to a client and not some distant relative in Australia. Not that she had any relations in Australia.

"No," said Alice. "I just couldn't."

"Is he violent?"

"James would never hit me."

"Then maybe you should outright ask him—are you cheating on me? He might confess and you'd save yourself some money." *Oh shit.* Roo didn't dare look at Niall.

"But if he isn't, I'd have wrecked everything. I'll call back this afternoon. Thanks for listening."

"You're welcome." Roo put down the phone and looked up at Niall. "Was that wrong?"

"Not my business. Come in the kitchen," Niall said.

Roo pushed herself up and followed him. "They should talk though, right? They might able to sort things out. I think people don't talk nearly enough and I blame television."

She sighed with pleasure when she walked into the room. A large red stove dominated one wall and the storage cupboards were constructed of old oak. A long wooden table sat in the middle of the kitchen, and there was an overstuffed crimson couch pushed against the back wall next to French doors that looked out onto a garden bursting with color. This looked so cozy and comfortable and homely, and so much like the kitchen Roo dreamed of having but knew she never would, that a lump rose into her throat.

Niall poured two mugs of coffee. "Milk, sugar?"

"Neither, thank you. Would it be terribly rude if I asked for a slice of toast?"

He laughed. "Terribly. One slice?"

"Four would be better." Roo slammed a hand to her mouth. "Sorry."

Niall pulled out a chair. "Sit down."

"This is lovely," she said. *You're lovely.*

Niall lifted the lids off the hot plates and put two—*darn it*—slices of bread between a couple of large wire disks.

"How are you getting on?" he asked.

"Fine. You don't work with Taylor then?"

Niall carried a butter dish to the table, together with a plate and a knife.

"No, though I did a job with him last night." He turned the toaster over and Roo's stomach rumbled at the smell of bread crisping.

"What did you do?" she asked.

"Decoy work."

"Like a wooden duck?"

Niall smiled. "We went to a club in Leeds and taped a woman who was prepared to cheat on her husband."

"Ah, so you flirted with her. Made like a drake to attract a...hen."

Niall put the slices of toast on a plate, pushed it in front of her

and sat opposite. "I danced with her."

Roo wondered how anyone could resist him. Didn't seem fair. Good thing she wasn't married. "Definitely entrapment." *Bother. I didn't mean to say that out loud.*

Niall cocked his head on one side. "You've never seen me dance."

He could have moved with the grace of a duck on ice and Roo would have danced with him if he'd asked. Not that he'd ask.

The butter melted on the toast and Roo could barely stand to waste time spreading it before she bit off a corner. She let out a moan. "Oh God, that is so good."

Niall laughed. "It's just toast."

Made by a handsome man.

"So what do you do?" Roo buttered the other slice while she ate the first.

"Take care of the garden. This house belongs to Taylor's parents. They've moved to Spain and they've let me live here rent free for the last few months in return for maintaining the grounds. The place is for sale but there doesn't seem to have been much interest so far."

"I didn't see a *For Sale* board."

"No point. There's no way out of this end of Thorpe Lane so no one's going to be driving past to entice with a board."

"How many bedrooms?"

"Seven."

"Whoa, that's a lot."

"Big garden too. Would you like me to show you outside?"

"I'd love to see the garden, but I better not. I'll take the coffee back into the office and get on with sorting stuff out before Taylor comes back with his whip." *God, rip out my tongue now.*

Niall edged closer. "It won't take long. The grounds look delightful first thing in the morning. Come and take a walk with me."

"That woman never stood a chance." Roo grabbed the coffee and fled.

Chapter Seven

Roo launched herself at the piles of paperwork and within minutes wondered what the hell Taylor's last PA had done all day. Nothing seemed to be in order. The wrong papers in files, everything jumbled inside them. She'd been right about one thing, doing this gave her a broad knowledge of ICU. The depressing side of the business, revealing cheats and fraudsters, by far overwhelmed the happier side, locating missing people and reuniting them with their families. No wonder Taylor was grumpy and disillusioned with life.

Over the course of the morning Roo took several phone calls and carefully logged and detailed each one. When she tired of staring at a blank wall, she turned her desk so it stood sideways to the window, then shifted Taylor's desk so it did the same. She tidied until there wasn't anything left to tidy and cursed herself for not getting the computer password before Taylor left.

At noon, Roo nipped into the kitchen to fill her water bottle. She put it back in her bag and bent to stow it under her desk.

"That looks good," Niall said.

Roo spun round and bumped her head. That guy had feet of air, and something about him had every cell in her body jumping up and down in excitement.

"My bum or the office?" Roo asked.

"Not sure. Want to bend over again?"

Roo raised her eyebrows. "That was a test."

"Office?"

She raised her eyebrows even higher.

"Office," he said in a firm voice.

Roo smiled.

"Going to break for lunch?" Niall asked.

"I forgot to bring sandwiches. I'll just keep working."

He walked across the room and it was all Roo could do to stand her ground. She'd flirted and was asking for trouble, but while part of

her wanted to throw herself into Niall's arms, the other part of her wanted to run. She ignored both voices and didn't move.

Niall stopped a foot or so away and frowned. "What are you frightened of?"

Roo bristled. "I'm not frightened of anything." She chewed her lip. "Well, I'm not keen on great white sharks. I think if I found myself in the water with one, I'd be scared sh—witless. And I don't like snakes that can launch themselves across a room, though I've only seen that happen in a horror film. And I'm really not keen on vultures because I can't help thinking that if I tripped over and hit my head, they might think I was dead, and I think I'd be scared if...I...saw...a...dragon."

A finger moving toward her lips slowed her down and then shut her up. Niall's mouth twitched. "I've made you a sandwich. Come and sit in the garden. A lot of dragons out there, but I promise to protect you."

"Thanks."

"And I don't bite," Niall said. "Not unless requested."

Roo let out a strangled whimper. "Neither do I unless something looks tasty."

He raised his eyebrows. "Join me?"

It seemed churlish to refuse and food was food. "Okay."

He gave her a slow smile and she melted. Not completely, but mostly. Niall went into the kitchen and emerged with two small paper bags and bottles of water.

"Picnic," he said.

Roo followed him over a perfectly striped lawn to a central door in a high stone wall that ran across the whole garden. Niall held it open and Roo went through.

"Oh wow," she whispered. "Wow, wow, wow, wow, wow."

As she stepped forward, the sun came out and Roo could almost sense the flowers turning their faces to the light. It was a riot of color everywhere she looked. Niall plucked a bud from the nearest plant and squeezed the neck. The flower opened as if it had a hinged jaw.

He smiled. "Quite safe to put your finger in the mouth of a snapdragon."

Roo put her little finger into the flower and Niall let it go. It closed on her and she laughed in delight. He pressed the neck to open it and then stuck the flower in Roo's hair. Niall walked around telling her the

names of everything, none of which Roo remembered. It wasn't that she had a bad memory, but she worked better with written notes. In all directions there was something different to see. A tree house, a hot tub, lines of vegetables, fruit trees, and lots and lots of flowers. She loved the fact that the garden was enclosed by walls, as if it were some secret magical place.

"Nothing ripe yet, but these are apple, pear and cherry trees," Niall said. "That's a mulberry bush. We could sit here under the walnut tree." He dropped to the grass.

Roo sat opposite and stretched out her legs next to his.

"What's your favorite sandwich?" Niall asked.

"Lettuce, camembert and cranberry."

He gave an astonished laugh. "You're joking."

Roo shook her head and when she looked in the bag, saw what appeared to be a lettuce, camembert and cranberry sandwich. "I'm a bit spooked now." *A lot spooked.*

But it didn't diminish her appetite.

When Roo licked her fingers and savored the last tasty mouthful, she glanced across at Niall to see he was only halfway through eating his. *He'll think I'm a pig.*

"Hungry? Even after that toast?" he asked.

"Well, I did ask for four slices and disappointingly you only gave me two."

He chuckled. "I thought you were joking."

Roo looked in the bag. "Cake as well?"

"A chocolate brownie. I made it."

"Oh yum. Don't watch me," Roo begged. "I'm such a monster with chocolate. Close your eyes and count to ten...no, three, and you can open them again."

Niall frowned. "You can't eat that in three seconds."

"Want a bet?"

"Go on then, but I have to watch."

Roo sniffed. "You think I'm going to cheat?" Actually, she *had* intended to cheat. She wanted to take it back and eat it in the tent tonight to compensate for cold SpaghettiOs.

"What do I get if I can do it?" Roo asked.

"What do you want?" He stared straight at her and Roo's organs

liquefied. *I could ask for a kiss. We're flirting after all.*

"Your brownie," she said.

He laughed. "Go for it."

Roo broke hers in half inside the bag as she pulled it out and held it in such a way that Niall couldn't tell. Staring him straight in the eyes, which she hoped would distract him from looking too closely at her hand, she pushed the whole thing in her mouth and chewed frantically.

"One elephant, two elephants, three elephants," Niall said.

"Gone," Roo spluttered and swallowed the last crumbs.

Niall narrowed his eyes. "Fibber."

Roo ran her tongue over her teeth and opened her mouth. "Not. See?"

His gaze dropped to the paper bag at her side.

"Better get back to work," Roo said and rose to her feet, the bag clutched in her hand.

Niall was up and in her face before she could take a step. "Show me."

"Show you what?" Roo took a step backward.

"You know what I do to little girls who tell fibs?"

She took another step backward, though she wasn't frightened. "Pin them out for vultures?"

He grinned. "Throw them to great whites."

He leapt at her and Roo squealed with laughter and ran. She raced all over the garden, down paths, past the tree house, through the vegetable patch and back to the orchard, and as she did she snatched bits of the brownie out of the bag and dropped them. Roo spun around a tree expecting to see Niall behind her, and he came at her from another direction. Roo squeaked and jerked the bag out of reach.

"Show me what's in there," Niall said.

Roo swallowed the words "make me" and shoved her hands behind her back. "I'm very hurt you don't trust me."

Niall held out his hand.

Roo sighed and pushed the bag into his fingers. He opened it and growled. It was an honest-to-God bearlike growl and for a split second Roo really *was* frightened.

"Where've you hidden it?" Niall asked and then looked at the

garden and laughed. "Playing Hansel and Gretel, you little cheat? I should spank you."

Oohh. Why did that sound so appealing? Before she did something stupid, Roo turned and fled. She smacked straight into Niall.

"Where the hell did you come from?" she gasped. *Wow, he's fast.*

He wrapped his hands around her back and pulled her close. Roo wanted to kiss him more than she'd wanted to do anything for a long time, but she needed this job, and she wasn't easy. She stamped hard on Niall's foot and he yelped but didn't let her go.

"You are the most—" Niall broke off, the smile slipped from his face and he took his arms off her. "Go," he said.

Roo ran back to the house, wondering what the hell had just happened. He'd still been smiling when she'd stamped on his foot, so that wasn't why he'd suddenly turned cold.

She'd hardly settled at her desk before the door opened and Taylor walked in holding a handful of mail. Had Niall heard him coming? She felt her face heat.

"Rearranging the furniture already?" Taylor quirked an eyebrow.

"I didn't like staring at a blank wall."

"You're supposed to be working, not staring at walls."

"I'll move them back," she muttered.

Taylor slumped behind his desk. "Leave it like it is. I'll see if I like it. I'll be able to tell if you're daydreaming now. How've you got on?"

"Fine." Roo's answer for everything. She was *not* going to think of what just happened in the garden with Niall. "I tidied and sorted, and itemized the calls on different sheets of paper. I've put a few observations on the bottom—what I thought about the potential client. You didn't tell me your computer password so I couldn't link the paper files to the digital ones."

"Marlowe with a four for the e."

"Thanks."

The phone rang and Roo picked it up. "Good afternoon. ICU Investigations."

"Hello. Do you look for animals?" asked a young male voice.

"Er..."

"Our dog's gone missing." There was a snuffled sob at the other end of the phone.

"What's his name?" Roo asked.

"Arthur. He's a black, flat-coated retriever. He's two years old."

Roo glanced at Taylor who was engrossed in his mail.

"Me and my sister have put signs up everywhere, but no one's called."

"Where do you live?"

Roo started to make notes. This was a youngster on the other end of the phone. Strike one. And Roo already knew Taylor wouldn't look for a lost dog. Strike Two.

Taylor looked round. His desk was much better at an angle like this. It made the room feel bigger. Everything looked tidy. How come she'd managed in half a day what the others hadn't in more than a week? Taylor checked through the pages Roo had left on his desk, and read the notes she'd made.

Pompous guy and *a cheapskate* and *a male chauvinist pig.* Taylor chuckled.

She wouldn't stop crying all the time she was talking. Sounded on the edge of a breakdown. Didn't they all?

Husband hits her. Told her to go to police or find a woman's refuge. Was that okay? Do we have a list of places to suggest? Yep and yep.

Teenager has been missing for ten years. Parents still can't give up hope. Mother said they know they're clutching at straws.

The paper fell from Taylor's hand and he swallowed hard. He glanced across the room at Roo. She was bent over, speaking urgently but quietly into the phone as she made notes.

"He likes biscuits? Right."

What?

"Does he do as he's told?" she asked. "He comes when you call him?"

Taylor stared at her.

"Is he micro-chipped?" she whispered.

What the hell? Taylor lifted his phone and pressed the switch that enabled him to listen in.

"And what do your parents say?" she asked.

"Mum says he might just turn up. Dad's...gone somewhere."

Taylor ground his teeth.

"Have you any idea what might have happened to Arthur?" Roo whispered.

"I think someone's taken him."

Taylor put his hand over the mouthpiece and said, "Roo."

She looked up and he shook his head. That caused her to frown but she kept talking. "Has he ever run away before?"

"Never. He always stays close to the house."

"I'll see what I can find out," Roo said.

"Thank you."

Taylor leapt out of his seat as she put the phone down. "Oh no you won't. I'm not running a fucking charity. And we don't look for bloody lost dogs."

Roo glared. "He said he'd pay."

Taylor put his palms flat on her desk and leaned forward. "How much?"

"Twenty pounds."

"That won't pay for shit and I can't take money from a kid," Taylor yelled.

"I wasn't going to take his money."

He backed away and leaned against his own desk. "So what were you going to do?"

"I thought I'd go and speak to his mother and the neighbors."

"And what are they going to tell you that he hasn't already heard?"

Roo chewed her lip. "He's just a boy and he's upset. He needs our help. There's nowhere else for him to go. Even if he just wants to talk, we can do that, can't we? At least by speaking to me he felt he'd *done* something."

Taylor's hands shook and he sat at his desk. That hit too close to home.

"I told you not to care," he said in a firm voice. "You can't bring emotion into this job. Leave it alone." He put his hand in his pocket and pulled out a Dictaphone. "Type this up. File it under Robinson. There are headphones in the drawer."

When Roo didn't move, he scowled at her. "And make me a coffee. Black, one sugar."

She rose to her feet, grabbed the Dictaphone and put it on her

desk, and then left the room. Taylor dropped his head into his hands. What the hell was wrong with him? He fancied her like mad and yet he kept yelling at her. It wasn't going to kill him just to make her happy over this. He jumped to his feet, pulled on his jacket and went after her.

"Where does he live?"

Roo turned to him with an eager look in her eyes. "17 Rathman Court, Ilkley."

"Come on then."

She gasped. "We're going now?"

"Isn't that what I just said? Switch on the answer phone, get your notes and tell me everything he told you before I started to listen."

Taylor wondered what the hell he was doing, but when Roo sat next to him in his car with that cock-lifting smile on her face and he glanced at her long legs, he knew damn well what he was doing.

Roo surprised him by managing to relay the salient facts of the conversation without veering off into another dimension. There wasn't much to go on. The chances of finding this dog were zero. The animal had wandered off and either been picked up by a passing car or knocked over by one. It was a legal requirement to report hitting a dog with a vehicle to the police, but that didn't mean shit.

Rathman Court was the other side of town, only a few minutes' drive. Taylor parked around the corner on Steadman Road.

"Watch and learn," he said. "Don't say anything."

"Not even hello?"

He sighed. "You can say hello."

"And goodbye?"

"Are you smirking?" Taylor restrained his own smirk. "Hello and goodbye and that's it."

"What if they ask my name?"

She grinned when he glared and he wanted to laugh. Then he did laugh and Roo beamed back at him. *Oh God, my dick.*

Taylor got out of the car and fastened his jacket. Fortunately it was long enough to hide the problem at his groin. He locked the car and walked over to a nearby lamppost. A laminated poster had been tied there—a picture of a jet-black dog wearing a red bandanna. Missing three days. Taylor turned, stared at the road and then walked down it, his gaze sweeping side to side.

"What are you looking for?" Roo asked.

"Signs of a car having swerved or even hitting the dog," he said. "It could have happened anywhere, but if this is a pet that's been well looked after, he might not have gone far."

But he found nothing.

Roo tagged along at his side as he walked into the small cul-de-sac. Expensive houses, but then most of them were in this town.

The Farrant residence was in the far corner, but Taylor headed for the first house he came to. He had a half smile on his face and his PI license out as the door opened. He was usually taken for a policeman or someone on a religious crusade if the occupier didn't spot the ID before they spoke.

The woman looked at him blankly. She was dressed for tennis in white shorts and white top.

"Sorry to disturb you," Taylor said. "I'm looking for Jason Farrant's dog."

"Who?"

"The boy who lives at number seventeen?" Taylor said. "The dog's a black retriever. Have you seen it?"

"Oh, I didn't know the kid's name. He's been and asked. I've seen him walking it, but not for the last couple of days."

"Is he well behaved? The dog, not the boy." Taylor turned on his smile and received one in return.

"He picks up after it. His dad made sure of that."

"I thought his father had moved away."

The woman frowned. "I haven't seen him around lately, but that's his car on the drive."

Five more houses, only two people in, but Taylor had more or less the same story. Boy was good with the dog. Always on a lead. Father not been seen for a week. Finally, Taylor knocked on the door of number seventeen. He assumed the boy who opened it was Jason. The kid's gaze immediately dropped to look for his dog and Taylor watched disappointment flood his face.

"We're from ICU Investigations," Taylor said and Jason's face lit up again.

"Who is it?" a woman yelled.

"Some people about Arthur, Mum," he called.

A pale-faced woman with frizzy brown hair came down the

hallway to stand behind her son. “What do you want?”

The slight aggression in her voice surprised Taylor.

“Your son called us to see if we could help find his dog,” Taylor said. “I’m a private investigator.”

“What did you do that for?” She glared at the boy. “I told you, someone must have taken him. There’s no way of finding out who.”

“Maybe your husband took him,” Taylor said.

Jason looked up at his mother. Taylor didn’t miss the tightening of her mouth.

“I’m sure he hasn’t,” she said.

Taylor smiled at her. “Have you asked him?”

She smiled back but it didn’t reach her eyes. “I’m not in touch with him. If that’s all?”

“Can we see where the dog slept?” Roo blurted.

Taylor turned and mouthed, “*What?*”

“No,” said the woman.

“Please, Mum.” Jason tugged on her arm. “Please.”

“What’s the point?” she snapped.

“Please.” The boy looked close to tears.

“Oh, all right.” She reached for a remote sitting on a table behind her and pressed a red button. “You can get to the garage round the front.”

Taylor and Roo followed Jason to the garage door, his mother behind. There was a red convertible on one side of the double garage and packed shelves on the other. Below them was a large blue dog bed sitting next to a chest freezer. Roo bent down and picked up one of the chew toys from the bed—a chicken.

“Useful?” asked the woman, who stood with crossed arms. *Why so defensive?*

“Yes, thank you.” Roo let the toy drop.

“Will you find him?” Jason asked.

“We’ll try,” Taylor said.

On the way out of the garage, with the boy out of earshot, he turned back to face the woman. “Why did your husband leave his car?”

She let out a short laugh. “I don’t know. I’ll ask Patrick if I ever see him again.”

Taylor walked out of the cul-de-sac back to the main road.

"Oh God, oh God, oh God," Roo muttered under her breath.

Taylor walked faster. "What are you oh God-ing about?"

Roo caught up with him and grabbed his sleeve. "Isn't it obvious?"

Taylor stopped. "No. What? And why did you want to see where the dog slept, for crying out loud?"

"She killed the dog."

Taylor rolled his eyes.

"But she killed her husband first."

Clung. That was the sound of Taylor's jaw hitting the ground.

Chapter Eight

Roo glared as Taylor laughed so hard he started to choke. "This isn't Cluedo," he spluttered. "Mrs. Frizzy Hair killed Mr. F in the garage with a candlestick."

She didn't know whether to kick him or thump him on the back.

"Get in the car," he gasped for air.

Roo dropped into the passenger seat.

Taylor clipped his seat belt and was still laughing as he headed down the road. "You're funny."

"I'm serious. She killed her husband and hid his body in the freezer."

"You're funny and insane. Such an attractive combination. How the hell did you figure that out, Sherlock? I didn't spot any bloody fingerprints or a blood-stained axe."

"There was a padlock on the freezer. Who padlocks their freezer?"

"Maybe she didn't want to risk her kids climbing inside."

Roo hadn't thought of that. "She had the setting on super-chill."

Taylor sighed. "Because she'd just bought a load of stuff to freeze?"

Damn, she hadn't thought of that either. "There were fresh scratches on the casing."

"Clumsy kids?" He glanced at her.

"No, the dog could smell the body of the husband and kept scratching to get at it. So she had to get rid of the dog."

"You do realize how crazy that sounds."

Roo frowned. *No it doesn't.* He could at least take her seriously. "His golf clubs were still in the garage. No man would walk out on his wife and leave his golf clubs behind."

"She definitely did it then."

"There's no need to be sarcastic. Should we call the police?"

"No." Taylor turned onto Thorpe Lane.

"Why not?"

"Because I'll be a laughing stock when they find a freezer full of pizzas and lamb chops."

"So you're more worried about being the butt of jokes than solving a murder?"

"For Christ's sake. They'd never get a search warrant. Drop it. You're fantasizing."

By the time Taylor had pulled up outside Sutton House, Roo was plotting but had her innocent face firmly in place.

"Thanks for driving over there, anyway," she said. "I guess I overreacted. The dog will probably turn up. It *was* micro-chipped. So if anyone takes it to the vet or the police, they'll be able to identify it."

Taylor turned and stared at her, and Roo had the feeling he wasn't taken in by her sudden reversal.

He sighed. "We can try and help the kid. Check with vets in the area, the local authority pound—both Bradford and Leeds. Contact the Kennel Club, the local breeders. Look online in chat rooms about the breed."

Roo smiled. "You *do* care."

"Twenty quid is twenty quid," he said.

The smile on her face broadened. She knew he didn't care about the money.

"Make us a coffee," Taylor said. "See if there's any cake. Niall bakes something most days."

Taylor disappeared into the office and Roo headed for the kitchen. Her heart jumped into her throat when she saw Niall. Would he have kissed her if she hadn't stamped on his foot and if Taylor hadn't come back?

"The master wants coffee and cake," she said. "He didn't say please so I'm thinking I should take him milky with no sugar unless you have a bottle of arsenic handy."

Niall's mouth twitched. "Don't make his mood any worse. You want coffee too?"

"Yes, please."

"Date and walnut cake?"

"Good grief. You baked that as well? Yes please, and you owe me a brownie."

Niall growled and came round the table. Roo yelped and fled the other way. Niall reversed direction and Roo laughed as they faced each other down the length of the table.

"Admit you cheated," Niall said.

"Or?"

"You know what I promised."

To spank her. Heat flared in Roo's cheeks.

"Okay. I cheated."

Niall smiled and pushed the plates across the table. "You'll enjoy it."

She wasn't sure if he meant the cake or the spanking. Roo picked up the coffees with one hand, balanced the plates on top and fled. She was being an idiot. As Roosevelt said, *"Keep your eyes on the stars, and your feet on the ground."* She needed this job and she wasn't going to keep it long at this rate, flirting with two guys who lived together.

Outside in the hallway, Roo paused. *Two guys who lived together and one of them baked?* Were they gay? Was Niall's flirting just a bit of fun? Disappointment settled over her like a heavy blanket. She went into the office and put the cake and coffee on Taylor's desk. He was talking on the phone and nodded his thanks.

Gay. Roo sighed. Why were so many good-looking guys gay?

She made a list of the places Taylor had said to contact about the dog and then looked up their numbers and called them. Arthur hadn't been handed in anywhere, but they all took details and promised to contact her if he was. Roo still had the sneaking suspicion the dog was dead. *Maybe he's in the freezer with the husband?*

When Taylor popped out of the room, she called Jason to find out where his father worked. Dorsey's in Guiseley. But a call to them elicited no information other than the fact that the guy wasn't at work. Roo decided she'd have to go in person as soon as she could manage.

At five thirty, Roo tidied her desk. "See you tomorrow," she said to Taylor.

"I'll give you a lift to the station."

Bugger. "Thanks, but there's no need. I'll be fine walking."

"It's no trouble."

No, no, no. I don't want to have to walk all the way back again.

"I'm looking forward to the exercise," Roo said in a firm voice. "It will do me good."

She picked up her bag, winced at the weight with the bottle of water inside and made for the door. "Bye."

"You did well today. Thanks."

Roo turned and smiled.

"Much better than I expected."

She sighed and headed down the hallway. One foot outside the door and the rain started. *Crap.* She didn't bother running down the drive. She was resigned to getting wet, but when she heard a car start up behind her, Roo groaned. Taylor pulled alongside, flung open the passenger door and she had no choice but to climb in.

"Thanks."

As they pulled out of the drive, Roo cast a lingering look in the vague direction of her tent.

"Will it take you long to get home?" he asked.

"Yes," she said in a glum voice.

"Pudsey, right?"

"Mmm."

"Do you live on your own?"

"Yes."

As Taylor approached the traffic lights in Ilkley, Roo spotted a fish and chip shop on her left and licked her lips.

"You can drop me here," she said.

"I'll take you to the station."

Damn.

When he pulled up on the road next to the ticket office, Roo started to get out of the car and he caught her arm. "It's throwing it down. Wait there."

Christ, now what? Taylor exited the car, took a large umbrella from the trunk and came round her to her side.

"I might as well walk you to the station. I can park here for thirty minutes."

Choked with frustration, Roo nodded her thanks.

"I'll wait while you get your ticket and walk you onto the platform."

"It's under cover. Thanks for the lift. See you tomorrow."

She skipped into the building before he told her he'd stay and make sure she got on the right train. In fact why didn't he come to Pudsey with her, see her to her door and make sure no murderous axe man waited inside? Roo lingered until she thought Taylor must have driven away and then came out of the ticket office. She almost expected to see him standing outside.

He wasn't.

The rain seemed to be coming down even more heavily and Roo debated forking out for an umbrella, but having decided to make the monetary sacrifice, the only shops open didn't sell them. She walked back toward the chip shop. If that was closed, she was going to slit her wrists.

It wasn't. *Phew.*

But Taylor was in there. *Bloody hell.* Roo retreated before he saw her and hurried back up the road to hide in a doorway. Once he'd driven off, she ran back to the shop.

"A large bag of chips, please," she said.

"You can have fish as well," said the white-coated assistant. "The guy who was just in paid for it. He said to tell you that you won't find the dog in this weather."

So that was why Taylor had lingered. He didn't really care if she got wet or not. "Fish too, please," she said. "And could I have a plastic bag?"

She sprinkled on salt, added vinegar, then more salt because the vinegar had washed the first lot off and her mouth watered. She put her purse and the bottle of water inside the plastic bag and went back to the doorway where she'd sheltered. Roo told herself not to eat too fast, but it was impossible not to. The chips were hot and crunchy and the fish in batter was delicious.

Roo hoped the rain might stop while she was eating but it didn't. The weather had turned the skies prematurely dark, though not dark enough to keep her hidden if Taylor drove past. Roo headed back out into the downpour and walked out of town. After she'd crossed the river, she spotted a sign for a public swimming pool and had another light bulb moment.

Ten minutes later, Roo had stripped to her underwear and was drying her skirt and blouse under the hand drier in the changing room.

"Cute bikini," a woman said. "Where did you get it?"

What? "London."

Roo looked down at her red-and-white-patterned bra and pants and smiled. Once her clothes were dry, she pushed them in a locker with her bag and went for a swim. She could shower, wash her hair, and if the gods were smiling, the rain would have stopped by the time she came out. If they weren't, she'd put her blouse and skirt in the bag and walk back in her underwear.

Taylor couldn't come up with another reason not to go back to Sutton Hall. He had to face Niall sooner or later. He'd intended to ask Roo to go for a meal and for some unaccountable reason had blathered on about getting her to the train. Since when was he nervous about asking women on dates? *When I worry about them saying no.*

After he'd left her at the station, he'd called Niall and asked if he wanted fish and chips, and as he'd glanced in the mirror behind the counter, Roo had reversed out of the shop. The sinking feeling in his stomach was hard to describe but he knew disappointment was part of it. She hadn't wanted the lift to the station because she either didn't like him or he made her feel awkward. Probably both. Or was the little minx planning to go and look for that damn dog? He wasn't sure what annoyed him more.

Now he felt relieved he hadn't asked her out for a meal. Taylor wasn't sure his ego could take further rejection. He skidded to a halt outside Sutton Hall, grabbed the bag of fish and chips, locked the car and ran to the door through the rain.

Niall was in the kitchen, plates and beer waiting.

"Don't say I never make an effort." Taylor tossed the bag of food onto the table.

Actually, he rarely made an effort. Niall had some internet arrangement to get groceries delivered and did all the cooking and cleaning. Taylor was happy to let him. It was Niall who showed potential buyers around the house, not that there had been many. Maybe a price reduction was needed. He'd email his parents.

Taylor might not have wanted to come back here, but he'd quickly settled into a comfortable routine thanks to Niall, and it was also thanks to Niall that he'd managed to not let the memories of sixteen years ago overwhelm him. He'd begun to tell Niall about Stephanie,

and when Niall said he already knew, Taylor had felt a sense of relief that he didn't have to explain.

He took off his jacket and hung it over the back of a chair while Niall plated up the fish and chips.

"How was her first day?" Niall asked.

Taylor sat at the table and took a swig of beer. "Interesting. She seems to be whipping the files into order, but she's a sucker for a hard-luck story. A boy called about a missing dog, and because I had a feeling she wouldn't let it rest, I drove her to the kid's house. Father's gone off somewhere, probably with the dog, but Roo reckons the man's wife has killed her husband and hidden his body in the freezer."

Niall raised his eyebrows. "Evidence?"

"Padlocked and scratched freezer, and the dad's golf clubs still in the garage."

"Ah, the wife did kill him then."

Taylor laughed. He glanced across the table at Niall who had his head down concentrating on his food and felt his heart skip. Taylor wished he'd said something this morning about what had happened last night—only what? And Niall could have said something too and hadn't.

"I like Roo," Taylor blurted.

Niall looked up. "I like her too."

Now Taylor was the one who lowered his gaze. "I mean really like her."

"Good," Niall said. "I finally got the hot tub working. The part I was waiting for arrived today. I'm letting it run for a while to make sure it's okay. The water's hot."

He lifted his head and stared straight into Taylor's eyes. *Fuck.* The chip Taylor was trying to swallow got stuck. Was Niall suggesting they go for a dip in the hot tub?

Why not follow up on that?

Because I'm not gay.

You don't have to be gay to use a hot tub.

Taylor gulped. The chip went down.

"Fancy taking a beer out there and getting wet?" Taylor asked. *Oh shit, did* I *say that?*

Niall smiled, just for a moment. "Sounds like a plan."

Yes, it did, but didn't mean anything was going to happen. Taylor speared the last few morsels of fish with his fork, and when he looked up, caught sight of Niall staring at his mouth. Niall abruptly rose to his feet and slotted his plate in the dishwasher.

He turned to Taylor. "Want dessert?"

Taylor's cock started to tent his pants. "Later."

Niall took two beers from the fridge, passed one to Taylor and walked over to the French doors. He peered out into the darkness. "Still pouring."

"Sure the water's hot?"

"As hot as *you* can stand."

Niall put his beer on the floor and, with his back to Taylor, began to strip. Taylor lurched to his feet and opened the dishwasher. He knew he was being pathetic, but he couldn't look at him. There was no way he was walking out to the hot tub with a hard-on.

"Join you in a moment," Taylor said and sighed when he heard the door open and close.

Niall's clothes lay in a neat pile on the floor. Taylor threw his next to them in an untidy heap. His willful cock was hard as stone. He grabbed the icy beer, held it against his shaft and yelped but didn't remove it. Ten seconds would do it.

It made no difference.

Taylor didn't think there was any point waiting for the damn thing to subside. He rejected the idea of having a quick wank, and refused to think about why that was. Maybe he could slip into the tub without Niall noticing.

He stepped out into the rain and shivered. His erection wilted a little. *Thank God.* Now he just needed to think unsexy thoughts until he was in the water. Taylor padded down the lawn imagining his parents sitting in the tub. Naked. That should be enough to dampen his ardor but—*ah damn it*—his mind leapt to an image of Niall, a memory of the way his hand had felt on his cock, the way he'd spurted into Taylor's fingers. *Shit, shit, shit.*

He squelched across the grass and pushed open the door to the walled garden. The glow from the hot tub was like a beacon in the darkness. Passing UFOs would probably use it as a bloody landing light. Niall sat facing him in the steaming water. Taylor kept the bottle at his crotch as he walked toward the tub. *Get in fast.* Taylor rushed up the steps, slipped at the top and nose-dived into the water.

Not that fast. Oh God, it's hot, hot, hot. And my bloody head.

Taylor reared up, spitting water out of his mouth, holding the beer bottle aloft, his bloody cock waving a flag.

Fuck it.

He slumped down in the tub, blinked the water from his eyes and pressed the bottle to where he'd banged his head.

"You didn't spill a drop," Niall said. "Impressive."

Taylor settled opposite him on a ledge under the water. He took a swallow of beer and sighed. He wanted to relax but he was wound as tight as a violin string. Slow release of tension seemed unlikely. A snap more probable.

"Cold rain, warm water, icy beer," Niall said. "Feels good, doesn't it. Eases aches and pains. Though you probably just managed to give yourself a few more with that fall. You okay?"

"I'll live."

Taylor stole a glance at Niall who leaned back with his head tipped to the sky, eyes closed. His hair was plastered to his skull, water dripping down his cheeks. Niall's nipples were tight, sharp—*Jesus.* Taylor closed his eyes and tipped his head back too. Maybe if he stopped looking, stopped thinking, stopped everything, his cock would subside. It was currently swaying under the water like an electric eel.

He shifted to sit in a spot where the bubbles were more intense and his foot touched Niall's. Taylor told himself to move it away but he didn't. Niall didn't either. Taylor peered out of half-open eyes and saw Niall's hand cradling his erect cock under the water.

Need roared through Taylor like an express train, gathering speed, racing out of control until thinking sent him crashing into the buffers.

"I'm not going to—" Taylor clamped his lips together.

Niall's eyes opened. "Not going to what?"

Taylor's mind struggled to come up with a lie, struggled to come up with anything other than what he *wasn't* going to do.

"I ask nothing of you," Niall said.

He'd said that before. What did he mean? That this was just sex, no more? Of course it was no more than sex. Taylor's gaze fell back to Niall's hand. The guy was playing with his cock in a lazy sort of way and Taylor became aware he was mimicking Niall, pulling at his own cock, squeezing and stroking. Warmth pooled in the pit of his belly and fire began to trickle through his veins. Taylor made himself look into

Niall's face and didn't see the cool, detached guy he knew. Instead, he saw a man uncertain of himself.

"What do you want?" Niall asked.

He wanted Niall's lips around his cock, to push his dick to the back of Niall's throat, to come in his mouth and for Niall to swallow every last drop.

Taylor's hand tightened on his cock. "Another beer?" he croaked.

Niall smiled. He lifted his hand from the water and Taylor lurched back and up so his butt landed on the step out of the water, but he couldn't make himself get out.

Niall brushed dripping hair from his eyes. "Alternatively?"

"Two beers?"

"What are you afraid of?" Niall asked, a slight smile on his face.

Liking it. Not being able to live without it, without you. Thoughts he'd never voice.

"Tell me what *you* want," Taylor said.

Niall stared at Taylor's cock. "Dessert."

Taylor's body tingled head to toe. He had to say only a couple of words and they'd both get what they wanted. The rain came down harder, sharp darts hitting his skin, striking his cock, as if a million tiny spears were urging him to make up his mind. Trouble was Taylor had already made up his mind. It was the trying to convince himself it was a bad idea that was his problem.

"Okay then." Taylor exhaled his response. *Please don't ask me if I'm sure.*

Niall slid across the hot tub to kneel in front of him, and Taylor's cock jutted toward Niall's face as if it had a mind of its own. Niall kissed the crest and Taylor shuddered. *Oh fuck, oh fuck, oh fuck.* His balls tightened and he clenched his butt cheeks. *As if that's gonna help.* He closed his eyes. *That's not going to help either.*

Hands slid up Taylor's legs, caressing from ankles to calves, sweeping over knees onto thighs. Fingers danced across his tense abdominals and up to his pecs. A low moan escaped when Niall rubbed his nipples, a louder moan burst free when hot lips slipped over the tip of his cock and a tongue trailed around the head. Taylor stretched out his arms, dropped the beer on the grass and wrapped his fingers around the edge of the tub.

He wanted and yet didn't want to watch. Wanted won. Taylor

opened his eyes to see and feel Niall wrap a hand around his cock, and then he rubbed it against his cheek. *Jesus.* Taylor panted as Niall trailed his tongue down his length and then lapped at his scrotum, laving the delicate skin in long, smooth strokes. When he took first one and then the other ball into his mouth, Taylor's toes curled on the lower step, his entire body tensing. He had to fight not to buck into Niall, fight not to show him how much he wanted this. Niall gently sucked and then released his nuts over and over, and as Taylor was on the point of sobbing, Niall switched his attention to his inner thighs and Taylor forgot how to breathe. He gasped and gulped as if all the oxygen had been hoovered into space.

"Oh Christ," Taylor moaned.

Niall licked up his cock and swallowed him, sucking hard, and Taylor's moan turned into a strangled grunt. His hands released their grip on the tub and his fingers threaded Niall's hair, pulling and pushing his head up and down until Taylor registered what he was doing and went back to holding the tub. Niall sucked and fisted Taylor's cock, squeezing and pumping, while his other hand massaged the sac beneath.

It was different with a guy. More physical, less mental. Niall had big, strong hands. Hands that knew what they were doing and an expert mouth that was driving Taylor steadily insane. A hot tongue that—*sweet Jesus.* Niall swirled his tongue around the crest at the end of each upstroke and flickered the tip down the sensitive underside on the way down. Taylor's hips flexed. He couldn't help it. He wanted his cock deeper. But then Niall dipped his tongue into the little slit at the crown and Taylor's head fogged to everything but coming.

And he *was* coming. Orgasm gathered inside him, pulling threads together from all over his body until there was a tangled, writhing knot low in his belly. Niall took his cock so deep into his mouth Taylor felt it hit the back of his throat, the sensitive head releasing more precome in response. Niall gripped tight around Taylor's balls, pressed down, and the need to come backed off.

Part of Taylor wanted to say something, wanted to tell Niall how good this felt, but his throat had seized up. *Coward.* Though he returned one hand to Niall's soft, wet hair while the fingernails of the other gouged holes in the tub. Niall grabbed his thighs and lifted him higher so he balanced on the edge of the tub. Taylor clung on to the sides. When Niall pressed his face behind Taylor's balls, pushing with his tongue against the point where his cock grew from his body, Taylor let out a loud cry.

"Fuuuuck."

Niall licked and sucked at the patch of skin between Taylor's balls and his anus and the pressure was—*oh God*—perfect. Not hard enough to hurt but firm enough to let Taylor float in uncomfortable pleasure.

But I need to stop him. Otherwise I'm going to fall over the edge of the tub.

Niall tilted him even farther back, licked at his anus and Taylor whimpered. Then coughed to try to disguise it. *As if that worked.*

Stop him.

In a minute.

A combination of Niall's rhythmic twisting pressure on his cock, and the silky slide of his tongue behind his balls was sending Taylor racing toward freefall. When Niall's mouth returned to his cock and began to twist as he sucked, Taylor's parachute failed to open.

I'm going to come.

In his mouth?

"Niall, I'm close," he grunted.

Niall wrapped his lips back around his cock, gave one hard suck and Taylor's knot unraveled in a blast of fire. He came so hard, white lights flashed behind his eyes. His shaft pulsed and jerked against Niall's tongue and Niall looked up into his face and swallowed every jet.

Taylor shook like a kitten. He felt as weak as one. As the spasms in his body died away, he managed to suck in a breath. Niall pulled back and knelt in the water, and the look on his face was one of shy pleasure. Taylor reached out to touch Niall's cheek and the guy turned into the caress and rubbed his face on Taylor's palm.

No, no, no. This was just sex, cold and impersonal. No touching like that, no looking at him like that. Taylor sprang out of the water and raced back to the house.

Chapter Nine

Niall sighed and sank beneath the water of the hot tub. He'd anticipated Taylor might run, but he was still disappointed. Then he reminded himself of how long he'd waited to even touch Taylor's cock, let alone suck him off, and he smiled. Slow, small steps. Once Taylor accepted there was nothing wrong with what they were doing and allowed Niall to love him, surely he'd return that love?

Hands yanked him out of the water and Niall found himself hauled from the tub onto the grass.

"Fuck it, fuck it. Don't be bloody dead," Taylor shouted.

And bad boy that Niall was, he kept his eyes closed and his body limp. Taylor pushed him onto his side and Niall allowed a trickle of water to fall from his mouth.

"Oh Goddammit, fuck, shit."

Taylor pulled him onto his back, pinched his nose, tipped his head back, and then a miracle happened—he pressed his lips against Niall's. Niall could have done without Taylor forcing air into his lungs, but it was a small price to pay. This counted as a kiss, didn't it? Taylor had made the first move. Niall knew he shouldn't push the moment, but he couldn't help himself. He forgot the slow, small steps and took one large leap. He slid his tongue into Taylor's mouth, wrapped his arms around him and kissed him.

"*Mmph—?*" Taylor tried to jerk free but Niall was much stronger, though he had to be careful not to show Taylor how much stronger.

Urgency flared between them. Taylor hovering between acquiescence and desperation to get free, and Niall torn between keeping him where he was and letting him go. And then Niall wondered what he was doing, forcing Taylor. All this time waiting only to wreck everything in a moment of lunacy. Maybe Taylor was right, maybe love was insane.

Niall let go and slithered away over the wet grass. He lay on his back and flung his arm over his eyes. This was hopeless. *He* was hopeless. All these years wasted, pining for a guy who'd never be his.

Those who'd mocked him were right. Niall *was* a fool. He'd been so sure he could make this work, his pride hadn't let him see the truth, that even without the terrible secrets that could destroy everything, Taylor would never be his.

Pain seared his chest as effectively as a shark's teeth. Niall just wanted Taylor to go now. Fuck off back to the house and leave him alone. Nothing mattered anymore. Niall couldn't go back to his old life and this one would soon be over. He didn't want an afterlife. He wanted the torment to end.

"Niall," Taylor whispered.

Nor did he want to hear soft, apologetic words—Taylor telling him he was sorry, Taylor telling him he wasn't into guys—but through the rain pouring over him, Niall felt the warmth of Taylor's body as he moved closer.

"I thought you'd drowned," Taylor said.

I wish I had. I wish I could.

"And I thought who'd bake for me if you'd copped it?"

Niall felt as though barbed wire was winding tighter and tighter around his heart. Taylor lifted the arm Niall had over his eyes and pushed it down onto the grass. Niall kept his eyes closed. Then the rain stopped hitting his face and he felt the wash of Taylor's breath on his lips as he leaned over him. He had to fight the urge to pull him down.

"I feel..." Taylor paused, "...comfortable with you and I don't want to lose that. I swear it's as if we've known each other for years."

We have.

"There's something about you," Taylor said. "I...what you just did surprised me, that's all."

It surprised me too.

"Want to try again?" Taylor asked.

Oh Christ. Niall opened his eyes, looked up into Taylor's beautiful face, and every cell in his body hummed back to life. *Try what again? Being friends? Being more than friends?* Niall couldn't move. Lightning bolt, blazing fire, raging flood—nothing could shift him, because *this* was what he'd waited for. Except Taylor seemed to be waiting for him. That look on his face—uncertainty, shyness—not Taylor at all. Niall couldn't speak. This *had* to come from Taylor.

"Oh fuck it," Taylor said and bent his head to brush his lips over Niall's in a rough, clumsy caress that almost burst Niall's heart with

joy. This time, he didn't drag Taylor down, didn't try to kiss him back, just left him to do what he wanted.

Taylor lay on his side next to him, supporting his weight on his elbow, and leaned over to lick the seam of Niall's lips. When Taylor's tongue pressed harder, they both groaned and Taylor released a choked laugh.

"Christ, I don't know what I'm doing," he whispered.

Taylor brushed away the water he was dripping onto Niall's face, and with it Niall's tears, and kissed him again, a wet, open kiss that set Niall's pulse jumping. The sudden thrust of Taylor's tongue surprised him. Then Taylor leaned against him, his leg pushing Niall's thighs apart as their tongues tangled. One moment of gentleness before the kiss turned rough and grew rougher. Their staccato gasps and cries rang out into the night sky as the rain fell more heavily.

Niall risked sliding his tongue into Taylor's mouth, and when Taylor kissed him harder, he melted beneath him. They rolled on the grass, hands everywhere, legs entwined, Niall's cock aching, Taylor's cock growing. Bodies plastered together, they writhed and humped and kissed until Taylor jerked his head back, gasping for air.

"Oh Christ, what am I...what the...?" Taylor gasped.

Don't stop, don't stop. "Don't think. Just feel."

But Taylor pulled away and pushed himself to his feet. "Can't," he blurted, and this time when he ran, he didn't come back.

Niall stayed on the grass, lying flat on his back, letting the rain beat his cock into submission. Only some time later, when he heard the sound of Taylor's BMW start up, did he slink back to the house.

Taylor didn't know where he was going, only that he had to get away from Sutton Hall and Niall so he could think. He'd yanked on his clothes over wet skin and run for his car. Taylor felt like he were being torn in two. He didn't know what he wanted and he thought his brain would explode trying to figure it out. He pulled out of the drive onto Thorpe Lane, windscreen wipers on full speed, and headed toward Ilkley with no better plan than to drive round for a while until he calmed down and didn't see things like...a woman wandering along in a bikini. Taylor blinked as he passed her and then checked his mirror.

What the hell was Roo doing? When she scuttled off the road into some bushes, Taylor fixed the point where she'd disappeared and

turned the car. When he pulled up there was no sign of her. Had he imagined it? The night was crazy enough.

He lowered his window and addressed the shrubbery. "Roo!"

A moment later, a bedraggled figure carrying a white plastic bag approached the car, her breasts level with his eyes, and Taylor forgot what he'd been going to say. Her nipples were sharp little peaks under the material. *Whoa, those breasts.*

"I can explain," Roo said. "I can see you'd think this looks a little unusual, but—"

"Are you hurt?" Taylor asked, looking up into her face.

"No."

"Get in the car."

"I'm all wet. There's no need."

"Get in the bloody car," Taylor snapped.

As he pulled through the gates, Roo said, "You could drop me here."

Taylor rolled his eyes and continued up the drive. "Why the hell would I do that? And start thinking carefully about what you're going to say."

He pulled up outside the hall and waited until Roo joined him on the steps before he locked the car. But as Taylor strode inside, he realized she hadn't followed. He went back to find her in the doorway, looking embarrassed and struggling to put a shirt on over her wet body.

"I'll get you a towel," he said and ran up the stairs.

By the time he came down, a dressed Niall stood in the hall with her and Taylor felt a surge of... *What? Jealousy?* Roo was barefoot and had a blue blanket wrapped around her shoulders. Taylor avoided Niall's gaze.

"I'll make a drink," Niall said. "What would you like?"

"Wine?" Roo asked.

Taylor glared. "Get her hot chocolate."

"I don't like hot chocolate," Roo mumbled.

Taylor sighed. "Fine. Bring a bottle and three glasses. We'll sit in the drawing room."

"Please," Roo said.

"What?" Taylor frowned.

"This might seem like an odd situation, but you could still say please? Niall's not your slave." She slapped a hand against her mouth. "Sorry if he is," she mumbled through her fingers.

"For fuck's sake," Taylor grumbled and then raised his gaze to Niall. "Please. Sorry."

Taylor wanted Niall to know he was sorry about running too, but Niall turned and walked away with no hint on his face of how he felt. *Have I fucked this up?*

"Drawing room," Taylor said.

Roo didn't move.

He exhaled. "You're on very dodgy ground. Drawing room...please."

Roo padded in ahead of him and curled up in a corner of one of the couches. "It's not a crime to walk along a road in a bikini," she said.

Taylor sat opposite and waited. The truth would spurt from her eventually. Niall came in with the wine and gave everyone a glass. He sat next to Roo and Taylor felt a jolt of disappointment.

"Did I miss anything?" Niall asked.

"Roo was just saying it's not a crime to walk along a road in a bikini."

"It's not a bikini," Niall said. "It's underwear."

Taylor gaped. *Is it?*

Roo's eyes widened. "Everyone else thought it was a bikini."

Taylor clenched his fingers on the side of the couch. "Everyone else? It doesn't matter what the hell you're wearing. What were you doing walking along Thorpe Lane half-naked at this time of night?"

Roo turned to Niall. "How did you know it was underwear?"

"Stop changing the subject," Taylor snapped. "And think before you speak."

Roo pressed her lips together and then sighed. "How long do you want me to think?"

Niall let out a snort of laughter.

"Okay," she sighed. "After I had the fish and chips—thank you for...yeah, er...I decided to go for a swim. When I came out I realized I'd lost my keys. I went back in, but they weren't there so I wondered if I'd left them here. Because it was still raining and I didn't want to get my skirt and blouse wet, I took them off and put them in my bag."

She stared straight at Taylor.

"Lying little witch," he whispered.

Roo bristled. "Here. Check my purse. You'll find the swimming ticket and no keys."

Taylor upended the purse on the carpet and stared in bewilderment. Along with a phone, lipstick and the normal sorts of things women carry, there were guitar picks, a screwdriver, a bottle of peppermint essence, a wind-up nun, an egg separator and a plastic lizard...condoms but no keys. Oh, and a ticket to the local pool. Taylor swallowed the lump in his throat. Maybe she wasn't lying. In her convoluted brain, it probably made perfect sense to do what she'd done.

"Why didn't you call?" Taylor asked.

"I did. No one answered." Roo bent to refill her handbag.

Ah. "So how were you going to get in the house?"

"I thought I'd just wait for you to come back." She started to tap her foot.

"Why didn't you go home and call a locksmith?" Taylor asked.

Roo glared. "What is this? The Spanish Inquisition?" Then she grinned. "Oh, I've waited years to say that."

Taylor bit back his laugh.

"I couldn't call a locksmith because I don't know any. I don't have internet access on my phone."

"You could have asked a neighbor," Taylor said.

Roo clapped her hand to her head. "You're right. Mrs. Dutton has a spare key. I'm so stupid. If you'd just call me a cab, I'll get out of your hair. Oh, you've both got wet hair. That's—"

"I'll drive you," Taylor said.

"No, you've had wine. I insist on a cab," Roo said. "Please phone for one. Sorry for being a nuisance. I'll go look for my keys just in case I did drop them here."

She fled from the room. Taylor took his phone from his pocket. He might be a private detective, but he couldn't figure Roo out at all.

How unlucky could she be? Roo carried her clothes to the office and got dressed. A couple more minutes and she'd have been safe in her tent, not frozen like a wide-eyed rabbit in Taylor's headlights. Now she'd have to pay for a cab she didn't need and tell him to drop her

outside the gates.

When Niall had come into the entrance hall and seen her standing there dripping in her underwear, his jaw had dropped and then he'd gulped. He'd been so fast to fetch the blanket, Roo wondered if he'd managed to slow time. One blink and he was back. But when he'd wrapped it around her shoulders, she felt his fingers tremble and maybe they'd lingered for a moment.

Wishful thinking, idiot.

Dressed again, she walked back to find Niall leaning against the doorframe of the drawing room while Taylor paced.

"Any luck?" Taylor asked.

What was he talking about? *Think!* "No, they're not there. I've called Mrs...B—Dutton and she's in all night." Why couldn't she make up names she'd remember? She'd picked it because it was like Sutton. Maybe too close to Sutton. And what happened to the not-telling-lies-unless-it-was-a-matter-of-love? Roo looked at Niall, her gaze settling on his lips. *Ah love.* That was okay then.

"Cab's here," Taylor said.

Roo picked up her purse and the bag with the water. "Thanks. Sorry to be a nuisance." Words that would no doubt be engraved on her tombstone. "Good night."

The elderly driver held open the door and then shut her in. He sat next to her and said, "Pudsey, right?"

Oh Christ. "No, I—"

"Mr. Sutton's paid. It's fine."

The end of the drive was approaching. Roo let the cab travel about fifty yards along the lane before she spoke.

"Stop, please."

"Forgotten something, love?"

"Yes."

"I'll just turn around."

"No, it's fine," Roo said. "I've changed my mind. We had a row, but I see I was in the wrong now. I don't want to go anymore. Obviously doesn't matter about the money."

"I'll drive you back."

What was it with bloody accommodating males? They were never around when you needed them and now Roo was plagued with them.

"I'd like to walk."

The driver peered through the window. "Still raining."

Yes, of course it is.

"No problem. Sorry about this." Roo got out of the cab.

"No bother to me. I get paid for a job I haven't had to do."

As his taillights receded in the distance, Roo blew out a sigh of relief and slunk back along the road. The moment she slipped past the gates, she pushed through the rhododendron bushes. All that effort to stay clean and dry and now her blouse and skirt were wet through and dirty.

Roo whimpered with joy when she saw her tent. It would have been the last straw if she'd not been able to find it straightaway. She stripped outside, folded her clothes and took off her sodden shoes before she unzipped the flap and crawled in. Roo fumbled for the lantern and switched it on, then zipped herself in.

Home. Not much of a home but she felt safe here. Though it was clear she couldn't keep this up. She had to look for a room to rent. Not in Ilkley, it would be too expensive, but maybe in Guiseley. She could check out the company Jason's dad worked for at the same time. She still thought he'd been murdered. Roo rubbed her hair with a towel. She needed to make the trip in working hours, and if she told Taylor she had a room to look at, he'd never suspect what she was up to, particularly when she was going to have to ask him for an advance on her salary.

Roo peeled off her underwear and pushed it into a bag with her wet clothes. Maybe she could sneak them into the guys' washing machine tomorrow. She pulled a short, tight T-shirt from her suitcase and slipped it on along with pair of hipster panties, then draped the sleeping bag around her. She was in the middle of brushing her teeth when the sound of voices filtered into the tent. Roo snapped off the lantern and swallowed the minty foam.

A high-pitched giggle was followed by a deeper voice. Roo couldn't make out what was being said, but knew they were close. More than close. Her heart pounded in embarrassment. Even in the gloom of the interior she could see hands brushing the outside of the material, fingers pressing. *Not funny, guys.* But all at once, Roo wasn't sure this *was* Taylor and Niall, and her heart pounded even harder. With fear. She reached for the zipper and held it down at ground level. Right in front of her, a face pressed against the nylon. It looked like a death mask and Roo bit her lip so hard she tasted blood.

She didn't understand why she couldn't work out what they were saying, but she was sure both men and women were out there muttering and whispering. They laughed, but there was a menace in it that seeped into Roo, soaking her as effectively as the rain. *Phone the police.* She reached for her purse but it was too far away to grab. Roo wondered about the point of holding on to the zipper when one slash through the material would reveal her, yet she was reluctant to let it go.

"Let us in," a woman whispered, her voice clear and sultry.

Oh God. There *were* such things as vampires? If books and TV were to be believed—and who else could Roo believe?—they couldn't come in a private residence unless invited—that had to include tents—so Roo was definitely not going to invite them. The outside of the tent rippled and dipped as hands, faces, God knew what else, rubbed against it. Roo wanted to scream "Go away," but if she did, it would be admitting there was something out there and Roo really didn't want there to be anything there except figments of her imagination.

She'd not been this scared since—ah, well remembering another scary occasion wasn't going to help. Roo closed her eyes, which got rid of one scary thing but not the sounds. *Oh crap.* Roo opened her mouth and sang a stupid yodeling song.

It was one she remembered her dad singing to her that always made her smile. Partly because her dad couldn't yodel. Though neither could Roo. Roo's eyes slid open as she sang louder. Somehow it felt worse not to look, except the tent seemed to be vibrating. She didn't *think* she was doing that. But it gave her an idea and she stopped singing.

"Harder, harder," she shouted. "That's it. Oh yesssss. So good. Just there. Oh wow. Yes. Yes. Yessss."

Bit of a leap from yodeling to sex, but Roo put everything she had into her screaming orgasm, and the sounds outside stopped. Just like that. Which was almost as scary. Then Roo's fingers where they held the zipper began to rise as someone pulled on the outside. By the time she'd come to her senses and lurched for her phone, the entrance to the tent was fully open and Niall's face came into view.

"Niall!" Roo threw herself at him, yanked on his arm and he fell inside the tent. "Oh God, something's out there."

He lay on his side, looking straight into her eyes. "Now something's in here."

"Not you. Well, not unless you can speak like a woman and sound

like a lot of people at the same time." She gulped. "You can't, can you?"

"No."

"What are you doing out here?"

His jaw twitched. "That's my line."

Roo stared into his eyes and gave up any thought of lying. What was the point?

"I hadn't paid my rent, and when I got back to my bedsit, my landlord had turfed out all my stuff and was repainting. So I bought a tent and a sleeping bag and I was going to stay here until I had enough money for the deposit for a new place. I was fine last night, but there's some people out here in the wood. They pressed their faces against the tent and kept whispering. I think they were..."

Niall edged closer and Roo flicked on the lantern.

"Vampires," she whispered.

Chapter Ten

Niall's heart thumped so hard he could hear it in his head, but when Roo had said the word—vampires—relief smothered the sound. Only the fact that she was deadly serious kept him from laughing out loud. Not vampires but others like him. He'd seen them flit off through the woods as he approached and he wondered what they were doing on this side. If it was bad or good news for him.

"Probably kids messing around," he said.

"It's a long way from Ilkley and they didn't sound like children."

Niall moved closer. She needed distracting. He was already well past distracted and into serious lust.

Roo frowned. "Perhaps there's a...oh I don't know the collective noun for a group of vampires—a colony?—somewhere in the vicinity?"

"A bite of vamps, a lick, a lap, a suck?" He stared at her mouth. "You smell of mint."

"Toothpaste. Had to swallow it. *Blurggh.*"

"I like mint."

Roo's eyes widened and she gulped.

As he looked at her, Niall felt a sharp blade of longing drag up his spine and nudge him closer. *I want her, I* want *her.* But maybe this wasn't really him feeling this. *They* might be interfering. Had they come through tonight because Taylor had finally begun to respond? But why threaten Roo? He swallowed hard. Maybe they knew that something drew Niall to her. And that feeling he had reminded him of that summer's day years ago when a blue-and-white model plane had flown over the wall of the garden to crash at his feet. And a dark-haired boy had followed.

Lightning flashed, followed by a boom of thunder, and the rain pelted the tent. Niall reached back to zip up the doorway and then lay down again in the cramped space. He'd stay for a while. They wouldn't hurt her while he was with her.

"I don't think I'd like to be a vampire," she whispered. "The

staying young sounds good, but I'm a vegetarian."

He smiled.

"Though I do lapse occasionally. I can't resist crispy smoked bacon."

Niall's smile broadened.

"And fillet steak," she said with a sigh. "Oh damn, I'm not a vegetarian at all, am I? Just a picky eater. But then vampires are picky too and they make such a mess when they feed. Living so long, you'd think they'd have better manners. Um...you're not a vampire, are you?"

"No. You've seen me in daylight, remember? Not sparkling. Eating a sandwich without dribbling."

"Yes, but you might have been wearing sunblock. Perhaps they've made scientific advances—"

"Roo, I'm not a vampire. And if there *are* any around, I'm not going to let them hurt you."

She clutched his arm as another rumble of thunder vibrated the tent. "But you won't be able to stop them. They're insanely strong."

"So am I." *At times.*

"Let me feel your muscles."

He laughed and flexed the biceps of the arm she held. When Roo squeezed, Niall swallowed hard.

"Oh God, you *are* insanely strong. That feels like a cannon ball."

Not the only hard ball he had.

It was no use. Niall couldn't help himself. It had to be worth the risk. He wasn't looking for love with her and this wasn't Taylor, so Niall should be safe and so should she. Lust pooled in his groin and his cock completed the journey north it started the moment he'd unzipped the tent. Niall cupped her face in his hand, rubbed his thumb over her mouth and kissed her.

The moment their lips touched, excruciating pain ripped through his body, running down every line of his tattoo, thousands of razor-sharp teeth biting into him. *Oh fuck.* He jerked, his hand striking her chin as he flung himself aside and his back arched in agony until he thought his spine would snap. His eyes closed and he clamped his lips together to keep from crying out. *Shit, I hit her. Fuck.* Niall forced his eyes open and saw Roo rubbing her cheek.

He tried to tell her he was sorry but no words came from his mouth, just unintelligible grunts as the pain maintained its grip, but

he lifted his hand to stroke her face and felt relief she didn't flinch away.

"S'okay," she said. "I know you didn't mean it. But what the hell's the matter? Did you get hit by lightning? Have a back spasm or something? Want me to rub it better?" She gasped. "Maybe you're in anaphylactic shock. That toothpaste is cheap stuff. Do you have an Epi pen?" She felt his pockets and touched his erect cock. "Oh, bit big for a—ah right. Need CPR? Well, no, because you're still breathing." She gulped. "Was it me?"

Even through her ramblings, the pain continued, whipping up and down his tattoo, sinking into him like poison. *I hit her.* He should say sorry, but if he opened his mouth, screams would burst out. Niall felt as though his body were being eaten while his brain boiled. This would have happened if he'd kissed Taylor, and maybe affected Taylor too, but Taylor had kissed him first and protected him. Niall didn't know the rules of this bloody game, had no idea if Taylor always had to make the first move to keep them both safe, but he now knew if he kissed someone first, the price was painful agony.

"Okay yet?" Roo asked, stroking his face.

What am I doing here with Roo when it's Taylor I want? He lifted his hand and touched the red mark on her chin with trembling fingers, then let his arm drop and his eyes close. Niall held himself rigid as the pain slowly ebbed away.

"Maybe you're allergic to me," she whispered. "I have that effect on people. They always seem to want to get rid of me fast."

I don't want to get rid of you. Her caress of his face was soothing. Niall didn't want her to stop. *She's cute. I want them both. And both at the same time would be perfect.*

His breathing eased, the pain faded to a dull ache and he opened his eyes to see Roo leaning over him, staring down anxiously.

"Just checking you're alive." She gave a little grin.

One bite of the apple and damn the result, he still wanted Snow White. Rain fell more heavily. Thunder rumbled.

"Feeling better?" she asked.

Niall nodded.

Roo smiled. "You had me worried there. I thought rigor mortis had set in. You went stiff in places that aren't usually stiff." Her cheeks flushed. "It wasn't the lightning, was it? Otherwise I'd have been incinerated. But what do I know? Do you think we should experiment

to see if you'll have that reaction every time you kiss me? Obviously, if you do, we'd have to stop." Roo frowned. "I need to know if I'm going to electrocute everyone I kiss. It hasn't happened before, but that doesn't mean it won't happen again. I could create Frankenstein. Kissing in a thunderstorm. Wonder if the tent's important. Something about the material."

He'd never met anyone with a mind like hers before.

"Could you act as my guinea pig?" she asked.

Niall wanted to speak but he couldn't. He wanted to kiss her and he couldn't. *Kiss me. Kiss me.*

Roo swallowed. "Sorry. Mouth running away with me again, nothing unusual there. Maybe you've got a girlfriend—um...boyfriend. Taylor? Sorry, sorry, sorry." She clapped a hand over her mouth but spoke through her fingers. "Niall, if you don't say something soon I'm going to freak out big time."

"I like your mouth," he croaked.

Roo let her hand fall. "You do?" She smiled. "I like yours too."

She lifted his hand to her lips and, looking into his eyes, she kissed the tip of his index finger, then kissed the next and the next before she sucked hard on the littlest finger. Niall's cock hardened and he groaned. How could something so simple be so erotic?

"Are you in excruciating agony and being brave?" she asked. "Or incandescent with lust like me?"

How could he not smile at her?

Roo held his hand tight, their fingers entwined. She took a deep breath and lowered her mouth slowly.

Please, please, please. Niall waited for the blast of pain, but her lips touched his, and when all he felt was desire, he relaxed and felt her melt into him.

"Thank God for that," she mumbled against his mouth.

She ran the tip of her tongue along the seam of his lips and Niall felt like he'd been zapped by lightning—but in a good way. Lingering pain ceded to growing pleasure and he pulled her on top of him and slid his hands under her T-shirt onto her back. As her tongue slipped into his mouth, a great chasm of longing opened up inside him for wasted time, wasted years, wasted love.

Roo was sweet, soft and sexy, so different to Taylor with his hard muscular body. Her skin felt satin smooth under his fingers and she smelled of coconuts. The slow kiss grew hotter as desire sparked

through him. Their tongues tangled and parried, and Niall danced his fingers down to her butt and squeezed. Roo mewled into his mouth and, as if putting a match to gas, Niall's body exploded with need.

He rolled so she lay beneath him, making sure he didn't crush her and that their mouths stayed welded together. Niall slid his hand onto her breast, letting the hard nub of her nipple rub against his palm. His cock struggled in the confines of his pants. He wanted to eat, devour, consume her. He wanted to know every contour of her mouth, her body, her sex. He wanted her under him, over him, beside him. He wanted—

Roo broke away, gasping. "Air."

Shit. He'd forgotten. Not breathing for a while was no problem for him, but she and Taylor weren't like him. Niall tried to calm his racing heart, his accelerating brain and particularly his overexcited dick. This was just lust. He'd spent so long without having sex, and it seemed those recent encounters with Taylor had opened the flood gates. Niall could never stop loving Taylor, but he wanted Roo. He took his hand from under her T-shirt and ran his finger along the line of her jaw to trace a path around her face. Roo lay panting, cheeks flushed, eyes cloudy with desire. Niall thought she was the most beautiful woman he'd ever seen.

Which totally confirmed he was not in his right mind because she couldn't be.

Except...

He dropped his hand to the bottom of her T-shirt and peeled it over her face and up her arms, using the material to trap her hands above her head. Niall raked her with his gaze. Long legs, cute, white hipster panties covered with pink lips, a gently rounded belly, perfect breasts, small tight nipples, a long neck and that mouth that made him laugh, made him smile and would make him come. He kissed his way from her neck down, smiling against her skin when he tasted the chlorine of a swimming pool, alternating licks with kisses as he danced his tongue over her nipples. He made the skin flutter around her navel while she writhed and groaned beneath him. When Niall was sure she was too far gone to stop him, he let go of her hands.

Roo groaned as he trailed his tongue along the edge of her panties. He tugged at the material with his teeth and her fingers threaded his hair as she arched her back.

"Oh wow," she gasped.

Niall peeled her panties down her legs and almost came in his.

Shaved. He stripped, tossed his clothes aside and lay beside her.

"Condom in my purse, but it's not going to fit," Roo blurted.

Niall laughed. He didn't need to use a condom. He couldn't get her pregnant, but the thought dragged sense back into his brain and his smile died. What the hell he was doing? If Taylor found out—*when* he found out, because Niall doubted Roo could keep her mouth shut—how would he react?

"That tattoo," she whispered. "Head to toe?"

He nodded. Roo climbed over him, kneed him in the chest, then the back and whispered, "Sorry, sorry." He sucked in a breath at the feel of her body pressed against his, his butt against her warm stomach, her leg hooked over his. Then she began to explore, her fingers and mouth brushing his upper back. *That feels good.* But Taylor was going to be pissed off. Niall knew the guy fancied Roo, so the fact that Niall had got here first wouldn't make him happy, and Niall needed him to be happy. *If I do this, Taylor's going to kill me.* He groaned as Roo trailed her tongue down his spine.

"You taste like a sunny day," she said. "All warm and comfortable."

She nibbled around his waist and Niall groaned. Why was his head full of Taylor? Niall knew he ought to stop this, but he didn't want to.

Could this be a trap? The breath caught in Niall's throat. *Were* they *interfering? Tempting him?*

"This is an amazing tattoo," Roo mumbled. "I don't think I've ever seen one so intricate. What other secrets are you hiding?"

Her mouth had reached his lower back, and Niall had to push down on his balls to stop himself coming.

"They wouldn't be secrets if I told you, would they?" he said.

"So long as you're not going to bite my neck."

"Not hard."

Don't flirt with her. I have to stop this right now. It wasn't Roo's fault. There were forces at play here that were beyond her comprehension. This was too big a risk.

Roo's tongue trailed down the crease of his butt and Niall lurched away and grabbed his pants.

"Sorry, I can't do this." Where had he heard that before?

Niall heard her swift intake of breath but she didn't say anything.

He didn't look at her as he dressed, but she reached past him for her T-shirt and panties. When Niall turned, Roo was curled up inside her sleeping bag facing away from him.

"Roo," he whispered.

She pulled the bag over her head until he couldn't see her.

Leave. Don't make this worse.

When Niall stepped out of the tent, the rain stopped.

Roo shuddered when she heard the rasp of the zipper closing her inside the tent. She wondered when she'd ever been so disappointed. Even when the big surprise her parents had promised turned out to be a sister and not the bike she'd hoped for. Sometimes it seemed Roo's whole life was one big letdown after another which was probably why she tried so hard to be happy. She didn't want to know why Niall had changed his mind.

Yes I do.

Something she'd said, not said, done, not done? *Because I licked his backside?* She squirmed. Because of Taylor? Roo lifted her head out of the sleeping bag and switched off the lantern. Everything was messed up. But maybe not if neither of them said anything. She could pretend this never happened. Nothing *did* happen except she'd fallen in love again with yet another asshole.

Roo rolled onto her front and slipped her hands inside her panties. She was so wet, so ready, so...annoyed. Yet it was still Niall she thought of which made her even crosser. Why not add Taylor? Roo imagined them in the tent with her, four hands stroking, two mouths kissing, two cocks inside her, the guys feeling each other through her. Roo rubbed harder at her clit, trapping the slippery nub between her fingers. She groaned as her orgasm rose in slow motion, spreading from her belly until her legs and arms tingled. Roo tensed as it broke and chewed her lip as the spasms hit.

Bitter-sweet pleasure and ultimately unsatisfying. And that was her, wasn't it? Occasionally annoying, fun to have around for a while, but not for long.

By the time Roo had dressed, ready for work the next morning, she had her happy face back on as well as her only decent pair of shoes that just happened to be open-toed, black high heels. Her more

suitable shoes were still wet through and her only other footwear was a pair of running shoes. As Roo bent to zip up the tent, her stomach rumbled. Her plan to eat SpaghettiOs for breakfast had been stymied by the lack of a can opener.

Never happened, never happened. It was a dream. She could do this, be happy and carefree. Nothing had happened. Not really. She could still love him. *Yes, I know it's not really love.* It didn't mean she was stupid, just lonely. Well beyond the age for crushes, Roo had yet to grow out of them.

She emerged from the bushes and headed down the drive toward the house.

"Hey," Taylor shouted.

Roo cringed as she stumbled to a halt. *Damn.* She turned to see him walking up from the gates. Niall was with him. Roo fixed her gaze on Taylor.

"What were you doing in the bushes?" Taylor asked as they reached her.

A question that told Roo everything. Niall hadn't blabbed to Taylor that she was living in a tent because he wanted her to keep quiet about last night.

"I thought I saw a squirrel," Roo blurted.

Taylor raised his eyebrows. "You're not going to be more imaginative than that? Sure it wasn't a moose or an elephant or a T-rex?"

Roo straightened up. "It was limping."

Taylor narrowed his eyes and walked toward the rhododendrons.

"Don't bother. It went up a tree," Roo said.

Taylor turned to stare at her. "With a bad leg?"

When he pushed his way through the bushes, Roo sagged. She could feel Niall at her shoulder but couldn't look at him.

"Roo!" Taylor shouted. "Get in here."

She sighed and made her way to the tent.

Taylor stared at her incredulously. "Have you been sleeping in this?"

Not even her vivid imagination could come up with an excuse, though she wasted a few minutes trying. "Yes."

"Why?"

"That's a stupid question. I was sleeping in the tent because..." Her defiant tone fell away as Taylor raised his eyebrows.

"When I got back to my bedsit after you'd said I'd got the job, my landlord had chucked out all my things. I didn't have enough money for a hotel or to rent somewhere so I bought a tent."

"Your landlord's not allowed to just throw you out," Taylor said.

"I hadn't paid last month's rent," Roo mumbled.

"He's still not allowed to put you on the street."

Niall had come to stand next to Taylor. "It's not safe out here."

No, it wasn't. Roo still couldn't look at him.

"I don't want to go back to where I lived," she mumbled. "If you could give me an advance on my salary, I should be able to find a room to rent locally."

Taylor stared at her for a while. "Fine. I need to go to Leeds at lunchtime. I'll drop you in Ilkley and you can go round the estate agents." He took out his wallet and offered her a twenty-pound note. "Get a taxi back and tonight I'll drive you and your...tent to your new place."

"I don't need the money—"

"You just told me you need an advance on your salary. Take it," Taylor snapped.

Roo put it in her purse.

His mouth quirked in a smile. "You're late for work, hurry up."

In these shoes? He had to be kidding.

Roo tottered along behind as they strode up the drive.

"You're wrong about the gates," Taylor said to Niall. "They're not dangerous."

"Just thought you ought to look at them."

And Roo guessed that Niall had somehow engineered this so she'd be caught out without him having to say anything. Her heart clenched. Niall wanted her gone. So what had last night been about? He'd wanted her one minute and not the next. Why had he even come to the tent?

Roo almost tripped as she remembered the voices, the faces pressed against the material. How the hell could she have forgotten that?

By the time Roo made it to the office, Taylor was already at his

desk.

"Coffee," he said.

"No thank you." Roo sat down.

He rolled his eyes. "Not for you, for me. Though you can have one too. I'll take it out of your wages."

Roo stared at him.

"Joke." He smiled. "Niall will have some ready."

Roo pushed herself up and headed for the kitchen. If she was lucky, Niall wouldn't be— *Oh.*

"Taylor wants coffee," she mumbled and took two mugs from the shelf.

She shouldn't still want him after he stalked off last night but she did. Roo reckoned lust killed brain cells. She set the mugs on the counter and turned her face straight into Niall's. He caught her head and held her there as he stared into her eyes. Every single one of Roo's erogenous zones caught fire. Niall flicked his tongue very lightly into her mouth and she felt the tension ease from him when no thunderbolt struck. He sighed and kissed her properly, exploring her mouth in languorous delight as if she were the most delicious thing he'd ever eaten. And Roo knew she should have stepped back, asked what he was playing at, kicked him in the shin or slapped his face, and she did none of that. Instead, idiot that she was, she kissed him back.

The floaty sensation in her head reminded Roo of when she'd been given a local anesthetic to have a dislocated shoulder slotted back into place. After the pain had come an incredible high, an energizing buzz, a feeling that the world was perfect as long as her shoulder stayed in—and Niall wanted her. When he let her go, his face was wreathed in a smile.

"Thank you," he whispered.

What for?

For once, Roo didn't know what to say. Was he interested or not? Roo's heart pounded. *I don't want to want him, but I do. I don't want to love him, but I do. Not really. Do I?* But those words weren't going to jump from her mouth because he didn't love her. More likely he wanted to check kissing her wasn't going to kill him. He didn't love her because he'd left her out there in the tent. He hadn't even asked her to move in here with him.

As if.

"You need to move in here."

Roo's jaw dropped. *He loves me?*

"Sutton Hall has plenty of bedrooms."

Ah no, he doesn't love me.

"No thanks," Roo said and reached for the coffee. "I can find a place to live. I don't need anyone—" That last part had slipped out. "Anyone's help," she added.

She poured the coffee with a shaking hand.

"Please don't say anything to Taylor," Niall asked.

He definitely doesn't love me. Didn't matter, she still loved him because she was an idiot.

"About what?" Roo walked out.

This was like pulling the petals off a daisy. *He wants me. He wants me not.* She might as well crush the flower in her fist.

Chapter Eleven

"Roo, are you listening to me?"

She looked up to see Taylor glaring at her from his desk. "Sorry." She hadn't been listening. She'd been too busy thinking about Niall's kiss and what it meant. Nothing probably. In fact it had probably been a peck on the cheek that she'd imagined into a full-frontal snog. She wished—

"Roo!"

"Yes?"

"Do you have any gym gear?"

She nodded and then furrowed her brow. Might have been a help to have had a clue as to what Taylor had been saying.

"We'll pick it up on the way. Come on."

Roo grabbed her purse and followed him. "So...the gym?"

Taylor *tsked.* "Jonas is watching a woman who's made a massive insurance claim for an industrial accident. June Barnette isn't supposed to be able to walk more than a few yards without a stick, but apparently she's a member of the Hollins Hall leisure club. Using the pool would be fine, but she's listed on gym classes."

Taylor opened the car door for her and then got in the other side. He did have nice manners. And nice hands. Roo pinched her thigh. *Concentrate.*

"Jonas went there this morning pretending to be a journalist writing an article about fitness so he could take a few snaps of the woman, but they won't let him without written consent from the manager."

"What do you want me to do?"

"She's booked into another women-only session at eleven. I want you to say you're thinking of joining but would like to try a class first."

Taylor pulled up on the drive parallel with her tent. "Go and get your things."

Roo hurried back with running shoes, a creased blue T-shirt and

black shorts. She'd hardly clipped her seat belt before Taylor accelerated out of the drive and down Thorpe Lane.

"What's the class?" Roo asked.

"Force her."

"Force her? How?"

Taylor laughed. "No, it's called *Forza.* Something martial arts related."

Roo cringed. *Oh God, it's going to hurt.*

"You want me to take pictures," she said. "What does she look like?"

"There's a folder on the backseat."

Roo reached for it and looked at several photos of June Barnette walking with a cane. She was thirty-two, had curly blonde hair and looked very fit—apart from the stick. She'd apparently slipped on a wet floor and injured her back. Roo was thrilled to be more directly involved in ICU. She could be much more than a PA and she was determined not to cock this up.

"Use my spare phone," Taylor said. "It takes high-definition pictures. Practice now so you know what you're doing."

Roo picked the phone up from the dashboard shelf, and after figuring out what to do, snapped Taylor. When she looked at the shot, she gulped. *He's really good looking.* There was already a shadow of stubble on his cheeks and chin. His nose was perfectly straight, his lips fuller than Niall's. *Ah, Niall.* Was it wrong to like two guys at the same time? Not when neither of them liked her in that way. Niall's kiss and the nearly-sex and then the earlier kiss—yeah, well Roo was inclined to think he was playing with her. She tucked the phone in her purse.

"You're very quiet today," Taylor said. "What's wrong? Apart from the fact that you were sleeping in a tent in my garden and I caught you?"

She shrugged. *I'm confused.* And if she opened her mouth, she was going to blurt something she shouldn't.

"Why didn't you stay with a friend when you were thrown out of your bedsit?"

"I don't...really know anyone that well. Since I moved up from London, I haven't been able to find a proper job and I don't have money to socialize."

"No boyfriend?"

"No." Roo pressed her lips together.

"Do you have family up here?"

"No."

Taylor glanced at her. "So why Leeds?"

"I did eeny meeny miney moe at St Pancras station. I quite fancied Hogwarts but Leeds came up."

Taylor chuckled. "Escaping from your lying, cheating, scumbag of a boss who I guess had also been your boyfriend."

Roo gave an overly dramatic gasp. "Wow, you're such a great detective."

"And you were doing so well not pissing me off."

Taylor pulled out to overtake a tractor. Roo clung to the seat and started to tap her foot.

"Have you always lived in Yorkshire?" she asked.

"I moved to London when I was eighteen. I only came back a few months ago."

"Did you do eeny meeny miney moe too?"

He smiled and Roo's stomach clenched. "I got tired of London traffic, the noise and the smell. I was born in Yorkshire. I guess the place somehow pulled me back. Plus Jonas was keen to move out of the capital."

"Nothing more than that? If your business was doing okay in London, it must have been a wrench to leave."

"Not really. I'm doing fine here."

Roo looked out of the window. "It *is* beautiful. Wild moorland on the doorstep." Heathcliffe sitting next to her. "The towns and villages don't blur into each other. And the people are friendly though it took me a while to understand what they were saying. I still don't understand—*Ah'll go to t'foot of ahr stairs.* Why would they want to go to the bottom of the stairs?"

Taylor sniggered. "It's just a polite way of saying—Really? An exclamation of surprise."

"Ah." Roo guessed she did a lot of surprising.

"Here's the Marriott." Taylor turned right at the traffic light and pulled up a steep hill, Shetland ponies grazing on the left, rabbits on the right. "Sure you know what you're doing?"

“Yes. Are you going to wait in the car?”

“No, I’ll have a coffee in the bar. Come and find me when you’re done. You don’t need to stay for the whole session. Should take no more than fifteen minutes. Get the shots and leave.”

Roo gathered her gym gear and got out of the car.

It was surprisingly easy to talk her way into a class. She left her clothes in a locker, tucked Taylor’s phone in her pocket and one of the uber-buff male staff members showed her to the Forza room where her heart dropped into her stomach. Fifteen women, five lines of three, faced an Amazonian female instructor standing in front of a mirrored wall. They all wielded three-foot-long wooden sticks in perfect synchronized precision.

“Forza means force in Italian,” said the guy who’d brought her to the room. “It’s based on samurai training.”

“Without the blood and beheading,” Roo mumbled. Though she’d not had a go yet. Plenty of opportunity for blood, hopefully not the beheading.

He laughed and waved to the instructor. “Jody, this is Roo. Interested in membership.”

“Hi, grab a sword and join in at the back,” the instructor called back. “Put one hand about twelve inches above the other and follow our moves.”

Roo picked up the wooden sword and immediately thought of Uma Thurman in *Kill Bill.* She shot straight into the role and thrust her shoulders back, and almost put her arm out of joint. *Christ, this is hard.* The sword had to weigh a couple of pounds, which might not sound a lot, but when she had to brandish it over her head and then slash and skewer, it soon made her muscles ache.

But it was fun. She swashed and buckled, stabbing Tom, her scumbag ex-boss, in the belly, slicing into his neck on one side, then the other. Roo hit Niall over the head time after time to try to knock some sense into him, wacked Taylor too until she was panting so hard she could barely breathe.

“Control the sword,” called the red-haired instructor, who looked as if she had muscles like Niall’s. “Don’t let it control you.”

Roo was gasping and sweating and having a great if exhausting time until the instructor called, “That’s it,” and Roo realized she’d been having *too* good a time. *Shit. No photos.*

She propped her sword against the wall and rushed to the front.

"That was so awesome. Do you think I could take a couple of pictures of everyone to show my friend? I'm sure she'll want to come too."

It was that easy. Roo made sure she had June in several shots, arms wielding the wooden sword over her head, and she even managed to video a few seconds of the woman lunging.

"You were pretty good at that for a beginner," Jody said.

"Was I? Thanks." Roo beamed.

"Want to try float?"

"I didn't bring my bathing costume," Roo said.

The woman laughed. "It's not in water. It's a combination of aerial acrobatics, Pilates and yoga. It's slow and controlled."

Roo watched as several of the women pulled at loops of cream material that hung from metal tracks on the ceiling. She realized they were silk hammocks. They locked in place, and as the women lay on them, the room was transformed into a cave of anemic bats. Roo looked to see if June was staying and she was.

"Okay." Roo smiled. "I'll give it a go."

"Watch the others for a while and then I'll come and talk you through."

It looked effortless, so of course it wouldn't be, but Roo stared in fascination as the women used the slings to lift themselves off the ground. They hung from them, entwined with them, stretched with them and Roo snapped June bending like a sapling. So much for her bad back. When Jody returned, Roo had all the material she needed but she couldn't leave without having a go at this.

"It strengthens your core," the instructor told her as Roo hung upside down three feet above the floor in the silky sling, clinging on for grim death. "Stretches tight muscles and eases aching joints."

"So good if you'd had an accident and hurt your back?" Roo asked quietly.

"Only if you were fully recovered. This is quite extreme. You okay on your own?"

"Yep, thanks."

Roo hung upside down and once she felt safe, found it surprisingly relaxing. But her arms and shoulders burned as she pulled herself up. When she finally stood, her legs shook, but this was the most fun she'd had exercising for years.

When Roo reached the entrance to the bar, she waved to Taylor, hoping he'd buy her a drink. He walked over, caught her arm and ushered out of the leisure club.

"I said fifteen minutes," he snapped. "You've been in there an hour and a half."

Damn, have I? "It was soooo good. It made exercising fun, but I had to shower and..." She caught the look on his face and shut up.

Taylor opened the door of the car and Roo climbed in, clutching her gym clothes. When he sat beside her, she handed him the phone and then waited as he looked through the pictures she'd taken. Taylor sighed, Roo tensed, and when a smile lit his face, she relaxed.

"Fantastic. Well done." He leaned over as though he was going to kiss her and then jerked away.

Roo felt flustered. What was it with guys flinching away from her?

"On the downside, I don't have time to take you back to Ilkley. I'll drop you in Guiseley and you can catch the train or get a taxi."

"Thanks. Can I leave my gym stuff on the backseat?"

"Yep."

"Anything special you need me to do when I get back?"

"The invoicing and you can chase up those who've not paid their bills from last month. Just a call, no threats."

Roo waved goodbye when Taylor dropped her off in Guiseley but he zoomed away and didn't wave back. She walked up the road toward the large supermarket and asked the first person she encountered for directions to Dorsey's, where Patrick Farrant, Jason's father, worked. The fourth person she asked directed her off the main street into a warren of terraced housing, in the middle of which was a small industrial estate.

Ideas for cover stories had rippled through Roo's head—she was Patrick's long-lost sister, she was unrelated but researching the Farrant name, Patrick had won a prize in some obscure African lottery—but decided it was easier to go with the truth. The receptionist was a woman Roo's age.

"Good morning," Roo said, producing one of Taylor's business

cards that had mysteriously appeared in her purse. *Oops.* "I work for a private investigation company and I'm looking for someone who's gone missing."

Well, almost the truth. Something rather than someone. Though while she was looking for the dog, she could look for Jason's father.

She started the next sentence hoping the receptionist would jump in. "Patrick Farrant..."

The pause grew longer and longer and just as Roo was about to give up, the receptionist spoke. "I think you better speak to our managing director." She picked up a phone. "Mr. Anstell? There's a private detective in reception asking about Mr. Farrant."

Roo's heart pounded. The secret to successfully winging it was to not say too much. Which was why blabbermouth Roo was generally crap at it.

The receptionist put the phone down. "He's coming to speak to you."

"Thank you." Roo glanced at the pictures on the wall. Dorsey's looked to be some sort of arty design company.

"What's the business?" she asked.

"Blast finishing, spray wash and ultrasonic cleaning equipment."

"Oh." So much for her observational skills.

A door opened and a harassed-looking forty-year-old emerged with his hand outstretched. "Sam Anstell."

"Roo Smith." She shook his hand.

"Come this way."

Roo followed him to his office and perched on the chair he gestured toward.

"Like to tell me why you're looking for Patrick Farrant?" He sat behind his desk and stared at her intently.

"It's a family matter," Roo said. "I need to speak to him."

The MD's fists clenched on his desk. "So do I."

Ah. "When did you last see him?"

"A week ago."

"You don't sound very happy about it." Roo crossed her fingers.

"No, I'm not. I'm thinking about calling the police. The fact that you're here makes me sure I should. Is it his wife you're working for?"

"I can't be specific, but it is a close family member."

He frowned. "When I called, she didn't seem too bothered Patrick had disappeared. I wondered—"

"If she has something to do with his disappearance?" Roo blurted.

The MD's eyes opened wider. "What?"

Damn. "That she knows where he is, I mean."

"But then why would she hire you?" He stared at Roo.

"I didn't say *she'd* hired me. I said a family member. What did Patrick do?"

He hesitated and then said, "Possibly swindled us out of thousands."

Bloody hell. Roo had meant—what was his role in the company, but she grabbed the answer and ran. "How many thousands?"

"Not sure yet and I might be wrong, but maybe a hundred." He huffed. "He's been my finance director for seven years. I trusted him."

Roo winced. She reached into her purse for the business card, wrote her name on the back and put it on the MD's desk. "If you hear anything about him, please call and ask to speak to me." She started to leave and then turned back. "Did you ever play golf with him?"

He gave Roo a puzzled look. "Yeah, a couple of times. He's very good."

"Did he ever mention his dog?"

Now the look was one of complete bewilderment. "No, why?"

"The dog's gone missing too. I'm trying to work out if the two are connected. I think you should contact the police, Mr. Anstell."

He straightened. "Do you know something you're not telling me?"

Roo swallowed hard. "Suggest that they check the freezer in the garage."

She left before he could ask another question and hurried out of the building as fast as her high heels would allow.

By the time Roo had dragged herself to all four estate agents in town, she had a list of precisely zero rooms to rent. Not only were they all more than she'd wanted to pay, none were available. The woman in the last estate agents told her to check the window of the post office and Roo spotted a badly written advert offering a room in a house with three others. She called the number straight away and found herself

saying she'd take it when she hadn't even seen it. It would be horrible. Any room of that price would be horrible, but Roo had little choice unless she moved her tent to another part of the woods and hoped neither the guys nor the vampires noticed.

She caught the train back to Ilkley and blew Taylor's twenty pounds on a cheap pair of comfortable sandals, and instead of going back to Sutton Hall, walked up to Steadman Road.

Ilkley Grammar School's day ended at three. Unless Jason went to a private school, he'd be home soon and walking back along Steadman Road. Roo thought it was worth waiting for half an hour to see if he turned up.

As she was on the point of giving up, she spotted Jason and another boy coming toward her. Jason's face lit up when he saw Roo and her heart sank.

"Not found him," she said quickly and watched his shoulders slump. "Can I talk to you?"

He nodded. "See you, Mark."

The other boy continued up the road and Jason leaned back against a garden wall.

"Your dad come home yet?" Roo asked.

"No."

"You don't think he might have taken Arthur?"

Jason shook his head. "Arthur's my dog. Dad said he was too much trouble anyway."

"Where do you think your dad is? Has your mum said?"

The boy scuffed at the path with his shoe. "Dunno. She's glad he's gone. They argued. I suppose they're going to get divorced." He spat out the last word.

"Has your dad called? You've not spoken to him?"

He lifted his head and looked at her through a thick fringe of hair. "I'm more worried about my dog than my dad."

Oh dear. "I'm just trying to work out if there's a reason why Arthur might have disappeared."

"Mum thinks a stranger's snatched him. If that's so, you won't be able to find him, will you?"

"I've called a lot of places and asked them to keep a look out. Don't give up hope."

Jason gave her a sad smile.

"I won't stop looking," Roo told him. "Are there any special tricks Arthur does so I'll know it's him?"

"One really cool thing. If I pretend to shoot him and say *bang bang* he lies on his back with his legs in the air."

Niall dropped the pea pods into the basket as he worked his way along the row. They'd be lucky to make it into the pot. The last batch he'd picked, Taylor had eaten them straight from the pod while he sat at the kitchen table watching Niall cook. Niall sort of hoped he'd do the same tonight.

When he saw bare feet on the path ahead, Niall knew who it was before he looked up. He straightened and said nothing, but his heart pounded as adrenaline surged.

"Hello, Niall."

Oisin tipped his head to one side and smiled. Niall bent again and continued to pick peas.

"Come home," Oisin whispered.

"No."

"Taylor doesn't want you."

Niall crushed the pod he was holding.

"You're running out of time," Oisin said. "Come home before it's too late."

When Niall continued to ignore him, he sensed Oisin's anger rising.

"The woman doesn't count. Her love is worthless."

Roo loves me? Really? Niall was careful to show no reaction.

"You grow weaker by the day. Taylor doesn't deserve you. He's self-centered and shallow. Come home."

A spike of pain pierced Niall's heart. "No, and leave Roo alone."

"We were just playing. She's a distraction you can't afford."

Niall stood and faced his brother. "Leave her alone and leave me alone.

Oisin gave a snort of disgust. "You can't win. Taylor will never love you."

"Can't? Why?"

Niall watched Oisin's gaze shift left. "Because he's too self-centered."

Oisin only had one arm, his right. So his glance left didn't mean what he'd said was a lie, but Niall thought it was. Taylor *was* self-centered at times, though that wasn't the reason he couldn't love Niall. Had they done something, interfered in some way, made this impossible?

"Please, Niall. Come back with me now."

Niall shook his head. "This is my choice. I live or die by it."

"Then you'll die."

"So be it."

Niall watched Oisin walk away and kept staring long after his brother had disappeared. Why had he come? After all these months, why now? To warn him he couldn't succeed because this was not something under Niall's control? Or because of Roo? *The woman doesn't count. Her love is worthless.* What if the opposite were true?

Was that why his mother had sent Oisin and the others? To frighten Roo off?

Niall headed out of the garden. If Roo did love him, could that save him? And in order for that to happen, did he have to return her love? Yet they'd tried to drive her off before they'd even kissed.

That kiss.

Well, not the first but after. *Sublime.*

Niall had been warned before he left. If he showed true affection first, kissed first, demonstrated his love, he'd pay heavily in the short and long term. Immediate pain and days off his life. But kissed who first?

He headed for the orangery and closed himself inside. The heady scent of plant life calmed his pounding heart. Niall lay on the couch and stared up at the vine-covered glass ceiling. He'd long decided this was where he'd come to die. But he found himself *thinking* for the first time in ages. And not about death. About irony and about love. And maybe finding a way to live.

Niall needed Taylor to love him and Oisin had told him Roo did. The truth or a lie instigated by his mother? How could Roo love him? She hardly knew him—didn't know him. There was *something* between them, some spark. Love wasn't exploding fireworks or erupting volcanoes or towering tidal waves. That was lust. Love was something that crept up on someone, wrapped around them and seeped into every

part of them until it was all they could think about, being with that person, looking at them, listening to them while the words *I love you* bubbled inside their head.

Niall loved Taylor. He'd loved him from the moment they met as boys, but it was a different sort of love then. A love that comes from playing together, laughing together, *being* together. That feeling had shimmered through Niall like a warm wind, whispering in his ear and trailing down his spine. Each morning he'd woken and thought of Taylor, of seeing him when he came home from school, hearing about what he'd learned, what he'd done with his friends. Niall didn't think about him *all* day, just sometimes, but when he did, his lips had curved in a smile that was only for him, despite his brothers demanding to know what he found funny.

He closed his eyes and sighed. Real love had snuck up on him before he'd ever thought of Taylor in any sexual way. Taylor had the life he wanted. He was everything Niall wanted to be, represented everything he valued. Then, one day, Niall had an erection when he'd been play-fighting with Taylor and life changed for both of them. The next day, not a coincidence, Taylor's sister disappeared and Niall lost Taylor. Sixteen years passed while Niall watched and waited for this chance to win him back, but what Niall thought possible a few months ago, seemed less possible now unless Roo's love gave him more time.

The kiss was the key.

If kissing anyone caused the same violent reaction, then Niall would have his answer.

He needed to find someone to kiss.

Chapter Twelve

Taylor drove toward Ilkley in a bad mood. After dropping Roo in Guiseley, he'd spent the afternoon negotiating with an anal-retentive company lawyer who wanted a complicated job done on a shoestring. After they'd finally agreed on a price, Taylor refused the suddenly genial guy's offer of a drink and went back to his car to find he'd got a bloody ticket.

Much as Taylor wanted to get out of Leeds, he also wanted to stay right where he was and not have *that* conversation with Niall. Taylor kept asking himself what he was afraid of. Niall had told him twice he asked nothing of him, and he had to be talking about commitment, right? Taylor had been so close last night to doing to Niall what Niall had done to him. He gulped. *Go on, think it. If I can't even think it, how can I say it?*

Sucking his cock.

Taylor's dick stirred and he groaned.

Before he talked to Niall—though maybe they didn't have to actually *talk*—Taylor needed to drive Roo to wherever it was she'd rented. He'd withdrawn a few hundred in cash to loan her. Taylor called the office number, got the answer phone and switched to the house line.

"Hello," Niall said.

"Put Roo on."

"It's six thirty," Niall pointed out. "She called a cab and left."

"I thought she'd wait. She doesn't even have any money." Taylor sighed. "What's the address of the place she's renting?"

"17 Vermont Avenue, Guiseley."

Damn and blast. He'd driven through Guiseley, now he had to drive back.

"Want me to bring anything?" he asked Niall.

"Dessert?"

Taylor broke the connection with a gulp. He pulled off the road

and sat for a minute wondering if Niall meant ice cream or...*Oh God.* Taylor didn't want him to mean ice cream and the admission sent heat pooling low in his belly.

He entered Roo's address into the sat nav and ten minutes later pulled up across the road from number seventeen. It was a rundown, post-war semidetached house with a front garden so overgrown the path was almost invisible. The house it adjoined was boarded up and the car parked outside looked held together with string.

As Taylor sat wondering about the wisdom of leaving his car unattended, a guy walking up the road stopped and faced the hedge in front of the house. Only when Taylor saw him shaking his dick, did he realize the guy had been taking a piss. It was a gloomy evening but still. Taylor got out of the car, locked it, begged it to stay safe, and headed to the door of number seventeen.

The young guy who opened it had a cigarette dangling from his mouth and a belly hanging over the waist of his jeans.

"Yeah?" he asked, looking at Taylor as though he was considering whether or not he could take him. *Dream on.*

"I've come to see Roo."

The guy moved back from the door. "You the one with the money? Upstairs, room on the left."

The smell hit Taylor the moment he stepped into the hall and he breathed through his mouth. Old food, farts, feet—he didn't want to think too hard about it. It was bad enough that he had to walk on the carpet. He didn't think of himself as a snob, but this place was a shithole. What the hell had Roo been thinking?

He knocked on the bedroom door and then wiped his knuckles on his pants.

"Come in," Roo said.

She was sitting slumped on the bed but straightened when she saw him and plastered a smile on her face. He wasn't fooled. Taylor took in the suitcase still packed, the bags lying on top, the pillow and sleeping bag on top of that, as little as possible touching the heavily stained carpet and he sighed.

"What are you doing?" he asked.

"Thinking."

Taylor held back his smile. "What are you thinking about?"

"Whether to paint the walls yellow or white."

He looked around. "Think it would make much difference?"

She sprang to her feet. "Course it would."

Even Roo was having problems sounding convincing. Taylor took in the tatty, cheap wardrobe, lopsided chest of drawers, the curtain pole half attached to the wall, the ugly light fitting, and turned his gaze back on Roo.

"Why did you take this?" he asked. What the hell had she been thinking?

"It was the only place available and all I could afford."

"Since I'm paying for it, I think you could have aimed a little higher."

"Darn it, why didn't you say? I quite fancy somewhere with a pool."

There was a knock at the door and the guy with the belly walked in. "You can pay me now. I'm going out."

"She's not staying here," Taylor said.

"What? Tay—" Roo began.

"We're leaving. Pick up what you can carry. I'll bring the rest."

"Hey, she said she wanted the room. I had to turn people down today."

Roo filled her arms with her belongings and left the case. Taylor was relieved she wasn't arguing. He grabbed the case and followed her downstairs.

"You have to pay for the room," the guy called as he clattered down the stairs after him.

"Fuck off," Taylor muttered.

Roo opened the door and headed down the path, Taylor a few feet behind her.

"Mitch, Sanjit, get out here," the guy shouted.

Taylor put the suitcase down and turned to face three guys. One of them taller than him, the other two smaller.

"Where's she going?" one of the new guys asked.

Taylor smiled. "She's leaving with me."

"She should pay us for the inconvenience," Beer Belly said. "You should pay us."

"How much are you charging for that shit hole?" Taylor asked.

"Two fifty a month," said the tall guy.

Taylor made a rapid calculation. "Eight-pounds-thirty a day. She's been here what, two hours at the most, so she owes you sixty-eight pence." He pulled a pound from his pocket and flipped it toward them. "Keep the change."

He heard them coming as he stepped onto the pavement. Roo stood across the road by the rear of his car, alarm written all over her face. Taylor waited until the last moment and then swung her case backward. He heard the grunt of pain but didn't linger. He pressed the remote, the trunk lifted and Roo tossed her things inside.

Taylor had almost made it to the vehicle when he was thumped in the kidney. He gasped, dropped the case, turned and swung. His fist made a satisfying connection with a nose, blood spurted and the two guys behind Beer Belly backed off. Taylor clenched his fists. He quite fancied a fight, particularly when he knew he'd win, but the guy turned and slunk away.

A tug at his arm and Taylor swung round again but it was Roo.

"Get in the car," she said, worry all over her face.

She didn't think he could take these guys? "Your case?"

"In the trunk."

Taylor waited until she was inside before he got in, and then drove away. Too fast. Adrenaline still raced around his bloodstream.

"Slow down," Roo whispered.

"I like driving fast. It's exciting." The BMW's wheels squealed as he turned a corner.

"It's even more exciting if you stick your head out of the window. Do it now. There's a bus coming."

Taylor let out a snort of laughter. And slowed.

Roo gasped. "Taylor, Taylor, Taylor, find somewhere to pull over."

"What?"

"Now," she shouted.

He turned into a side street and Roo leapt from the car and raced off toward the main road. *What the hell?* Taylor locked the car and followed.

When he turned the corner, he groaned. Roo was heading for a man walking a large black dog on a lead.

"Roo!" Taylor shouted and ran after her.

"Arthur?" Roo called and the dog turned.

Taylor almost tripped over his own feet. *No way.*

"Excuse me," Roo shouted. "Could I have a word?"

The guy stopped and glanced from her to Taylor. Big guy, thick, muscular arms. A man Taylor didn't want to tangle with. This had to be done carefully, tactfully.

"That dog doesn't belong to you," Roo snapped.

Oh shit.

"What are you talking about?" The man scowled.

"How long have you had him?" Taylor asked before Roo wrenched the lead from the guy's hand.

"A few days."

Roo exhaled noisily. "He went missing in Ilkley a few days ago."

"I bought him in Skipton. I paid good money for him. How do you know he's the dog you're looking for?" The man's voice sounded belligerent. "There are lots of black dogs around."

"He's a pedigree," Roo said. "A flat-coated retriever. Arthur's been micro-chipped. The boy he belongs to has put notices on lampposts and hired me—us—to look for him."

"His name's Riley, not Arthur." But the guy sounded less sure of himself.

"Arthur?" Roo said and the dog wagged his tail. "See?"

"Riley?" said the guy and the dog wagged his tail harder.

Bugger.

Roo pointed two fingers at the dog and said, "Bang, bang."

The dog dropped, rolled over and put his feet in the air.

She smiled and turned to Taylor. "Jason told me he'd do that. This *is* Arthur."

The guy clung tighter to the lead. "I bought him fair and square. I paid five hundred pounds."

Taylor stared at him.

"Okay, two hundred. I knocked the price down from five hundred."

Taylor took out his wallet and peeled off four fifty pound notes.

"I'd rather have the dog," the guy said.

Roo was crouched down, tickling Arthur's ears. "Give me your

number and if Jason says it's not Arthur, we'll bring him back to you."

"If I call the police, and it's proved he's Arthur, you won't get anything," Taylor said.

The lead was thrust into his hand together with a scribbled number.

"One last thing," Taylor said. "Describe the guy who sold the dog to you."

"Wasn't a guy, it was a woman. Medium height, frizzy brown hair, pale face."

Christ, Jason's mother. The guy stroked Arthur's head, sighed and walked off.

Roo stood up. "It might not be her."

"You don't think mothers can do bad things?"

The look of sadness that flashed over Roo's face almost felled Taylor.

"If I've just paid two hundred quid for a dog that Jason's mother wanted to get rid of..."

"But she won't be able to say that, will she?" She tugged the lead from Taylor's hand and led the dog back toward the car.

Taylor didn't bother parking on Steadman Road, but drove down into the cul-de-sac and parked outside number seventeen.

"I can't believe we found him," Roo said. "If I hadn't taken that room, if you hadn't come, if—"

"Life's all about ifs," Taylor interrupted before she went back to "if he hadn't been born" but she was so excited and pleased, he didn't want to burst the bubble. "You did well to spot him."

Roo pulled the dog out of the car. "Jason is going to be so happy."

Taylor followed her to the front door. It was part-opened by Mrs. Farrant who, the moment she set eyes on the dog, looked far from happy. Arthur woofed and strained at his lead. He jerked out of Roo's grip, collided with the front door, pushing it fully open, and jumped at Jason who screamed with joy. The hall was full of suitcases and bags.

"You found him, you found him," Jason shouted. "Arthur, you good boy. Where've you been? I was so worried."

"Aren't you going to say thank you?" Roo smiled at the boy's

mother.

"Thank you," she said through gritted teeth.

"I'm never going to let you out of my sight again." Jason wrapped his arms around the dog's head.

"Going away?" Taylor asked. Something was off here.

"Holiday," she snapped. "Though now I have to find someone to look after the dog. Perhaps you'd like him."

"We can take him, can't we, Mum?"

Jason was joined by a girl a couple of years younger and she hugged the dog too.

"I think being honest with your kids is very important," Taylor said in a quiet voice. "You can't protect them from everything. You owe me two hundred pounds."

The woman blanched. "I don't know what you're talking about."

"I think you do."

"Wait," Jason said, and fiddled in a backpack that lay with the bags. He walked over to Roo and offered her a handful of coins and notes. "I said twenty pounds, right?"

"No, it's—" Roo began.

"Take it," Taylor said.

Roo glanced at him and then put the money in her purse. "Thank you, Jason."

The woman scribbled a check and thrust it at Taylor.

"You have any more problems with Arthur, give us a call," Taylor said to the boy and then glared at his mother before tugging Roo back to the car.

She was still grumbling about taking the money when they got in the vehicle.

"It's a lesson to both of you," Taylor said.

"Phone the police."

He gaped at her. "What?"

"Stop when we've turned the corner and call the police."

Once they were out of sight of the house, Taylor pulled up. "Now what?"

Roo winced. "Don't be cross."

"Tell me what you've done."

Roo blurted out what she'd discovered at Dorsey's and Taylor felt his jaw drop.

"You need to phone the police. She's obviously running."

"Obviously."

Roo glared. "No need for sarcasm."

"So what do you think's happening?" *This should be good.*

"Maybe her husband isn't dead. Maybe he embezzled money from Dorsey's and he's hiding and she and the kids are running to him. They couldn't take the dog because...they're going abroad so the mother had to sell him and lie to the kids. Alternatively, her husband stole the money, he's in the freezer and she's running to Rio."

Taylor waited.

"What?" Roo frowned.

"Maybe she couldn't cope with the dog and misguidedly thought it was kinder to pretend it was missing than tell the kids she'd sold it. Maybe she's going for a holiday because her husband has walked out and left her with a mountain of problems."

Taylor started when there was a knock on the window. He turned and exhaled when he saw the face of Dan Newlyn, a police detective he'd had dealings with before. Not good ones. Taylor let the window down.

"Like to tell me what the hell you're doing here?" Dan asked.

"Returning a missing dog," Roo said.

Dan laughed and then glared. "Bugger off, you're interfering with police business."

"Okay," Taylor muttered.

"Check the freezer," Roo called as Taylor put the window up.

In the rearview mirror, he saw Dan stare after them as they drove off.

Roo let out a heavy sigh. "I just solved my first case and got paid. Why do I feel bad?"

"Because it was ICU's case and that twenty quid isn't yours?"

"I didn't want to take it."

"I know. You can keep it as a reminder not to take jobs where kids are involved. I warned you."

"Sorry. Thanks for taking me away from that house. I'll be fine in the tent, but could I pitch it closer to the hall?"

Taylor pulled over the bridge and up the hill. "You're not sleeping in the tent. There are plenty of bedrooms."

He'd been mulling the idea over for a while and hoped he'd not just made a stupid mistake.

Niall took a deep breath before he walked into the pub. He didn't mind the noise and the smell and the mass of humanity when he was with Taylor, but he wasn't with Taylor. Not only that, his reason for coming here was not to be sociable and have a drink, but to find someone to kiss.

He'd asked the cab driver to wait for him, and the guy insisted on being paid up front. Niall hoped this didn't take too long. He bought a glass of wine and leaned back against the bar, looking around the room.

A group of four women sat at a table near the window. Niall didn't fancy any of them, so one of them would be fine. No point hanging about, he might as well act fast. He bought a bottle of Prosecco, asked for four glasses and carried them over to the table.

"I've had the day from hell and looking at you four cheered me up," Niall said with a smile. "I bought you some sparkling wine. I hope you don't mind."

No, he didn't think they would. A chair was dragged over for him. Another glass brought from the bar so he could drink with them and four women were soon commiserating about his slave-driver boss. Niall didn't have to say much. The women were quite happy to chat, particularly when he told them he didn't have a wife or a girlfriend. Only then he got stuck, wondering how to proceed.

Easy enough in a club once you were dancing, but kissing one of these women suddenly seemed impossible. He couldn't just launch himself at the nearest one. And for that matter, why one of them? Why not all of them?

"Want to play a game?" Niall asked.

The woman on his right smiled. "What sort of game?"

"I guess one fact about each of you and if I'm right, I get a kiss."

"Okay." The word sprang from four mouths at the same time and they laughed.

Niall turned to the blonde on his left. "Melody, you crashed your parents' car."

She gasped. "How the hell did you know?"

He didn't.

She pulled him into her arms.

"Hold on. *I* get to kiss *you*," Niall said and pressed his lips to hers.

Nothing happened. No searing pain, no twinge, nothing. He waited until he felt her tongue run along the seam of his lips and then he tugged free.

"Wow," Melody whispered.

Niall made three more random guesses. All three declared him correct and he gave three more kisses. *Nothing happened.*

"You're amazing," Grace said.

"Sure you don't have a girlfriend?" Donna asked.

"Want me?" Sheena whispered.

Please don't fall for me.

Niall stood. "I have to be going. I promised my mother I'd go and see her." Over his dead body.

But when he stepped outside the pub, Melody went with him.

"Kiss me again," she whispered. "Something...I just want to see...please."

Maybe that wasn't a bad idea. A proper kiss, in case he hadn't gone far enough. A kiss like the one he'd given Roo. *Don't think about Roo.* Niall eased Melody into his arms and pressed his mouth against hers. Her lips opened and he slid his tongue into her mouth. Her hands slipped down to his backside and pulled him closer.

Hands yanked him away and Niall found himself heading for the pavement.

"What the fuck do you think you're doing with my girlfriend?"

As Niall pushed himself up, a foot landed in his ribs and he groaned. Hands hauled him upright and a fist slammed into his stomach, another caught his cheek. Niall fought back and managed to land a couple of blows, but this far away from Sutton Hall he was weak. He fell again and more blows rained down on him until he heard voices yelling, "Stop." Which was great. And "Police." Which was not.

Niall staggered to his feet and headed to where he'd asked the taxi to wait, only to find the driver wouldn't take him.

"I don't want blood in my cab."

"Phone my friend, please." Niall gave him Taylor's number and collapsed.

Chapter Thirteen

Taylor skidded to a halt on the gravel in front of Sutton Hall and switched off the engine. *Say something nice.*

He unclipped his seat belt, turned to Roo and sighed. "I knew you were going to be trouble." *Oh Christ. Kill me now.*

But to his relief, she smiled. "My chicken costume tip you off?"

"That and those long legs that seem to walk you straight into problems. What the hell possessed you to go to Dorsey's?"

"I wanted to find Jason's dog. And I did."

She looked so pleased with herself, Taylor melted. *I want to kiss her.*

"But you were right," she said.

He widened his eyes. "Tell me more. I don't think a woman has ever said those words to me before."

Roo grinned and Taylor's cock tented his pants. He shifted position to try and disguise it.

"I mean right to avoid cases involving kids. What if we hadn't found Arthur? I'd have felt so bad. It was a miracle really, not even good detective work."

"I don't object to miracles. I need all the help I can get." He edged a little closer. "This is Make Your Boss Happy Day. How else am I right?"

"That I couldn't stay in that house in Guiseley. The guys were having a belching competition when I arrived. I don't think it would have been long before they set fire to their farts. The kitchen looked like the aftermath of Armageddon and the bathroom..." She shuddered. "I've lived in some bad places but that was *bad.* Even my university—" Roo pressed her lips together.

"It didn't say you'd been to university on your application."

"It was preventing me getting interviews."

Taylor slid his arm over the back of her seat, his fingers inches away from her hair. "How?"

"Because I have academic qualifications but no experience of graduate jobs. Better to pretend I don't have a degree and at least I get work. I desperately wanted to find a job in an advertising agency and I thought, once I'm in I'll be able to show them what I can do, how far I can go. Only when I finally landed my dream job, my boss had something else in mind when he wanted to see what I could do and how far I'd go." She gave a rueful smile.

Taylor's fingers paused as they were about to stroke her hair. *Was that a warning?* "What did you do for your degree?"

"Russian."

He gaped at her.

Roo grinned. "What were you expecting? Media studies? Tourism and Leisure? Golf Course Management?" She sucked in a breath. "Sorry. Did you do one of those?"

Taylor laughed. "No I didn't, you little..." His phone buzzed and he ignored it. *No use. I can't wait any longer.* "Roo..."

"That's your phone."

Of course it was. *Damn thing.* Taylor didn't recognize the number, considered ignoring the call and instead thought about Roo's comment about her former boss coming on to her, sighed and pressed the button. "Yes."

"Is this Taylor?" asked a man.

"Yes."

"I'm calling about your pal Niall. There's been a bit of an incident."

Taylor felt his stomach launch into freefall and he shot upright in his seat. "What sort of incident?"

"A fight. He's outside the Three Horseshoes in Ilkley."

"Christ, is he okay?"

"No, but he won't let me call an ambulance."

"Give me five minutes."

Taylor ended the call. What the hell was Niall up to? Taylor couldn't believe he'd gone into town alone, nor that he'd get into a bar fight.

"Niall's in trouble. Do you want to get out?"

"Drive," Roo said, looking as worried as Taylor felt.

His heart banged in his chest as he shot out of the drive onto Thorpe Lane. Had whoever was looking for Niall found him? *Fuck it.*

Why the hell hadn't he pushed Niall harder to confide in him?

"I'm not sure what the situation is," he said to Roo, "but do exactly as I tell you when we get there."

"Okay."

"If I have to get Niall out fast, I need to know you're safe."

She gasped. "Why would you have to get Niall out fast?"

Taylor glanced at her. "When I moved in here, he told me he was hiding from someone. It's why he rarely leaves the house. This is the first time I've known him to go out on his own. Jesus, I hope he's okay."

"Oh wow. Who's he hiding from?"

"I don't know. He won't say except the trouble he's in is some sort of family thing." Taylor braked. "Damn lights."

"Can't you help him?" Roo asked. "I mean find out what it's about and sort it out?"

"Not if he doesn't want to be helped," Taylor snapped, guilt winding its fingers around his heart. What the hell had Niall done that he had to keep himself hidden away? Was anything so unforgiveable? A shiver of unease trickled down Taylor's spine. Some things were. *I should have pushed harder.*

Taylor pulled up outside the pub and unclipped his belt. "Stay in the car."

"I can see him." Roo scrambled out her door. "He's up there."

Taylor called her back but she ignored him. *Little idiot.* He spotted Niall sitting on the path with his back to a garden wall, blood all over his face, a couple of guys leaning over him. *Oh shit.* Taylor drove farther up the road and parked next to Niall. Roo was already by his side, holding his hand. Taylor sprang out and left the door open.

"Get me home," Niall muttered. "Home. Please."

"Someone's hit you? What's happened?" Taylor was filled with fury and worry. "Who did it? I'll fucking kill them." He glared at the two guys with Niall.

"Nothing to do with us," one of them said, holding up his hands.

"We were trying to help," said the other.

"Taylor," Roo snapped. "Home. Now."

Niall groaned as they helped him to his feet.

"You need to go to the hospital," Taylor said.

Niall looked straight at him. “No.” His voice was weak, his conviction strong.

Roo scrambled into the back with Niall, and Taylor passed her a box of tissues and a bottle of water. As Taylor pulled back onto the main road, a police car turned onto the road they'd come down and he slowed.

“No,” Niall said. “No police.”

“Okay, okay,” Taylor muttered and sped up again.

“What hurts?” Roo said. “Have you broken anything important?”

“No.”

Taylor braked to let a pedestrian cross and Niall gasped as the car lurched.

“If this isn't a good enough reason to get a mobile phone, I don't know what is,” Taylor barked. “You could have been lying in a ditch. How would I have known? Christ, Niall. A fight?”

In the mirror, he could see Roo wiping the blood from Niall's pale face.

“Don't worry. You haven't lost your good looks,” she said. “I'm sure they'll be able to straighten your nose and your lips won't always look like bananas.”

“What?” Taylor checked again in his mirror.

“Don't worry, he's fine,” Roo said.

“He could have internal bleeding. He ought to see a doctor.”

“No,” Niall said.

Taylor pulled up in front of the house, ran to unlock the front door and then rushed back to help Niall. Now Roo had wiped most of the blood from his face, he didn't look so bad. Niall eased himself out of the car and stood on shaky legs.

“I'm okay,” he muttered.

Taylor put his arm around him. “Let's get you inside.”

Roo scurried after them and Taylor turned and threw her his keys. “Get your stuff out of the car. Pick a room. I'll look after Niall.”

Her heart was still beating hard enough to hurt. She wanted to help with Niall but something in Taylor's manner, the worry on his face, the concern in his voice, the way he snapped at her, told her how much he cared for the guy and that she wasn't wanted. Strange,

because Roo had thought just before that phone call, Taylor had been thinking about kissing her. And she'd been thinking about letting him. What sort of tart did that make her?

In a way, Sutton Hall was the worst place for her to be. One guy she fancied who wanted her one minute and not the next, and one guy she hadn't fancied—much—who hadn't seemed to fancy her at all, who now suddenly did. And despite his crankiness, Taylor was growing on her, which just made the situation worse.

She dragged her case and the rest of her things out of the trunk and carted them into the house. Roo hadn't been upstairs before. The place was massive. They'd hardly know she was there. She could find a bedroom and keep quiet. Though that might be a problem. If she couldn't keep quiet, she could offer to clean.

After lugging all her gear up to the landing, Roo went exploring. The first door she opened was clearly Taylor's room. A bed unmade, clothes she recognized and shoes strewn on the floor. Roo closed the door again. Three bedrooms didn't have beds. She found a bathroom that didn't look used so maybe Taylor had an en suite. Two more doors to try. One held a massive four-poster bed and Roo shivered. It wasn't quite a phobia she had about four-posters, but she really didn't like them. She quickly closed the door.

The other room stole Roo's breath.

At first she thought someone must live here with the guys, but when she saw the dust, Roo realized she'd been mistaken. This was a young girl's room with pink curtains and a line of faded soft toys in the window seat. A single bed, with a pink-and-white-checked cover, had a pretty wooden headboard, a heart cut out in the middle. There was a matching wardrobe and chest. There were even books on the shelves. It had to belong to Taylor's sister.

Now it could be hers. Roo carried her things into the bedroom and rolled out her sleeping bag on the bed. She'd wash the sheets tomorrow. Roo tiptoed out to use the bathroom and then returned to lie down. She had nothing from her early childhood, no teddy bear, no doll, no books, no photos, only memories of good times and bad, memories that were so mixed up she was no longer certain which were true.

"I'm fine, I'm fine," Niall said. "I just need to rest. The orangery."

Taylor frowned. "You sure? It's a mess in there. I need to sort it

out. Well, you can do it. You're the gardener. I'm surprised you haven't done it already."

"Yep, leave it to me," Niall said. *Don't touch it, please.*

But at least Taylor helped him in there and onto a couch. Niall toed off his shoes and wriggled his bare toes. He felt better already.

"What the hell are you smiling about?" Taylor snapped.

Because I kissed a girl and it didn't hurt. "Thinking about the other guy."

"Liar."

"Oh fuck. Did my eyes shift left?"

Taylor smirked. "You'd think after I'd told you about that, you'd remember not to do it. Now, what can I get you? A drink? Frozen peas?"

"Frozen peas would be good."

Although he really didn't need them. Niall was healing already. He could feel the aches and pains fading, his anxiety receding now that he was back at Sutton Hall, particularly in this room. It was annoying he'd been assaulted like that. If he'd been at normal strength, it wouldn't have happened. Taylor returned with a bag of frozen peas and a dish of the peapods Niall had picked in the garden.

Niall nodded at the fresh peas. "I was going to cook those."

Taylor perched on the end of the couch. "I'd rather eat them like this."

Niall smiled, pressed the icy bag onto his ribs under his shirt and shuddered. Maybe his cock would take the hint.

"So what happened?" Taylor asked.

Niall sighed. He should have known Taylor wouldn't let it go.

Taylor's jaw twitched. "If you stare straight at me, I'll know you're lying."

Niall was tempted to close his eyes. "I kissed a girl. Her boyfriend took exception." Just as well he hadn't gone with his next thought, which had been to ask her to come back to Sutton Hall so he could kiss her here and check whether that made any difference.

He saw the flicker of confusion cross Taylor's face.

"I told you I'm not gay," Niall whispered.

Taylor opened his mouth as if he were going to say something and instead pushed in several peas and chewed. He swallowed and said, "I

nearly kissed Roo."

Niall didn't let a whisper of emotion cross his face. He wasn't sure how he felt about that. "Why didn't you?"

"I had that call about you."

"Ah." That was good, wasn't it, that Taylor had come for him? Only Niall felt a surge of desperation leap in his chest. He couldn't lose Taylor now, and if he told him he'd already kissed Roo, Niall suspected he'd sustain further injury.

"What happened with Roo's new place?" Niall asked.

"A dump. I wasn't leaving her there. Oh and can you believe we found that missing dog? Took it back to the house and the mother looked as though she wanted to kill us. Cost me two hundred pounds because I suspect the check she gave me will bounce. The police arrived as we left. Seems the father was embezzling. I doubt I've heard the last of that. That wanker Dan Newlyn was there."

He tossed a pea toward Niall's mouth and he caught it.

Taylor smiled and then his face fell. "I panicked when I had that call. I thought your past had caught up with you. You never go out on your own. I..."

Niall rubbed Taylor's back with his foot.

"Want to tell me why you're hiding? Maybe I can help."

Niall wondered what would happen if he told Taylor the truth. Would they come and drag him away in front of Taylor's astonished eyes? Would they kill Taylor? It was possible. More likely they'd take his memory again.

"My family wants to control my life." Niall chose his words carefully. "My mother...is a difficult woman. She and I don't see eye to eye. She had someone in mind for me to marry. It's not going to happen. I'm just laying low until it all blows over." That was a joke. She could carry a grudge forever.

"But you're never in touch with any of them. If they wanted to contact you, they wouldn't be able to. There could be some sort of emergency. What if...what if a friend or a family member was ill or dying? Shouldn't you at least tell someone where you are?"

Niall had managed to work Taylor's shirt out of his pants with his foot and he was now rubbing his toes on Taylor's lower back. He was encouraged by the fact that Taylor hadn't moved away.

"My brother knows where I am," Niall said. "This won't go on much longer."

Taylor stiffened. "You mean you'll leave?"

Niall slid his toes higher. "You're selling the house, remember?" He hadn't missed Taylor's reaction to the thought of him leaving. Disappointment. Niall felt a rush of delight.

"Mmm." Taylor groaned, closed his eyes and arched his back as Niall pressed on some aching muscle. "What are you doing?"

"It's not obvious?" Niall whispered.

"You're supposed to be injured."

"I've recovered."

"Why did you kiss the girl?" Taylor blurted.

"Actually, I kissed four girls."

Taylor let out a snort of laughter and then pinned Niall with his gaze. "And did you like it as much as you liked kissing me?"

"Can't quite remember," Niall whispered.

"Like me to remind you?"

The word *yes* stuck in Niall's throat. He could only nod. Taylor turned and knelt on the couch, one hand resting on the back, the other against Niall's hip. He leaned over and lowered his head until their lips were only inches apart.

"Sure you're up to this?" Taylor asked.

"All of me is up for it, despite the frozen peas."

What am I doing? What am I doing? What the fuck am I doing? But Taylor dropped his head until his lips brushed Niall's, and when he felt the electricity arc through him and need roar along his veins, he knew full well what he was doing. Taylor licked the seam of Niall's lips, tasting beer and a hint of salt, and then Niall's lips parted and Taylor's tongue slipped inside. Niall's groan vibrated in Taylor's mouth and he felt it all the way down to his dick.

Their lips attached, they unfastened shirts, button by button, fingers drifting over nipples as they moaned into each other's mouth. Taylor's cock surged against his zipper. He tugged his shirt from his arms as Niall pushed himself up to remove his. The bag of peas fell to the floor but their lips remained loosely connected, tongues dancing as they panted and gasped.

Taylor kicked off his shoes, heard the dull clunks as they hit the floor, then Niall's fingers rubbed his cock through the material of his pants and Taylor sucked in a hiss. It filtered through Taylor's brain

that they'd be more comfortable in his bed, but the thought of lying in a bed with a guy stopped the breath in his throat.

What am I doing? rushed back into his head.

Niall popped open the button on Taylor's pants and unzipped him. The relief that his cock had room to grow drowned out his worries. They wriggled out of the last items of clothing, mouths still sucking greedily at each other until they were naked, Taylor with his knees planted on either side of Niall's hips, and Niall lying there with his hands holding Taylor's head.

Taylor pulled back to breathe and gulped as he looked down at Niall, all long limbs and fluid muscle. No sign of any injury, except for that graze on his chin, which was good and bad. What if he'd—

"I'm fine," Niall whispered. "I just had the wind knocked out of me."

"You're gorgeous," Taylor muttered.

Moonlight filtered through the vine-covered glass ceiling, casting Niall in an ethereal glow. The tattoo running down the side of his leg had such sharp definition in the dim light that Taylor blinked, thinking he was seeing things that weren't there. *Barbed wire? Thorns?* Hadn't it been ivy? But his gaze was drawn to Niall's cock, all thick and long and hard. It was a thing of beauty, and the fact that he could think that brought Taylor one step closer to acceptance of his sexuality not being as clear cut as he'd once thought.

Niall pulled Taylor down to lie on top of him, the base of Niall's cock gloving the delicate skin of Taylor's balls as their shafts rubbed together. Niall's arms wound around Taylor's back and his legs spread until he hooked his ankles over Taylor's calves. They kissed more deeply now, the thrusts with their tongues matching the rocking of their hips.

Taylor's head swam with excitement as they rutted against each other. He slid his hands under Niall's shoulders, holding him tight as they bucked and rubbed their cocks together. Precome wet their bellies and the warm, slippery sensation tipped Taylor closer to release. And he knew Niall was holding back, waiting for him to take the lead, tell Niall what he wanted. Only Taylor didn't know what that was, except that he had to come. Soon.

He slid his hand between their bodies, reaching for Niall's cock. Wrapping his fingers around it, he squeezed and pumped, sliding his thumb over the sensitive crown, feeling Niall's shudder ripple through his body. Niall groaned and slid from under him, forcing Taylor to let

go.

"You're too good at that," Niall said with a half laugh.

His eyes. *Oh fuck.* How could Taylor see the color in this light? But he could. A brilliant green. He'd never seen anyone with eyes like that before—*yes I have.* Where? When?

"What do you want to do?" Niall whispered.

Christ, he's asking me*? Everything. Nothing. No, not nothing.* Taylor forced his bloodless brain to think. No condoms around, no lube—*oh God.* Letting Niall fuck him or him fucking Niall was a big step and one too far for Taylor.

Niall sat up on the couch, watching, waiting, and Taylor dropped to his knees in front of him. His heart was racing, his mouth dry, his breathing too noisy. Taylor clenched his fists to stop his hands shaking. It didn't work. Niall leaned back and spread his arms along the back of the couch. Taylor got the message. He wouldn't push. But Taylor would have liked a bit of a shove.

"You don't have to do this," Niall said.

Taylor smothered his laugh.

"What's funny?" Niall asked.

"I need encouragement, not an out."

"Be nice and I'll make carrot cake tomorrow."

Now Taylor released his laugh. He *loved* Niall's carrot cake.

Niall grinned. "Extra frosting."

Taylor laid his hands flat on Niall's thighs and slid his palms over firm muscles until his thumbs brushed the fragile skin of Niall's sac. The sound of Niall exhaling tightened his chest. Niall's balls were drawn up around the base of his cock, much like Taylor's. Taylor could smell Niall's musky arousal, hear his rapid breathing, see the bead of precome at the tip of his cock growing like a liquid pearl. Every sense seemed heightened. Every cell in his body ached with arousal. His mouth no longer dry, Taylor leaned forward to sweep his tongue over the silk-covered slit.

Niall hissed and Taylor's eyelids fluttered as he tasted another man for the first time. Salty and sweet, the tangy flavor sent a rush straight to his brain like a fast-acting drug. Taylor slid his hands higher until his fingers curved over Niall's angular hip bones. He wrapped his lips around the head of Niall's cock and sucked. Niall's thighs quivered and he moaned.

"Oh fuck, fuck."

Taylor licked down the length of the swollen shaft, trailing his tongue along the prominent veins, tracing their path. He lapped at Niall's balls and then licked his way back, bringing his hand up to squeeze Niall's cock. Taylor's other hand had crept to his own balls, and he pushed down, trying to win some time. Seconds probably. Niall's breathy gasps were turning him on as fast as if he pumped his cock.

When Taylor let Niall's cock slide in and out of his mouth, he felt fingers thread his hair and a palm settle at the back of his neck, but Niall didn't push, didn't pull, just held him. Taylor gripped Niall's dick and dipped his tongue into the slit, and Niall gave a violent twitch.

"Let's do this together," Niall mumbled.

Taylor leaned away and Niall swung round so he lay on his back on the couch, his legs dangling over the end. He caught Taylor's hand and pulled him up, turning him until he faced his feet. Taylor groaned when Niall caught his cock and bent it back to his mouth. Then Niall took him so deep, Taylor shuddered.

A moment later, his cock was back in the air and Niall was tapping it against his cheek. Lick and tap. Lick and tap.

"Want a race?" Niall asked.

"Ready, steady, go—oh it's over?"

Niall laughed. It seemed to Taylor that Niall had never laughed so much.

"The one who comes last wins," Niall said.

"Wins what?" Taylor choked out.

"Just wins. The sheer bloody joy of it."

Taylor lifted Niall's cock to his mouth and took him as deep as he could. The bastard did the same to him. Heat flashed through Taylor and his balls tingled. He wrapped a hand around Niall's cock, folded his mouth around him and tightened his lips as he pushed his head down over the silky length. It was hard to concentrate when Niall was sucking his cock, not just sucking but licking, blowing, teasing the length of him. Orgasm was a breath away, a suck away, the slightest touch away.

He bobbed his head over Niall's crest, pulling at the top few inches, tightening his lips, moving faster while Niall worked his own magic. They were both grunting and moaning. Taylor kept stopping to gulp air but Niall just kept going and going. *How can he breathe?* The

telltale tremors of eruption grew in Taylor's brain. Niall had his hands on his butt, fingers digging into the crease as he deep-throated him. Taylor sucked harder and faster and as he felt himself sliding down a huge wave, Niall's cock grew in his mouth and went hotter just as Taylor's balls exploded.

As he erupted into Niall's mouth, so Niall erupted into his. Thick jets of come hit his tongue, his teeth, his throat, and Taylor swallowed and swallowed and loved every moment of it.

But when the wave rolled away to leave him stranded on the beach, Taylor wondered what the hell he'd done. Niall licked him clean and let him out of his mouth. His firm grip kept Taylor from bolting, and he pulled him down to lie at his side, heads together. And finally Taylor didn't want to run because this felt perfect.

Chapter Fourteen

Roo backed away from the door, her heart jumping. She'd come down to find something to eat and heard groans coming from the orangery. She'd only looked because she worried Niall might be in pain. The expression on his face wasn't pain, it was ecstasy. They had their mouths around each other's cocks and Roo had never seen anything as sexy or frustrating in her life.

Well, that settled one question. Not straight. But raised another. Bi? Unless Niall had been playing with her in the tent and Taylor was pretending he'd wanted to kiss her a few hours ago. Maybe she was just some pawn in a stupid game. She sagged with disappointment and edged toward the stairs. They wanted each other, not her. Roo felt like a sumo wrestler was sitting on her chest. She didn't take another breath until she was back in the room she'd chosen with the door closed.

Roo brushed the back of her hand over her eyes and slumped on the bed. That *wasn't* a tear. Now she was not only pretending *not* to cry, she was wide awake and starving, her mind tearing along like a racing car. She was *not* going to think about what she'd seen downstairs. Definitely not going to admit that she did more than take a quick glance before she moved away. More than a long look. *Oops.*

Wow, they were hot. Really hot. Am I sick to be turned on by two guys getting down and dirty?

Now Roo was hot. *Shit.*

She pushed herself up, walked over to the bookshelf and ran her fingers over the spines. Harry Potter, Harry Potter, Harry *bloody* Potter. Roo had already read those. The last two in the series weren't there. All but one of them looked brand new. *Strange.* She pulled out Charlotte's Web and the book next to it came out as well and fell from its slipcover. Roo picked it up and could see it didn't belong to the cover. It was a notebook, not *Captured by Indians.* She flipped through the pages and smiled at the childish writing. If it had been a diary, she'd have put it back. Probably. But this looked like a story. Roo took it back to bed, crawled into the sleeping bag and started to read.

Once upon a time, there was a boy who lived in a big house with a big garden. His name was Taylor.

Roo stopped. Maybe she shouldn't read it. But her gaze was drawn inexorably back to the page and she kept going.

Taylor had a sister called Stephanie, who was very beautiful even though she was only ten years old. She had long, black hair and dark eyes.

Roo smiled. Within a few lines it was established that Stephanie was sugar and spice and all things nice, and Taylor was loud and rough and all things trouble. Roo curled up and lay on her side.

But this story started when Stephanie was five and Taylor was nine.

Taylor was playing with Stephanie in the garden and his blue-and-white plane flew over the wall. They weren't supposed to touch the wall, their mother and father had told them time after time, but Taylor climbed over to get his plane. He came back a few minutes later and told Stephanie to go back to the house because he was going to play with the boy who'd climbed back with him. Only there was no one with him. Stephanie stomped off to complain to her mother that Taylor wouldn't play with her and he was pretending a boy liked him.

An imaginary friend. Roo had never had one of those, though she had made up imaginary boyfriends based on the TV show she liked at the time. They used to walk to school with her and be waiting at the end of the day to walk home again. She used to dream of going to America and meeting them, and of course they'd love her at first sight. *Yeah right.*

She turned the page.

Poor Stephanie. She'd had all Taylor's attention and now she had none. Well, according to the story. As soon as Taylor finished his homework, he went to play in the garden and made it clear his sister wasn't welcome. He wouldn't even tell her the name of his friend. He was growing up, their mother said, and she'd started to show Stephanie how to cook, paint pictures and make necklaces so she didn't bother Taylor. But Stephanie spied on him sometimes, heard him talking to himself and then laughing as if someone answered.

Then one day Stephanie crept out to the garden when Taylor wasn't home, and she'd seen a boy with sun-streaked blond hair sitting in the tree house. She'd called out to him and he'd leapt over the wall and disappeared, right in front of her eyes. Stephanie had bolted to the end of the garden but he'd gone.

It hadn't just been an ordinary boy she'd seen. There was something special about him. He had wings. Stephanie knew without a shadow of a doubt that Taylor's friend was a faery.

Roo smiled. *That's so cute.*

The next page was the last one Stephanie had written. She wanted to see where the faery had gone, so she planned to creep out after dark when everyone was asleep and climb over the wall. *Maybe not when it's dark,* she'd added. *Tomorrow afternoon in the sunshine.*

Wish me luck. The last words in the book.

Roo was disappointed there wasn't more. She tucked the book under the pillow and closed her eyes. Then opened them. She needed to switch the light off. But before she could move, the door flew open and she sprang up.

"What the fuck are you doing in here?" Taylor yelled.

Roo moved to a sitting position, yanked up the sleeping bag to her chin and stared at him. He bracketed the doorway, his face filled with fury. *What have I done?*

"Get out of this room." Taylor's face was pale and his fists were clenched.

Niall appeared at his back, put his hand on Taylor's shoulder and Taylor shrugged him off.

"Now," Taylor snapped.

Roo crawled from the sleeping bag and picked it up, along with her pillow, keeping it pressed against her chest. She bent over her case and fastened it with shaking fingers. Taylor was frightening her. For a moment she'd been transported back a few years to when a guy had yelled at her like that, except Mike had less control than Taylor and he'd hit her. He'd taken her to a country house for the weekend, they had a room with a four-poster bed and he'd wanted to tie her up. Mike didn't listen to no.

"Taylor, come on," Niall said. "How could she know? What harm's been done?"

Roo scuttled out of the room, dragging her things with her. She turned to see Niall push Taylor into his bedroom farther down the corridor. Niall went inside with him and closed the door. She sagged. The floor in an empty room or that four-poster?

The floor won.

Roo took her things to the smallest room, luckily as far away from Taylor as she could get, and dropped her sleeping bag on the wooden

floor. She'd slept in worse places. At least this was dry and warm. When she laid her head on the pillow and felt something hard beneath her cheek, Roo realized she'd accidently slipped the book inside the pillowcase. She pulled it out and laid it in her case. The mood Taylor was in, he'd accuse her of stealing it. She'd put it back tomorrow and he'd be none the wiser.

Oh God. What had caused *that* outburst? If he hadn't wanted her to sleep in his sister's room, why hadn't he told her? Though she should have registered how it looked, how it was preserved and used some common sense. Roo wished she could leave now, but she had no money and nowhere to go.

I'm not going to cry. But she struggled against the tightness in her chest and the choking sensation in her throat.

She was Happy Roo, the woman who dressed as a chicken for fifty quid, the woman who found something to smile at in almost everything. Because if she didn't smile, bad things would creep up and strangle her, remind her she wasn't wanted, that the one person in the world who really should have wanted her, hadn't and didn't.

Not going to think that.

Not going to think at all.

Niall held a silent Taylor while he shook. He could feel the guy's tears falling onto his shoulder, and every drop felt like a dagger in his heart. Niall didn't let him go. Taylor finally pulled free, turning to wipe his eyes before he flopped back on the bed.

"I saw the light and for one crazy moment, I thought Stephanie had come home. Oh shit. Roo will think I'm a complete asshole. I should explain."

He tried to sit up and Niall pushed him down. "It'll wait until tomorrow. Let her sleep. You sleep." *Let* me *comfort you, not her.*

Taylor looked up at him. "Stay with me."

Always. Niall swallowed the lump in his throat.

Taylor settled on his back and Niall lay on his side facing him. Maybe what Taylor felt for him wasn't yet love, but he'd cared enough to rush to Ilkley to help him and he'd cared when he'd dragged him from the hot tub. Now Taylor wanted Niall's comfort. It meant something, didn't it?

"I need to clear that bedroom," Taylor whispered. "That's what my

parents want me to do because they can't. They never gave up hope. They still haven't given up hope. How can they when there are stories about women emerging after years in captivity, held in gardens, in underground bunkers, under bloody beds—held by warped men, and sometimes their warped wives? Stephanie could still be alive. How can you ever give up that hope?"

Niall said nothing. Taylor's pain was his pain and Niall stroked his face.

"My fault," Taylor mumbled. "I was supposed to be looking after her and I didn't even notice she'd gone. I was..."

Niall froze.

"Playing," Taylor whispered. "Was I with someone? I don't...I don't..."

Taylor slipped into sleep and Niall relaxed. He needed Taylor to remember the happy times they'd had, not the day his ten-year-old sister had vanished into thin air.

Roo woke at six and couldn't go back to sleep. She ached from sleeping on the floor and stretched until she'd worked the kinks out of her spine. After a quick shower, she dressed and slipped downstairs. If Taylor sacked her and asked where she was going, she'd invent a friend to stay with. In reality, Roo would camp in a field and renew her relationship with Dorothy at the employment agency.

It didn't take long to finish the invoicing. Roo printed out payment reminders for the few who still owed money, made a list of several to phone, and opened the mail on Taylor's desk, sorting it into piles. There wasn't enough to do in this job. Unless Roo was involved in some of the detective work, she'd quickly get bored.

Jonas arrived before either Taylor or Niall made an appearance.

"Morning." He tossed a folder onto Taylor's desk and yawned. "Where's the boss?"

"I don't know." *In bed with Niall?*

"Is the printer on?"

Roo nodded. Jonas took a memory stick from his pocket and slotted it into the printer. A moment later, the machine whirred as it began to print.

"Holiday snaps?" Roo asked.

Jonas grinned. "No sun, no sand, but plenty of sex. I had to crawl through a ventilation shaft to get these."

Roo came to stand by his side. The photo emerging was of an almost bald guy tied up in some complicated leather strap work. It didn't hide much, his cock erect in a cage, saggy balls dangling and a ball gag in his mouth. Roo cringed. He was on his knees in front of an ordinary-looking woman wearing a flowery blouse and a knee-length gray skirt, though she held a whip. The incongruity of it didn't escape her.

"Oh dear. His wife's not going to be pleased," Roo said.

Jonas *tsked.* "Now that's very sexist. It's actually *that* woman's husband we're working for and that's not the guy in the picture. He wants to know what she does every Thursday night because she never seems to open the book for her weekly reading club."

"Wow."

"They don't actually have penetrative sex. I'm not sure whether that will be of any comfort."

Roo frowned. "It's sad, isn't it, that people don't talk to each other? I mean, she might find her husband's quite keen on the idea of playing with leather. She could be a dominatrix in her own living room and not need to go out."

"Her husband's a vicar."

"He'd definitely be up for it then."

Jonas laughed. Roo's smile slipped when Taylor walked in and her heart began to gallop. He didn't even glance at her.

"Morning, boss." Jonas put the photos on the desk. "Hope you haven't eaten."

Taylor glanced at the pictures.

"I've written the report and emailed it to you," Jonas said.

"Thanks."

"I haven't anything on this morning. Like me to show Roo how to do some searches?"

"That's fine. I've things to do." Taylor walked out.

"What did you do to Mr. Sunshine?" Jonas asked.

He was joking, but Roo knew this was because of last night. At least he hadn't sacked her. Yet.

"He probably got out of bed the wrong side," she muttered.

"Whose bed?"

Roo glanced at him, but Jonas had moved to grab Taylor's chair. He dragged it over next to hers and sat.

"Right. We'll do a search on you and you can see the procedure."

"I'm boring. How about we make that a search on you?"

He smiled. "Okay. Me first, then you."

"Let me get a pencil."

Roo grabbed a pad of paper and looked at him expectantly.

"We're looking for coffee," he said. "First place to search. Kitchen. Check cupboards for mugs."

Roo elbowed him hard on her way past.

Taylor went out to the garage to get some cardboard boxes and carried them upstairs. No point putting this off any longer. Yet after he'd put down the boxes, he still managed to not open the door of Stephanie's room. Instead he went into the room next door. Taylor slumped on his parents' bed. If Stephanie hadn't disappeared, would his mum and dad still be living here? Was Spain their escape? London hadn't been his, no matter how much he wished it so.

He looked round the room. Hardly anything left in there. He'd emailed about the bed and they wanted to sell it. He probably ought to go round the house with stickers and get the local auction house to come and take it all away. Taylor frowned. So where was Roo's stuff? Was she exceptionally tidy or—he gulped—hadn't she slept in here?

Taylor couldn't believe she'd go back into his sister's room after the way he'd exploded. He wandered down the corridor, checking the rooms, and groaned when he saw the sleeping bag in the corner of the smallest bedroom. *Shit.* She'd slept on the floor. Taylor closed his eyes and dropped his head against his arm where it rested on the doorframe. *I am such a dick.*

He'd speak to her later.

Do it now.

Taylor glanced back at the boxes piled up by Stephanie's door. He wasn't going to put this off again. As he walked along the corridor, he heard Niall coming down the stairs from the attic. When Taylor had woken this morning on the bed, still dressed, the covers had been warm and he knew Niall had slept next to him. A little bit of him was

sorry Niall hadn't stayed, a larger part of him was relieved.

"Morning," Niall said.

Taylor nodded. "You okay?"

Hadn't Niall's chin been scraped last night? There was no sign of it now.

"Fine." Niall looked at the boxes. "You want a hand?"

"No thanks. I need to do this on my own." Taylor had wanted to say yes, but this was his burden.

Niall continued down the stairs.

"Hey," Taylor called. "Don't forget you promised carrot cake."

Niall smiled and Taylor felt like he'd walked into a rainbow. *Christ, I've got it bad.* He hurried into Stephanie's room with the boxes.

Taylor didn't get very far inside. He leaned back against the door and sighed. Apart from the dust, it looked as though his ten-year-old sister had just stepped out for a moment. His parents had wanted to keep everything the same, for the room to be waiting for her. But she'd never come back. And every day, instead of life growing easier, it grew harder.

The press had been full of speculation for weeks. *Ten-year-old disappears from her garden*—a continual headline. The moors were searched, the river too. They used helicopters, dogs, even a psychic, but Stephanie really did seem to have vanished into thin air. His father had been questioned over her disappearance and Taylor had been horrified to think anyone could imagine his kind, decent, distraught father would kill his own child. Then they'd taken his mother to the police station and she'd come back broken, her tears unstoppable, unable to speak for hours.

Then they'd questioned Taylor. Had he been playing with his sister and something had gone wrong? Everyone would understand if there had been an accident. But where was she? Had his father ever tried to touch his sister in an inappropriate way? Had Taylor? Had they both touched her? Where had he hidden her body? Was there a well he knew of? A cave? An old mine? It wasn't fair to his parents to keep quiet. He needed to tell the truth, all of the truth. The questions were relentless, the pressure intense. Taylor could see why people confessed to stuff they hadn't done, but he wouldn't.

Taylor had been left reeling, trying to crush that niggle of doubt the police had planted. What if his dad *had* killed her? Taylor couldn't believe that and he hated the police for ever making him think it. They

didn't listen to the truth. It was as though they wanted to find Stephanie lying someplace dead because that would be easier. They wanted someone to have killed her, someone they could arrest and put on TV, put in the paper, put on trial. Solve the crime. Close the file. Move on.

His parents were more worn down and exhausted with every day that passed. His mother ended up in a psychiatric hospital, and finally the papers delegated stories about his sister's disappearance to the inside pages. Smaller and smaller column inches. No more photographers lurking in bushes to take pictures of the family. No more snide remarks from Taylor's mates who obviously weren't mates at all. Time passed and people forgot.

Not his parents. Not Taylor.

He began to pack her books in one of the boxes, shaking each of them and flipping through the pages in case she'd written a note, something the family or the police had missed. And as he handled the volumes, an iron fist squeezed his heart because Taylor remembered how much she'd loved her books, how she'd adored Harry Potter. She'd only got to read the first book, but his mum had told him she'd bought the others and stored them in there for when Stephanie came home.

Her clothes still hung in the wardrobe, but no scent of his sister remained. The dresses looked limp and faded. Taylor folded her clothes and piled them in a box. Handling her teddy bears and soft toys increased the lump in his throat to painful proportions. Little things that she'd bought, or been given, filled another box. His parents had taken the photos, school reports, swimming certificates, her special treasures—the personal stuff. Taylor lifted the girly pictures off the walls, folded the bedding and boxed that too until all that was left was the bed, the wardrobe and her chest.

The police had searched this room more than once and found nothing. Taylor had looked, so had his mum and dad. Taylor walked around, tapping the walls, even though the wallpaper was intact and the same as when Stephanie had vanished. There were no hollow spots, no hidden niches, no secret rooms. Finally, he inspected the floor. On his hands and knees, looking for loose boards, Taylor worked his way across the room. The only place he hadn't checked was under the furniture. But everything would have been too heavy for his sister to move. Taylor gave the bed an experimental shove but it didn't budge.

He jumped when Niall appeared in the doorway holding two mugs.

"Coffee?" Niall asked.

"Yeah and a hand."

Niall put the mugs on the floor by the door.

"I want to move the bed, chest and wardrobe."

"Didn't the police do that?"

Taylor glanced at him. "Probably. So what? Bed first."

A thin layer of dust covered the area under the bed. Taylor checked the boards but they were all firm and they put the bed back in place.

"What are you looking for?" Niall asked.

"I don't know. I just feel as though there's something I've missed."

They edged the wardrobe away from the wall.

"You've looked through all her books and toys?"

"Yep."

"Nothing missing?"

Taylor gave a short laugh. "You think I'd remember after all this time? I know nothing went missing with her."

The only things under the wardrobe were one of Taylor's mini transformers and a pink comb Stephanie used on her doll. Taylor tapped the back of the wardrobe, checked the wall but found nothing.

When the chest was back in place, Taylor picked up a coffee and sat on the bed.

Niall stayed leaning against the wall. "Is this why you became a private detective?"

Taylor looked up at him but didn't answer. He didn't need to. The answer was yes.

"What are you going to do with her things?"

"I'll ask my parents, but I guess they can go to a charity shop. Not sure anyone would want the clothes." He stared at Niall. "You don't seem as battered as I'd expected. Where did all that blood come from?"

Niall rubbed his chin. "I heal fast."

"Was I a complete fuckwit last night? Over Roo being in here, I mean." Except he didn't only mean that. What they'd done in the orangery still heated his blood. He and Niall had dressed afterward, and until Taylor had spotted the light on in Stephanie's room, he'd been on the point of inviting Niall into his bed.

"She doesn't know about your sister. You need to tell her," Niall said.

Taylor sighed. "I thought Roo would use my parents' bedroom. She slept on the floor in the room at the end of the corridor."

Niall raised his eyebrows. "Why would she do that?"

"I've fucked it up with her and I was on the point of..."

"On the point of what?"

"Making a move."

Taylor looked Niall straight in the face. *What's he thinking?*

"You better apologize then," Niall said, and walked out.

"Niall!" Taylor lurched after him.

When Niall turned and Taylor saw the...*what the hell?*...he stumbled. Was that fear on his face?

Chapter Fifteen

Roo and Jonas started when they heard the door slam.

"Damn, is that Taylor leaving?" Jonas jumped to his feet and rushed out of the office.

Roo's shoulders slumped. At least Taylor hadn't burst in and told her she was fired, but she needed to apologize. She ought to have registered the room had been left like that for a reason. Jonas came back a couple of minutes later holding his phone to his ear.

"Is there a fire somewhere?" he asked. "I wanted a word with you about... No, not yet... Still doing searches... Okay." He glanced at Roo. "No problem."

She smiled. *No problem?* That would be a first then.

Jonas put his phone back in his pocket. "Looks like it's you and me for the rest of the day." He picked a file off Taylor's desk, took a sheet from it and copied it on the machine. "Amy Banks. Trying to trace her mother's sister. Mother's dying, so it's urgent. See what you can do." He ticked a few numbers on Roo's sheet. "I'll call those and you call the others. We'll share what we get. Then we'll have lunch."

"Is it a race?" Roo asked.

"Only if I win." He grinned and sat at Taylor's desk.

Roo employed all the techniques Jonas had just shown her. Checking websites, databases and a few sites she suspected they weren't really supposed to access. She liked doing this. It was a combination of a step-by-step approach but combined with a lateral curve. In other words, thinking outside the box helped because research often led up cul-de-sacs.

Just after she'd set the phone down from a call, it rang. "Good morning," Roo said. "ICU Investigations."

"Is Taylor there?"

"Not at the moment. Can I help you?"

"How about Jonas? It's Simon Blake."

"Hold on one moment, please. I'll see if he's in." Roo pressed the

receiver against her thigh. "Simon Blake?" she whispered.

Jonas nodded and picked up the phone on Taylor's desk. "Simon, what's up?"

Roo put her phone down and went back to what she was doing, though she couldn't help but listen to Jonas.

"No, she left over a month ago," Jonas said. "Well, yes, name's Roo... No, I doubt she's done this sort of thing before... Yeah, yeah... Yep, she's gorgeous. Brains and beauty."

Roo pulled a hideous face and Jonas snorted. "A total babe... Okay. What time? Text me the details and send a photo."

Jonas put the phone down and stared at her.

Roo narrowed her eyes. "What?"

"Another PI firm could use a favor. Needs you, gorgeous." He grinned at her.

"To do what?" Roo tried not to sound too excited.

"Decoy work."

She raised her eyebrows. "Like Taylor and Niall did in Leeds?"

He nodded.

"You've already said I'll do it, haven't you?"

Jonas gave her a sheepish look.

"You'll have to tell me what to do."

"Wear a recorder in your bra and flirt."

"What if I don't wear a bra?"

His jaw dropped.

The phone went again and Roo grabbed it. "Good morning. ICU Investigations."

"It's Kim Singer," a woman whispered.

Roo gulped. This was the woman whose husband hit her. Roo fumbled on her desk for the list of women's refuges Taylor had given her.

"What's happened?" Roo asked.

"I need you to come."

"What, now?"

"No, this afternoon. Not before three in case he comes home for lunch." She let out a sob. "I don't know what to do. I need to talk to someone."

"Give me your address."

Roo wrote it down.

"Just you. No one else. Not a man."

"Okay, okay."

Roo put the phone down and looked across at Jonas who had his eyebrows raised.

"She called the other day. Her husband hits her. She wanted to hire a detective to watch the house and her for a week so she could prove she hadn't been seeing anyone. Her husband came home while we were talking and she broke off. I wrote her number down, but Taylor said not to call her back."

"With good reason."

"She needs help. Taylor gave me the addresses of some hostels in case she called again."

Jonas sighed. "But you didn't give her the addresses, did you? She's expecting you to go and see her."

Roo nodded. "Please, Jonas. I'm doing you a favor. Would you take me to see her? She wants to speak to a woman. She lives in Skipton. That's not far, is it? She said after three."

"Ever ridden a bike?"

"A few times."

"I've got leathers in the pannier that should fit you. What's the address?"

That afternoon, Roo emerged from the bathroom wondering if she'd have to be cut out of the leather pants. She'd had to lie on the floor to pull up the zipper. The jacket was almost as bad. Her boobs were forced up and almost out there scenting the air. Her poor feet were going to freeze, but dressed in tight black leather and high heels she looked like some kick-ass vampire slayer. A slash of red lipstick and Roo hardly recognized herself.

Niall almost fell down the stairs when he saw her.

"Roo?" he blurted. "What the hell are you wearing?"

She bristled. "My dominatrix outfit."

"You... Oh shit."

Jonas came in through the front door and whistled. "Bloody hell.

You look better in them than Elise, and she was a babe."

Roo sighed.

"Where are you going?" Niall asked.

"To buy a whip." Roo strode out and nearly went headlong down the steps. Darn it.

Jonas laughed and handed her a helmet and gloves. "We can talk to each other through the headset. Tell me if you think you're going to fall off."

"Can I hold on to you or would you prefer me not to?"

"I'll be upset if you don't."

Roo fastened the helmet tightly, lifted her feet onto the foot pegs and tucked up behind him on the bike, her hands on his hips.

Even before they'd reached the end of the drive, Roo buzzed with excitement, but her feet tingled with cold.

"You okay?" Jonas asked.

"Fantastic. I've never had anything so impressive throbbing between my legs."

He laughed. "Listen, I might as well run you through what you need to do in the club later."

"Going to give me a lesson in how to flirt?"

"Nah, I think you've got that covered. One look at you and any guy's tongue would hang out. Don't give your real name. Roo's too unusual. How about Candy Kane?"

"Fuckwit," Roo muttered.

"That doesn't have a good ring to it. Chastity Belt?"

She laughed. "No I'm going to be boring. Paige Turner."

"Not sure you could ever be boring."

Roo curled up her poor toes against the wind. The chill was creeping up her legs. By the time they reached Skipton, Roo had lost feeling below her waist. She climbed off the bike and almost fell over.

Jonas caught her and smiled. "You need boots for next time."

Roo removed the gloves and helmet, and dragged her fingers through her hair. "Apart from frostbite in my extremities, that was fantastic. I wish I had a bike. Want to teach me to ride? Although I should add I can't actually ride an ordinary bike."

He laughed. "Then the answer is no. I'll wait for you in case there's trouble. I can see the front door from here."

Roo left the helmet with him and walked up the path. She knocked, and when the door opened, Roo's exhilaration evaporated in a flash.

"Kim?" she asked.

"Roo?" The woman spoke through puffy lips. She had a black eye and a cut on her cheek she'd tried to disguise with makeup.

Roo nodded. Kim pulled her inside and glanced down the street before she closed the door.

"Are you okay?" Roo asked. *Idiot question.*

"I don't know what to do." She led Roo through an immaculate living room where two small, neatly dressed children sat on the carpet in front of the TV. *Oh hell.*

The kitchen was just as pristine.

"He won't believe I'm not seeing anyone," she whispered. "I've tried everything to convince him. I thought if you could watch me, do a report, next time he accuses me I'd have proof I was telling the truth."

Roo stared into Kim's dark-circled eyes. "You know, I don't think it would make any difference. He'd say you paid us to lie for you. He doesn't want to believe you. He's using it as an excuse to hit you. You have to leave him."

"I can't. I've got kids." The woman glared. "And no, before you ask, Christopher's never touched them. He doesn't mean to touch me. He loses his temper. I get things wrong, make mistakes."

Roo wished she hadn't come, wished she hadn't seen Kim's face, Kim's kids, Kim's much-too-tidy house. She put her hand in her pocket and took out an ICU card. On the back, she'd written the name and address of a hostel in Headingly that took in women who feared for their safety. Kim put her hands behind her back.

"Put it somewhere safe. Just in case." Roo waited. "Please."

Kim snatched the card, opened a cupboard and put it in a jar marked *Vitamins.*

"Now will you watch me?" Kim asked.

Oh damn.

"I can pay. I've saved up."

Roo swallowed hard. "Think about this, Kim. It can't work. No one can watch you 24/7. Even if they did, your husband would—"

"Her husband would what?" a man's voice asked behind her.

Kim's cheek twitched. Roo spun round to find herself facing a

good-looking guy in a pinstripe suit. He'd come in through the back door. She plastered a smile on her face.

"Her husband would need to give permission for his wife to attend," Roo said and held out her hand. "I'm from the Fundamentalist Ewaja Christian Evangelical Spiritual Mutual Church." Roo hoped that covered everything. "We're trying to—"

"We're not interested," he snapped, ignoring her hand.

When he eyeballed her outfit, Roo blurted, "We're very progressive."

"Why did you invite her in?" He glared at his wife.

"I needed a drink of water. Your wife was kind enough—"

"Get out."

"I'm so sorry to have bothered you. May the Lord shine upon you and your children. May you live in peace and harmony 24/7. That's our motto." Roo beamed at him and then gulped once she faced the other way.

He followed her to the door and she could feel him watching as she walked down the path.

Roo waved to Jonas. "I just need to go next door," she called loudly. "Last one of my quota. Have you done the other side?"

He nodded. Roo knew Christopher was still watching. She walked up the path next door and rang the bell. Roo's heart sank when an old lady answered. She'd been hoping no one was in.

"Hello, I'm a representative of the Fundamentalist Mutual Spiritual Ewaja Evangelical Mormon Church." *Blast, that isn't right.* "I wondered if you could spare me a few minutes of your time." *Please say no.*

"Come in, dear. I'd love to talk to you. The chiropodist's just cancelled so I'm all yours." She looked Roo up and down. "I'll give you some advice about what young ladies should and shouldn't wear."

And didn't that serve her right?

Taylor pushed open the door of his office, expecting to see Roo, and blinked. He reversed and went into the kitchen. No Niall. Taylor walked out into the back garden and headed for the walled section at the rear. As he stepped through the gate, the sun came out and Taylor looked up to see a small break in what had so far been an overcast

day. Taylor followed the path of a ray of sunlight to where it reflected off the glass of the greenhouse. And Niall. Niall was in the greenhouse with no shirt, sweat trickling down his back over the tattoo, and Taylor gulped.

He moved toward the door and Niall turned before he'd even called out.

"Hi," Niall said.

The moment Taylor stepped inside the glass house, the heat hit him and he backed out. "It's like an oven in there. Where's my aggravating PA?"

"Jonas took her out."

"Any idea where?"

Niall shook his head.

"Did he take her on his bike?" Taylor asked.

"He put her in his ex's leathers. She looked...amazing."

Taylor paused for a moment, thinking about both Roo in leather and Niall's reaction to it and whether Jonas had ideas about Roo.

"I'll give Jonas a call."

As he walked off, Niall called, "I made the carrot cake. Extra frosting."

Taylor turned and smiled as he walked backward. "Good."

He turned the right way round, pulled his phone from his pocket and called Jonas.

"Explain," Taylor said.

"You're not going to like it."

No, Taylor didn't think he would. And by the time Jonas had finished, Taylor found no satisfaction in being right. At least Roo wasn't still in the wife-beater's house.

"How long has she been in the neighbor's?" Taylor asked.

"Quarter of an hour. If she doesn't come out in the next few minutes, I'll have to go and get her. I had a call from Simon Blake asking if we had anyone for a decoy this evening and I said Roo could do it."

Taylor tensed so fast his teeth snapped together. He opened his mouth and no words came out.

"That's okay, isn't it?" Jonas asked. "I mean, Emma did it a few times. I didn't think you'd mind. Roo's up for it. Oh, here she comes."

"Where?" Taylor blurted.

"Pussycats. I need to leave straightaway. I've a few leads to follow up on the Dickerson case. Roo can help. I'll call you later."

Taylor was beyond furious, with himself for not apologizing to Roo, with Jonas for volunteering her for something Taylor didn't want her to do and with Roo for going into the house of a guy who beat his wife.

"Like some carrot cake?" Niall asked behind him.

"Got to go out."

When Taylor turned, he didn't miss the stricken expression on Niall's face. *What have I done now?* But Taylor still grabbed his keys and left.

The microphone and recorder attached to Roo's bra itched. Jonas had pulled off the road before they reached the club in Leeds and had helped her attach it.

"You're such a disappointment," he said. "Teasing me like that. No bloody bra. Huh!"

"Sure you can't see it?" Roo asked. "Even if I unzip?"

"Try it."

Roo eased down the zipper on the jacket to reveal the pink top beneath.

"Nope, you're fine."

"So who's the guy I have to flirt with?"

Roo was quite looking forward to this. She'd worked out a story already. Paige Turner. In Leeds for the week. Looking for some fun.

"It's a woman."

Roo groaned. "You're joking."

"Annette Foster. Age thirty-eight. Married three years. Husband suspects she's a lesbian and plotting to kill him."

"What?"

Jonas laughed. "I only threw that last part in to make you take it seriously. Husband thinks she's having an affair with one of the pole dancers."

"Then why would she be interested in me?"

"Maybe you fancy the same dancer?"

"How do I know which one that is?" Roo could feel panic welling inside her. She might be good at fibbing when necessary, but this could be tricky. She wasn't into women.

Jonas showed her the picture of Annette. "Sit next to her. Strike up a conversation. See where it takes you. And walk in as if you own the place. You need to be an alpha bitch."

Ten minutes later Roo slid her hand into her bra to switch on the recorder and then strutted into the Pussycats club on the Headrow in Leeds. Jonas had given her money to get in and to buy a few drinks. He was coming in to keep an eye on her, and Roo was relieved about that.

The place heaved with businessmen unwinding after skipping out early on a Friday. Music pounded. To Roo's surprise, most people weren't gathered around the stage, instead they leaned against the bar. Roo swept the crowd with her gaze. Not many fully-dressed women, which should make her job easier. *Just a job,* Roo told herself and looked away from the bare breasts on the long stage, groaned, and then looked back. *I'm supposed to be interested in women.* None of those curling around the poles looked as though they were enjoying themselves. Their smiles were too forced.

"Hello, gorgeous, buy you a drink?" a voice slurred in her ear.

A young guy wobbled at her side, his tie skewiff, shirt half hanging out of his pants, a cute smile on his face.

"No thanks, little boy."

Roo made her way to the bar and ordered tonic water, which she hated, so it would take ages to drink. A hand reached over her shoulder and put down a black credit card. Roo was ready to get uppity about him pushing in until he spoke.

"Give the lady champagne." The guy's French accent made her weak at the knees.

"Tonic water," Roo said to the barman.

"You can have both," said the man behind her.

She turned to look at him. In his forties, tall, quite good looking with dark curly hair, a lecherous smile and a revolting swirly-patterned tie.

"You're not my type," Roo said.

"You're my type, leather girl."

Good grief. Roo dropped her money on the bar, picked up the tonic water and walked off. When she felt lips against her ear and someone mutter, "Bottom left of stage. White shirt. Gray slacks," she almost spilt her drink. It was Jonas.

Then he was gone.

Roo headed over and saw Annette sitting at a table nursing a drink. The tables either side of her were occupied by guys, but there was a free chair at the table on Annette's left. Roo sat on it and swiveled away from the men so she faced Annette.

"Hey, that seat's taken," a guy shouted.

Roo turned and smiled at him. "Yes, it is." Then she turned back and said loud enough for Annette to hear. "Don't mind, do you?"

The woman looked at Roo, shook her head and turned back to the stage. Roo sagged. Not going to be easy then.

A bottle of champagne appeared on the table with two glasses. Roo looked up at the French guy smiling down at her.

"Piss off," Roo said.

So of course, he found a chair from nowhere and sat next to her.

"I prefer to work for my pleasure. It makes it far more enjoyable," he said in her ear.

Shit. "Sod off," Roo said. "I prefer to vary my fuck-off lines."

He laughed. She grabbed the bottle of champagne, poured two glasses, kept one for herself and nudged Annette's arm with the other.

"Please," Roo mouthed.

The woman couldn't have missed what was happening even though her gaze was glued to the stage. When Annette took the glass and her mouth curved in a slight smile, Roo gave a silent sigh of relief. She glanced at the guy to see how he was taking it and he looked as though his ship had come in laden with gold. *Darn it.*

"You make my heart pound," he said to Roo.

"Maybe it will stop in a minute," she said. "Too bad I don't know CPR."

Annette sniggered.

His hand crept onto Roo's leather-clad thigh and she pressed her heel into his foot. The moron groaned as if she'd stroked his cock.

"I wish you'd walk all over me in those shoes," he said.

"Ooh, and then you could put rings in your balls where I'd made holes."

"Maybe I've already got rings. Like to check?" he asked.

Roo had the horrible suspicion he'd pull his pants down if she said yes.

"If you're smaller than ten inches, don't bother. If you're bigger than ten inches, don't bother."

"Come to the bathroom with a ruler."

Roo exhaled. "For Pete's sake, take a hint. I'm not into you. Your choice of tie says everything. I wouldn't want it anywhere near me. I'd probably catch something."

He edged his chair closer. "I don't want to touch you with my tie." He fluttered his tongue in a stomach-churning move.

As the dancers moved offstage, Roo caught Annette's gaze and rolled her eyes. The woman glanced at Mr. Wonderful, pulled Roo to her feet and kissed her.

Oh my God, oh my God, oh my God.

Roo had never kissed a woman before. Her mouth had opened in shock as she groaned. Annette obviously saw that as an invitation to keep going and slid her tongue into Roo's mouth. *Do something, idiot.* Roo lifted her arms and wrapped them around Annette, relieved she felt not a glimmer of excitement. In fact, it reminded her of her first kiss. Boney Mason behind the school gym. Terrible. She'd found out where the well-padded guy got his nickname though.

Annette broke away with a smile and sat. Roo could hear clapping and it took a moment to realize it was her and Annette who were being applauded. Her knees gave way and she sank onto the chair.

"Thought it might get rid of him," Annette said.

The French guy sat open-mouthed and wide-eyed at their side.

"Well, you've struck him dumb, that's a huge improvement," Roo said.

Annette laughed. "What's your name?"

"Paige. You?"

"Annette."

"So what brings you here?" Roo asked and leaned closer so the microphone would pick up the conversation.

"My girlfriend's one of the dancers."

"Oh, which one?"

"The one with the tail. Susie."

"Cute. She won't mind that we kissed, will she?" Roo asked.

"I think she might like to kiss you too."

Crap, crap, crap.

"That sounds interesting. Been going out long?" Roo asked.

"A year."

"You live together?"

"I'm married."

"To Susie?"

Annette sighed. "To a man."

Roo gasped. "Seriously? Why?"

"He's rich." She laughed. "Men are useful for something."

"Do you want another bottle of champagne?" asked the newly revived guy at Roo's side.

"See?" Annette said.

"You're going to kiss again, right?" He grinned.

Annette sighed, and then she looked over Roo's shoulder and smiled. "Here's Susie. Fancy coming back to hers?"

Do I have enough evidence? "Well..."

"I've been looking for you everywhere."

I know that voice. Roo looked up at Taylor glaring down at her.

"Oh it's you," she said and raised her voice. "No, I will not fuck you for a hundred pounds."

His lips twitched. "A thousand?"

Roo sighed. "All right. But bring your penis pump."

Chapter Sixteen

"Out. Now," Taylor snapped in Roo's ear and followed her as she made her way to the exit.

Christ. He could see what had Niall so wound up. Tight little arse in black leather, long slender legs and those shoes. By the time they were out on the street, Taylor's cock was rock-hard. Jonas was on their heels as Taylor tugged Roo around the corner.

"Did I do okay?" Roo asked.

"Like you were born for it," Jonas said and winked.

Taylor glared. "Penis pump? Where did that come from? You're never doing this again."

"I wasn't okay?" Roo's voice had a tremor in it, and guilt twisted Taylor's gut, but he was too worried about what could have happened to deal with it.

"You did great," Jonas said. "Let me get the recorder off you."

"I'll do it," Taylor snapped.

Roo batted their fingers away. "I think I can manage on my own." She put her hand into the top of her jacket, unhooked the equipment and handed it to Jonas who slipped it into his pocket.

"Can I play?"

Taylor spun round to see Simon Blake standing there, holding an open bottle of champagne and grinning.

"What part of piss off don't you understand?" Roo glared at Simon and then she frowned. "Hey, what happened to your accent?"

"Roo, this is the guy you spoke to on the phone this morning," Jonas said. "Simon, meet Roo."

"No, don't," Taylor said and caught her elbow. "We're leaving."

"I'll email you the footage," Jonas told Simon.

Taylor caught Jonas's eye and made it clear he wanted a copy too. He'd arrived just as Roo and the woman broke apart and he wanted to know what had Simon Blake so hot under the collar.

Simon offered Roo the bottle. "The client's paid for it, you deserve to drink it. Well done. Oh, and by the way, next time we meet I'll have a ruler. And I don't need a pump."

Roo sniggered and Taylor tugged her down the road. "What was that about a ruler?" he asked.

"Nothing."

Taylor aimed his remote at the car. "Do you realize how pissed off I am?"

She climbed in the passenger side. "What else is new?" she mumbled. "So what specifically pissed you off this time?"

"Going to that woman's house. What were you thinking? I blame Jonas as much as you. He should have had more sense."

"I wanted to help. Her husband had beaten her, Taylor. She had a black eye and a thick lip, and they have two kids. I gave her the address of the hostel in Headingly, but I don't know if she'll go. I did tell her we couldn't do anything else."

"You didn't give her one of our cards, did you?"

"Oh shit. She hid it though."

Taylor gritted his teeth. "Never do that again."

"Sorry."

He pulled out into traffic and headed for the A65. "What the hell would you have done if her husband had come home?"

"But he d— Oh bugger."

Taylor swallowed his growl of anger. That was a little nugget Jonas had failed to pass on.

Roo took a slug of the champagne. "It was okay though, I pretended to be from some religious group and I went to the next-door neighbor's. Unfortunately, she wanted company. She went on and on about the Bible and insisted on knowing my favorite parable. I could only remember the one about the lost sheep. You know, when the shepherd leaves his flock and goes to look for the one that's lost. He finds it and brings it home and then they have lamb stew for supper."

Taylor almost ran into the curb. "You didn't tell her that."

"It might not say that, but I bet they did." She took another swallow.

He laughed. It was impossible to stay cross with her. And when he looked at her, being cross was the last thing on his mind. His cock was still semi-hard. He wondered if she'd noticed.

"Did you hear from that policeman you know about Patrick Farrant?" she asked.

"Only that he wasn't in the freezer."

"Oh." Roo drank again.

Taylor smiled. "Don't sound so disappointed.

"Ooh...ooh...ooh...maybe she moved him. She might have buried in him the garden. No, that won't work. The dog would have dug him up. And she was going away, wasn't she? I hope the police are suspo...sp...curo...curious about that." She hiccupped.

She's drunk already? "When did you last eat?"

"Lunchtime."

Taylor pulled off into a gas station. "Stay in the car."

He went into the shop and then realized he ought to have asked her what she wanted. Chocolate was always right, wasn't it? He snatched up several bars and a bottle of water, and paid. When he walked back onto the forecourt, Roo was zigzagging toward him. Did she *ever* do as she was told?

She pulled him down to whisper in his ear. "I need to pee."

"Okay." Taylor restrained his snigger.

"I need you to come with me."

Amusement gone, Taylor gulped. "Why?"

"I can't get these pants back up when I'm on my feet. Not gonna lie on the floor in a gas station bathroom."

He laughed. "Can you get them off on your own?"

"Ye—p."

She didn't seem too sure, but it sounded like he had a good deal either way. "Go on ahead. I'll put these in the car."

"Chocolate? I love you." She landed a kiss on Taylor's cheek that he was much too slow to respond to before she wobbled off.

Sexy and slightly tipsy. He shouldn't take advantage. Yes, well, Taylor had stopped listening to his conscience a while ago. He tossed the chocolate and water inside the car, locked it, and followed Roo.

"Bathroom?" he asked the Asian guy behind the counter.

"In the corner."

Taylor pushed open the first door and banged on the second. "Need a hand with your pants?"

The door flew open. A big guy lumbered out and pinned Taylor against the wall by the throat.

"Like to repeat that, dickhead?"

No, but Taylor couldn't speak anyway. He'd clenched his fist ready to strike when the door next to the one he'd knocked opened and Roo peered out. "Don't hurt him. He was looking for me."

To Taylor's immense relief the guy released him and walked off. He rubbed his throat and sighed. "Come out then."

"I can't get them over my backside."

Good. "I won't look." *Much.*

She waddled out of the bathroom with the leather pants around the top of her thighs. "Don't laugh," she warned.

Taylor wasn't going to laugh, he was too busy drooling. *Tiny red panties.* He caught hold of the waistband and tugged. Roo came up on tiptoe.

"Try to push down as I pull up," he said and yanked.

The leather slid up a little way.

Roo groaned. "It's because I'm all hot and sweaty."

"Turn round. It might be easier tugging from the back." *Liar. You want to see her backside.*

"You just want to look at my bum. You could still pull at the back from where you're standing."

"Do you want to walk out of here with no pants on?"

She glared and turned round.

Sweet Jesus. The thinnest of strips of material crossed her lower back and disappeared into the cleft of her butt. Neat, cute, round, sweet, biteable, fuckable... He'd never run out of words. His cock tented his pants and he groaned.

"Taylor?"

He pulled hard and the leather slid up her hips. Roo gave a grunt of relief.

"Okay?" he asked.

"Nearly. If I hold the front together, can you zip me up?"

He gave her what he hoped she saw as a pained look, but finally the zipper was up.

"Well that was a first," he said as they walked back to the car. "I'm usually keener on enticing women *out* of their clothes. Bang goes any

hope of getting to third base on the way home."

Roo laughed but Taylor wasn't joking.

He pulled back onto the road and glanced at her as she took another swig of champagne.

"Don't you want the chocolate?"

"Yes, but it'll make the champagne taste sour. I'm going to finish it off first. I didn't offer you any because you're driving, but do you want some?"

"Nope, you're fine." *And drunk.*

And he was bad.

Watching her eat one of the crumbly sticks of flaked chocolate he'd bought sent him farther down the path to damnation. That particular bar figured highly in one of his fantasies. It hadn't been by accident he'd picked up three of the same type, much as he'd like to convince himself otherwise. Taylor was desperate to kiss her. He had to know whether this thing with Niall had fucked him up.

More lies? That's not why you want to kiss her, his cock said.

Once they were on Thorpe Lane and away from any houses, Taylor stopped the car.

"Run out of fuel?" she asked.

"No."

"Forgotten the way home?"

"No." He unclipped his seat belt.

"Going to kill me and hide me in the bushes? Can I finish the chocolate first?"

"I notice you didn't offer to share that."

Roo chewed her bottom lip. "Damn. Sorry. You want a bite?"

She took the wrapper off another Flake bar and held it to his lips.

"You first," he said.

I'm already rock-hard, his cock yelled. *Do you have to play games?*

Roo put it in her mouth and bit down. She used her other hand to catch the crumbs and Taylor grabbed hold of her wrist. He licked the bits of chocolate one by one from her palm. He wasn't sure if the low groan came from her or him, maybe both of them. He wrapped his fingers around her other wrist, brought the stick of chocolate to his mouth, and sank his teeth into it so flakes again dropped into her palm. Another lick of her hand and Roo gulped.

One small length of Flake left in her fingers.

"Going to share?" Taylor asked.

He took it from her, put half of it in his mouth and Roo moved forward to wrap her lips around the exposed end. She tickled him under his chin, Taylor gasped, and she sucked what was left of the bar out of his mouth, into hers, and chewed.

"You little cheat," he said with a laugh.

"Never get between a girl and her chocolate."

"You've left half of it round your mouth." Taylor stared at her lips. "Seems only fair I should have those bits."

The kiss started slow and hot and slipped straight to fast and incendiary. His fingers scrabbled by the side of her seat until he'd unclipped the belt, and then Taylor pulled her closer, held her tighter, kissed her harder. Arousal boiled in his groin, his cock thrust against his zipper, and Taylor sucked her tongue into his mouth. She tasted of chocolate and of sex, and he explored every inch of her mouth with a greedy delight.

When they came up for air, they were gasping.

"Roo." Taylor panted into her hair. "I want to touch you. I want to feel your skin, not leather. Only I suspect I'll break my fingers if I try to get you out of those pants."

"I swear they're getting tighter, the seams will leave lines down my legs like Niall's tattoo."

Her words hit like a thump in his gut and Taylor pulled back to sit square on his seat.

Roo knew the moment she'd said it she'd made a mistake, but could see no way to recover. Taylor didn't say anything. He fastened his seat belt, started the engine and drove back to the house. Maybe it was just as well she'd messed that up. Did she really want to come between Niall and Taylor? And what if she was just a way for Taylor to experiment with his sexuality?

As the pleasant buzz from the alcohol, chocolate and Taylor's kiss faded fast, Roo was torn between two truths. She went for the easier one and didn't break her promise to Niall.

"I saw the pair of you last night," she said. "In the orangery."

Taylor whipped round to look at her. The car swerved and he yanked the wheel back a split second before they ploughed through the

rhododendrons.

"Spying?" he snapped.

She glared. "Foraging for food." Then she sighed. "Sorry, though, sorry about the room too. I didn't realize you didn't want me to sleep in there. I should have guessed."

"Why didn't you sleep in the four-poster?"

"Don't like them," Roo muttered, a shiver of unease running down her spine like a skeletal finger.

"It's a bed. What's not to like?" Taylor pulled up in front of the house. "I shouldn't have shouted at you. I apologize. You can sleep in Stephanie's room. I've emptied it now. I'll find you some sheets."

Roo put her hand over his on the wheel and held on when he tried to pull free. "What happened to your sister?" *Please don't let it be anything bad.*

A muscle in his cheek twitched. "She disappeared when she was ten and no one's seen her since."

Oh no. Roo swallowed hard. "Did it happen here?"

"She...she came home from school, went out to play, and I was supposed to be keeping an eye on her. I didn't notice she wasn't there until Mum called us in for dinner. We thought she must be in the garden, but she wasn't. She wasn't anywhere."

"Had she climbed over the wall?" Roo asked.

"What? Don't you think we looked outside the garden?" Taylor sighed. "I'd never seen her try to climb the wall. If she had and she'd fallen, we'd have found her."

He jerked his hand free and got out of the car. Roo exhaled and followed. By the time she walked into the hall, there was no sign of him. She trudged upstairs to the room she'd slept in last night. She could stay in there. It wasn't a problem. The fact that she'd kissed Niall *and* Taylor was.

Roo took off her shoes, struggled out of the leather pants and jacket and sighed with relief. She folded them in a neat pile to give back to Jonas, took a pair of shorts and a T-shirt from her bag, and saw Stephanie's book. If Taylor had emptied the room, how was she going to put it back?

The high from the champagne had gone and Roo felt a bit sick. She had no idea of the etiquette of this situation. Was she supposed to stay in the room? What should she do about food? What should she do about the fact that she'd kissed both guys? Gone a little further than

that with Niall. What would they do if they found out? Roo suspected they'd not told each other.

Just as she landed a job she actually liked, it seemed probable she'd lose it. In that case, there was little to be gained from skulking in her room. If they threw her out, she still had her tent.

The guilty look on Taylor's face when Niall went into the office sent his heart plummeting into his stomach. *What had Taylor done?*

The answer had to be Roo.

"Three for dinner?" Niall asked. "Or are you going to take Roo to a restaurant?" He tried to keep his voice neutral but wasn't sure he succeeded.

"Eating here sounds good."

It did to Niall too. "Did everything go well?"

"Maybe a little too well. Come and look at this."

Niall moved to stand behind Taylor.

"Jonas got a video clip of Simon harassing Roo, which pushed her into the arms of the woman he had under surveillance. It's all the proof her husband needs."

Niall gulped when he watched the two women kissing. Instant Viagra. Looking at Taylor's groin, it seemed he had the same reaction.

"She saw us," Taylor said, and turned to face him. "She knew about your tattoo. She admitted she'd seen us in the orangery."

Ah, but not that I'd kissed her?

"I kissed her," Taylor whispered. "I fancy her. Really fancy her."

Taylor's words forced Niall toward a decision that could make or break his dream. His heart raced, but lying wasn't an option.

"I've kissed her too," he said in a quiet voice.

The silence stretched between them.

"More than kissed her?" Taylor asked.

Taylor sounded curious more than angry. Niall shook his head. *Not much more.*

"Want to watch her kiss the woman again?" Taylor blurted.

Niall nodded. Not the response he wanted but he'd take what he could get. At least Taylor hadn't thumped him.

They watched it twice before Niall retreated. Taylor wasn't going to say anything and Niall didn't know what to say. Well, he did but he couldn't push out the words. *If we're turned on by two women kissing, why shouldn't Roo feel the same about two guys?* Though that was the best-case scenario. Worst case, it turned her off.

He picked up a pair of secateurs and headed to the garden. He needed to think.

Taylor had been nine years old when his plane had flown over the wall and landed several feet from Niall. Of course, Niall hadn't seen a wall, all he'd seen was something flying through the branches of a tree that was neither bird nor insect. Then something larger had fallen to crash at his feet. Taylor.

It was the most extraordinary and exciting thing that had ever happened to Niall, and he could replay that afternoon in his head as clearly as if it had occurred a moment or two ago.

"Where did you come from?" Niall had asked.

"Over the wall."

"What wall?"

The dark-haired boy turned and gasped. "Where's my house?"

And Niall realized this was a mortal, the very first he'd seen. He'd been so thrilled, his knees had trembled. "What's your name?"

"Taylor."

"I'm Niall." He pointed to the plane. "Is that yours?"

Taylor went to pick it up.

"How does it work?" Niall asked.

Taylor showed him how to turn the propeller to tighten the elastic band, and then gave it him.

"Throw it forward and up, but not too hard," Taylor said.

The plane soared across the field of wild flowers and landed thirty feet away. Taylor ran after it, but Niall didn't move. He wanted to see where the boy had come from, and if he moved, he might not be able to find the place again. He stared up into the tree.

Taylor came back. "Don't you want to play?"

Niall nodded. "Can I see your house?"

Concern filled Taylor's face. "I don't know where it is."

"I haven't moved since you landed at my feet. We can work it out. There must be a tear."

"In the sky? That's not possible."

Niall smiled. "Anything's possible. Find things for me to throw and I'll see if I can get them back into your garden."

Taylor offered him the plane.

Niall shook his head. "Something that won't break."

Taylor picked up a handful of stones. The pair of them took turns throwing them into the tree. It was Taylor's that went up and didn't come down and he yelped with delight.

"Come on," Taylor said. "I'll stand on your shoulders and then I'll pull you up."

The pair of them sat side by side on a thick bough, looking out on Niall's side, feet dangling, and Niall had pointed out his home.

"It's a castle," Taylor said and laughed.

"I'm a prince."

Taylor had rolled his eyes and Niall's heart had swollen with joy. They swung their legs to sit the other way and Niall had his first glimpse of the mortal world through a shimmering rip in the sky. He caught a glimpse of a walled garden and a stone house beyond. Taylor clambered through the hole onto the wall and Niall followed, his heart pounding. When Taylor climbed down into his garden via a tree house, Niall took out his knife, leaned back through the rip and scratched the letters NT into the bough, entwining them together. He came back fully onto the mortal side and did the same on the stone where he sat. Then Niall climbed down too.

When he saw a girl playing under an apple tree, Niall made sure she couldn't see him. It was forbidden to show yourself to a mortal, and Niall instinctively felt he was safer if he only trusted Taylor. Plus he hadn't really broken the law because Taylor had come onto his side. When Taylor tried to introduce Niall to the girl, he realized he should have told him he'd made himself invisible.

Taylor scowled when the girl said he was lying, that no one was with him. She stomped back to the house. Niall thought Taylor would be angry, but he just turned, smiled, and said, "Let's look for a tiger."

Niall gulped. The only tiger he'd seen had been in the palace of his aunt and it had been in a cage. But when he realized Taylor was pretending, he crept through the undergrowth after him and hid among the fruit trees. They launched themselves at a snarling beast, both of them rolling on the ground trying to pin the animal down. At the sight of the delight on Taylor's face, Niall vowed they'd be friends

forever.

When Taylor was called in for his meal, he went back to the wall with Niall to make sure he could get through. Niall climbed up and found the stone where he'd carved their initials. Taylor sat next to him and ran his finger over the letters.

"Aren't you curious about my side?" he asked Taylor.

"Course. Are you curious about mine?"

Niall smiled. "I knew about your world, I just never expected to see it or find a friend in it."

Taylor grinned.

"We should make a pact," Niall said. "A promise sealed in blood."

He took out his knife and offered it to Taylor. "You cut my palm and I'll cut yours."

Niall gritted his teeth as Taylor drew the blade carefully across the fleshy pad below his thumb. His lack of hesitation pleased Niall. Niall made the exact same cut on Taylor and they clasped hands.

"I promise to come here every day that you want me to," Niall said. "My side is dangerous. Yours isn't. You have to promise not to come onto my side unless I'm with you."

"I promise," Taylor said.

Niall sighed. If Taylor was caught on the other side, all Taylor's blood would be spilt.

"I promise not to tell anyone about you," Niall said.

"I promise the same, but my sister saw you. Don't know why she said she didn't."

"She didn't see me. I'll never let her see me."

Taylor smiled. "I'll say I have an imaginary friend but I'll never tell them your name."

When their hands fell apart, there was no blood and no mark on either of them. Taylor's eyes looked about to fall out of his head. Niall wasn't sure if Taylor thought he really *was* imaginary.

"I have to go," Niall said. "Please don't come over or try to follow me. We'd both be punished."

"I swear I won't," Taylor said.

In the end, it hadn't been Taylor who'd crossed on his own but his sister, Stephanie.

"Niall!"

Roo's voice broke into his thoughts and he looked up to see her at the far end of the walled garden sitting in the tree house, her legs dangling, no shoes. Niall left the basket filled with lettuce, radishes and tomatoes and walked over. One glance at her long legs and his cock reacted. Niall stuck his hand into the pocket of his chinos.

"I'm stuck," she wailed.

"How?" Niall climbed the ladder and stopped with his face level with her stomach.

"I think my shorts are caught on a nail or something. I don't want to rip them."

Niall slid his fingers under her butt, feeling for where she was attached. His heart ricocheted round his chest.

"Nice as that is, I'd feel guilty if I didn't tell you I'm snagged on the other side."

He laughed, felt for the loose nail, and lifted Roo backward. She came free with the sound of tearing.

"Oh damn. Is there a big hole?" She looked over her shoulder.

Niall slid his finger into the rip in the material, Roo groaned and he yanked it out.

"What are you doing out here?" he asked.

"I wanted to walk on the wall."

Every cell in Niall's body seemed to freeze. "What for?"

"For fun, to check out the view, see what's on the other side."

She climbed back into the tree house, swung through a window and pulled herself onto the stone. Niall stared up at her. Roo stood with her back to him, looking out over the forest side, down into the Wharfedale valley. At least, he hoped that was what she saw.

"Anything interesting?" he asked.

"Herd of zebras at a waterhole. Euuw, two of them are trying to play leapfrog."

He forced a laugh. Roo walked along the top of the wall with her arms outstretched. Niall kept pace below. He knew she wouldn't be able to see anything, not unless she looked through at a very specific point. A little part of him hoped she found the tear between the worlds. A larger part of him knew that was the worst thing she could do.

"Oh shiiiiit."

Niall stared in horror as Roo lost her footing and began to tumble.

Chapter Seventeen

As Roo fell off the wall, she had a split second to see the ground rushing up to meet her before Niall got in the way. She landed on top of him and they sprawled in the dirt.

"Oh God, sorry," she blurted. "Are you okay? Have I bruised your bruises?"

"I'm fine."

Roo stared down into his face and felt his cock growing hard between them.

"Taylor kissed me," she blurted.

"He told me." Niall's hands slid over her butt, his thumbs stroking along the line where her shorts finished, a finger sliding in the hole made by the nail. Tingles raced down her legs and her toes curled.

"And I told him you kissed me too," Roo whispered.

"He told me that as well."

Roo swallowed hard. "And that—"

"You'd seen us in the orangery."

"Are you both angry with me?" She rolled off Niall and pushed herself up, torn between telling him how she felt and running. "I'm sorry. I can leave. I—"

Niall sat up and caught hold of her hand. "We don't want you to leave."

Roo's heart hiccupped. "We?"

Niall nodded. "We."

Roo read everything into that and then talked sense back into her thick skull. Kindness not lust. A place to stay, not a bed to share. Two guys having fun flirting.

"I'm cooking for three," Niall said. "Pasta with wild mushrooms, asparagus, ginger and cream."

He stood and didn't let go of her fingers. Friends didn't hold hands like this. As fast as she'd talked herself into believing nothing was

going to happen, she shot straight to thinking it was.

"Sounds delicious. Any pudding?" she croaked.

"Carrot cake."

"Extra frosting?"

Niall smiled. "You'll have to fight Taylor for it."

They walked back to the house hand in hand, and Roo's heart bounced around in her chest like a ping pong ball while her head tried to grab thoughts and hang on to them long enough to dissect them. When she'd become unbalanced on that wall, it was because she'd noticed something on the stone, only now she couldn't remember what. Something carved? She could have fallen either way.

Maybe it was fate she'd tumbled into Niall's arms. *Oh yeah.* But wow, he'd been so fast. *How*— He squeezed her fingers as if he could read her mind. And *thinking* about the wall was just a distraction from the real issue here. It was all very well thinking about having a relationship with two men, but now that it seemed possible...probable...definite... Roo gulped.

Yet holding Niall's hand made her feel safe, as if she were on a fairground ride and he was the security bar. Safe yet excited. Niall led her into the kitchen and sat her at the table before he let her go. Had he thought she'd run? *Should* she have run? Niall poured her a glass of white wine. Despite the half bottle of champagne she'd already consumed, Roo felt surprisingly sober.

"Can I help?" she asked. "Slice the mushrooms, crush the ginger, or shall I just sit and admire your fantastic butt—I mean technique."

He laughed.

"Are you feeling okay now?" she asked. "All recovered?"

"Yep."

"What happened exactly?"

He glanced at her. "Taylor didn't tell you?"

She shook her head.

"I kissed a woman and her boyfriend took exception."

Roo pushed back the sting of disappointment that he'd kissed a woman other than her. *Stupid.*

Niall turned to face her. "I wanted to know...I needed to see if it was different from when I kissed you that first time."

Roo brightened. "Oh, the electrocution thing. You were experimenting. Yeah, that was...weird."

"I didn't have a problem kissing her."

Her shoulders slumped and she stared at her glass. "Right."

"There was no spark at all. Not like there is with you and with Taylor."

She looked up to see Niall smiling at her. How could she not put two and two together? Niall wanted her. He'd told her Taylor did too. Anyway, she wasn't blind or stupid. She'd seen the way Taylor looked at her, and there had been that kiss until he'd got uppity.

"Want to tell him the food's about ready?" Niall asked. "He's in the office."

As Roo pulled opened the kitchen door, Taylor pushed from the other side.

"Good timing," she said. "Dinner's ready."

Taylor grinned. "My timing's always perfect."

Roo felt her face heat. *Shit.* She was hearing sexual connotations in everything. When she turned, the table had been set, two places one side, one on the other. How had Niall managed that so quickly? Her wine stood next to the single spot so she sat there.

The pasta was fantastic. Roo couldn't remember the last time she'd eaten a proper home-cooked meal. When she put her fork down on her empty plate, she looked across to see the guys were barely halfway through their food.

"Oops," Roo said. "I'm not usually such a pig, but that was delicious."

"Thanks." Niall smiled at her.

"No carrot cake until we've finished," Taylor said.

"Hurry up," Roo said. When they both slowed, she scowled. "Quit teasing."

The looks they gave her were identical. They might as well have had *lust* written across their foreheads. Roo picked up her wine, gulped more than she'd intended and coughed.

"I like teasing," Taylor said quietly. "How about you, Niall?"

"Yep."

They carried on eating slowly as they stared at her, and a gush of cream wet her panties. Niall's nostrils flared. *Oh God.*

Taylor slurped up a strand of pasta and licked his lips. "Very tasty, but I can think of something tastier."

Roo let a whimper escape.

Taylor frowned. "I was talking about Niall's carrot cake. What did you think I meant?"

Niall laughed.

The bastards. Well, Roo could tease too.

She slid her bare feet up their legs and into their groins. *Uh-oh.* They both had erections. Roo almost came off her chair. The pasta fell from Taylor's fork and Niall's hand froze on the way to his mouth.

Put your feet down! Before she could, hands gripped her ankles and held tight. Maybe they didn't know they both held her. But Niall smiled at Taylor, and Roo let out a quiet groan. The bastards ate even slower. Despite their hold on her, Roo managed to wriggle her toes over their crotches.

"Tell me you can unbutton and unzip with your toes and I'll give you a raise," Taylor said.

"Only on Mondays." It was Friday. "And isn't that a raise I can feel?"

The guys laughed.

When Niall stood to fetch the carrot cake, Taylor let her ankle go and Roo shuffled back on her chair. She hadn't actually believed eyes could smolder, but Taylor's were doing a good impression of it, like coals getting ready to blaze.

Niall put three plates on the table, and as Taylor reached for the one with the most frosting, Roo swiped her finger over the sweet topping and put it in her mouth. Every taste bud tingled.

"Hey," Taylor barked.

Roo snatched a different plate and jumped out of reach.

"Why don't we take dessert into the drawing room?" Niall suggested.

"Great. I think *The Sound of Music* is on." As Roo bolted, she heard twin growls behind her.

She settled on the rug in front of the coffee table and put her plate down. When she spotted a pack of cards sitting on top of a pile of books, Roo took them out and shuffled.

"Want to play cards?" Taylor settled on the floor on the other side of the coffee table while Niall sat adjoining her, leaning back against the couch.

"Hearts?" Roo suggested.

Taylor forked a chunk of cake into his mouth and took the cards from her hand. He flicked through until he found the two of diamonds and set it aside. "Lowest deals."

Roo won. And she was going to win the game too. They just didn't yet know it.

"Loser takes off an item of clothing," she said as she dealt. "Winner chooses what item." Silence followed that. She hadn't thought they'd object.

Niall was the first to lose his shirt then Taylor. *They have such great bodies.* Taylor was slightly broader than Niall, a little more muscular. She could only see part of Niall's tattoo where it wound up his neck, but it looked impossibly clear, as though the ink hadn't bled into his skin. Roo wanted a closer look but needed to concentrate on the game.

By the time the guys were down to their boxers and Roo had yet to remove one item of clothing, there were rumblings of discontent. She made sure she lost the next hand.

"Shorts," Taylor said.

Roo shuffled out of them without standing up and Niall laughed. Her heart was conducting a lively symphony with her other organs, firing them up into a state of acute excitement, priming every cell in her body for lift off. The three of them knew where this was leading, what was going to happen. And Roo understood that how far they went was up to her. They had to have guessed she was cheating, but not calling her on it was their way of letting her take control.

Niall lost the next hand. Taylor won. Niall hopped to his feet, pulled down his boxers and stepped out of them. His cock reared up, dark with arousal, the tip glistening, his balls hanging full and heavy beneath. Roo's jaw dropped, and when she realized she was staring, she stuffed more cake into her mouth.

Taylor's turn to lose. He wriggled out of his boxers without getting up and Roo giggled. She made sure Taylor lost again and she won.

He shrugged. "Nothing left to take off."

"Your toupee," Roo said and he glared at her. "Or your false teeth, I don't mind."

Niall let out a choked laugh.

"No clothing left, you have to pay a forfeit," Roo said. "Suck Niall's nipples."

One moment of hesitation while Roo held her breath before Taylor

slid round the table to Niall. Her nipples tightened as Taylor's tongue fluttered over Niall's pecs. Niall arched back, groaning, his arms outstretched, his eyes shut tight. Taylor's hand closed over Niall's other nipple and Roo pressed her thighs together. *Hot, hot, hot.* She was torn between watching Niall's face or Taylor's mouth. When Taylor eventually pulled back and licked his lips, she was drooling.

"Deal," Taylor croaked.

Roo messed up the cards and lost. *Damn.*

"T-shirt off," Niall said.

The hypnotic draw of her low-cut blue lace bra gave her chance to reorder the cards and make certain Niall lost the next game. Both men looked at her expectantly. How far could she go? How far would *they* go?

"Kiss Taylor's—"At the last moment, she lost her nerve. "Lips."

Watching the pair of them lock mouths made her instantly hot enough for spontaneous combustion. She'd always been turned on by the sight of two guys kissing, but these two guys did more than turn her on. They made her sizzle. But as Taylor pulled away from Niall, she saw something in Niall's eyes that made her heart ache so fiercely a sob slipped out. Roo forked the last bit of cake into her mouth to stop her making another sound. *Love. Oh God.* Niall loved Taylor. The way he touched him, looked at him, reacted to him, it all said the same thing.

But the heat was different in Taylor's eyes.

Then Taylor looked at her, and as Roo glanced at Niall, she watched pain flash across his face. At that moment, Taylor wanted her more than he wanted Niall. And Niall knew.

Oh fuck. This isn't going to work.

The only thing that stopped Roo running was the awareness that it was nothing more than lust for her that she saw in Taylor's face. She didn't want Niall to get hurt, but lust was okay. It was all she ever had from guys.

"You're thinking too much." Niall's gentle voice snapped her back, his fingers tracing circles on her back.

"And cheating too much," Taylor said. "We'll be here all night trying to get you naked. Who taught you to play cards?"

"No one." No point arguing about the cheating and they hadn't asked who'd taught her how to do that.

Taylor arched his brow. "You're too quiet. No veering off on a

tangent? No worry that aliens are about to land on the house or a flash flood's going to rip down the valley and sweep us away?" He sat up straighter, the smile falling from his face. "Don't worry, angel. None of us know what we're doing. We're all struggling. There's no right or wrong. You don't *have* to do anything."

"I can just lie there?" Roo whispered, unable to stop her mouth twitching.

Taylor smirked. "I bet you *can't* just lie there."

Roo pushed herself up. Niall's hand stayed on her back. "I bet you can't either," Roo said.

"If we both just lie there, nothing would happen." Taylor raised his eyebrows.

Roo looked at Niall. "You'd have all the fun."

"Not if neither of you move." Niall turned to her. "What's worrying you?"

What wasn't worrying her? *Is there room for me too? I know you love Taylor. You might both want me for now, but I don't want to cause problems. For me or for either of you.* Roo wanted them to love her, but knew it was asking too much, too soon. Yet she'd already slid down that slope. All the pep talks she'd given herself about not falling in love had paled into insignificance. She loved them. Didn't matter if they didn't love her. Well, it did, but that wasn't going to hold her back. *I am such an idiot.*

"What is it?" Taylor whispered.

"You can tell us," Niall said.

I love you and you don't love me.

"The usual." Roo sighed. "How to solve the issues in the Middle East. Whether wind turbines are a blight on the landscape or a necessary evil. If my legs are bristly."

Taylor almost choked laughing, but Roo knew Niall understood that she had to hide what she felt.

Niall looked from one to the other. "How about we each write down ten things we'd like to do and put them in a bag. Then we pull them out one at a time. That way no one has to choose who goes first at anything."

"That's a great idea," Roo said. "Do you have a whip and a couple of cock rings?"

"In the drawer with the nipple clamps." Taylor leapt at her over

the table and she squealed.

He pulled her into his arms and pressed his mouth against her throat. "Niall, grab pencils and paper out of that drawer. Since Roo cheated at cards, she has to pay a forfeit—we'll follow her up to my room."

That didn't sound so bad. "No spanking?" *Darn it.* That slipped out.

Taylor grinned. "You have to go upstairs on your hands and knees. And yes, spanking is involved. Thanks for the suggestion."

Bugger.

Her panties didn't cover much of her backside, but Roo could play the game too. She thought about racing up, but instead went slowly. The first smack from Taylor was just hard enough and she shuddered. Roo turned to look over her shoulder and both guys had their hands around their cocks.

"Not sure this is such a good idea," Niall croaked.

Niall was far gentler with his smacks, though Roo's butt still tingled. She wasn't into the infliction or receipt of serious pain. There was no pleasure for her in that, but this highly charged sexual reprimand made her gasp with delight. Her nipples throbbed and she suspected one touch between her legs would flip her over the edge.

By the time he and Taylor reached the bedroom door, Roo still crawling, her delectable butt flushed from their slaps, Niall's balls were as hard as his cock. Roo wavered between confident seductress and skittish kitten. He could hear it in her voice, see it in her eyes. She worried that Taylor wanted her more than he wanted Niall, but she didn't see that as much as Niall wanted Taylor, he was desperate for Roo as well. Niall had never met a woman he liked better, never met a woman he wanted more.

As they watched Roo crawl toward the bed, Taylor's fingers entwined with his. Niall swallowed. All this time waiting and now Taylor's bed beckoned. Had this been what they'd needed? A woman to bridge the gap between them, to bring them together? His heart leapt in excitement and not regret that he alone wasn't enough for Taylor. There was no doubt in Niall's mind that he wanted Roo just as much as the man he'd spent so long pining for.

Roo flopped belly down on Taylor's bed and leaned up on her elbows, facing them.

"You better make it worth me missing *The Sound of Music*," she said.

Taylor looked at Niall and laughed. "Think we're up to it?"

"I'll score you," Roo called.

Taylor looked as though he was going to jump on her until Niall pushed pencil and paper into his hand and gave the same to Roo. Niall sat on the bed. Not difficult to think of ten things he wanted to do to the pair of them. If all thirty actions were different, it was going to take some time to get through them.

"Rip three sheets into four and when you've written on ten pieces, fold them twice so there's no cheating." Niall pinned Roo with his gaze and she gave him a bright smile. *Yeah, she's going to cheat.*

"I've only written three things I'd like to happen," Roo said. "My toes licked, my fingers licked and my ears licked. Then I'm off to watch the Von Trapps."

Taylor laughed.

They put the folded papers inside Taylor's leather wash bag. Niall could have cheated too and ensured one of his came out first, but why waste his energy when he knew he'd get what he wanted sooner or later? In any case, what he wanted had become blurred.

Taylor went into the bathroom and came back with a long strip of condoms, a towel and lube. The last made the breath catch in Niall's throat. When had Taylor bought that?

"Ready?" Taylor asked.

Niall held the bag out to Roo. "You first."

Roo pulled out a scrap of paper. She opened it and read, "A turkey sandwich, hold the mayo. Oops, sorry. A Taylor sandwich. Can't read my own writing. Oh damn. That wasn't very anonymous."

Niall caught the telltale wander of Roo's eyes. *Lying.* He turned to look at Taylor who was staring at the lube as if it were a poisonous snake. Roo screwed up the paper and threw it aside.

"And very tasty I'll be too." Taylor's attempt at bravado didn't mask his anxiety.

"Lie down next to Niall, and to get you in the mood, I'll attempt to remove my underwear in a provocative manner." Roo smiled and then swallowed hard.

"Sweetheart, *any* way you remove your underwear will be provocative," Taylor said. "I'm not sure I can be any more provoked or

in the mood." He gestured to his bobbing erection.

Roo moved to the foot of the bed, the mirror behind showing them everything.

"Count," she said.

"One—" Niall laughed.

She'd whipped off her bra and pants so fast, he might have thought magic was involved, and then he got sidetracked by the beauty of her body, her perfect proportions and her smooth, tanned skin. She was tall and slender with long legs, her pretty breasts topped by dusky nipples. And the truth was, a little bit of him was disappointed he didn't get to fuck her first, even though the man of his dreams lay there waiting for him. Though Taylor was clearly nervous, and Niall still wasn't certain this was what Taylor wanted.

Roo threw herself to land between them on the bed and rolled onto her back. Her smaller hands clasped theirs and squeezed.

"Shaved?" Taylor croaked.

"Not shaved?" Roo let go of Taylor's hand to twist her fingers in his pubic hair.

"Oh Christ, touch my dick and I'll go off like a rocket," Taylor said with a moan.

"Well, maybe we should start with some pyrotechnics." Roo slid down the bed, rolled onto her stomach and wrapped her hands around their cocks. She held Niall tight, pressing hard where his dick met his balls. When she licked the head of Taylor's cock and then did the same to his, Niall's brain turned to soup. Roo tugged them closer together, and then suddenly Taylor was kissing him while Roo kissed their cocks. Taylor threaded his fingers in Niall's hair and plunged his tongue into his mouth, and any thought that Taylor might not want this evaporated.

Roo's mouth was much smaller than Taylor's, and she licked and sucked and drove Niall crazy in a different way, but when she held their cock heads together, swept them with her tongue and sucked them both, it was a miracle Niall didn't come. Judging by Taylor's loud gasp, he felt the same. The friction, the heat and the pressure made his balls draw up.

As hands and mouths drove him faster toward release, Niall managed a few words. "Supposed to be a sandwich."

Roo lifted her head. "I don't want to be short changed. Men have no stamina." Then she was on him again with that hot, wet mouth and

coherency moved beyond his reach. As Niall's tongue thrust against Taylor's, their hips rocked, pushing the heads of their cocks into Roo's mouth. The combination of the feel of Taylor's cock rubbing against his and the play of Roo's lips around the sensitive head catapulted Niall toward completion.

He and Taylor came within an instant of each other, gasping mouths welded together, hands entwined in Roo's hair, their fingers touching, and Niall shuddered with the sheer unadulterated bliss of it.

As the wrenching spasms died away and the afterglow seeped through his body, their mouths drifted apart and Niall answered Taylor's smile with one of his own. The brush of Taylor's fingers over Niall's cheek meant more than Taylor could know. They reached to pull a panting Roo to lie on her back between them. Taylor snagged the towel and wiped come from her mouth and face.

"I thought I was going to drown," she said. "Reminds me of the time one of my so-called friends gave me a can of Coke on the school bus. I didn't know they'd shaken the can, and when I opened it, I had to put my mouth over the hole so it didn't spray everywhere. I think it even came out of my ears."

Taylor looked at Niall and laughed.

"Maybe you ought to check," Roo whispered.

The moment their mouths were around her ears Roo began to writhe like an eel.

He and Taylor pulled back.

"Arrggh, don't stop. I'm wriggling in pleasure. Can't you tell the difference? Learn fast."

"Your perfume tastes of peppermint," Taylor said.

"It *is* peppermint. I can't afford perfume." They chuckled and she glared. "Peppermint tastes a lot better than scent, believe me."

"You don't need anything to make you smell or taste nice," Niall said and bent to bury his face against the pulse in Roo's neck. She tasted of innocence and kindness, and...well, peppermint.

His hand roamed lower as he licked and kissed and trailed his tongue down her body. Caressing her breast with his lips made his mouth water, and when he opened his eyes to see Taylor fluttering his tongue over Roo's other nipple, blood surged back into his cock. Roo groaned and panted and made all sorts of desperate little sounds as they explored. She couldn't keep still and Niall laid his leg over hers to try to hold her down.

As he and Taylor lay face-to-face with their heads on her stomach, hands clasping her inner thighs, Roo's fingers tugged their hair.

"It's too much," she whispered. "You're too much."

Taylor leaned back to look up at her. "You need to come a few times. Let yourself go, Roo. Trust us. We won't hurt you. Say stop and we will. Want to choose a word in case you get carried away?"

"Supercalifragilisticexpialidocious?" Roo asked.

Taylor raised his eyebrows. "Try again."

Roo frowned. "I don't think I'd say super—"

"Roo!" Taylor flicked her nipple.

"Ouch."

"That won't work either," Taylor said laughing.

"Pregnant," Roo said.

Maybe it shouldn't have made them laugh but it did. Niall chortled into her stomach and could feel Taylor doing the same.

Chapter Eighteen

Nerves either made Roo's mouth open too often or not at all. Lying in bed with the guys acting like her sex slaves, she really needed to shut up. They licked her stomach and a kittenlike mewl burst through her clenched lips.

Two guys. How lucky am I?

Two tongues.

Four hands.

Twenty fingers.

Two... Oh God. Not thinking about that.

It was hard to think about anything when she was being played with so expertly. As they kissed her breasts, they pulled her thighs apart and stroked the damp folds between her legs. When they slid their fingers into the valley on either side of her clit, a hard throb of sensation exploded in her belly. Her hips rocked into their caresses, trying to get them to touch her faster, harder, a little to the left—no right, and she heard Taylor chuckle.

Pointless attempting to delay this, senseless thinking she could, hopeless to want to even though it felt so good. Roo teetered on the brink with no way back. At the first rub of her clit, her spine arched, her legs stiffened and tremors rippled through her. She unraveled with a series of breathy cries. *That. Was. Lovely.*

Roo opened her eyes and lifted her head. The two faces looking back at her appeared much too smug.

"Eight," she said. "Beaufort Scale."

Niall arched his brows.

"I'm scoring you, remember?" she asked.

"A small gale?" Taylor glanced at Niall. "The Beaufort Scale describes wind conditions."

"Force eight. Some twigs broken from trees, cars veer on the road, progress on foot seriously impeded," Roo said.

"What does the scale go up to?" Niall asked.

"Twelve. Hurricane," Roo said. "You've a lot more work to do to make the earth move for me."

Taylor snorted. "You cheeky monkey. Trying to tell us you were pretending? Those moans and cries?"

"I didn't want you to feel bad."

Taylor dropped his head and licked her clit in a lightning-fast motion that made Roo buck hard into his face, and a moment later she came again, heat rolling through her body. She gasped and dropped her butt back on the bed only for Niall to take Taylor's place. He pressed his tongue deep into her, and as Roo opened her mouth to groan, Taylor slid up and kissed her.

Cast adrift in a sea of heightened awareness, Roo floated in bliss. Fingers stroked, tongues danced and cocks rubbed against her. Each man had his own scent, Niall's sweeter, Taylor's musky. Taylor's fingers were softer, Niall's tongue longer. Taylor's nipples were more sensitive than Niall's, but kissing Niall's neck had him gasping for air. Breathing for Roo became tricky, and her inhalations turned into jagged sucks, her exhalations noisy grunts. Her body was no longer under her control but theirs, and Roo loved it. *Loved them. Damn it. Damn it. Damn it.*

They positioned her on her hands and knees, and Niall lay beneath her, his legs pointing the same way as hers, his head under her belly, his fingers on her thighs, pulling her down onto his face. Taylor knelt behind her, astride Niall, his hands on her hips, sliding his cock in the valley of her butt cheeks. Then it wasn't Taylor's cock rubbing her but the stubble of his cheeks as he licked her backside. *Oh fuck, fuck, fuck.* If Niall hadn't been supporting her, she'd have fallen, but between them they kept her exactly where they wanted her.

Roo planted her face in the pillow and groaned. Niall was licking her clit, teasing her back to orgasm. Her stomach tensed, her nipples tightened and she felt the nibbling sensation in her lower belly that heralded the flurry of spasms to come. *Again?* Roo raced toward the finish line like an Olympic sprinter, and the guys' hold tightened as she came apart, orgasm riding her body head to toe.

"Oh God, God," Roo muttered into the pillow.

Taylor and Niall changed places. They shifted her around on the bed until Roo no longer knew who touched her where, or how many times she'd come, only knew that she didn't want any of this to stop. Fingers and tongues explored every part of her, three pairs of legs writhed and entwined, their faces pressed together, kisses greedy until

she couldn't breathe, and then the guys were so gentle her heart ached with happiness.

The rip of foil brought her back to some sort of reality. Roo lay on her back, licking her kiss-swollen lips, her nipples almost painful, her inner thighs soaked with her cream and their precome. The guys panted beside her, slick chests heaving, each holding a flat foil packet. Taylor looked...petrified. *Damn.*

"What's wrong?" Roo reached out to touch his arm.

"I've never...done this before." Taylor gulped.

She stroked his wrist. "A virgin? You missed sex ed? Quick lesson. You put that," Roo pointed to his cock, "in here." She pointed between her legs. "And move it in and out."

Taylor let out a forced chuckle. But Roo had guessed what he meant and made sure her surprise didn't show. He and Niall had never fucked? She could feel the tension grow in the air, thickening it, squeezing out the fun. Niall's cheek twitched and resignation crept over his features. The moment was slipping away.

She turned to Taylor. "Don't you want this?"

Taylor's mouth opened but no sound came out.

He's afraid. He wasn't the only one. Roo took a deep breath and looked at Niall. "Want me to go first instead? I'll be the filling in the sandwich. You'll go slow, right?"

But Niall was staring at Taylor. "You don't have to do this."

"I want to," Taylor said. "It's just that I'm having trouble getting my head round it. Thinking too much."

Roo shuffled up the bed and hugged her legs. *Don't say a word. Let them sort this out.*

"It's okay," Niall muttered and stood.

Roo caught his arm and pulled him down. *Don't give in!* When Taylor wrapped his hand around Niall's, she sighed with relief.

"Sorry to be a pain in the butt," Taylor said and his mouth turned up in a smile.

Roo laid her hands on their necks and twisted their heads to face her.

"Are we three?" she asked. "Because I don't want two against one, no matter who's the one. If we don't trust each other, it won't work. If you two want me to go, just say so. I've never done this before either. And in that toiletry bag there's a piece of paper—ah darn it—at least

five pieces of paper that say *Roo Sandwich.* Two guys at the same time? Two cocks? Don't you think I'm nervous too?" She took a deep breath. "So, are we three?"

Roo put her fist in the space between them. The guys knocked her knuckles at the same time.

She smiled. "I've got the best seat in the house. I'll hold the condoms and watch until it's my turn onstage." She sighed. "Last time I was onstage, I was the back legs of a cow. I had to drop a milk carton—"

"Roo!" They spoke at the same time.

"Sorry." She zipped her lip but knew it wouldn't last.

Taylor didn't have to talk himself into this. He wanted it. His nerves were more borne of fear of coming too fast inside Roo once Niall was fucking him. How impressive would that be? But Roo was right. They couldn't hide anything. If they weren't open about what they wanted, they shouldn't start this.

He reached out, trailed his fingers over the depression between Niall's pecs and heard the breath catch in the guy's throat. Taylor let his thumb drift over Niall's smooth skin, following the contours of his chiseled abs down to the ridge of his hip bone. One gentle push sent Niall to lie against Roo. She crossed her arms over his chest and stroked Niall's neck with her fingers.

God, that cock. Taylor ran one finger down the line of fair hair below Niall's navel and brushed his thumb over the crest of his dick. Why did it look twice as big as it had before? The foreskin had drawn back from the rounded head. The veins that snaked down its length were dark and thick, and his balls hung heavy beneath. Taylor shifted his gaze and watched Niall's chest rise and fall, watched the flex of his muscles as he stroked Roo's arms. She had her face pressed against his hair, but her gaze was fixed on Taylor.

Taylor grabbed a condom and slid it on. *Ouch.* He had to take it off and try again and felt his face heat. Niall did his in one smooth move, though his fingers shook.

"Did you practice on bananas?" Roo asked and Taylor snorted. "Hey, I'm serious. In our sex-ed lessons, we all had to bring in a banana. School provided the condoms. Course, I'd eaten my banana for lunch before I remembered. They had extra though. Then I got into trouble for putting the condom on with my mouth. Well, trying to."

Niall shook with laughter.

"I thought it might be a useful skill. A bit like tying knots in cherry stalks. I can do that, but I still can't do the trick with the condom."

"You can practice on us another time," Niall said.

He reached for the lube and Taylor's heart zoomed into his throat. He watched Niall rub the glistening fluid down his shaft, his fingers circling his cock, dragging up and down his length, and Taylor stopped breathing. Right at that moment, if anyone touched Taylor's cock, he'd explode. Roo let Niall go and Taylor allowed Niall to pull him down so he lay on his side with Niall tucked up behind him. Roo slithered down the bed until she lay facing him. *A Taylor sandwich.*

Taylor sighed and flexed his shoulders as Niall kissed his way down his spine, sighed louder when hands spread his butt cheeks, and went silent when Niall kissed his asshole. Taylor felt his upper leg being lifted to give Niall better access and he trembled as cold lube hit the valley of his butt and trickled down to his balls. Roo ran her thumb over his lips and smiled at him. Niall pressed himself against Taylor's back and slid his lubricated finger back and forth over the puckered ring of Taylor's anus.

"Chriiiist." Taylor's whisper was shaky.

He flinched as Niall pressed harder and the tip of his finger slipped inside. Goose bumps erupted on his arms, and even as he told himself not to, Taylor tensed.

Roo slid forward and cocooned his head between her breasts. "Shhh," she whispered into his hair. "Don't freak out or you'll scare me."

Her soft breasts distracted only for a moment before Niall's finger slipped deeper. Taylor felt the slide of every inch, the first knuckle, the next, until Niall had pressed in up to the webbing. The flare of pleasure surprised him, the burn strangely erotic.

"Okay?" Niall asked.

Roo pulled back a little and looked Taylor in the eyes.

"Feels good," Taylor blurted as he stared at her.

One finger became two, and as Niall slid them in and out of his butt, Taylor's breathing quickened. Then as Taylor was getting used to the feel, settling into the unfamiliarity of the action, Niall scissored his fingers and Taylor groaned, but with pleasure not pain.

Niall pressed his mouth to his ear. "You sure?"

"Yes." It meant a lot that Niall had asked.

The heat against Taylor's back disappeared, and then Niall's cock slid down the wet crease of his backside. Taylor sucked in a breath and Roo stroked his lips with her thumb. Niall's hand settled under Taylor's leg and held him steady as he pressed his cock home.

"Push back against me," Niall whispered.

Shit, it hurts. As Niall pushed, Taylor bore down, braced for the pain, gritting his teeth so he didn't call out. The moment the rounded head of Niall's cock popped through the tight muscle barrier, his anus burned as it stretched to accept the intrusion. Niall's fingers tightened on his leg as his rapid breaths washed Taylor's back. Roo's eyes were wide with excitement, and as Niall slid deeper, Taylor opened to him, flexing his hips and rocking back so his butt nestled into Niall's pelvis. Discomfort had morphed fast to enjoyment and Taylor's eyelids fluttered as the awareness of being filled overwhelmed him. Was this what it was like for a woman?

"Roo," Niall said.

Taylor opened his eyes as Roo shifted forward. He wasn't sure he could—oh, seems he could. Roo lifted her leg and hooked it over both of them as she slid onto Taylor's cock.

"Jesus," Taylor blurted.

Roo sighed. "No, he's not here. Only me and Niall." She kissed him.

Niall drew back and then pushed into him, and as he slid into a rhythm, Taylor caught hold of Roo's waist and tugged her down on him as Niall surged forward. He wanted to cry with the joy of it, the feel of thrusting into Roo's tight, hot pussy and the sensation of Niall pumping into his ass. Roo broke free to breathe and Taylor gulped air.

Roo made little cries as he drove into her, her cheeks and chest flushed with heat. Niall slid harder, deeper, then changed the angle of his thrusts and hit Taylor's prostate. Taylor grunted as his muscles gripped Niall's cock in response to the touch on his gland.

They were all slick with sweat, Niall's speed dictating the pace Taylor fucked Roo, and now he was fast. *Shit.* Very fast. Roo wailed as Taylor held her tight against him as he powered into her. Her pussy contracted around his cock and he felt the moment she flew. Taylor couldn't hold off any longer. Every sense pushed to the limit, his libido in outer space, he let go of the thread holding him and orgasm raced down his spine to set fire to his balls. They drew up tight, his cock swelled and then he was jetting into her, crying out with each spurt as

he buried his face in her shoulder.

As his remaining brain cell clicked into gear, he registered Niall had held off, but now his speed picked up again. Short jabs with his cock while his grip on Taylor's leg tightened. "You feel perfect," Niall gasped. "So bloody perfect."

And even though Taylor had come, the pressure on his prostate as Niall pounded into him, hips circling, sent sparks of heat dancing around his belly while his semi-hard cock still stroked Roo's pussy. Taylor clenched around Niall's shaft and Niall cried out and shuddered against him. Roo's arm sneaked under Taylor's to wrap around Niall, and the three of them lay tight together as aftershocks racked Niall's body.

Taylor wasn't going to think about the wet sensation where Niall leaned on his shoulder, and that the guy was crying. This was nothing more than red-hot sex.

When can we do it again?

Niall blinked back his tears and lifted his head to press his face against Taylor's hair. Roo's fingers drifted up Niall's arm to his neck, and then she stroked his cheek. When Niall shifted to look at her, she was staring at him. *She knows how I feel about him.* Without her, maybe this wouldn't have happened. And even though what they'd just done was a huge leap forward, it still wasn't enough to save Niall.

But it was a start.

"He's asleep," Roo mouthed.

Niall nodded. She kept touching his face with her fingers, running them over his lips, down his nose, along his chin.

"I love you," she mouthed.

Niall's heart swelled and he smiled at her. "I love you," he mouthed back.

Roo sighed. When she closed her eyes, she had a smile on her face.

How could he not love her? She'd made this happen. It was Roo who'd brought them together, Roo who could keep them together. He did love her. It wasn't a lie, no automatic return of her words. He loved her. Hope burned in Niall's chest.

Love. It had the capacity to induce incredible happiness and the ability to ruthlessly destroy what it had created. He could have walked away from Taylor long ago, but to spend his life pining for what might

have been? Niall had felt compelled to give love a chance even if by doing so he lost his right to exist. What was existence worth without love? Without Taylor? Without Roo?

Niall knew he'd been obsessed with the guy and it wasn't healthy. When he had moments of lucidity, he even wondered if somehow he'd been maneuvered into the obsession. Had someone in Faeryland been pulling his strings? And if that was the case, had someone spun a web around Taylor to stop him from ever returning Niall's love? Niall believed true love could break his mother's spell, but what if he was wrong?

Whatever the case, he owed Taylor. Niall had come back because he loved him, but also because he wanted to make things right. Now he'd dragged another into the mess. Had he made things worse or better? Roo's hand lay motionless on his shoulder, her breathing even, and Niall knew she'd drifted into sleep.

Would Taylor remember now? Wake to realize he'd played with Niall as a boy? Would he understand the depth of Niall's feelings? And if he did, what should Niall do? Tell the truth or lie? He couldn't live on this side without Taylor's love but when Taylor learned what he'd done, would he still love him?

Niall had thought holding Taylor in his arms would be a step toward making everything right, and now he worried he'd made things worse. He could leave, walk into the garden and go home. Taylor and Roo would worry for a while but they'd forget him just as Taylor had years ago. Niall could make them forget him. And when he got home, what would happen then? He'd be forced into marriage, forced to spend his life pretending he was happy.

So was this all about him? Some selfish desire to ensure his own contentment at anyone else's expense? Niall tried to swallow the lump in his throat. He wanted to make Taylor happy. Ever since that day when he'd gone back over the wall for the last time, leaving Taylor in tears, Niall had wanted to make his world right again. He'd had to wait, bide his time until he was strong enough to return, until he could bargain with his mother. But Niall should have remembered she never lost at anything.

Niall jerked when he saw Oisin standing in the doorway. *What now?*

"They won't wake, don't worry," his brother said. Oisin walked over to the bed and stared down at Taylor and Roo. "He doesn't love you."

"Not yet," Niall murmured.

"You think our mother will let that happen?"

Niall's tattoo prickled. "There was supposed to be no interference."

Oisin laughed. "Your path was marked from birth as was mine. You really believe you can defy her?"

"My life is my own, to do with as I wish."

Oisin dropped to his knees at Niall's side and caught hold of his hand. "I don't want you to die," he pleaded. "If you persist in this, that's what will happen. And what will you have achieved? Nothing."

"I'm happy."

Oisin stroked Niall's face. "You're dying."

Niall swallowed.

"You knew the price and yet you still spread yourself too thin. Everything you do on this side is paid for heavily."

"I have months."

Oisin shook his head. "You have another week."

Niall exhaled. No use protesting. Their mother could make and break rules at will. He'd felt the tattoo tighten when he'd fucked Taylor, and known it was a message from her.

"Come home with me," Oisin said.

"I am home, brother."

Chapter Nineteen

Roo woke to the sound of water running and no guys in bed with her. A flutter of worry started up in her belly. She wanted to feel confident, but she wasn't there yet. She shuffled to the edge of the mattress, stood and sat right back down. *Wow, wobbly legs.* Her next attempt to stand succeeded and Roo crossed to Taylor's bathroom. A peek around the door showed the pair under the shower, Niall on his knees sucking Taylor's cock. A bolt of lust almost took Roo's legs out from under her again.

She considered backing away, and then steeled herself and took a step forward. *She* was the one who'd said they needed to be open, and Roo didn't feel jealous, maybe a little shy, which was ridiculous. She should be well past the point of being coy. Odds were this wouldn't last, but Roo felt happy and...safe for the first time in a long while. She wanted to make the most of it.

"Can I play ball?" she asked.

A smile and a hand held out to her answered her question.

"Very gently," Taylor said.

Niall let Taylor's cock slide from his mouth. Roo knelt by his side and blinked as water hit her face.

"Good morning," Niall whispered.

He slipped warm, wet hands around her throat and stared into her eyes before he pulled her lips onto his. The kiss was bruising in its intensity, and the sheer possessiveness of it made her ache in the pit of her stomach. Water poured over their heads, and the feel of Taylor twisting his fingers in her hair made her heart soar. When Niall broke away, she was gasping.

"Want to see if we can bring Taylor to his knees?" Niall asked.

Taylor barked out a laugh, though judging from the hungry glow in his eyes, he had no objection. As Niall trailed his tongue up one side of Taylor's cock, Roo licked up the other.

"This isn't going to take long," Taylor said with a low moan.

He leaned back against the tiled wall. As Roo and Niall teased him with their fingers and tongues, their mouths traded kisses at the same time. They kissed each other, kissed Taylor's cock and his balls while Roo's heart beat harder and harder. Niall had one hand on Taylor's butt and one on her neck, stroking with his thumb while she sucked Taylor's cock.

Even through the force of the shower, Taylor tasted salty, his precome leaking into her mouth. Roo ran her tongue around the smooth ridge of his cock while Niall sucked his balls. When Roo opened her mouth and swallowed his shaft as deep as she could, Taylor's breathing became choppy. She felt Niall's fingers moving on her throat and knew he was tracing the movement of Taylor's cock.

"Oh fuck, fuck," Niall grunted. "That is so hot."

Roo pulled back, panting, and Niall took over, his cheeks hollowing as he sucked hard and took Taylor deep. And Roo did what Niall had just done, put her fingers on Niall's neck and felt Taylor's cock slide in his throat. Need spiraled through her and Roo slipped a hand between her legs. Without looking at her or taking his mouth from Taylor's cock, Niall's hand settled around her wrist and tugged her fingers away. When Roo tried to pull free, he tightened his hold and took his mouth off Taylor.

Looking straight at Roo, Niall whispered, "That's mine."

"I ache," Roo wailed.

"Good." Niall smiled.

"Hey, I'm still here. You haven't finished with me yet," Taylor said.

"Come on our faces." Roo looked up at him and Taylor's breathing became more ragged.

With no hesitation, he wrapped his fingers around his cock and began to pump and twist as he looked into their eyes. A vein pulsed at Taylor's temple. Roo ran her tongue over her upper lip and stared straight at him.

"Christ," Taylor gasped and ribbons of come flew to splatter Niall and then Roo when she pushed Niall out of the way.

Taylor snorted and tried to aim the next jet at Niall.

"Ooh, *Top Gun*." Roo chortled and licked her lips, licked Niall's lips and then Taylor pulled them both up to join in.

"Our very own porn star," Taylor whispered to Roo. "Do you have any idea how sexy you are?"

"You didn't think that when you first met me."

"Even as a chicken you were irresistible." Taylor licked the water from her eyelashes and turned her to face Niall. "I want to watch you fuck her."

"Don't blink," Niall said, his hand pushing down on his balls.

The look on Niall's face was a mix of desire and desperation. Roo almost pinched herself to make sure she wasn't dreaming. Even as her sensible part kept saying *This won't last*, the part of her brain she most listened to told her *Seize every chance for joy that you can.*

Niall lifted Roo by the hips, and as he shifted her against the wall next to Taylor, she raised her legs and wrapped them around him. When Niall pressed the crown of his cock against her folds, he groaned as if the world were ending. Roo slid her arms around his back and kissed him, digging her heels in the muscles of his butt.

"Roo," Niall whispered her name, drawing it out like a caress.

Taylor slid behind her and supported her as Niall worked into her slowly, prolonging the entry. Roo gulped against his mouth, tangled in the kiss. *Bliss, bliss, bliss.* Her head turned to mist as heat gathered inside her and liquefied her organs. Niall spread his legs, changed the angle and pressed in a little deeper. It was as if he'd pushed the air from her body, and Roo threw back her head to take a breath.

Then as Taylor licked her neck, Niall began to move, small, gentle thrusts that quickly grew longer and harder. With every drive of his cock, she tightened her muscles around his shaft and he panted into her face. Roo crossed her legs on his back and clung on as Niall began to pound into her and Taylor slid away. Her breath hitched as Niall went deep, the feeling— *Oh fuck. No condom.*

As if he'd realized at the same time, Niall froze and buried his face in her hair as he clutched her. "It's okay. Sorry. I forgot," he whispered. "But I can't get you pregnant and I'm clean. Trust me."

Roo took a contraceptive pill but she'd never had sex without protection. And she knew better than to trust any guy who said *trust me* particularly when it related to contraception. But something told her to believe Niall.

Taylor moved closer. "What's wrong?"

"Nothing," Roo said, and smiled at Niall.

He should have stopped. He could have pulled out and put a condom on, but he didn't want to. Roo felt perfect and he wasn't lying. He couldn't pass on any disease, though he wasn't sure about the

pregnancy part. He doubted it could happen, but he didn't *know.* Though he barely moved inside Roo, his cock sang with the pleasure of each slide. He could feel the texture of her cunt, the wet folds caressing his cock, his precome mixing with her cream.

Niall slid his hands under her thighs so he could pull her down more strongly, and each time their bodies pressed together, his need to come grew more powerful, the grip tightening on his body, creeping through his limbs. Roo's fingers threaded his hair, stroked his face, held his head. Niall wanted to do this forever, to never let her go.

Roo is our center, our balance, our heart.

The moment that thought came into his head, his tattoo burned like acid and Niall's knees buckled.

Taylor slid behind him, his hands on his hips as if he'd sensed Niall had a problem. He did. Poison leached into him from every mark on his body, and if Roo and Taylor looked closely enough, they'd see the tattoo grow. But even that pain wasn't enough to stop him coming. As Roo flew and tightened around him, the muscles of her sex pulling at his cock, fire licked up his spine, flared in his belly and Niall exploded inside her.

They clung together and Niall knew that without Taylor holding him, he'd have collapsed. The aftershocks of release were overwhelmed by the hurt in his body, and Niall had no choice but to lift Roo off his cock before he sank to the floor of the shower. He hadn't expected Taylor to let him fall. Niall groaned when his knees collided with tile.

"You stupid fucker," Taylor snapped. "What the bloody—"

Niall saw a fist coming toward him but Roo grabbed Taylor's arm. "Don't. It's okay."

"It's not fucking okay. He didn't use a condom."

Roo moved between him and Taylor. "It's my fault as much as Niall's. We got carried away. I'm on the Pill. I trust Niall. I trust you. Don't make this an issue."

Roo bent at his side. "You okay?" She reached to turn off the water and laid a hand on his forehead. "Wow, you're burning up." As she touched his neck, he gritted his teeth. When she ran her fingers down his tattoo, Niall groaned.

"Why is this so hot?" Roo asked.

He couldn't speak, even if he'd wanted to tell her. A message from his mother. Perfect fucking timing.

"Stop sulking and feel him, Taylor. He's too hot."

Niall cringed as Taylor ran his hand down his leg, the brush of his fingers like sharp needles.

"What's wrong?" Taylor asked, sounding worried now.

"An infection from the tattoo?" Roo suggested.

Bright girl. Though she'd never guess the truth. Niall closed his eyes. *Shit, it hurts.*

Taylor shook his head. "Maybe if it was new, but I don't think it is. It's not red and inflamed, it looks—blacker if anything. Sharper."

"Could it be some sort of fit, an allergy to the soap? Do we need to call an ambulance?" Roo asked, clutching at Niall's hand.

"Niall?"

"No," Niall grunted.

"Don't try to talk yet." Roo squeezed his fingers.

"Let's get him to bed," Taylor said.

Between them, they helped Niall to the bedroom and he lay on his back, gasping like a fish. The pain was fading now and he had to think of a lie to tell them before they called someone and made matters worse. Roo wiped a towel over his face then down his body, wicking away the moisture, avoiding his tattoo. Any fabrication would have to include something about that damned mark.

Taylor wasn't so careful in the way he handled Niall. He touched the tattoo on his leg and Niall writhed.

"Is it the tattoo?" Taylor asked.

Niall kept his eyes closed.

"Should we call the doctor? Take him to the hospital?" Roo asked, panic clear in her voice. "Maybe he's been poisoned. You said he was hiding. What if he's been found? He could have been stabbed by a poisoned umbrella, or maybe picked something in the garden that was coated in a drug. We need to do something."

Niall opened his eyes, grabbed her hand and squeezed hard.

"No?" she asked.

He squeezed again and managed to shake his head once, though the action brought on a fresh burst of pain.

"Niall, do you have medicine?" Taylor asked. "Upstairs in your room?"

"I'll go look." Roo dashed out.

I don't have the energy to sustain the mirage.

Taylor took his hand and stroked the back of it with his thumb. "Why didn't you tell me you were sick?"

"Sorry," Niall whispered. *Sorry about everything.* He shouldn't have come back. He'd made matters worse and he wasn't sure he could stand a week of this pain.

Taylor kissed his forehead. "You don't have anything to be sorry about. But I think we need the truth now, mate. Otherwise I'm going to carry you to the car and drive you to the nearest hospital whether you like it or not."

Roo raced up the stairs, burst through the door into Niall's room and came to a crashing halt. She'd thought this was his room but it couldn't be. The attic was practically bare except for a pile of blankets in one corner topped by a blue cushion. She frowned. If Niall had been sharing with Taylor, wouldn't he have said and not let her rush up here?

As Roo stepped over the threshold, the room seemed to shimmer and the outlines of the sorts of things she'd expected to see took shape. A bed, a chest of drawers, a wardrobe. *What?* Roo blinked and rubbed her eyes. No, the room was almost empty. That was weird. Roo headed for the corner and lifted the blankets to check for a bottle of pills, but her attention was snagged by something else. Hanging from the eaves, dangling a couple of feet above the makeshift bed was a tatty blue-and-white plane.

Was that the one Stephanie had written about?

Roo ran back down the stairs and into the bedroom. Niall was sitting up, leaning against the headboard and looked less pale.

She took a deep breath and stared straight at him. "I didn't find anything."

Niall's cheek twitched.

Taylor turned to Niall. "No medication?"

Roo sat on the bed. "No, I mean I didn't find *anything*. There's nothing up there. No bed, no clothes. Just a few blankets and dust bunnies." She turned to Taylor. "And your toy plane."

Niall caught hold of her hand and squeezed. Was he trying to tell her something?

"What the hell are you talking about?" Taylor snapped. "Did you look in a bloody cupboard?"

Roo bristled. "No, I didn't. It was the attic and it was empty."

Taylor hesitated and then left the room. Roo heard him running up the stairs. She turned to Niall. "You said you'd been here six months. Where's all your stuff?"

Niall summoned the energy to grunt a few words. "How d'you know...Taylor's plane?"

Ooops. Blue and white. She'd assumed it was the plane Stephanie had written about, but Roo still hadn't come clean about the book. "I said *your* plane. I didn't say Taylor's."

"You looked at him."

Taylor came clattering back. "What the hell was that about? Bed, wardrobe, chair, clothes all over the place. No pills though. Unless they're in a drawer?"

"No pills," Niall said.

Roo frowned. *Had* she somehow gone into the wrong room? A door she'd missed?

"Are you okay now?" Taylor asked Niall.

"Pain's going."

"So what was it?" Taylor asked.

"You think I could have...a coffee and some toast?" Niall asked.

He lifted a shaking hand to his head and dragged his fingers through his hair.

Taylor sighed. "Okay."

"I'll stay," Roo said.

"Go help him. Give me a minute," Niall said. "Please."

Roo sighed but pushed herself off the bed and put on the white shirt Niall had been wearing the night before.

Taylor stepped into boxers and followed her out of the room.

"Are *you* okay?" he asked as they went downstairs.

Roo took his hand. "If Niall wasn't ill, I'd say I felt fantastic."

"Good." He tugged her to the kitchen. "We're going to have to work on him to tell us the truth, who he's hiding from and why, and explain what the hell just happened in the shower. There's nothing that can't be sorted out. Well, not much. As long as he's not murdered anyone. We need to persuade him to talk to us."

"You'd better bring a sledgehammer up with breakfast."

Taylor smiled. "I'll do the toast while you make the drinks. Hey, what was that crap about the attic being empty?"

Roo furrowed her brow as she pulled mugs from the cupboard. "Is there another room up there? A split attic?"

"No."

Her frown deepened. "That's weird. You saw your plane though, right?"

"A plane? No. My toys have long gone." Taylor slipped slices of bread between the metal holders. "Why think it was mine when it's in Niall's room?"

Roo spooned coffee into the mugs. Something wasn't right here. Roo had thought it was Taylor's plane, Niall said it was and now Taylor denied it.

"Pass the marmalade," Taylor said.

Roo handed it over and then poured boiling water into three mugs. When she put the kettle down, she turned to find Taylor had moved closer. He pulled her into his arms and gave her a long, slow, leisurely kiss that made her toes curl and her heart thump.

"Thank you," he said after he let her go.

"For what?"

"For helping make this happen, for making me happy, and for being you."

Roo gulped. She didn't know what to say. Then suddenly she did. "Toast's burning."

Taylor leapt for the stove. "Shit."

"See you upstairs." She put the mugs on a tray and carried them out of the room. Roo was fighting not to cry. No one had ever said anything like that to her before. She should have said something nice back, but she'd blurted out about the toast. Stupid, even though it *was* burning.

Niall lay on his back with his arm over his eyes. Roo put the tray on the bedside table and slipped back up the stairs to the attic. One glance and she blew out a heavy breath. Bed, wardrobe, a chair strewn with clothes. Her gaze drifted to the corner where she'd seen the blanket and the plane, and it was empty. But this was the same room.

Roo wandered to the corner and kicked the empty space where the cushion and—*what the hell?* She dropped to her knees, reached out and squeaked. The blanket was here. She could feel it. *Impossible.*

Roo's mouth lost all moisture. Was she dreaming this? Had the guys slipped her some drug?

She waved her hand above her head and her fingers snagged the plane. Heart pounding, she traced the line of the string to the ceiling and tugged it free. She had to fight the urge to giggle. She knew she was holding something yet couldn't see it.

"Roo?" Taylor shouted. "Where are you?"

"Coming."

Roo held her hand up so the plane didn't hit the floor, but as she walked out of the attic, she almost let the thing drop because suddenly it *was* visible. Roo made her way down the stairs, nipped into her room to get Stephanie's book and tucked it under her arm, hidden beneath Niall's shirt.

When she went into Taylor's room, they were sitting on the bed eating toast, Niall, under the duvet, leaning against the headboard, and Taylor on top with his back toward the door. When Niall saw what she was holding, his mouth tightened.

Taylor turned and his reaction was a puzzled frown. "Where did you get that?"

"The attic," Roo said. She put the plane down on the floor and slipped the book under the bed before she sat next to Niall.

"Why've you bought it down here? You shouldn't touch Niall's stuff."

The press of Niall's fingers at her back told her to keep quiet. The look in his eyes begged her to.

"Er—I'll put it back later."

Taylor turned his attention to Niall. "Right, now you've got your toast and coffee, explain what happened in the bathroom."

Niall's fingers pressed more insistently into her spine.

"Take your private detective hat off for a minute," Roo said. "This isn't quite the loving cuddle I'd hoped for after such stupendous, sensational sex."

Taylor grinned. "You think we were stupendous and sensational?"

Roo shook her head. "I was talking about me."

Taylor sighed and rolled onto his side, propping his head up with his hand. Roo's heart was racing. She felt as if a monster storm were brewing, the air full of electric charge, making it hard to breathe. The three of them had to be open for this to work and already there were

too many secrets, particularly what was going on in the attic and what was wrong with Niall. Roo thought about the book lying under the bed. She had secrets of her own.

Maybe she had a way to help them open up.

"Do you have any brothers or sisters?" she asked Niall.

"Three brothers."

"Younger? Older?"

"Older."

"Are your parents still alive?" she asked.

"Yes."

Thank you, Mr. Chatty.

"My father died seven years ago." Roo felt a jolt of pain when she said that. "My mother and my sister live in Greece, I think."

"You think?" Taylor stroked her knee, drawing circles with his finger, making her quiver.

"They moved there eighteen years ago. I haven't seen them since."

Taylor's finger stopped moving.

Niall wrapped his arms around her. "How old were you when they left?"

"Ten."

Taylor's eyes widened. "Sure they're still alive?"

"Until seven years ago, they sent Christmas and birthday cards. I moved house then. Maybe they're still sending them."

"No return address?" Taylor asked.

The private detective in him. "No. Just a Greek stamp."

"What happened when you were ten?" Niall asked.

Roo choked up as she remembered. "I went to school as usual. Madison didn't go because she said she felt sick. When I came home, she and Mum weren't there." She swallowed hard. "Madison's room was almost empty. All my mother's things had gone." And Roo's money box. Her mother wanted her money but not her. She'd saved up more than two hundred pounds of her pocket money and birthday money over the years. Maybe her sister had taken it, but it still hurt.

"What did you do?" Taylor asked.

"Made some weird dinner for my dad with potatoes, cheese and bacon, and did my homework while I waited for him to come back from

work. He smashed a vase and a plate and he kept saying, 'What am I going to do? What am I supposed to do with you? How could she do this to me?' I didn't understand then, but later I did. She'd left me to punish him. He'd been going to leave her and instead she left him.

"The woman he'd been seeing didn't want him with a child in tow, so it was just me and my dad. And he never resented me for it." Roo gave a sad smile. "We were happy most of the time. I was better off without my mum. She was hard and brittle as toffee, not soft and cuddly. She was angry all the time, shouted if I didn't eat all my dinner, if I didn't get full marks on a test, if she caught me reading under the covers in bed."

"All mothers do that." Taylor looked at Niall for confirmation.

"Mine gets pissed off very easily," Niall said. "I only have to have the wrong look on my face."

Roo had always seemed to have the wrong look on her face for her mother. "My dad turned out to be the best dad in the world. Once there was just the two of us, we did everything together. I think he tried harder because he felt bad about what had happened, guilty because he'd been going to leave me. He said he hadn't wanted to see how much Mum hated me and that it was his fault she was so angry, his fault she liked Madison better. He'd had an affair and Mum found out, and in an attempt at a new start, she got pregnant with me. So I wasn't born out of love. But my dad made up for it by loving me so much."

Roo smiled as she remembered him kissing her every night before she went to bed, the stories he'd read to her, the way he collected her when she was out late.

"I wanted to live at home while I went to university, but he wouldn't let me. He said I had to learn to make myself happy and not rely on anyone else."

He'd been right to make her move out. Roo hadn't had many friends at school but she'd blossomed at college. She'd just completed her year in Russia when her father had fallen ill and Roo moved to a different university so she could live at home and look after him.

"What happened?" Taylor asked.

"Cancer. It spread very fast. He tried so hard to hang on until I graduated." Roo's throat began to close. "I was going to take him in a wheelchair, and when I went to help him out of bed the morning of my graduation, he was...he was dead."

Roo had never cried so hard or so long.

Niall pressed himself harder against her back and Taylor wrapped his arms around her too.

She'd lost love that day and had been looking for it ever since.

Chapter Twenty

As the three of them lay in bed together, Roo couldn't help but think of another mother who'd lost her little girl. Taylor's mother probably still cried for her daughter whereas Roo doubted her mother even gave her a second thought. "Are the police still looking for Stephanie?"

"Not actively. It's an open case but nothing's going to happen unless someone comes forward and admits taking her or if they find… Christ." Taylor rubbed his jaw with his hand.

"What was she like?" Roo pulled Taylor down so his head lay in her lap while she leaned against Niall.

"Beautiful. Huge brown eyes and long dark hair she tied in a pony tail—too tempting not to pull." He chuckled. "She was inquisitive and funny and a pest and I used to tell her to get lost." He groaned. "God, I wish I'd never said that."

Niall held Roo tighter while she stroked Taylor's hair, her fingers massaging his temple. "I bet all brothers say that to little sisters."

"Except they don't actually get lost," Taylor muttered.

"Did you play with her in the tree house?" Roo asked. "Did she want to be the princess and you were some monster who'd captured her?"

He gave a short laugh. "I used to leave her up there for ages. I just wanted to play with…"

"Who?" Roo asked.

Niall sucked in a breath and Taylor turned his head to look at him. "I don't remember."

"You don't remember your friends' names?" Roo asked.

"One friend," Taylor blurted. "Why the hell can't I remember? I can recall my mates from school—Pete, Robin, Ginger, Tommo. Who did I play with here?"

"Maybe you had an imaginary friend," Roo said. "Maybe you played with that plane."

Roo felt Niall stiffen behind her. Taylor didn't miss Niall's reaction either.

"I didn't have an imaginary friend," Taylor said. "And that's not my plane."

Roo sighed. "Yeah, you did and it is."

Taylor rolled over to look up at her. "What are you talking about?"

"Promise you won't be mad?" Roo asked.

Taylor rolled his eyes. Roo slid from under him and leaned over the edge of the bed. When she couldn't feel the book, she shuffled further so she could look underneath.

The book wasn't there.

"Roo, what the hell are you doing?" Taylor asked. "Not that I'm complaining." He slid his fingers under the shirt and onto her backside.

Roo slithered off the bed. She lay flat on her stomach and patted the boards. Maybe it was invisible. She let out a strangled laugh and sat up. *What the hell am I thinking?* But the book had been there a moment ago and now it wasn't. No holes in the floor. The guys hadn't moved. Where the hell had it gone?

"What are you looking for?" Taylor asked.

Roo's mind started to jump to impossible conclusions. She stared at Niall, not Taylor and said, "I found a book. Stephanie had written in it."

The look on Niall's face lasted only a moment, but it was shock, which meant he knew something. But then if Niall had hidden the book, why would he be shocked? Unless he was pretending to be surprised.

"Stephanie's book?" Taylor's voice was arctic cold. "Where is it?"

"It *was* under the bed. I put it there a moment ago."

Taylor dipped his head to look and then sat back on the bed. Roo stayed on the floor. He looked pissed.

"Where did you find it?" he asked.

"In her room. I was looking for something to read and it fell out of a slip cover for *Captured by Indians*."

"Was it a diary?" Taylor's fists were clenched in the covers.

"A story. It began something like, *Once upon a time, there was a boy who lived in a big house with a big garden. His name was Taylor. Taylor had a sister called Stephanie who was very beautiful even*

though she was only ten years old. She had long black hair and dark eyes."

"She wrote it when she was ten?" Taylor whispered. "What else did it say?"

"That years before, when she was five and you were nine, you lost your plane over the wall and went to get it. When you came back you said you were going to play with your new friend, but Stephanie couldn't see him so she thought you'd made him up. Then one day she *did* see a boy in the tree house. Well, not a boy as such." Roo glanced at Niall who stared at her without blinking. *Is he even breathing?* "When the boy realized Stephanie had seen him, he went over the wall and she decided to go and find him. The last words in the book were—*Wish me luck.*"

"Oh my God." Taylor swallowed hard. "How come we didn't find that? How come the police didn't find that? Who was the boy?"

"You don't remember?" Roo stood, picked up the plane and pushed it into Taylor's hands.

There was no mistaking the look of raw hope on Niall's face, and Roo began to tremble. Niall couldn't be that boy. Couldn't really be a faery. Just Stephanie's imagination. Except everything told Roo that Niall was Taylor's boyhood friend and he was more than a boy. Why had the attic looked empty to her and full to Taylor? Where had the book gone? And the biggest question of all—why didn't Niall tell Taylor who he was?

Niall took the plane from Taylor and, as their fingers touched, Taylor caught his breath.

Time seemed to hang. No one spoke while thoughts whirled. At least they did in Roo's head, random images and fragments of memory spinning in a centrifuge while she tried to grab them and turn them into sense. Or nonsense.

Niall's speed in the garden when he'd chased her.

The sandwich he'd made that had been exactly what she wanted.

His sudden appearance at her tent. Those voices.

The strangeness of his bedroom.

His silence now.

Roo gulped. And the very first time she'd seen him, she'd thought she'd seen wings. She raised her head and stared straight into Niall's eyes. His lips were pressed tight together, but there was a wistful expression on his face that made her stomach lurch.

Oh my God.

Taylor took the plane from Niall, unfastened the string and tossed both aside. "Maybe it was mine. I don't remember."

Roo heard the disappointment in Niall's exhalation. He needed Taylor to remember but he couldn't tell him? Was that what was wrong?

"I need to see this book of Stephanie's," Taylor said. "You obviously didn't put it under the bed, so where is it?"

"I don't know," Roo said.

"Well, bloody think where you put it," Taylor snapped. "There could be a clue in there, something to tell us where she might have gone."

Roo swallowed hard. "She went over the wall."

"I already told you, we checked. The police went through those woods on their hands and knees. They found nothing."

Roo chewed her lip, but she had no choice. "She went into Faeryland."

She risked a glance at Niall. He was staring at Taylor.

Taylor scowled. "This isn't a fucking joke, Roo. Some bastard likely raped and murdered my ten-year-old sister. That boy could be the clue."

"I'm not joking," she whispered. "I know it sounds crazy, but you have to believe."

"What planet are you on? Faeries at the bottom of the garden?" Taylor gave a snort of annoyance.

"Let me show you something," Roo said.

"What?"

"In the garden. Maybe you'll remember then. Bring the plane." She walked to the door. "Please."

"Niall? You coming?" Taylor asked.

But when Niall tried to stand, it was obvious he wasn't up to walking that far. "I'll stay here."

Taylor turned at the door. "Don't think I've forgotten I want answers from you. If what happened in the shower was some mental thing because of the people or person you're hiding from, I can help. If it's medical, I'm taking you to the hospital whether you like it or not."

"Wow, Taylor. You almost sounded as if you cared," Roo said.

"You're both pissing me off, so don't push it," he snapped.

Taylor quickly dressed and followed Roo down the stairs and out of the back door, the plane clutched in his hand. If it hadn't been for the sudden chill of the morning air, he might have tried to convince himself he was still asleep. The sex between the three of them had been fantastic, but since Niall had freaked them out, the world had gone crazy.

Roo headed toward the door leading to the walled garden, Taylor on her heels. He liked that she was a bit weird, but believing there were faeries at the bottom of the garden? No, that was a step too far. He could just see himself telling the police. Pitying looks and a suggestion he visit a shrink.

Taylor followed her through the door in the wall and stiffened as he took in the garden beyond. "What the hell?"

"Oh my God," Roo whispered.

It looked as though someone had run amuck with a scythe. Hardly a plant remained standing. Flowers and vegetables had been tossed everywhere. Taylor was rigid with fury.

Roo gasped. "Who'd do something like this?"

"It had to have been done overnight. It was fine yesterday evening." Taylor bent to pick up a decapitated flower and then dropped it. "Bastards." He exhaled. "Right. I need the truth out of him now. Looks as though whoever is after Niall has found him."

Taylor turned to go back to the house and Roo caught his arm. "Please. Let me show you the wall."

"What about the damned wall?"

"I can't remember."

"Look, this has gone far enough," Taylor snapped. "We need to talk to Niall."

Roo tugged him forward. "I was on the wall and I nearly fell. Well, I did fall and Niall caught me, but I saw something. I just can't remember what."

She gave up on tugging him and ran to the bottom of the garden. By the time Taylor climbed into the tree house, Roo was already on the wall and wobbling. His heart lurched into his mouth.

"Be careful," he called.

Roo made her way along the stones with her arms spread like a

tightrope walker. Taylor was torn between following her or going back down the ladder and getting ready to catch her. Still, she might fall on the other side and then he'd be no use at all. He looked down onto the other side. Shrubs and forest. A boring sort of Faeryland. He tossed the plane into the air and watched as it hit a tree and tumbled to the ground.

A spike of pain in his head made Taylor tremble and he grabbed at the tree house roof.

"It's here," Roo said.

I did throw a plane over this wall. Not just now, before. He gulped.

Taylor made his way to her side. Something had been carved into the stone. Letters entwined. He crouched and ran his finger down the grooves. NT. The marks weren't new. Had he made them? He didn't remember doing it, yet his heart pounded as though it was trying to tell him something. Roo stared at him as if she expected some massive recognition.

"T for Taylor," she said.

N for Niall?

As if a wave washed over him, memories flooded back and Taylor sat before he fell. Niall had been his boyhood friend. A friend who'd vanished at the same time as his sister. Not a bloody faery, well, not the supernatural sort, but maybe a bloody murderer. *I'll fucking kill him.*

"Taylor," Roo said.

He wanted answers—now. He stood and made his way back along the wall, climbed into the tree house, down the ladder and ran across the lawn.

"Taylor," Roo shouted.

He turned to glare at her. "Are you in on this? What the hell are the pair of you doing? Trying to fuck up my head with lies?"

He stalked toward the house.

Roo scrambled to her feet. She had *not* liked that look on Taylor's face. Roo thought he'd be happy to remember. She needed to get after him fast and stop him from doing something stupid. As she took one small step, a stone gave way under her toes and she fell.

A shriek burst from her lips as she nosedived to the ground on the wrong side of the wall. Roo collapsed in a heap with a long groan.

She lay facedown, eyes closed and didn't move. Gradually, the pain from the impact faded, didn't return when she wriggled her fingers and toes, and Roo sighed with relief. When she opened her eyes, the sigh died on her lips.

She lay on soft, lush grass in bright sunlight. Which was wrong. There should be forest on this side. She rolled onto her back. The sun was high in the sky and it was warm. Had she been knocked unconscious? Lain there until lunchtime? She didn't think she'd banged her head.

Roo pushed herself into a sitting position. She was next to a tree in the middle of a grassy plain with a hill in the distance. No forest anywhere near and no wall in sight. *Am I dead?* It didn't look much like heaven, but at least there were no everlasting fires or pits of tar or little red men with horns and pitchforks. And if it was heaven, where was the welcome committee with tea and scones? In Roo's heaven there were always warm scones, strawberry jam and clotted cream. If you couldn't have what you most longed for in heaven, what was the point in believing in it?

So unconscious and dreaming?

Maybe.

Her stomach rumbled. That didn't seem like something she'd dream.

There was only one other explanation, and no matter how hard Roo tried to back away from it, it kept surging into her head.

I'm in Faeryland.

Niall really does have wings.

Shit. Shit. Shit.

She rose to her feet and bent to brush her knees, pulling down Niall's crumpled and dirty shirt. Roo felt a waft of wind blow over her bare butt and groaned. Why hadn't she put panties on? After taking a couple of steps to test she could walk without falling over, Roo realized her mistake. She spun round and looked for the crushed grass at the foot of the tree where she'd landed, bit back a sob when she saw it and stepped back. If she landed here, the way back was from here. Roo spread out her arms and turned in a circle, feeling for the wall.

It wasn't there.

Panic bubbled in her throat as fear tightened its hold, and her heart thumped faster. She yanked a white button from the top of Niall's shirt, placed it on the grass in the middle of where she'd fallen,

checked she could easily see it and began to explore.

There was no wall. It wasn't invisible. It wasn't there. Roo groaned. She supposed it made a strange sort of sense. Invisible walls in the middle of fields were death traps. *Don't think about death traps.* Roo looked at the gnarled tree on her left but had no way to climb it, particularly without shoes. The nearest branch was out of reach. Would Niall realize what had happened and look for her? But maybe he couldn't come back. Maybe this was what he was running from.

She didn't know what to do. Stay where she was and hope Niall came? Scream and run round in a circle? Or head out to try and find someone who could show her how to get back, hoping she met a kind faerie and not some flesh-eating monster?

Roo looked over her shoulder just in case. Instinct told her to stay where she was, that it was her best chance of rescue. She'd watched the documentaries on the TV, and they always said—stay with your car, stay at the first spot someone would look for you. But the emergency services weren't rushing to her rescue, Taylor didn't know about this place, and Roo suspected Niall couldn't come back.

She began to walk toward the hill.

The farther she moved from the tree, walking through the ankle-deep grass, the more worried she became. What if she couldn't find it again? It might be the only tree standing on its own here, but once she crested the brow of this hill, there might be a plain dotted with isolated trees. Roo sighed and kept going. *"If you could kick the person in the pants who's responsible for most of your trouble, you wouldn't sit for a month."* Roosevelt's words made her smile. It was her own fault she was stuck here, so up to her to get herself out again.

So what should she say when she met someone? Tell them she knew Niall or not? Might not be an issue. This place was like a huge deserted oasis.

Ah, maybe not. As Roo reached the top of the slope, she dropped down into the grass, lay on her belly and stared at the scene below. She might as well have wandered onto a movie set. A mile or so ahead of her was a high stone wall and behind it a city with red-roofed houses. A large castle topped a central mound. Beyond that was a huge body of water.

Roo didn't hear anyone come up behind her but she felt a draft of air on her backside when something lifted the shirt. Her heart stuttered as she rolled over and then sat up to face three guys in their thirties holding spears, three horses behind them. *Not good, not good,*

not good. She hadn't heard a thing. Roo clenched her fists to stop her fingers shaking.

The nearest man, who had silver hair to his shoulders, and only one arm, brought his spear to her throat. "What are you doing in the hinterland?"

"I fell in by accident. If you could just show me the way out, I'd be very grateful."

A black-haired guy smiled. He had teeth like her dentist. Much too white and even. "There is no way out."

Roo bristled. She pushed the spear aside with her fingers and stood. "Of course there is. If there's a way in, then there's a way out."

"Only if we want to let you go," said the third guy who was shorter than the other two.

She couldn't outrun horses. "I'm a lot of trouble," Roo said.

All three of them laughed.

Taylor slammed back into the house and raced up the stairs. When he flung open the bedroom door, Niall wasn't there. Nor in the bathroom.

"Niall!"

Taylor didn't wait for a reply. He ran up to the attic, glanced inside and blinked. Must be dust in the air or something, because everything seemed to shimmer for a moment. There was no sign of Niall so he went back to the ground floor.

He found him in the orangery, lying on the couch in his jeans. Bare chest, no shoes and the jeans weren't fastened.

Taylor slapped back a surge of lust. "I remember."

Niall turned to him and smiled, but the smile faded as he stared at Taylor.

Taylor clenched his fists at his sides. "I remember that you were my friend, and when Stephanie disappeared, you did too. Did you hurt her?"

Niall pushed himself to a sitting position, his face grave. "No."

"Do you know what happened to her?"

"Yes," he said in a resigned voice.

Taylor couldn't help himself. He flew at Niall, knocked the couch

over and rained punches on him.

"You bastard," Taylor yelled. "What the hell do you think you're doing, worming your way into my parents' lives, into my life, into my bed? Why the fuck didn't you come forward at the time and tell me or the police what had happened?"

Taylor registered his hands were around Niall's throat, choking him, that Niall wasn't fighting back, and he let him go. Blood trickled down Niall's face from a cut at his temple. He looked...gray. *Shit.*

"What happened to my sister?" Taylor snapped.

"She followed me over the wall."

"Did she hit her head? Is that how she died? It was an accident? Why didn't you tell someone? Jesus Christ, Niall."

"She isn't dead."

Taylor slumped onto his backside in shock. "What?"

"Stephanie's in Faery...land." Niall gave a gasp of pain.

Hope evaporated and Taylor groaned. "Niall, you're crazy. Is that why you're hiding out here? You escaped from a mental hospital?" Taylor's mind jumped from one thought to another. "You killed my sister and your family took you away."

"No," Niall said, panting. "Well, no and yes. I didn't kill Stephanie, but my family did take me away. They stopped me coming over the wall by threatening to kill her."

Oh God. The guy's delusional. Taylor thought his heart was going to explode in fury, sadness and confusion. Last night, everything had been perfect. Now he was in the middle of a nightmare. And where the fuck was Roo? Why hadn't she come back to the house?

"What do you remember?" Niall asked.

Taylor swallowed hard. Remembering Niall had brought back memories of the time Stephanie disappeared. Not that he'd forgotten any of it, but it all seemed clearer, closer, more painful.

"You climbed into the garden over the wall," Taylor said.

Niall frowned. "Before that."

Taylor shook his head, trying to sort out his thoughts. "My plane went over, I got it and brought it back. You came too."

Niall pushed himself to a sitting position and wiped the blood from his mouth. "And?"

"And what? You came over. We hung out. You said you lived locally but you were home-schooled. We played in the evenings and at

weekends. You were my best friend." *Christ, a best friend who killed my sister?* Niall seemed completely sane and utterly insane at the same time, and Taylor's heart verged on collapse.

"Did you introduce me to your parents?" Niall asked.

Taylor frowned. "You...wouldn't let me. You said you'd be in trouble if your mother found out you'd come into the garden."

"Did Stephanie see me?"

"Course she did, she must have, but she always claimed you weren't there. She was just jealous."

Niall's shoulders sank. "Did you tell the police about me?"

Taylor faltered. "I-I must have done. I don't remember. I'll tell them now. You need to speak to them." He ran his fingers through his hair. "Christ, Niall. Why did you come back? You'd have got away with it, but you—"

Niall bristled. "I didn't lay a finger on your sister. She's not dead, but it's my fault she was taken, my fault you don't remember." Niall looked around. "Where's Roo?"

"She showed me the mark on the wall. The entwined NT. I remembered then."

Niall's eyes widened. "She didn't come back with you? We need to find her."

"How is she involved in this? Did you know her before she came for the interview?"

Niall shook his head. "I'd never seen her before and she's not involved. *Wasn't* involved. We need to look for her."

"You have to tell me everything," Taylor said. "Does your family have Stephanie? Whereabouts in the country is she being held? Does she remember me?"

"She's in Faery...land." Niall gritted his teeth and cried out as his body spasmed.

Taylor groaned. "If you care anything for me, tell the truth."

Niall started to shake. "It is the truth."

His back arched and Niall groaned. The beads of sweat and the agony on his face told Taylor he wasn't pretending. Fury and worry competed in Taylor's gut and worry won. Niall was sick, both in body and mind. Taylor had no idea how he'd come up with the fantasy of Stephanie being in Faeryland, but the physical issues he had were real. And what was it with this room? The vegetation smelled wrong. It

didn't seem a healthy place to be.

Taylor reached out and stroked Niall's face. "What can I do? Is there something you need?"

Niall stared into his eyes. "I'm dying."

Chapter Twenty-One

Taylor pulled his hand away from Niall's face. The scorn in his expression made Niall flinch.

"Dying?" Taylor snapped. "Another lie to make me feel sorry for you?"

"It's not a lie."

As Taylor stared at him, disappointment deadened every one of Niall's senses, even his pain receptors, which should have been a blessing but wasn't because he deserved to hurt. What the hell had he thought would happen when Taylor remembered? That everything would suddenly be bright and beautiful? Well, yes, that's exactly what he'd hoped, that Taylor would remember him, realize he loved him and they'd live happily ever after.

"Niall, mate, you need help," Taylor said, his voice quieter.

"Yes." He did, but not the sort of help Taylor had in mind.

Niall had been under the mistaken belief that deep down Taylor must have known Faeryland lay the other side of the wall, and with the right memories triggered, everything would become clear as if he'd emerged from a fog. After all, Taylor had been over the wall and found his plane not in the forest he could see from his side, but in a sea of grass, so surely Taylor had realized Niall came from another world.

The answer was no, he hadn't. He'd believed Niall's lies about home schooling and living like a gypsy, he'd not wondered why Niall never invited him to his house, he'd not wondered anything. It was amazing the guy had ended up as a private investigator.

"Christ, what a mess." Taylor slumped and put his head in his hands.

Now Taylor not only thought Niall was crazy, but that he'd killed Stephanie, and pretty soon Taylor would call the police and that'd be the last time Niall would see him. Death held Niall in its claws. Until now, he'd kept to the agreement with his mother and stayed silent, knowing that with a few words he could so easily forfeit his right to live on this side, but Roo had spoken out, talked about Faeryland and Niall

assumed that would allow him to speak too. The pain told him he was mistaken.

The orangery could sustain him no longer. The plants were dying, the smell of decay grew stronger. The tattoo had tightened its strangling hold and now Niall walked toward death knowing Taylor didn't love him. How could he? Why should he? Niall clenched his jaw. Roo's love wouldn't save him, but he wished she was here.

"Where's Roo?" he asked.

Taylor lifted his head from his hands. Dark shadows bloomed under his eyes and Niall's heart ached that he'd caused more pain to the man he loved.

"Did you watch her get down from the wall?" Niall asked. She'd fallen before. She might again. His heart beat faster. "Taylor? Go and see if Roo's okay."

"Only if you come with me."

It hurt not to be trusted, but Niall knew he deserved it. He pushed himself up on shaky legs, pain skittering down his spine, and forced himself to follow Taylor outside. Niall pulled up short when he saw the devastation in the walled garden.

"Fuck," Niall muttered.

"Looks like your past's catching up with you," Taylor said.

It didn't need to catch up. It was always here. The destruction was borne of anger and a reminder of time running out.

"There's no sign of Roo," Taylor said.

There was no place to hide inside the garden.

"Check the other side of the wall," Niall said, his pulse racing. He stumbled to lean against the tree.

Taylor climbed the ladder of the tree house, hopped onto the wall and looked down. "She's not there. She must be in the house."

Niall really wanted her to be in the house, but by the time he'd staggered after Taylor through every room, and returned to Taylor's bedroom, it was clear Roo was nowhere to be found.

"Has she run now that the gig's up?" Taylor spat. "Left you to face the music on your own?"

"All her things are still in that bedroom," Niall pointed out. "And there's no plot here. I'd never seen her before she came for the interview."

"So where is she?" Taylor asked and Niall was grateful the guy at

least looked concerned.

Taylor's face hardened. "I'm taking you to the police."

"If you do, I'll be dead before the end of the day."

"More dramatics?"

"If I leave Sutton Hall, I'll die."

Taylor snorted.

Niall sagged with disappointment that Taylor didn't believe him. It wasn't going to happen anyway, not the taking to the police. Niall was weak, but this close to Faeryland he was not without power, only heart sick and struggling with a tattoo that burned as if phosphorus licked his body.

Taylor picked up his phone and a few minutes later, it was done. Niall had sat on the bed and listened to Taylor report he had a man in his house who knew something about the disappearance of his sister sixteen years ago, and in addition, another woman appeared to have gone missing.

Niall's choices were few now and he didn't want anything to remain hidden between him and Taylor. He watched Taylor get dressed, aware that was the last time he'd see him unclothed. Painful as that was, Niall braced himself for further hurt and said the words he'd held in his heart for so long, "I love you."

Taylor's face showed nothing but derision. "Yeah right. Great timing, you sick fuck."

Niall gritted his teeth. "When my mother discovered I'd been coming over the wall to play with you, she told me to stop. I didn't. She beat me. She...found other ways to punish me. I still came. Then one day, Stephanie saw me, caught sight of my wings."

Taylor snorted and headed out of the room. Niall followed.

"My carelessness cost everyone dear. Stephanie came over the wall to look for me and she was found. Her return was then impossible. My mother made me come back one more time. She wanted me to see you and your family drowning in despair, suffocating in sorrow and know that it was my fault. My selfishness in wanting to keep playing with you, my carelessness in letting myself be seen by another mortal."

"You making this up as you go along?" Taylor barked as he walked downstairs.

Niall took a deep breath, fighting against the pain that was now so fierce his vision wavered. "It's rare for any mortal to enter the faery

realm. Those who do are usually killed. My mother wanted me to see the consequences of my actions. You sat next to me and cried and said you'd give anything for Stephanie to be alive. I went home and pleaded with my mother for your sister to be returned with her memory wiped, so she'd remember nothing of Faeryland or me."

Taylor turned to stare at him, but Niall knew he didn't believe him. Taylor walked into the drawing room and dropped onto a couch. Niall sat opposite.

"My mother said she'd spare Stephanie for a price, but the girl had to stay in Faeryland. The price was yours and mine to give, willingly or not." Niall's spine felt as though it was cracking. "My mother removed your capacity to accept love. Your life was to be one where no relationship lasted."

Taylor raised his eyebrows and sprawled like a starfish, spreading his arms. "Maybe my relationships don't last because I haven't yet found the right person. I work a job that shows me the so-called value of love, how people lie and cheat on those they'd promised to love forever."

"We've had this discussion before. You're blind to the other side of the coin and it's my fault. I thought I could teach you to love again, not just another person but to love life. We were happy here."

Niall saw Taylor swallow hard and a spark of hope struggled to gain strength in Niall's weakening heart.

"And what did your mother want from you?" Taylor asked, though Niall knew he still didn't believe.

"My love for you couldn't be revealed until you loved me. If I kissed you first, I'd suffer intense pain and the time I could spend here would be adversely affected. If I told the truth, if I mentioned Faeryland, the deal I'd brokered would end and I'd die. I thought I had a year, but turns out that's not true. The destruction of the garden is a final message from my mother. My time has run out."

Taylor leaned forward, resting his arms on his knees. "If they gave you a year or six months or whatever, they know you're here, so why are you hiding? See how lies come back and bite you?"

"I'm not hiding from faeries. I'm hiding from other supernaturals who'd like to get their hands on a faery. There's a werewolf pack not far from here, and vamps love faery blood."

Taylor snorted.

Niall's cheek twitched. "I had to give up some of my power in order

to live on this side. The orangery keeps me safe. *Did* keep me safe, but it's dying because I'm dying. That and the garden are my lifeblood, my links to Faeryland. When I went with you to Leeds, you remember I was ill? The pub in Ilkley? I can't stray far from this place without consequence."

Taylor leaned back again. "If you're a faery, prove it. Show me your wings."

The atmosphere between them set like cement.

Niall gave him a sad smile. "If my words aren't enough, what's the point in actions? I wanted to win you with love not magic." Though he suspected he was now too weak to make his wings come out this side of the wall. In this instance, better not to try than try and fail.

"Stop this, Niall. You're talking nonsense."

Niall trembled with the effort of keeping the pain at bay. "Call Jonas. Ask him to come here and tell you the truth. Watch his face and say the word moon-gold."

The doorbell rang.

"That will be the police," Taylor said. "Stay there. Try telling them the truth instead of a fairy story."

Taylor walked out of his life and Niall's heart shattered.

Dan bloody Newlyn. Of course it was, Taylor thought as he opened the door.

"Taylor." Newlyn nodded and gestured at the short guy next to him. "DC Whitby."

"Come in." Taylor led them to the drawing room.

Niall had gone.

"Oh shit," Taylor muttered. He turned and pushed past the two policemen as he ran back into the hall. "Niall!"

There was no answer. Taylor couldn't figure out how Niall had gotten past without him seeing, but no point dwelling on that.

"Who's Niall?" Newlyn asked.

"The guy I suspect was involved in the abduction of my sister. I was talking to him a minute ago. My parents employed him to look after the garden. He's been living here for close to seven months."

Newlyn pointed to the back door and the other detective hurried

toward it.

"Description?" Newlyn asked.

"My height and build. Blond hair, green eyes. Jeans, no shirt, barefoot. Tattoo from his neck to his ankle, diagonally crossing his back. Like some sort of barbed vine. He's—he's not well."

"And the girl who's just gone missing?" Newlyn asked as he began to search the downstairs rooms, Taylor on his heels.

"Roo Smith. You saw her with me. Five nine, slender, short dark hair. Mid- to late-twenties. Last time I saw her she was only wearing a guy's shirt. Niall's shirt."

Newlyn turned and looked at him and then gestured toward the stairs.

"Yes, look anywhere, everywhere."

When Newlyn took his time looking around Taylor's bedroom, Taylor regretted not tidying first. Condom wrappers and lube told their own story. The raised eyebrows when Newlyn opened the door on Roo's suitcase and makeshift bed made Taylor cringe.

"You sleeping with her?" Newlyn asked.

"Yes."

"Both of you?"

Oh shit. "Yes."

Newlyn came back out onto the landing. "Another floor?"

"Niall's room. The stairs are there."

"So what happened? Fall out over her?" Newlyn asked as he walked up.

"No. We...share." *Oh God, don't go there.* "Niall told me he was here when my sister went missing. I must have blanked it from my mind. I didn't remember, but I do now. We were friends. After Stephanie disappeared, he did too."

Newlyn pushed open the door to the attic room. All that was in there was a pile of blankets and a blue cushion. Taylor rubbed his eyes but it made no difference. *What the fuck?*

"I'm surprised you have any guests let alone lovers if you make them sleep on the floor." Newlyn smirked. "If he's been here seven months, where are his things?"

"I don't know," Taylor whispered.

He staggered and hit the wall. This was impossible.

"You sure this guy exists? I had a quick look at the file before we came out. There was no mention of a boy disappearing at the time."

Taylor's knees gave way and he slipped to the floor. He felt like he'd been sucker-punched by a wrecking ball. Breathing was as much as he could manage. Newlyn knelt beside him.

"You okay, Taylor? Need a doctor?"

"No, I— Where's Roo? She was here. She was in the garden."

Newlyn patted him on the shoulder. "Maybe this got too much for her and she split."

"Without her stuff?" *With Niall?*

Newlyn shrugged. "She'll come back for it. If I didn't know you better, I'd worry you might have done something to her. If she's not been in touch by Monday, I'll open a file."

"What if Niall's hurt her?" Only Niall wouldn't hurt her. He wouldn't have hurt Stephanie. Taylor thought his head was going to explode.

"Like I said, let's wait until Monday. And I think you need medical help."

Newlyn made his way downstairs and Taylor spotted the other cop shake his head.

In the hall, Newlyn turned to Taylor. "Make an appointment to see a doctor and get some sleep. You look terrible."

The door opened and Jonas walked in.

Taylor sighed. "They think I'm making Niall up."

"Who's Niall?" Jonas asked.

Roo stared at the horse and the horse stared back.

"Get on," said the silver-haired faery with one arm. She'd heard the others call him Oisin.

The other two were already mounted.

"I'm not dressed for riding," Roo muttered, wondering if she had any other options.

She shrieked as she suddenly found herself wearing umpteen petticoats, a thick skirt, matching jacket and a top hat.

"Stop it, Ardal," Oisin snapped.

"Too hot," Roo gasped as more layers were added.

"Tell me when to stop," said Ardal, the dark-haired one.

Stop what? But one by one her clothes began to disappear. Roo shouted, "Stop," but the corset and pantaloons vanished and she stood there naked. She was too annoyed to be embarrassed.

"Oh very clever. Can you pull coins out of your ears and a rabbit from up your arse as well?" she snapped.

Oisin laughed.

"Don't make fun of magic," her tormentor snapped back and glared at Oisin.

"Why not? You're making fun of me. I bet you have to add a couple of inches to your dick before you strip off."

He shifted his horse to her side and his hand shot out to grip her around the throat. "Want me to give you a dick of your own?" he snarled.

"Ardal, let her go," Oisin said.

Roo pulled at the man's fingers as he squeezed. Her big mouth was going to get her killed. Her vision wavered.

"Ardal!" Oisin shouted.

As his grip relaxed, Roo found herself wearing a butt-ugly shapeless brown sack of a dress that might have passed for high fashion at the time of the Vikings. He released her and she rubbed her throat. *Don't say anything else to upset him.*

"Get on my horse," Oisin said.

Roo glared at Ardal. "No jewelry?"

So many beaded necklaces appeared around her neck that she almost collapsed under the weight, but it gave her an idea. *Thank you, God.* Roo climbed onto the horse and positioned herself behind Oisin. As they set off down the hill, following the other two, Roo broke a necklace and began to drop beads. She'd read a sexy story about a cowboy and an English dude where the latter had dropped beads and it had saved his life. It might save hers.

"Did Niall send you over here?" Oisin asked in a whisper. "Does he need help?"

Was she supposed to trust this guy? He'd behaved better than the other two, but until Roo knew for certain who was friend and who was enemy, she had to be careful.

"I told you, I fell. It was an accident. If you'd just take me back to

the hole or whatever it is and push me through, I'd be grateful."

"I can't," he said.

Damn.

"You don't seem disturbed by where you find yourself." He turned in the saddle to look at her and Roo's fingers froze around the beads. "You think you're dreaming? Going to wake up soon?"

"No. I can smell you. I don't smell things in dreams." *Careful.* "You don't smell bad. I didn't mean that. It's just that I know how things are in dreams. This isn't a dream. And what's the point freaking out? I can't run away. Well, I could but you'd chase me down and I'd be back where I started and you'd be pissed off. So I figure I might as well cooperate for the time being." She might not be running, but her mouth was. Roo's nerves had taken charge of her tongue. "It's quite pretty here. Soft grass, blue sky. Is that water the sea or a big lake? How can there be another world like this? Is it part of the Earth or—"

Oisin sighed. "Do you ever shut up?"

"Sorry. I don't get why the sun is so high. It's midmorning not noon. I—"

"Stop talking."

"Stop talking at all or stop talking about the weather? Because the weather's such a safe topic of—"

"Not another damn word," Oisin barked, but she heard him laugh.

Roo glanced over her shoulder and her eyes opened wide. Something galloped soundlessly through the grass toward them. It looked like a cross between a tiger and a velociraptor. *Ooh, that's a lot of teeth. Oooooh, more than one of the things.*

"Oisin," she muttered, fear slithering down her spine while she gripped harder at his shirt.

"What did I say? Shut up."

"One question. Are there things to avoid in the hinterland?"

"Yes. Me when I'm angry." He turned in the saddle and gasped. "Shhhiiit. Ardal, Eoin, four stabilos behind."

Roo clung on as he urged the horse into a gallop. *Don't look back.* Roo couldn't help it. The creatures were gaining on them, the one in the lead no more than twenty yards away. Why the hell had she sat *behind* Oisin? She was the one they were going to grab first. Roo peeped over her shoulder again. The stabilo sort of lollopped along baring its teeth in a strange sort of smile. If Roo hadn't been staring at

one, she wouldn't have believed her eyes. Between the orange stripes on its back were small, sharp-looking spikes. The claws on its feet were like eagle's talons. The whole thing was lethal.

"Go faster," she shouted in Oisin's ear.

The lead stabilo lunged left.

"Right," she yelled.

Oisin swung right and the creature missed them. Her heart pounded so hard she could hear it in her head. Roo pulled at the beads around her neck and gathered them in her hand. When the lead stabilo attacked, she flung the necklaces. They wrapped around his feet and he fell.

"Woohoo," Roo yelled.

"Duck," Oisin said.

"Where?"

Even as Roo thought it was an odd time to be telling her about a fairly ordinary bird, she flew off the horse to land on the ground, pinned by one of the creatures. Adrenaline surged and Roo struggled to get free. It opened its mouth and roared. *Shit, a great white shark with halitosis.* Roo shot from severe panic to catastrophic organ failure in the blink of the stabilo's indigo eye. Its jaw opened wider, its head dropped and Roo brought up her knee hard into its balls. *Thank God it was male.* Its shriek was so high pitched it made her ears ring.

The stabilo rolled off to one side and a hand reached down to wrench her up and back onto the saddle. Roo wrapped her arms around Oisin and hung on. For a guy with only one arm, he'd handled all that quite impressively.

When she risked a peek back, the creatures had gone. A glance forward showed her they were almost at the city walls. The horses slowed to a walk and Ardal and Eoin pulled round to ride at Oisin's side.

"I said duck," Oisin said.

"I thought you meant a flying one."

They all laughed.

"You did well for a mortal," Ardal said.

Oisin slipped from the saddle and held out his hand to help her down. Roo dismounted the other side. Her brown sack changed to a shimmering, short blue dress. Ardal fluttered his tongue and stroked her bum.

Uh-oh.

Taylor waited until the two detectives had driven away before he slammed the door and turned on Jonas.

"Why the fuck did you say you didn't know Niall? You made me look a complete and utter wanker."

"What's happened?"

Taylor strode to the office. "Niall's gone crazy and Roo's just...gone."

"Crazy in what way?" Jonas asked.

Taylor slumped behind his desk. "I remembered him from when I was a kid. We played together in the garden. He disappeared at the same time as Stephanie. I think..." He swallowed hard. "Oh fuck, I don't know what I think. I sort of accused him of killing her. He told me he was a faery. He said he was dying." Taylor put his head in his hands.

"What about Roo?" Jonas asked.

Taylor laughed. "No reaction to what Niall told me? And you still haven't explained why you said that to the police."

"I'm always careful what I say to the police until I know all the facts. Where are Roo and Niall?"

"No idea. Roo was with me in the garden and now she's not anywhere. Niall was in the drawing room and he's vanished. Maybe the two of them are working together."

"To do what?"

"Drive me crazy? I'm halfway there." Taylor raised his head and looked straight at Jonas. "Niall said to say something to you and watch your reaction. You're supposed to be my partner, Jonas."

"I work part-time for you, I'm not your partner."

Taylor sighed.

"What did Niall tell you to say?"

"Moon-gold."

Jonas's eyes widened and he let out a deep sigh. He leaned his butt on Roo's desk and his mouth tilted in a half smile. "Niall's a faery."

Taylor let his head bang on the desk. Then he looked up at Jonas.

"Yeah, and I'm a fucking werewolf."

"No, that would be me," Jonas said.

"Not funny."

Jonas laughed. "How long have you known me?"

"You know how long. We met at university twelve years ago."

"I've been working for Niall for twelve years."

Taylor's jaw dropped. "Doing what?"

"Keeping an eye on you."

Taylor's mouth lost all moisture. "How did you meet him?"

"That's not something you need to know. He paid me in moon-gold to keep you safe. Lucky for him I was happy to work as a private investigator. Remember those times when you were in trouble and I turned up unexpectedly? The Greene case. Mrs. Jenkins and her lunatic husband. There were other occasions when I saved your ass and you knew nothing about it. Les Thompson—hospitalized. Dave Teague—confessed to the police. Chris Robbins—broke both legs."

Taylor could feel his jaw twitching.

"Whose idea was it to come to Leeds?" Jonas asked.

"Mine."

"Was it?"

Taylor's head ached so much he could hardly think, but now Jonas had said that, he recalled moaning about London and Jonas bringing up the subject of Yorkshire, saying he'd go with him. Taylor's shoulders slumped. So Jonas and Niall had plotted together to get him here?

"I'm worried about Roo," Jonas said.

"Didn't she turn up to your rendezvous?" Taylor snapped.

Jonas glared. "Roo isn't part of what's going on here."

"Yeah, right."

"Why would I lie about that?"

If Roo wasn't part of whatever the fuck this conspiracy was, then where was she? Had she pissed off anyone enough to make them come after her? Apart from him? Did the destruction of the garden have something to do with her?

Think. Think. Who'd want her shut up?

Patrick Farrant and his wife, the dog-napper. One or both of

them. Had Roo done more than she'd confessed to?

Kim and Christopher Singer. The wife-beater. Not such a leap for him to hurt Roo, especially if his wife had run to the refuge. And Roo had told him the guy had come back while she was at the house.

Annette Foster. When her husband confronted her, she'd realize she'd been set up in Pussycats. Would she want to get even with Roo?

They had motives, but how would they know where Roo lived?

"Finished thinking things through?" Jonas asked. "Made sense of any of it?"

"No." Taylor looked up and did a double take. Jonas had taken off his leather jacket and was unbuttoning his shirt. "What the hell are you doing?"

"Proving a point."

Christ, he's ripped. Taylor gulped. He wasn't Niall though, and the pain of betrayal clamped around Taylor's heart like an iron fist.

Jonas took off his boots and unfastened his pants.

"I'm not interested," Taylor blurted. "And you're not gay or bi." He didn't think.

The leather pants landed on top of the jacket and Jonas peeled down his boxers.

Wow, long cock. Only I'm not looking.

"I'm trisexual. I'll try anything once. Even you, but that's not why I've stripped. Are you watching? I'll never do this in front of you again. If anyone discovers I've done it, even once, I'll likely be killed. So pay attention and prepare to be blown away—in the nicest possible way."

Jonas's body contorted, arms and legs shortening, his face elongating as he fell to all fours. Taylor pushed himself up and stared down in shocked disbelief as the transformation completed and a wolf stood where Jonas had been. *Can't breathe, can't breathe.* Taylor worried his brain was going to explode. This could not be happening.

Told you I was a werewolf.

Taylor sucked air. "Jesus Christ."

A large black wolf sat between him and the door.

"Jonas?"

Who the fuck do you think it is?

"You're talking in my head?"

I don't have the vocal chords to make myself understood. I'm going

to see if I can track Roo.

"What about Niall?"

I can already guess where he's gone. Back to Faeryland.

The wolf bounded out and Taylor slumped back in his seat, his legs refusing to support him. He felt as if the Earth had tilted and he'd slid onto another planet. What else was real? Vampires? Father Christmas? Martians?

Chapter Twenty-Two

Everyone stared at Roo as Oisin, Ardal and Eoin led her through the town on foot. She kept her head high. She'd walked through the streets of Leeds dressed as a chicken, she could cope with this. People came out of shops and houses to watch, their faces curious rather than hostile. In one way, it was as if Roo had stepped back in time into an old-fashioned world of crooked buildings and cobblestone streets, and yet everyone wore modern clothes. And they were all beautiful. Shining hair, perfect teeth, tall and short, but no one too thin or too fat.

Roo hadn't noticed children until a little girl ran from a doorway and tripped right in front of her. Roo caught her before she hit the ground and set her on her feet. Ardal reached out and knocked Roo's hands away.

"Don't touch her," he snapped. "You have no right."

Roo bristled. "It isn't as if I want to be here. You're the ones who hauled me away from the way to get back."

"Shut up," Oisin said.

"No I won't shut up."

Ardal dragged her up the road while she struggled to get out of his grasp.

"I should have let her fall on her face, should I? How would that have been the right thing to do?" She dropped her voice. "You fuckwit. I should have kicked you in the nuts instead of that stabilo. In fact, I'd rather take my chances with them." Roo yanked free, turned and walked back the way they'd come.

The next moment, Ardal slung her over his shoulder and carried her toward the castle. When Roo beat at his back, he slid his hand under the dress onto her bare backside.

"You stop or I won't," he snapped.

Roo lay still and he took his hand away.

When he put her down, they were inside the castle, but they could

just as easily have been in some modern hotel. No brick walls or suits of armor or displays of weapons, instead smooth white walls, marble floors and flowers everywhere.

"I'll see you two later," Oisin said, and Ardal and Eoin peeled away.

Oisin pushed her down the corridor and into a large room. Ahead of her were open windows with views onto a sundrenched sea. Roo tried not to think how this could be possible. It just was and she might as well accept it.

"Mother," Oisin said and Roo turned.

Several men and women lounged on cream-colored leather couches placed on either side of a platform holding an ornate throne made of silver leaves and flowers. Roo dragged her gaze from the amazing chair to the woman with long golden hair who sat on it. She wore a floaty white dress that brushed her ankles, and looked too young to be Oisin's mother.

A shove in the middle of Roo's back sent her tumbling to her knees.

"Show respect to our queen," Oisin said. "You've shown none so far in trespassing in her territory."

Roo pushed herself to her feet, only to be knocked down again. She gasped as she jarred her hands and knees on the hard marble floor. Instead of feeling scared, Roo was angry. She was quite capable of showing respect, but she'd not been given chance to do so. She swiveled round and launched herself at Oisin, yanking his legs out from under him so he ended up on the floor too. Roo sat on his stomach.

"You were the one who dragged me here. All I wanted was to go home."

Oisin bucked her off and Roo grabbed his leg and twisted it.

"You little bitch." He wrapped his arm around her chest.

"I didn't mean to come here. I fell in by accident. If you don't want people to come, then you should mend the bloody tear. Ouch."

He'd pinched her backside. Hard.

"Oisin! Enough," said the queen.

Oisin glared at Roo but stood and pulled her up, his fingers tight around her arm. Roo straightened her dress and turned to face the woman on the throne. She did a little bob. "Sorry if I trespassed, Your Majesty. I didn't mean to. If you could spare someone to show me the

way back, I'd be very happy to leave. I wouldn't say anything about this place. I mean, there'd be no point. No one would believe me. Well, Niall would but—"

Not a word was said, but it was as though all the oxygen had been sucked out of the room. The queen rose to her feet and walked over to Roo, her face blank. Roo started to think something not very complimentary and stopped herself. Maybe this woman could read her mind.

"How do you know my son?"

Oh God, Niall is her son?

"I love him and I love Taylor too, and they both love me," Roo said with as much defiance in her voice as she could muster.

She wasn't sure why she said what she did, just some inner desperation that made her want to say the words out loud that she'd only whispered to Niall. What she hadn't expected was for the queen to laugh.

When the wolf padded back into the office, Taylor still sat behind the desk. He swallowed hard as he watched Jonas emerge, fur dissolving back to skin, face reforming, tail shrinking, and wondered if he'd been slipped some hallucinogenic drug. Or he'd gone mad. Or Jonas was a werewolf. *Oh God.*

Jonas pulled on his clothes. "I lost her scent at the wall."

"Meaning?"

"You and Roo walked to it. You came back, she didn't."

"What about Niall?"

"I can't track faeries. They have no scent discernible to werewolves."

Jesus. I'm going to have a heart attack. The damn thing pounded so hard in his chest, his whole body hurt.

Jonas leaned on his desk. "Suspend disbelief, Taylor."

"The world isn't flat."

"Well, that's just being stupid."

"She might have run away or been taken by someone," Taylor muttered. "Christopher Singer—"

"Is in hospital and will be for some time. Multiple fractures. He

won't be hitting his wife again anytime soon."

Taylor stared into Jonas's face and gulped.

"Annette Foster isn't yet aware her husband knows about her lesbian tendencies," Jonas said. "Patrick Farrant and his wife are in police custody. They were arrested at Manchester airport. They have nothing to do with Roo's disappearance."

"Right."

"Niall is a faery. A way into Faeryland lies at the bottom of your garden. I can't be certain Roo is there, but I suspect she is. I can't be certain Niall is there, but the word he gave you signals the end of my relationship with him. He no longer requires me to guard you. I no longer need to work for you. And at the moment, I no longer *want* to work for you."

Taylor straightened. "Why not?"

Jonas stamped away from the desk and then stamped back. "Because I've trusted you, shown you something that could at best get me expelled from my pack, at worst get me executed, and you Still. Don't. Fucking. Believe."

"If they're in Faeryland, go and get them back," Taylor said.

Jonas shook his head. "I can't invade the territory of another species without permission. I had enough problems changing packs from London to Leeds. My Alpha was not particularly understanding of the fact that I showed more loyalty to my employer than I do to him. Nor can I ask my new Alpha to request permission for me to cross over to Faeryland or he'll know I've been working for a faery. In any case, it's too late. You've blown it, Taylor. You've lost them both."

Taylor pushed himself to his feet. "The fuck I have."

Once Taylor reached the hall, he came to a grinding halt. Maybe the way to deal with madness was to play along with it. If he'd really lost his mind, he needed to find it—fast. Taylor took the stairs two at a time and flew into his room. The plane lay on the floor. As Taylor bent to scoop it up, he saw a book poking from under the bedside table. He dropped the plane on the bed and pulled the book out.

When he opened it, Taylor slumped onto the bed with a groan. Roo hadn't been lying. He read quickly and his heart almost stalled on Stephanie's last three words. *Wish me luck*. It was what he needed too.

Taylor pulled out his mobile and called his parents.

"Hey, how are you?" his father asked.

"I've been better, Dad."

"What's wrong?"

Taylor swallowed hard. "I was sorting out Stephanie's room and there was a book, she'd written a story." He licked dry lips. "Do you remember me having a friend I used to play with in the garden?"

His father sighed. "Yes, your imaginary pal, the one we never saw and whose name we never knew."

"Mum never saw him either?"

"You can't see someone who's not there. We thought you'd grow out of it, and after Stephanie...vanished, you never mentioned him again. Why do you ask?"

"Stephanie had written about me and the boy. She said she'd gone over the wall to look for him."

There was a short silence. "We looked the other side of the wall. So did the police."

"Yeah, I know." He sighed. "How did you get to know Niall?"

"He knocked on the door one day and asked if he could help with the garden. He came every now and again for years and then when we were ready to leave Sutton Hall, he offered to take care of everything for us. Why?"

"Did you like him?"

"Yes. He's a good lad. Trustworthy. What's happened?"

Taylor heard the worry in his father's voice and didn't know what to say.

"Are you all right, Taylor?"

"No. Not yet. Love you."

He heard the gasp before his father replied, "We love you too."

Taylor didn't say that often enough. He ended the call. There was only one thing he could do to try to make things right. Grabbing the plane, he left the house and made for the wall.

As he walked through the debris of the garden Niall had worked so hard on, Taylor faltered. He'd been tempted to tell his father everything but the words had dried up on his tongue. Taylor still searched his brain for a way to explain everything to himself but continually came up blank.

He reached the tree house, climbed up and stepped onto the wall. All he could see on the other side were trees and then the land fell away to drop to the River Wharfe in the valley below before it rose up to heather moorland. As a boy, Taylor remembered thinking Niall's family

must camp somewhere in the woods. *I looked.* Taylor exhaled. He *had* looked but he'd never found anything. He'd never pushed Niall. Why not? Taylor had always been inquisitive, so why hadn't he wondered more about a boy who always seemed to be there when he wanted him?

Taylor walked along the wall until he reached the place where NT had been carved into the rock. One of the stones was missing. Had Roo slipped and fallen? Taylor could see the stone lying on the other side. So it hadn't dropped into Faeryland, but that didn't mean Roo hadn't. *I'm nuts. This is crazy.* He put down the plane and sat on the stone with the carving. Seemed only one way to do this if he was going to find both of them and put things right. He jumped.

And landed hard on the ground facing the view he saw from the top of the wall. He almost gave up then. This was ridiculous. He climbed back up and hauled himself onto the wall. He jumped slightly to the right then to the left, and both times landed exactly where he'd expected to land. All he needed to do was break his ankle and he'd be in trouble. His mobile was back in the house.

Taylor perched on the wall, fingering the carved letters, and looked at his toy plane. If all this crap was true and he still couldn't convince himself that it was, then the plane could have flown some distance before it went through the rip or tear or whatever.

I can't fly, but I went through. A tree. Taylor stiffened. There'd been a tree. But there was no tree close to the wall. *This is such crap.*

Taylor picked up the plane in a rage and threw it.

It didn't land.

Fucking, fucking hell.

Before thinking could stop him, and before he lost track of the point the plane vanished, Taylor flung himself after it.

He landed with a thud facedown in soft grass. *Grass?* Taylor lifted his head and looked around. *Oh Christ.*

Niall had been in the room while the police talked to Taylor. Being invisible took its toll on his body, but Niall needed to hear. Even knowing it was all over between them, he couldn't walk away, not that walking anywhere would be easy. There was an old story about a faery who'd died on this side, and the dust of her body had worked magic for the mortal she'd loved.

If Niall died in this house, he'd likely be swept away and thrown in with the garbage.

If he returned to Faeryland, he'd live, assuming his mother allowed it, but for what purpose? To be ridiculed for loving a mortal who despised him? To be forced to do his mother's bidding? To spend his time wondering had he done things differently, might he have caught his star?

But what happened to him wasn't important now. Taylor and Roo were all that mattered. Until Jonas told Taylor he'd tracked her *to* the wall but not back, Niall had clung to the hope that Roo hadn't found a way into Faeryland. Now he was certain she was there and his choice of what to do had vanished. Roo had done nothing to deserve any of this. She was sweet and kind, and he wasn't going to let his mother hurt her.

When Jonas told Taylor he'd lost them both, Niall had held his breath. *The fuck I have* Taylor had said, and though Taylor hadn't seen the smile on Jonas's face, Niall had. Jonas probably thought he was doing the right thing in pushing Taylor, but if Taylor followed Roo into Faeryland, that just gave Niall another problem. Hard enough to get one mortal out, let alone two.

Taylor stamped out of the house and down to the garden, carrying his plane, and Niall followed at a slower pace, each step more and more painful. Niall paused to pick several peapods from the wreckage of his plants and pushed them in his pockets, then climbed into the tree house and slumped to sit, exhausted, on the wall. He watched Taylor try time after time to find a way through and fail. Even if it was only Roo Taylor wanted to help, Niall loved him even more for that. But if Taylor found a way through, Niall would have to follow and send him straight back. He needed Taylor to give up and go back to the house, and then he'd go after Roo.

Taylor threw the plane, gasped when it disappeared and then jumped.

"Oh shit," Niall said and followed.

He landed on top of Taylor who let out an *oomph* of surprise and collapsed beneath him. Niall rolled off onto his back and braced for the fist in the gut or on the chin. Instead Taylor kissed him and Niall's eyes and mouth opened in wonder. The scent of him, the feel of him rocketed Niall into instant arousal. Taylor's eyelashes stroked his cheeks as softly as feathers while his tongue dipped into his mouth. It was the gentlest, most seductive kiss they'd ever exchanged. Niall

could feel Taylor's erection pressed against his thigh, and the knowledge that Taylor still wanted him made his heart leap.

"This is unbelievable," Taylor whispered. "Everything I thought I knew has been turned upside down. I came looking for you and Roo. I didn't think I'd find you. I didn't think any of this was true until I landed here. I'm not dreaming, am I?"

Niall pinched his butt.

"Ouch. Still, I might be dreaming I'd been pinched."

Niall smiled. "You sound like Roo."

Taylor sighed. "We have to find her."

"*I* have to find her. *You* have to go back."

"I'm staying with you."

"It's too dangerous." Niall rolled to a sitting position. He felt stronger already.

Taylor glared. "You want to find Roo and keep her for yourself?"

"No, idiot. I'd never do that. Go back to Sutton Hall and wait for Roo. I'll find her and get her out of here."

"I'm coming with you."

Niall groaned. He should have known he wouldn't be able to make Taylor go back.

Taylor gasped. "Oh Christ. What the fuck are they?"

Niall turned. Two stabilos bounded toward them. He pushed himself up, and as Taylor stood, he shoved him behind him.

"Keep quiet. Copy me," Niall whispered.

As the creatures bounded closer, Niall bowed, relieved Taylor did the same.

"Good afternoon, Evestes, Shanta." Niall bowed again to each of them. Taylor dipped his head.

"You not been here long time," Evestes rasped.

"I was visiting my friend." He gestured to Taylor.

The stabilo sniffed Taylor who held himself rigid. "Why you bring him here?"

"We're looking for another mortal. A female."

Shanta roared right in Taylor's face and he flinched. Evestes laughed. A stabilo's version of a laugh.

"She kicked Shanta in balls," Evestes said. "Oisin took to city."

Niall was disappointed Oisin hadn't sent Roo back to the mortal side. He pushed a handful of peapods into Taylor's hand and offered those in his to Shanta. Taylor gave his to Evestes.

The stabilos yipped with pleasure. They lay down and carefully opened the pods with one claw and then skewered an individual pea and raised it to their lips.

"Until next time," Niall said and bowed again.

Taylor did the same.

"What the hell were they?" Taylor asked when they were well away from the creatures.

"Stabilos. Employed by my mother to deter us from searching the hinterland for ways into your world. Specifically to deter me, but they amuse her so they remain. If they catch any faeries and return them to my mother, they're rewarded. I'm the only one the Stabilos seem to tolerate. Probably because I treat them with respect." He smiled at Taylor. "They like peas."

"So I see."

Niall strode toward the hill, Taylor beside him.

"Why did you change your mind about me coming with you?" Taylor asked.

"Because you'd found your way through once, you'd probably find it again. You're safer here with me than on your own." Niall didn't add that he wanted Taylor with him, that he felt stronger with him by his side. He should have tried harder to persuade him to return.

"If your mother didn't want you to get out of Faeryland, why didn't she seal the tear or rip or whatever it is?"

"She can't." Niall smiled and walked faster.

"You have your energy back," Taylor said.

"Not all of it."

"Is it connected to that tattoo?"

"Yes. It's her hold on me."

"So are you still dying?" Taylor whispered.

"Yes, but not as quickly, unless my mother has something else planned."

Taylor grabbed his arm, swung him round and smothered his face in kisses. "I'm sorry, I'm sorry."

Niall pushed him away and held him by the shoulders. "You have

nothing to be sorry for. Because of my love for you, you and your parents lost your sister. You should hate me. I deserve it."

"I didn't believe you. I should have trusted you."

"I was expecting too much. This is all my fault." Niall strode on. He'd lost Taylor now but he could at least try to get him and Roo back to safety.

"I don't hate you," Taylor said at his shoulder. "I love you."

Niall stumbled to a halt. Three words a world too late. Niall had failed and could never return to the mortal side. He turned to face Taylor.

"You lost your sister because of me."

Taylor shook his head. "Your mother kept her when she could have let her come back. "

"Because of me," Niall said.

"You were a kid. This is down to her, Niall, not you." Taylor slipped his hands around Niall's waist. "I remember playing with you. I remember sharing comics, kicking a ball around, games of hide and seek in the woods, eating peas and strawberries in the garden, making snowmen, having snowball fights. You were my best friend. You still are."

Taylor pressed his forehead against Niall's and Niall's heart ached.

"I don't deserve you," Niall said. "I should have left you alone."

Taylor pulled back to look Niall in the eyes. "What's happened is done. What matters is what we do now. What's the plan?"

Niall's shoulders slumped. "I have no plan."

Chapter Twenty-Three

Roo folded herself tighter and tighter like a piece of origami, wrapping her arms around her head and pressing her face into bent knees. She'd been dragged away from the queen and thrown into this dark space where she could hear things slithering and hissing. Roo wasn't good with anything that slithered, especially if it hissed as well because that could only mean one thing. *Sn— Oh shit. Not even going to think the S word.* In retrospect, telling the queen that she loved her son hadn't been the wisest move. Classic case of not being good enough for her boy. Well, if Niall was a prince, Roo could see that was true.

The sound of a door opening made her lift her head. There was a flash of light in the blackness and Roo gulped and closed her eyes. If she looked, she might see what surrounded her and she was close to full-out panic. Her heart banged so hard against her ribs, she felt sick.

"Roo," a woman whispered.

If she answered, would it bring the slithering things closer?

"Tell me about Taylor," the woman asked.

Roo put two and two together and tensed. "Are you Stephanie?"

"Yes."

Oh God. Roo opened her eyes and peered toward the light. *Mistake.* The floor heaved with S words. Big ones and small ones all tangled together in a knotty mess. *Fuck, fuck, fuck.* Roo tied herself in an even tighter pretzel. She could hear a high-pitched keening leaking from her mouth but couldn't stop herself.

"They won't hurt you. Tell me about my brother."

Roo wasn't giving any information without something in return. "Why did she laugh so hard when I said I loved Taylor and Niall?"

"The queen stopped Taylor from loving anyone. Taylor is incapable of love."

"She did what?" Roo snapped and unfolded. "What an absolute bitch."

"Don't," Stephanie whispered. "She only wants the best for Niall. Tell me what's happening with Taylor."

"Not unless you get me out of here."

"Is he all right? My parents?"

"Help me and I'll talk to you."

Stephanie sighed. "I'm sorry. I can't."

The door closed and Roo shuddered as the hissing grew louder. Stephanie said the snakes wouldn't hurt her. Was that the truth? It didn't make Roo any less frightened. She said aloud, "'I have often been afraid, but I wouldn't give in to it. I made myself act as though I was not afraid, and gradually my fear disappeared.'" *Thanks, Teddy.*

Roo doubted Roosevelt had been trapped in a room full of s-s-snakes, but why stay in there a moment longer than she needed to? Was it test of her mettle?

She lifted her head and slowly stood. There was the faintest chink of light coming from her right. A door? The only snag with that was Stephanie had talked from the left. Left was dark.

"In any moment of decision," Roo whispered, "the best thing you can do is the right thing, the next best thing is the wrong thing, and the worst thing you can do is nothing."

She slid a foot forward and a snake slunk over her toes. Roo squeaked and clenched her fists. She took another small step and another. Inch by inch she worked her way toward the sliver of light. The right way? Or the wrong way?

"We ought to have some sort of plan," Taylor said as he followed Niall across the grassy plain.

Niall gave him such a bleak look that Taylor's confidence took a nosedive.

"What were you thinking when you threw yourself after the plane?" Niall asked.

"To find you and Roo and bring you back."

"What about Stephanie?"

Taylor exhaled. He still couldn't believe he was going to see his sister again. "Well, I'd want to take her back too."

"What if she doesn't want to leave?"

He swallowed hard. "But—"

"She's grown up now," Niall said gently. "She's spent more of her life on this side than the other. This is her world."

"And whose fault is that?" Taylor retorted. "She was kidnapped. We thought she'd been raped and murdered."

Niall put his hand on Taylor's arm. "I only want you to think about what *she* might want."

Taylor shrugged him off. "My parents need to know she's alive."

"You didn't want to believe. Why should they?"

"Because she'll be there, telling them."

Niall stopped walking. "And they'll accept she's been living with faeries? Or will they have her committed to some psychiatric nursing home for the rest of her life?"

"You said memories can be wiped. Mine was. That could be done to Stephanie."

Niall shook his head. "Not sixteen years of her life. It can't be done."

"Roo won't want to stay," Taylor blustered.

"You're right. She needs to go back with you. There's just the not-so-simple matter of persuading my mother."

With me? Not all three of them going back? Taylor opened his mouth and then closed it again.

Niall changed direction.

"Where are we going?" Taylor asked.

"Plan B. To speak to my father."

"I thought you didn't have a plan A?"

Niall smiled. "I don't."

"Doesn't your father live with your mother?"

"No." Niall stopped abruptly. "This will take too long. I need to see if I can carry you. Keep still."

"You can't— Oh fuck."

Taylor gasped when iridescent blue wings erupted from Niall's back. Niall stepped in front of Taylor, hooked his arms under his and lifted him. A moment later, they were rising into the air and Taylor grasped Niall around the waist. The strain on Niall's face was clear and Taylor felt relieved they stayed close to the ground, though they were traveling at some speed, so if Niall dropped him, it was going to hurt.

Wings? At first Taylor didn't think they were flapping until he realized they were moving so fast they appeared stationary. Over Niall's shoulder, and receding into the distance, Taylor saw a city with the sea or a large lake beyond. Everything around it was very green. He didn't want to distract Niall by turning his head, but looking down, he could see the grassy plains had gone. They were traveling over rough, stony ground and moving uphill.

"This is incredible," Taylor whispered. "You're amazing."

"I hope you'll say that after we've landed," Niall grunted. "Oh shit, hold tight."

Taylor heard something whizz past his ear just as Niall dropped to the right, and then they were tumbling together through the air. Even as Taylor tried to protect Niall, Niall was doing the same to him and it was Niall who collided with the ground, Taylor landing on top. Niall arched in agony and Taylor lurched to the side. As he rolled to his feet, Taylor could see one of Niall's wings lying crumpled beneath him, the other flapping feebly.

"No," Taylor gasped. "Niall, talk to me. Are you okay?"

As Taylor leaned over, he saw bare feet approaching and looked up into the face of a man too much like Niall not to be related. But no way was this guy old enough to be Niall's father. He held a bow and Taylor realized the prick had shot at them.

"Damn it, I missed," the guy said, turned and walked away.

"Hey." Taylor pushed himself up on shaky legs. "Why the hell did you do that?"

Niall struggled to his feet, one wing dangling. "Father."

The man stopped, muttered, "Fool," and stalked off.

Taylor wasn't sure who the "fool" comment referred to. Niall stumbled after his father and Taylor grabbed his arm.

"You sure this is a good idea? He just fired an arrow at us."

"And missed. He doesn't miss. Come on."

They headed toward a house set into the rock, all glass and gleaming steel, but Taylor's attention was on Niall's broken wing. The other had presumably retracted to leave this one hanging. His back was gashed and streaked with blood.

"Father," Niall called.

"Go away," his father snapped. "I'm busy."

Niall dropped to his knees, gasping. Taylor ripped off his shirt and

pressed it to the wound.

"Please help him," Taylor pleaded.

The guy stood by the door of the house.

"He's your son," Taylor barked. "Don't you care about him at all?"

"About as much as he cared for me sixteen years ago."

"When he was still a child and you were a grown-up?" Taylor spat through gritted teeth.

Two women appeared in the doorway of the house and stared at Taylor and Niall.

"Who are they, Endor?" one of them asked.

"Nothing."

Taylor's temper spilled over. "We are not nothing." He stomped across to the house and stood in front of Niall's father. "You're the one who's nothing. What sort of father are you to walk away from your son when he needs you? He's hurt."

Endor tilted his head to one side and frowned as he pinned Taylor with his gaze. "I'm a father who did everything for his sons. A father whose sons turned on him when he needed them." He straightened. "You shouldn't be here. She'll have you killed and who knows what she'll do to him." He turned his gaze on Niall.

"You could stop her," Niall muttered.

"Could I?"

"You *should* stop her."

"Why?" his father asked.

"You bastard," Taylor whispered. "I can understand you not caring about me, but he's your son."

Endor sighed and then nodded to the two women. "Bring the idiot inside."

They picked Niall up as if he weighed nothing and carried him into the building. Taylor followed. What looked stark from the outside was the exact opposite inside. They moved through rooms cluttered with plants and artifacts, past walls lined with heaving bookcases and into a glass conservatory, the roof open to the sky. The women laid Niall facedown on a couch.

"The water," Endor said and the women slipped away.

Niall groaned. Taylor gulped when he saw blood flowing from the gash. *My fault.* Endor gaped at Niall's back and Taylor wondered if the

wound was even more serious than it looked.

"That bitch," Endor gasped. "How far does this go?"

Ah, the tattoo.

"Down to his foot," Taylor said.

Endor reached under Niall and a moment later, taking care not to jar Niall's wing, he tugged down his pants and boxers and stripped them off Niall's feet. Endor sagged as he stared at the complex marking that ran across Niall's back from shoulder to toes.

Taylor stared at Niall's butt. *Do not get an erection.* This was *not* the time. Taylor hoped his cock was listening.

The women came back with bowls and towels and bent over Niall's back. Endor put his hand around the break in the wing and straightened it. Niall cried out and grabbed hold of Taylor's hand.

"You can retract it now," Endor said. "But you can't use it until it's healed."

Taylor watched in fascination as the wing seemed to melt into Niall's body. The women bathed the wound between his shoulder blades, and with each wipe, the injury healed more and more. Niall's grip on Taylor's hand gradually loosened, but Taylor didn't let him go. Endor signaled the women to leave.

"You're very weak," Endor said. "The tarsis holds you tight."

"Tarsis?" Taylor asked.

"The mark on his body. His mother's way of maintaining control." He turned to look at Taylor. "Why are you here?"

"We seek another mortal," Niall spoke before Taylor could. "The stabilo said she was taken to the city. She came over by accident. I want her back safe on the other side."

"There'll be a price," Endor said.

"Of course." Niall sighed, his eyes closing.

"You need to sleep. You can do nothing until you recover. She won't hurt this mortal she holds while she waits for you to come to her." Endor tugged a cover from the back of the couch, laid it over Niall, and signaled Taylor to follow him.

The moment Taylor was out of the room and the door was shut, Endor grabbed him by the throat. Taylor tried to wrench his hand away and couldn't. *God, this guy is strong.*

"What are you to my son?" Endor demanded.

"I love him."

Endor dropped him so fast, Taylor's knees buckled. He waved off the women and led Taylor to a room overlooking the grassy plain with the sea and city in the distance.

"Sit down." He spoke gently. "Tell me everything."

Taylor hesitated.

"If you want help, I have to understand. This is the first time I've spoken to Niall for sixteen of your years."

Taylor's jaw dropped. "What—?"

"Talk. Niall brought you here for a reason. I know you're his boyhood friend. I know about your sister."

Endor leaned forward, listening intently.

"I returned to Yorkshire from London, back to my parents' old house at their request to put the house on the market. My father told me a guy was living in the attic rent-free in return for work on the garden. Niall. I moved in a few weeks ago. I didn't remember Niall. He says his mother wiped my memory. That was part of the price for Stephanie's safety."

A muscle in Taylor's cheek twitched. "I can see *now* how much Niall wanted me to remember but I didn't. Then along came Roo." He smiled. "We interviewed her, gave her a job as my personal assistant, we both...

"Niall and I..." Taylor had no idea how to say this to a parent. "The pair of us were growing closer. Roo was helping. She didn't know about Stephanie and I freaked out when Roo slept in her room. Roo said she'd found a book Stephanie had written just before she disappeared, where she said she'd gone over the wall to look for a boy she'd seen in the garden. Everything unraveled then. The room Niall had been sleeping in seemed to have furniture one minute and not the next. Niall told me he was a faery, and that the rest of the price paid for Stephanie to stay safe and for Niall to come back to me was that I could never fall in love and Niall couldn't make the first move on someone he loved."

"The tarsis. If he defies his mother, it poisons and strangles him from the inside out."

Taylor gulped. "Niall told me if he stayed on the mortal side, he'd die. That even on this side he's still dying, but the process is slowed."

"Perhaps, but my wife, Vanda, makes the rules up as she goes along. Niall was a fool to trust her."

Taylor's hopes of the perfect ending dwindled. "Roo's who we're looking for. We suspect she came here by accident. Or maybe she came

to plead for Niall. The stabilo told us she'd been taken to the city. I don't think Niall had a plan for what to do, so he flew here to you."

"You're a three with this woman?"

"I love them both."

Endor twisted his mouth in a half smile. "That was very quick. If my wife has bespelled you incapable of love, how do you know this is love you feel?"

"Because I can't contemplate life without them." The moment the words came from his mouth, Taylor knew he'd spoken the truth.

Endor laughed. "The power of true love is strong. Maybe you're right. But what if to save Niall's life, you have to give him up?"

Taylor's heart stuttered to a halt. "Give him up?"

"Do you remember seeing the tarsis on him when you were boys?"

Taylor closed his eyes. He hadn't thought so, but... He looked at Endor. "On his foot, when we were paddling in the brook. He said it was a birthmark."

"The punishment started once his mother discovered he was seeing you. I tried to protect him by stopping you from thinking too deeply about where he came from. Perhaps I made things worse. If you'd been too curious and tried to cross to this side, things might have been very different."

Oh God.

"His refusal to give you up has strengthened the spell's hold. Even if you walk away from him, there's no certainty he will survive. But if you leave and tell him you don't love him, he has a chance."

Taylor lost all moisture from his mouth. "I can't do that. He's waited so long for me to say I love him. I won't take it back. I *do* love him. I'll stay on this side with him."

Endor shook his head. "The queen won't allow it."

Taylor clenched his fists. "My sister's here. Why not me too?"

"Vanda doesn't want you. She wants her youngest son back in the fold, doing her bidding, helping maintain her control over the kingdom."

"While you sit here abdicating responsibility?"

A faint smile crossed Endor's face. He stood and unfastened his shirt. Oh shit, another guy stripping for him? But what Taylor saw stopped the breath in his throat. Every inch of Endor's chest and arms...*oh fuck*...and his back were covered in the same entwined

marks as Niall's.

"Do I need to take off my pants?"

Taylor shook his head.

"She's very powerful. I thought she loved me, and chose me for who I was, what I was. The son of a noble, but no threat to her. More importantly, from a fertile family. Faeries are not known for their fertility. We live a long time. It's nature's way of controlling our numbers. I am one of seven. My brothers and sisters all have children. Vanda saw me only as a means of providing her with offspring. She used me, but I wasn't supposed to leave her. I walked out sixteen years ago and the tarsis was my punishment. I'm marked with the queen's displeasure and shunned. Once my face is covered, I'll die. She likes her punishments to last. I asked my children to come with me when I left. None would."

"Because from where you went to live in Rigat all those years ago, I couldn't continue to see Taylor," Niall said from the doorway. "Because she said if one of us left, the others would pay. Because she said she'd leave you alone if we stayed with her. I thought you might have a chance of happiness without us."

Endor gestured to his exposed chest. "Every woman I touch increases the mark. She sends them my way and knows they won't love me. I'm denied that comfort. I shouldn't have married her. I loved another and she knew it."

Niall walked across to his father. "You're still king. You must be able to do something."

"And where's my army? I can't even get rid of the tarsis. God knows I've tried. What chance would I have against her?"

"How do you know if you don't confront her? People are tired of her rule. Fewer and fewer children are being born. With no communication allowed between us and other kingdoms, we decay."

"I've tried. The result is not much of my skin remains untouched. I've reached a measure of happiness and will spend my remaining time here. I have my plants, my work, and an occasional fuck. I'm a lot closer to death than you are, boy. Priorities change." He nodded toward the door. "Those two will tell her you're here. Better go to her than let her come for you. Better still, send Taylor back to his world and go to the castle alone. Bargain for your third."

Taylor opened his mouth and then closed it. He no longer knew the right thing to do. He wanted to support Niall, save Roo, and for them to live happily ever after, but he had no idea how to make that

happen in a world where magic held sway.

"Do you have a shirt I can put on?" Niall asked.

His father handed over the one he'd been wearing. Niall pulled it on and fastened the buttons. He bent his forehead to his father's and put his hands on his shoulders.

"I never forgot you," Niall said. "You always had a place in my heart."

"And you in mine," Endor replied. "My youngest, my bravest. You've grown so tall. I didn't recognize you. I'm sorry I shot at you. I didn't realize how weak you were. I'm sorry about your wing."

Niall moved away and beckoned to Taylor.

"Take two horses," Endor said. "Look out for the stabilos."

"Unlike you, they were pleased to see me." Niall put his hand in his pocket, pulled out a peapod and tossed it to his father.

Endor gasped. "You remembered?"

"I remember everything."

Roo was quivering by the time she reached the door. Each slide of her foot had been accompanied by hissing and slithering and the occasional flick from a tongue, but nothing had bitten her. She fumbled for the door handle and groaned in relief when she wrapped her fingers around it. It hadn't occurred to Roo that the door wouldn't open, which in retrospect was a bit stupid, but when she turned the handle the door moved outward.

She screamed. An honest-to-God, ear-splitting, horror-film scream because there was nothing the other side of the door. It was a sheer drop down a rocky face into a churning sea hundreds of feet below. Roo teetered on the edge of the room, her hand still locked around the handle. This didn't make sense. Why have a door to nowhere? She looked up, down and to the side but there was only rock, though higher up she could see the rock had been smoothed and jutted out as if it supported something. Even so, there was no way she could climb to it.

Roo wondered if this was some trick, and that a path was here but invisible. Unlike Harrison Ford, she had no handful of sand to throw out to mark the route, only a handful of snakes, and no way was she touching those, apart from the fact that she didn't want to throw them to their death. As Roo remembered her namesake's words—*the*

worst thing to do was nothing—a snake shot past her foot and out into midair. Roo's jaw dropped and splashed into the sea. It was no more than twelve feet before the snake disappeared. Hopefully into another room. Twelve feet of invisible path.

She slipped one foot out while she still clung to the handle and her toes connected with something solid. *Oh God, oh God, oh God.* Her pulse raced and she struggled to slow her breathing. *Don't throw up. Don't look down. Jesus, that's a hell of a long way down.* Roo moved her toes from side to side to calculate the width of the path. Maybe twelve inches. *Not nearly wide enough.*

Now she had a choice. Go back with the snakes and try to find the other door now she had some light, or move forward and hope there was a way ahead. She let go of the handle, put her weight on her front foot and swung her back foot round in front of the other. It landed on something firm. Not the time to wobble. Nor was it the time for the snakes to decide they'd like a breath of fresh air. Roo squealed as one squirmed past her foot, but it made her next couple of steps easier. Her heart nearly stopped as she trod on its tail and then it moved fast and vanished, and she was on her own again, standing in midair.

It was hard to think when she'd been more frightened, which sort of explained why she'd not thought this through properly. She had no idea what lay ahead of her. The snakes could have slithered through a tiny gap. There might not be a room there at all. Mouth dry, stomach churning, her heart pounded with fear while the need to pee gathered pace. Even that stabilo hadn't scared her as much as this.

When Roo slid her foot forward and only touched air, she realized there was another level of terror. *How can there not be anything there?* The snakes hadn't fallen into the sea. She hadn't noticed either of them swerve to one side. Arms outstretched to keep her balance, Roo tapped around with her foot and could feel nothing solid. She brought her foot back behind her and there was nothing there either.

Oh fuuuuck. She pressed one foot against the other, realizing she was balancing on a pillar with no way of knowing how far it was to safety. Roo wasn't into leaps of faith. She could go neither backward nor forward. Maybe this time Roosevelt wasn't right. The worst thing wasn't to do nothing. If she did nothing, she lived a little longer.

Chapter Twenty-Four

"Hate to sound like a broken record, but what's the plan?" Taylor asked as they neared the city wall.

"Follow my lead." Niall tried to sound confident, but he had no clue, no idea what his mother would do and no means to protect the two mortals who were in the kingdom in direct defiance of her orders. He had nothing to barter with but his willingness to do whatever she wanted if she allowed Taylor and Roo to go home. He already knew Stephanie would *not* be going with them. The guilt of that would remain.

The city gates opened as they approached and sentries emerged. When they saw Niall, they bowed. He slipped from the horse's back and Taylor did the same. Riding within the city was forbidden.

"Return to my father," Niall whispered in his horse's ear and the animal turned and cantered away, followed by Taylor's.

Niall greeted almost everyone they passed, nodding, smiling or exchanging some pleasantry. His mother wasn't popular and by default neither were her sons, but everyone pretended because they feared the queen's wrath. The faeries of this kingdom wanted a chance to grow, to build different homes, to travel, but were trapped by laws that forbade new development and exploration. In keeping them confined within the city, his mother maintained her hold. Those who wished to leave were persuaded by one means or another to change their minds.

Niall and Taylor had barely entered the castle before they were surrounded by guards. Niall opened his mouth to reassure Taylor, but a voice came from behind them.

"Hello, Niall."

Niall turned to see Oisin leaning against a doorframe.

"Where's Roo?" Niall narrowed his eyes.

"Not far away. How are you, brother?"

Taylor tensed and Niall wrapped his fingers around his arm.

"Pissed off," Niall replied. "Taylor, this is my oldest brother, Oisin."

Oisin pushed himself upright and walked over. He stared at Taylor and then turned to Niall. "Our mother wants love from you."

"Then she should show she deserves it." And Niall knew just as well as Oisin that it wasn't love his mother wanted, but allegiance.

"Do any of us deserve it?" Oisin sighed and headed down the corridor.

Niall beckoned Taylor to follow.

"Bow to my mother," Niall said quietly. "Show respect at all times. You're not welcome here and she's within her rights to destroy you."

Taylor exhaled.

When they walked into the throne room, conversation ceased. His mother turned and headed toward them. Niall saw Stephanie staring wide-eyed at Taylor, but Taylor hadn't seen her, maybe hadn't recognized her. Niall met his mother's gaze.

I should love her, but I can't. I should show her true allegiance and I can't do that either.

"Niall," she exhaled his name.

He bowed and then kissed her on each cheek.

"You brought contamination with you." She glared at Taylor.

Taylor made a deep bow. "I'm—"

"Did I give you permission to speak? Keep your mouth shut or I'll shut it for you. Permanently." The scowl faded as she looked at Niall. "You've had what you asked for. This is an end to it."

"You gave me permission to live on the other side for a year. I've not had my year and you—"

His mother waved her hand in the air. "Yes, yes." She turned her gaze on Taylor. "You love...this thing but weren't allowed to show affection before it was shown to you, or speak of love until love was spoken of to you, or to reveal our secrets." Her eyes glittered as she faced Niall.

"I kept to the agreement."

"Then why is he here? In our world? Is that not our greatest secret?"

"I love him," Taylor blurted.

Niall flashed him a warning glance. Words Niall had waited so long to hear were going to get Taylor killed.

His mother frowned as she stared at Niall. "You were a fool to

think this would work when you knew he'd had the capacity to love removed years ago. He doesn't love you. He can't."

Niall straightened. "But he does. And so does Roo. You said I could stay on that side if I was loved. You gave your word."

His mother stepped up to his face and smiled. "You're not loved."

Niall stared into her eyes. "I am, but you're not."

She laughed and twirled away, gesturing to those in the room. "Everyone loves me."

"My queen."

"My queen."

One by one the couriers bowed and kissed her outstretched hand.

This was a battle Niall couldn't win. She'd never let him go.

"What do you want of me?" he asked in a quiet voice.

"Marry tomorrow." She gave him a triumphant smile and beckoned to Stephanie.

Niall wished he'd told Taylor. Now it was too late.

"Get her with child," his mother said.

Taylor gasped. "Stephanie?" He rushed toward her and threw his arms around her. "On my God, oh my God."

Niall saw how desperately Stephanie clutched at Taylor's shirt and guilt gnawed at his gut.

Taylor pulled back and held her by the shoulders. "I can't believe it's you. Mum and Dad paid an artist do an impression of what you might look like now. He was spot on. My God, you look... We thought... Oh Christ." He tugged her back into his arms and pressed his face into her hair. "Are you happy?" he whispered and pulled back to look into her eyes.

Niall saw the nod she gave Taylor, and didn't miss the glance she shot Oisin, nor the one his brother gave her. Nothing had changed there then. The queen snapped her fingers and Stephanie scurried to her side.

"No," his mother growled. "You are to marry her, not Oisin. I want perfect grandchildren, not ones who are deformed."

Niall couldn't look at Taylor or his brother, knowing the hurt he'd see on their faces, but he could try to put some things right. He owed them that. "If I do this, will you let Roo and Taylor return to the other side with their memories of me wiped?"

"No," Taylor blurted. "This isn't fair."

The queen turned on him then, her face filled with fury. "You challenge me?"

"No he doesn't," Niall said and stepped between Taylor and his mother.

Taylor gently pushed him aside. "If Niall doesn't do this?"

"Then the tarsis will eventually cover his body and he'll die."

"I'll do as you ask if you give us one last night," Niall said, fighting not to let his desperation show. "The three of us together. Me, Taylor and Roo."

His mother pursed her lips. "If they admit they don't love you, you can have your last night."

"Majesty," someone called.

Niall turned. A young courtier he didn't know stood by the open window.

"What is it?" she asked.

"The woman...she must have broken the spell."

Niall followed his mother to the window. He gasped when he looked out and the blood drained from his head. Roo stood about twenty feet below them, in the middle of the sky, with her back toward them. The crashing sea lay another hundred feet below.

"What the hell?" Taylor snapped and shot Niall a desperate glance.

"How did she get out of the room?" Niall's mother demanded. "Who let her out?"

Roo wobbled and Taylor groaned. "Do something, Niall."

Niall sagged. "My wing." He'd kill them both if he tried to fly to her.

"Who released you?" the queen called to Roo.

Roo's arms shot farther out as she reacted to the voice. Niall held his breath until she regained her balance.

"The snakes," Roo shouted.

Niall shot a pleading glance at Oisin but his brother shook his head with a sad smile. He wouldn't risk their mother's ire. She despised Oisin because of his missing arm and yet he still clung to the hope she'd love him. If his brother wouldn't help, there was no one else to ask. His other brothers had escaped this city to live miles away.

Niall slipped to the far end of the window and climbed onto the sill. If Roo fell, he'd try to save her.

His mother rubbed her hands together. "Well, isn't this splendid?"

"Please," Taylor pleaded. "Don't let her fall."

"I *could* save her." The queen ignored Taylor and stared at Niall. "If she admits she doesn't love you." She leaned out of the window. "Do you hear that, mortal? Admit you don't love my son and I'll have someone fly down and pluck you to safety."

"I love Niall and Taylor," Roo shouted.

The queen shrugged. "Looks like it'll just be the two of you tonight."

"Don't," Niall whispered. "Please."

"Hold him," the queen ordered, and hands wrapped around Niall's arms as he prepared to launch himself from the window.

"Roo," Niall called as he struggled in their grasp. "Just say it. Say you don't love me."

Roo's heart jumped when she heard Niall's voice somewhere above and behind her. Her legs had started to shake a while ago and she figured it wasn't long before she fell. A gust of wind would do it. If someone was close enough to breathe on her, well, that would work too. Would Niall put out his wings and save her? Maybe his bitch of a mother was stopping him. If she was going to die, she wouldn't do it with a lie on her lips.

"I love you," she shouted. "I love the way you tease me. I love the way you look at Taylor. I love your smile. I love your eyes. I love your chocolate brownies." *Don't get distracted.* "I love every bit of you and I'm not going to say I don't."

"Stupid mortal," the queen snapped.

"I'm not stupid. I'm honest. The person I was named after said, 'Only those are fit to live who do not fear to die; and none are fit to die who have shrunk from the joy of life. Both life and death are parts of the same Great Adventure.' I finally found love and you can never take that away from me."

"I wouldn't be too sure of that," the queen shouted.

The support under Roo's feet vanished and she plummeted toward the water. No breath to scream, time only to realize this would be like hitting concrete, and hope she didn't survive long enough to drown.

As her toes grazed the tip of a wave, she was swept to one side and scooped into strong arms.

OhmyGodohmyGodohmyGod. The force of the rescue locked her lungs.

"Breathe," said the faery.

Roo was trying but nothing worked.

The faery bent his head and blew air across her lips. There was a noisy gurgle and Roo gulped oxygen.

"Better. Good girl. Keep breathing. I won't let you fall. You're much too precious."

She managed a strangled grunt as they zoomed over the ocean.

"I'm Endor, Niall's father."

"Roo," she rasped.

"Named after Theodore Roosevelt. I recognized the quote."

"Yep."

"Bit cruel for a girl."

"Quite like being different. Could have been worse. Hoover. Eisenhower." She paused. "Polk."

He laughed.

"Thought I'd had it. Thank you for saving me."

"You're not saved yet. You have to do that yourself."

Roo sighed when he flew in through a window and landed in front of the bitch-queen. *Bugger.* The only reassuring thing was that as he set her down, Taylor rushed forward and wrapped his arms around her. Niall pulled free of the men holding him and pressed himself against Roo's back. Roo suspected without their support, she'd have collapsed. *I nearly died.*

"Endor. What a surprise." There was so much venom in the queen's voice, Roo could almost taste it.

"You don't like to be defied, do you?" Endor gave a deep sigh. "These three believe in love and you can't deal with that."

"I believe in love," the queen said.

"You have a strange way of showing it. You inflict your youngest with the tarsis because you don't want him to leave you." He glanced at Oisin. "You keep your eldest here, yet you foolishly despise him because of something he can't help. Love is about letting go as well as keeping hold. These three would sacrifice themselves for each other.

Niall would do your bidding to save Roo and Taylor. Roo would accept death rather than deny her love. Taylor is willing to give up the mortal side to be with the man he loves. Oisin bites his tongue because he seeks a kind word from you."

The queen shrugged. "I've offered them one last night together. It's generous of me. Tomorrow they leave, and Niall marries Stephanie."

Roo gulped and felt the guys' hold on her tighten.

"You challenged Niall to find love with Taylor and you lost. Remove the tarsis and let them make their own decisions."

The queen laughed. "What right do you have to come here and make demands of me?"

"I'm still the king, your husband."

"In name only."

"Let them go." Endor walked toward her.

"And what do I get?" she asked.

Roo watched in horrified fascination as the pair circled each other like panthers waiting to pounce.

"A night with me," Endor said.

The queen sneered and gestured to the others in the room. "For what purpose? I can have all the sex I want. Finlay and Rubin are very inventive. They last such a long time compared to some."

"I'm not offering sex. I'll talk to you about love, teach you what it means."

"I know all I need to about love."

He shook his head. "You can't bear the idea of anyone having love in their life because you don't."

Endor raised his fingers to her face and Roo held her breath, wondering if the queen would bite them off.

"I *am* loved," she snapped. "I'm queen."

"A title doesn't make you loved. You have to work for love, deserve it."

She scowled at him. "What do you know?"

"I know that when you have love and lose it, it takes time to survive the pain. Your heart doesn't want to accept it. You cling to every bit of hope, and while you're still together, you listen for a kind word, for a smile aimed at you, the slightest look that you're something worth fighting for. And even when all hope is gone, the flame is never

completely extinguished."

A muscle ticced in the queen's cheek as Endor moved closer until his lips were inches from hers.

"I could kill you where you stand," the queen hissed.

"If you love someone, you have to take risks. I'm dying anyway. You send me a few more women and it will be the end." Endor sighed and stepped back. "Better to have loved and lost? No, I don't think so. My happiness is gone, crushed by you. My memories of the good times have been corrupted by those that weren't. I want to be loved. I want to be happy. Isn't that what everyone wants? Don't you want that too?"

The queen's lips were compressed in a tight line.

"If you make yourself happy," Endor said, "then you attract others with your happiness. You could be a queen who loves and is loved. Not having love doesn't make you strong and independent. It makes you lonely. It makes you cling on to your children when you should let them fly. It makes you rely on the old, familiar ways. You can't make people love or not love. It's beyond your power. You might push love back for a while, but it will always shine through, even on the darkest day, at the darkest hour."

He glanced at Roo and smiled, and then tipped his head to one side as he regarded the queen. "Do you understand how hard it is to look at someone, knowing you love them and that they don't love you? Have you any idea of what Niall went through? Any understanding of why he was prepared to risk all?"

Roo glanced up at Niall who smiled at her and Taylor.

Endor reached to stroke the queen's cheek and she slapped his hand away.

"You take me for a fool?" she snapped. "You think I assume you talk about me? You still want that woman."

"You never gave me a chance." Endor glanced at Niall, Roo and Taylor. "Give them a chance."

"They've had it," the queen said. "Now they have one night." Taking Stephanie's arm, she walked out, most of the faeries following.

Roo felt Niall grip Taylor tighter and guessed he was worried he'd try to get his sister. When the queen had gone, Niall relaxed his hold.

"Let's get Stephanie and run," Taylor whispered.

"We wouldn't get out of the castle," Niall said.

"So do you have a plan this time?" Taylor asked.

"Yes. Excuse me a moment."

Niall walked over to his father and took him in his arms. "Thank you for trying." He lowered his voice to a whisper. "Tomorrow, if you can, will you make sure Taylor and Roo reach the other side safely? I'd ask for Stephanie too, but I fear that's impossible."

"I saw who she loves. She mustn't leave," said his father. "Your mother is as much a manipulative bitch as she ever was. But I haven't given up yet. You mustn't either. Take your night. Use it well. If all fails, you can keep the memory in your heart."

Niall nodded and turned to Oisin. "My quarters?"

"Ready for your return, brother. Use the pool. I'll lock my side."

Niall moved to hug Oisin but he turned away, his face downcast. Niall wanted to tell him he'd rather die than come between him and Stephanie, but for the time being it was better left unsaid. This was Niall's mess to put right. His responsibility. His sacrifice. Niall put a smile on his lips and held out his hands to Roo and Taylor. "This will be the best night of our lives."

A tear slipped down Roo's cheek and Niall kissed it away. "Only tears of joy allowed." He pressed his face close to theirs. "No talking until we're alone."

Niall led them down the maze of corridors to his suite of rooms. Once they were inside, he put a ward on the door. It likely wouldn't stop his mother for long, but it afforded them some degree of privacy. When he turned, Taylor stood staring at him.

"Marrying Stephanie? Why didn't you tell me?"

Niall swallowed. "How could I? What was the point? I won't marry her. She loves Oisin."

Taylor frowned. "Then why does your mother want her to marry you?"

"Oisin was born with only one arm. Our mother won't take the risk of him passing the deformity to his children. She only wants perfection."

"Why is she so full of hate?"

"I'm not sure. I *do* know that I don't want to waste any more time thinking about my mother. Through that door is an area shared between Oisin and myself. All ours tonight."

"Is there chocolate?" Roo asked. "I really feel in need of chocolate.

Did you see me standing in midair? I almost wet my pants. Though that would have been tricky because I'm not— Why are you both looking at me like that?"

"Like what?" Taylor asked as he advanced on her.

Roo laughed, but as she turned to run, Niall slipped in front of her and she bumped into his chest. He slid his arms around her and Taylor moved up to her back.

"I don't know of any woman who could have almost died in the way you did who'd bounce back as though it were the sort of thing that happened every day," Niall said.

"Well, I'm sort of thinking I must have fallen over while I was dressed as a chicken, knocked myself out and I'm dreaming all this."

"Do you want to be dreaming?" Taylor kissed her neck.

"No."

"Open that door," Niall said.

Roo walked toward it, tugging Taylor. "Promise it's not a hundred foot drop on the other side?"

A little dart of worry teased Niall's stomach and he did a mental check. He also conjured something to make Roo happy.

"You hesitated," Roo wailed. "Does that mean you're not sure?"

Niall rolled his eyes and pushed open the door.

Roo gasped and ran toward the pool, then saw what Niall had created on a table and changed direction, then spotted the waterfall and headed for that only to jerk to a halt and run back again to the table. She stared at the chocolate fountain and started tapping her foot.

Taylor laughed. "Rather dive into that?"

Niall never took this room for granted. It was an open-air courtyard between his room and Oisin's, which they either shared or took turns to use. In the center was a heated, sunken pool with a waterfall at the far end. There were small trees around the sides festooned with lights so that at nightfall it looked like a glade in a star-filled forest. It was a place to relax, to float free of worries. Tonight it was a place to make memories.

Roo circled the table and swallowed hard. "A whole fountain of chocolate? I was thinking of a bar. How does it work? How can dark, milk and white chocolate stay separate like that? And fruit?" She picked up a strawberry, swiped it through the dark brown liquid and

popped it in her mouth. “Mmmmm.” Roo swallowed, licked her lips and said, “So what are the options?”

“You on top, me on top, Taylor—”

“You know that’s not what I meant,” Roo said, sliding her finger under the flow and lifting it to her mouth to suck.

Niall lost his train of thought. He shook his head. “No options,” he said. “You go back tomorrow and I stay here. I won’t marry Stephanie. My brother loves her. I’ll find a way to make them happy.”

And from Taylor’s face, Niall knew he’d guessed how far he’d go.

“We could run tonight. Now.” Taylor wrapped his hand over Niall’s shoulder. “We’ll find a way past the guards. We should at least try. Maybe get those creatures to help.”

“If I go back to the other side, I won’t last another day.”

“So we run on this side,” Taylor whispered. “Find another city and live there.”

“We’d never be safe and Stephanie would face my mother’s wrath.”

“She comes too,” Taylor said.

“She won’t leave Oisin and he won’t leave here. He should be the next king, and our mother promises him he will, and yet he fears she plots to make that not happen. She would track and destroy us. You go and I stay, and if you love your sister, you’ll leave her here. I promise she’ll be happy, loved.”

Taylor’s mouth tightened but he nodded.

Niall took hold of each of their hands. “I want this night to sustain me when you’re no longer here. I want this night to be perfect. No more talk of what we could do when there is *nothing* we can do. Once I know you’re safe, and the tarsis is removed from me, I’ll try to return to you. Let that be enough.”

Niall knew they’d never see each other again, that his mother would find some way to stop it, but hoped the lie would make the parting easier. Yet looking at their faces, he suspected they saw the truth.

“Right. Clothes off,” Roo said. “I’d like two chocolate popsicles. White and dark.”

Chapter Twenty-Five

Roo trailed her fingers in the chocolate fountain, the silky liquid warming her fingers. She couldn't fathom how the three types of chocolate stayed separate, but guessed it was Niall's magic, along with the fact the temperature was perfect and this room was fantastic.

She had a plan of her own to put in place tomorrow as long as the queen listened. Roo would go back, drop dead, do whatever the bitch wanted as long as Taylor could stay with Niall. They could share a different woman, though not Stephanie of course. The thought of her guys with another made her heart ache, but Roo plastered a smile on her face. Niall was right. This night was special. It was all about now and not what was to come.

"Hey, chocolate girl!" Taylor called. "You want that or us?"

The two men stood naked in front of her in the silvery light, muscles rippling, cocks erect and a wave of heat swept over her, every cell instantly aroused. Roo swallowed the lump in her throat.

"Turn round and don't look until I tell you," Roo said.

They did as they were told and Roo stripped out of her blue dress, staring at their cute backsides and admiring the solid muscles of their thighs. Her mouth tightened as she looked at the mark running down Niall's body. How could his mother do that?

Roo used the dark chocolate to paint a bikini on her body. Not as easy as it sounded. She dripped everywhere.

"Oh damn," she said. "You might as well look. I'm not much of an artist."

They turned and laughed.

When Taylor reached for her, Roo pulled back. "Ah, no touching me. Not yet."

She trailed the fingers of one hand in the milk and the other in the white chocolate and wrapped them around their cocks, smearing the velvety liquid up and down. The guys groaned in unison. Three more coatings until Roo was satisfied. She twirled chocolate-covered index fingers around their nipples and sighed. "We're going to make a

mess."

Taylor laughed. "You've already made a mess. It's even in your hair."

"It doesn't matter," Niall said, his gaze fixed on her eyes. "It's easily fixed and there's a shower in the corner."

He pulled them to a lounging area, kicked cushions aside and tugged them down onto a padded mattress. In moments they were a tangled knot of sticky limbs as they laughed and licked and sucked wherever they could find chocolate. Roo ran her tongue along Niall's cock while Niall worked on Taylor's. Taylor buried his head between Roo's legs, and she groaned and moaned around the cock in her mouth, which in turn made Niall buck into her.

The sweet taste combined with the salty tang of precome sent Roo's head into a spin. Not just her head. She felt as though tornadoes swirled in her body, every part of her teased into excitement so that the slightest touch on her skin sent bolts of fiery current shooting along her veins. And when the guys pinned her on her back and tussled over who licked her where, she thought she was in heaven.

Taylor's tongue lapped the hollow of her throat while Niall sucked her nipple. Someone's finger was sliding over her clit. *Niall's?* Roo's fingers sank into their hair, twisting, turning, tugging. When Taylor's mouth drifted to her ear and then his tongue slid inside to trace the curves, Roo's body quivered with pleasure.

"You even have chocolate inside your ear," Taylor whispered.

"It's everywhere," Roo moaned.

Taylor laughed. "I'm not complaining."

Nor was Roo. Niall trailed a half-coated strawberry over her lips and then dragged it down her body and gently pressed it inside her. Roo whimpered.

Taylor's eyes darkened. "What a good idea."

Niall licked the chocolate path he'd made, pinned her legs apart, fluttered his tongue over her clit and then ate the strawberry.

"Ooooh," Roo wailed as she felt her body begin to tip over the edge.

Taylor tickled her nipple with another strawberry and Roo groaned. Torn between hanging on to stretch out the pleasure or letting go, the decision was taken from her as Niall sucked hard at her clit and she flipped like a switch. Taylor caught her cry of release as he pressed his mouth to hers. Roo wrapped her arms around him and

clung on as aftershocks rocked her body.

When awareness returned and she sensed them about to trade places, Roo shuffled down to lie between their hips and shoved at Niall to make him move up so she could lick from one cock to the other. Roo held their hot shafts tight together and ran her tongue as fast as she could over the velvety plum-shaped heads. Chocolate long gone, Roo's mouth filled with the taste of them. She glanced up to see the guys kissing, and smiled. Taylor rubbed Niall's cheek with his fingers and the gesture of tenderness tugged at Roo's heart. She pressed her thighs together to capture the rush of pleasure. All three of them were covered with smears of chocolate, and usually Roo hadn't imagined she'd like this sort of messy play, but obviously she hadn't fantasized with the right guy. *Guys.* They groaned into each other's mouths, sounds of excitement, lust and pleasure echoing around them as she licked and nibbled and lightly nipped their cocks.

Roo explored with her fingers as well as her mouth. She ran her tongue over the smooth, slick heads, traced the thick veins, laved the wrinkled skin of their balls, feeling it tighten under her caress. Roo caught both cocks in one hand and with her other massaged Niall's balls, his thighs tensing and then relaxing against her. She switched her attention to Taylor's and sucked gently at the heads as she squeezed their cocks.

"Ah fuck," Taylor gasped.

"Hold your cocks together," she said.

Once the guys had done as she asked, she kept her mouth moving over their crests and slid her sticky fingers to the sensitive area behind their balls. Roo rubbed gently, and with each wet slide drew closer to the puckered holes beyond. When Roo pressed against the entrances to their bodies, circling with her fingers, a low cry broke in Taylor's throat, echoed by one from Niall. When the tips of her fingers slipped into them, both men groaned loudly.

"Can't wait any longer," Taylor muttered. "It's going to be embarrassingly fast anyway. One hour instead of two."

Roo and Niall laughed. She pulled her fingers out and Niall pressed a wet towel into her hand. *Where did that come from?*

"Roo sandwich?" she asked.

Niall's green eyes glittered and he tugged her until he was pressed against her back.

"Condom," Taylor said.

"I'm on the Pill," Roo blurted. If this was the last time she'd do this, she wanted to feel Taylor as she'd felt Niall.

Roo could tell from the expression on Taylor's face that he wanted to do this unprotected, the flare of his nostrils, the widening of his eyes. Niall produced a string of condoms from nowhere, just as he had with the towel.

"In case," he said.

"Can we wash first?" Roo asked.

A second later, she squealed because all traces of chocolate on their bodies had gone.

"I can't wait," Niall whispered.

Taylor lay on his back and Niall pulled Roo round to position her with her knees either side of Taylor's hips while he remained at her back, his hands over her breasts.

"Jesus," Taylor gulped, and he wrapped his fingers around the base of his cock and squeezed hard as he pushed down on his balls. "You two look so beautiful."

Roo arched back to drop her head onto Niall's shoulder. He slid his fingers between her legs and pinched her nipple with his other hand. Niall kissed her neck then her throat, and as her body flooded with heat, Roo whimpered. Taylor reached up to catch her as Niall lowered her down and it was Niall's hand that guided Taylor's cock inside her. Roo sucked in a breath.

Niall pressed her down onto Taylor as Taylor lifted his hips to push into her. One long slow slide controlled by them both until Taylor was as deep as he could go.

"Fuck me," Taylor whispered.

Roo lifted her hips until he'd almost slipped out, and then sank down again.

Taylor let out a shaky breath as he stared into her eyes. "That feels so good. Too good. I'm not going to be able to hold off for long."

"Think unsexy thoughts," Roo said. "Think about emptying the dishwasher. Though I've never had a dishwasher."

Taylor laughed and she felt his cock jerk inside her. He pulled her down so she lay on his chest and then kissed her.

"Angel, the chance of thinking of anything unsexy is zero. I don't think I've ever been so primed." Taylor brushed her hair from her eyes.

Niall leaned over them both, kissed Taylor then Roo, and worked

his way down Roo's spine with an alternate lick, nibble and kiss. She gasped and wriggled.

Taylor clamped his hands around her hips. "No moving allowed. I'd just about conned my dick into thinking it was nice to lie still for a while."

Niall's tongue swept down the crease of her backside, his hands spreading her butt cheeks, and then there was oil everywhere, or some slippery substance. Roo melted into Taylor as Niall's hands squeezed and pressed and molded her butt cheeks. When his tongue fluttered against her anus, it was competing with the sensation of his slick hands stroking her sides, her back, her inner thighs.

Taylor jerked. "Bastard," he gasped.

Roo guessed Niall had licked him too and she giggled.

"No laughing," Taylor said through gritted teeth. "You're gripping my cock like a vise."

"I can't help it," Roo blurted. "You're big." There was a long pause before Taylor spoke. "You don't have to do this."

Roo gave a nervous smile. "Hey, you coped with his big dick. No one's going to call me a pussy."

"Very funny," Taylor said. "That might be my new name for you."

"I *am* here," Niall said.

Yes, Roo knew. She could feel the bell of his cock sliding up and down the seam of her butt, slipping in the oil or lube or whatever magic juice it was.

"I want you both. Like this," Roo whispered.

Taylor slid his hands onto her hip bones and held tight.

"I love you," Niall whispered and pressed his cock against her anus.

Roo inhaled, braced for the pain, and pressed her lips together to keep from crying out. Niall's breath washed her back as he panted and his fingers threaded Taylor's on her hips. She felt the thick head of Niall's cock pop through the tight barrier and her muscles burned and spasmed around it, already stretching to accept the invasion. Roo took another deep breath, spread her legs and bore down, imagining herself opening to him.

Niall groaned as he slid the rest of the way inside her, and for a moment, Roo couldn't breathe.

"Roo," Niall whispered. "Are you all right?"

"Don't move," she gasped.

"Too much?" Taylor asked.

"No, it just feels so good, so bad, so...perfect."

Niall stared into Taylor's eyes and guessed he saw a mirror image of his own desire. Roo was right. This was perfect. Whichever way round, they were meant to be together and he wasn't going to think about tomorrow and spoil this. Roo's muscles tightened around him, maybe around Taylor too, and they both smiled.

"Oh, so it's okay for you to move?" Niall asked.

"I'm not doing it on purpose," Roo wailed.

"Let us move, sweetheart. We'll make it more than perfect," Niall whispered.

He could feel Taylor's cock through the thin barrier in Roo's body.

"Okay," Roo said. "You can move now. But slow."

Niall shifted his hips back and then gently eased into her, his hands sliding to her breasts to support her weight. As he pulled back, Taylor pushed into her, their thrusts and withdrawals matched in speed and strength. Niall's breathing became ragged as he fought to keep control, the desire to pound hard roaring in his head. Ripples of tension ran through his body and pressure built.

"More," Roo whispered.

The word he'd wanted to hear and Niall increased his speed and began to drive more firmly into her wet heat. Taylor matched him, stroke for stroke. Niall felt Roo come. Her muscles clenching around his cock, she cried out, but neither he nor Taylor stopped. He could feel the caress of Taylor's cock, the brush as Niall withdrew and Taylor surged forward.

"Oh, oh, oh," Roo gasped.

Then their rhythm changed and they were both pushing into her at the same time. Niall felt his cock swell, tension coiling at the base. His balls were rock solid, drawn up tight to the bottom of his dick. *So close.* Roo clamped down around him again and there was no way to hold back. Niall felt Taylor come at the same time, saw pleasure-pain erupt on his face, and as lightning flashed from his brain to his groin, Niall's balls exploded. Hot, liquid ribbons of pleasure spurted from his cock, spasm after spasm until he wondered how much he had in him. Niall kept pumping, kept grinding until he'd emptied his balls, and then barely let a heartbeat pass before he pulled out of Roo and

flopped onto his back.

Niall kept his eyes shut. *Shit, I hurt her. Too much, too soon but I couldn't stop.* It might be the last time he touched them both and the pain of that seared his soul. Then he felt little kisses being landed all over his face and he opened his eyes to see Taylor and Roo looking down at him.

"You did it," Roo said.

"Did what?" Niall asked.

"Widespread damage to vegetation. Windows might have broken—luckily there aren't any. Mobile homes and poorly constructed sheds and barns could be damaged. Debris may be hurled about. Force twelve on the Beaufort scale. The earth definitely rocked."

Niall laughed and tucked her head under his chin as he smiled at Taylor.

"I love you," Taylor said. "Both of you."

Roo turned in Niall's arms.

"It's not the sex speaking, though you—" Taylor kissed Roo, "—were—" he kissed Niall, "—stupendous." Roo's turn again. "And sensational." A final kiss for Niall. Taylor gulped. "I've never had sex before without a condom. Thank you for trusting me."

"It *was* great," Roo said. "Only problem is I can't move. My legs have turned to jelly."

"A swim?" Niall asked.

"I'll drown," Roo wailed.

"Think we'd let you?" Taylor whispered.

"Shower first," Roo said.

Niall rolled to his feet and Taylor pushed himself upright. Roo lay sprawled on the mattress.

"I told you I couldn't move," she said.

Niall scooped her into his arms and carried her to the far corner of the room. The shower came on as they approached. He let Roo slide down until her toes touched the tile and then they supported her between them.

This hurts. It was impossible not to think of tomorrow, not to remember this was the last time they'd be together. As he and Taylor soaped Roo's body, Niall accepted this might be his last night for anything. His mother would waste no time pushing him into marriage with Stephanie. Christ, she'd probably want to supervise their

coupling. As soon as he was sure Taylor and Roo were safe on the other side, Niall would run. *Just like my father. And I'll die. And their memories of me will likely be severed at that moment.* And though Niall regretted staying behind when his father had gone, he knew his mother would have brought him and his brothers back. She was still taking her revenge on his father.

"Stop thinking." Roo wrapped her arms around his neck and kissed him.

She slid her tongue into his mouth and let it dance with his while her hands crept down to rub their cocks.

Taylor groaned. "I thought you were tired."

Roo lifted her mouth from Niall's. "I've got my second wind, though it's only two on the Beaufort scale. Light breeze."

"You're funny," Niall said.

"Is the pool warm?" Taylor asked.

Niall nodded.

"Yippee." Roo slipped from between them and ran toward the water.

"Make it cold," Taylor whispered.

Niall grinned.

They headed for the water and watched as Roo threw herself in. She came up spluttering. "Bastard, bastard, bastard."

When Roo finally fell asleep lying between them, Taylor thought his heart was going to break. He looked across the top of her head at Niall who stared back at him, and wondered if there was a way of killing the queen. Taylor sighed. Even if there was, he couldn't do it. And what basis was that for a future relationship with her son?

Taylor was torn between wanting to stay with Niall yet knowing he should leave with Roo. And then there was Stephanie. He'd hardly had the chance to talk to her. What could he say to their parents? Niall had promised he wouldn't marry her and Taylor suspected he'd be punished for that.

"Would you want to remember me?" Niall asked. "Think before you answer. You could forget all of this, knowing I'm here, knowing Stephanie is here."

"Christ," Taylor whispered.

"It would make me happy to know that you and Roo are content and not mourning me."

"Is there no other way?" Taylor asked. "We can't go to another part of your world and stay together?"

Niall touched the mark at his neck. "This will kill me."

"But your father has the tarsis all over his body."

"The speed with which it spreads is determined by my mother. She could kill me right now. Running is pointless."

Taylor swallowed hard. "So if you plan not to marry my sister, what *do* you plan to do?"

"Once the two of you are safe, I'll leave with my father."

And die together? Taylor didn't voice the thought. There had to be a way out of this.

Chapter Twenty-Six

Roo's fist was tightly clenched, except it wasn't her doing the clenching. Not that anyone else's hand was anywhere near, just that she couldn't uncurl her fingers. But she'd seen the marks on her palm the moment she'd woken and fear had galloped through her—was still galloping through her. The black twisting threads looked the same as those on Niall, so did that mean the queen was killing her too? A couple of times Roo had opened her mouth to tell the guys but something stopped her. Maybe the same something that kept her fingers in a fist.

Niall had produced a pale-blue floaty dress for her while he and Taylor wore cream linen pants and loose, collarless shirts. None of them wore shoes. They looked like they were about to start a new life and instead, this was the end. Roo kept swallowing, but the lump in her throat didn't shift.

"We should have run," Taylor muttered. "We should have at least tried."

"Hush." Niall put his finger over Taylor's lips. "There is no perfect solution here, but pissing off my mother is very unwise."

Under curled fingers, Roo rubbed at the marks with her thumb.

"I have something for both of you," Niall said.

He held out his hand and opened it. On his palm lay a silver heart. Niall touched it with his finger and it fell into three pieces. He took three chains from his pocket and threaded a section of heart onto each, then hung one round Roo's neck, one round Taylor's and one around his own.

Roo gulped.

"Don't be sad," Niall whispered.

Might as well tell her not to breathe.

"A last kiss." Niall bent his head to hers and pulled Taylor in too, so the three of them were kissing one to the other while Roo's living, beating heart threatened to shatter.

She didn't want to let them go, wanted to kiss forever, but Niall broke them apart.

"It's time."

They walked side by side in silence down the corridors, not touching now.

The queen sat on her throne, a sparkling crown on her head and an ugly sneer on her face. Niall's father stood to one side, and groups of courtiers gathered on the other, Oisin and Stephanie among them.

"You've had your night," the queen said. "I hope you used it well."

Roo stepped forward and made a deep curtsy. "Please, Your Majesty, may I ask you something?"

"Roo," Niall whispered.

The queen beckoned and Roo moved toward her, her namesake's words echoing in her head. *"Knowing what's right doesn't mean much unless you do what's right."*

Roo took a deep breath before she spoke. "I'm sure you wish Niall to be happy." Though Roo actually was sure of no such thing except for the fact that the queen might want it to look as though she cared. "I've thought of a way that could happen. Let Taylor stay here in Faeryland with him. He's no threat to Niall's marriage."

She heard the guys sigh behind her.

"You expect Niall to have a relationship with a brother and sister?"

Ouch. Niall had promised not to marry Stephanie, but the queen didn't know that.

"Of course not. I only know that without Taylor in his life, Niall will be devastated," Roo said. "He loves him so much. He went through a great deal to be with him."

"And what about you?" the queen asked.

Roo straightened her shoulders against the ripples of discomfort running through her. "Do what you like."

"Roo, no," Niall snapped and moved up behind her.

"What I like?" The queen laughed. "What if I'd *like* for you to be dead?"

Niall and Taylor both groaned. Taylor's fingers wrapped around

hers. Niall's hand settled on her shoulder.

Roo swallowed and then released a shaky breath. "Well, okay. If that's what you want, if you let Taylor stay."

"No," Niall and Taylor snapped together.

She kept her back resolutely toward them. "I don't want to die, but this whole mess can't end in a way that pleases everyone. Without Niall and Taylor, I'd be swamped with unhappiness. If I left with Taylor, how could we ever smile again knowing Niall suffered? If you send us back and wipe our memories, you leave Niall miserable. It seems to me you're punishing people for being in love and I don't understand why."

Endor smiled at Roo before he turned to the queen. "See what this mortal would do for those she loves? Is there not a lesson to be learned here?"

"You forfeited the right to speak here long ago," the queen snapped.

"I speak while I still can," Endor said. "Before your tarsis silences me forever."

He ripped open his shirt, and as Roo gasped, she heard exclamations of surprise and mutters of, "All this time?"and "He's had it so long?" and "Who gave consent?" from the faeries. Endor had the same mark as Niall, but it smothered his body.

Endor walked up to Roo, took her wrist and turned her hand. "Unclench your fingers, sweetpea."

Roo's fingers uncurled to expose her palm. Dark lines twisted and turned in an intricate pattern, one thorny strand creeping onto her wrist. Wow, it hadn't been so big earlier. Taylor stepped forward and put his hand out next to Roo's. His palm was covered with identical markings. Roo groaned.

The queen rose to her feet, shock evident on her pale face.

"Recognize your mark on these humans?" Endor asked.

She shook her head. "I didn't do that."

"Apart from the fact that permission from at least four members of the high court is needed for this spell, it's expressly forbidden to interfere with mortals in this way," Endor said.

"This is a trick," the queen whispered.

Roo could hear murmurings of shock and anger coming from the faeries, but wasn't sure if they were against Endor or the queen.

"I didn't do this," the queen barked, and the voices were silenced.

"It's your mark," Endor said. "Let it be checked if you dispute it."

Two faeries came forward and examined Roo's and Taylor's palms.

"It is the royal tarsis, Your Majesty," one said. "Only your blood can make it. Only your blood can remove it."

The queen seemed to shrivel, her face etched in distress.

"You and Niall have done this," she whispered.

Endor shook his head. "Those with the mark cannot create it on another. In any case, my blood could not make this."

Roo gasped as dark lines began to creep up her arm. She glanced at Taylor and pushed up his sleeve to see the same was happening to him. Roo sucked in a breath as pain stabbed her, needlelike pincers biting into her skin. She felt Taylor stiffen and they exchanged glances. *It hurts.* Roo panted. How had Niall coped with this all over his body? Taylor grunted and clasped his arm against his chest.

Stephanie cried out and Oisin silenced her with a finger.

Niall pulled Roo and Taylor close. "Mother, stop this," he pleaded.

Stephanie pulled away from Oisin. "Please, Your Majesty."

"Enough." Oisin stepped between Stephanie and his mother. "Mortals can't cope with the tarsis. It spreads too fast." He turned to the queen. "You said you'd let them go."

"This has nothing to do with me," she barked.

Roo could see several faeries casting worried glances at each other.

"Remove the tarsis from all three of them," Oisin said. "Niall is here, doing as he's bid. There is no longer a requirement for this punishment. He stays. They leave. And show compassion to our father."

The queen looked at him in shock. "I didn't do that to the mortals."

"Perform the retraction spell," Oisin said. "It will lift any tarsis you created. If you didn't make those on the mortals, what have you to fear?"

"This is a trick to make me remove Niall's tarsis," she spat, and turned to face Endor. "As I lift the mark from Niall, so will you lift their marks too."

Endor fixed his gaze on her. "I cannot create or remove the mark, but to prove I do not, let the court bind my magic."

Roo didn't have much idea what was going on, but she could tell

the queen was rattled, which had to be good.

"Do it," the queen ordered.

Endor stepped into a ring of faeries who all held hands. The air seemed to crackle and Roo felt as though her hair were standing on end.

"Secure," someone called.

The queen held up her hands in front of her, palms facing the three of them. Her eyes glazed and she whispered, "My blood, unwind what thou hast made."

Niall agreed with his mother on one thing. This was some sort of trick, but he couldn't figure it out. He'd been horrified when he'd seen the marks on Taylor and Roo. Neither had seemed shocked, so why hadn't they told him? The court confirmed the marks were royal, so why would his mother deny doing it?

What's my father up to?

With the tarsis gone, Niall could survive on the other side, build a life with Roo and Taylor, but all his mother had to do was repeat the spell and he was back where he started. *Ah, but she couldn't act without the court's permission and would they give it again?*

Perhaps his father was giving him the chance to run? Did the three of them have time to cross before his mother blighted him without consent of the court? The only certainty was the sensation of the mark lifting from Niall's body. He could feel it dissolving, his full strength and power returning. His muscles hummed, his body tingled with energy, and Niall felt better than he had for years. Strong again, though not strong enough to defeat his mother.

Niall stared down at his foot as the last dark lines slipped away. He turned to look at the hands of Roo and Taylor. The marks had gone and joy filled his heart.

Endor stepped out from the circle of faeries. "There's the proof. The tarsis was yours."

"It was not, but it little matters," his mother said, sounding confident again. "Niall is free of it sooner than he would have been and these *nothings* can leave."

The door opened and Niall gasped with surprise when his other two brothers walked in. He'd not seen Aedon or Daire for many years. Their mother staggered back to her throne and sat. *I'm not the only one who's shocked.* Her face had lost all color.

Aedon and Daire nodded to Niall, Oisin and their father, and then bowed to their mother.

"How delightful to see both of you," she said, clutching the sides of the throne so tightly her white knuckles looked as sharp as chiseled marble. "You'll be able to attend Niall's wedding tomorrow."

"Sadly, Mother, you will not," Oisin said.

The queen sprang to her feet. "How dare you!"

"You acted without the high court's permission in inflicting the tarsis on the mortals," Oisin said. "Your power is weakening, your mind deteriorating along with your abilities. The illegal spell you placed on Taylor didn't work. He's shown himself to be not only capable of loving Niall, but Roo as well. Your abuse of power has gone on long enough. You're not fit to rule. I claim the throne."

Niall's heart jumped to lodge in his mouth. His mother looked too horrified to speak and his father had a grim smile on his face. Aedon and Daire beckoned to Oisin and Niall. Niall stepped forward, away from Roo and Taylor, his pulse racing, and clasped Aedon's fingers. Oisin took Daire's and their father completed the circle.

This was beyond Niall's comprehension. He could do nothing more than offer his support. In a rush of heat, powerful magic shifted through him and he stiffened as if he'd been brushed by lightning. He felt as though some transfer was taking place, part of him, his brothers and father passing to Oisin. His mother gasped and Niall turned to see Taylor groaning on the floor and the queen dragging Roo toward the open window. Niall tried to pull free but his brothers held him firm.

Roo! He couldn't even speak her name, magic held him fast. Niall gulped in partial relief when Stephanie tugged Taylor to his feet, but Roo was still in danger. The circle broke open, but his father's grasp stopped him from racing for Roo.

"Wait," Endor whispered. "Look at your mother's arm."

The tarsis. Niall shuddered.

"What is this?" the queen shouted. "Stop it or I'll kill her. Finlay, Rubin, to my side."

Neither man moved and Niall saw the moment realization dawned on his mother that she'd lost the support she counted on. Yet while she held Roo, she held half of Niall's world.

"Oisin," his mother whispered his name. "My eldest, my favorite, how can you do this?"

Oisin shook his head. "Never your favorite. I'm your imperfect son,

the flawed son, the one pushed to the back, the one overlooked, the one you wish had never been born. Hard words to hear from your own mother. Born with one arm, my powers less well developed, I needed you more than the others and yet you loved me the least. I worked harder than my brothers, stayed by your side when I could have left, supported you even when I didn't agree with you because I still hoped somewhere inside you there was affection for me. Yesterday I finally saw the truth. Last night, the woman I love made me see what I had to do. Why would you want Niall to marry Stephanie when she loves me and I love her?"

"Stephanie," the queen called.

Taylor pulled his sister closer and Oisin stepped in front of the pair of them. "She's not yours to command."

"Help," Roo gasped. "Something's happening to me."

Roo was turning to stone, her skin fading to gray, her panicked breathing clearly audible.

Niall followed Roo's gaze down to her feet and groaned. "Mother, don't," he pleaded. "Please. I'll do whatever you want but don't hurt her."

"What's happening?" Taylor moved to his side.

"Stop this now or you kill your first grandchild," Endor said.

Taylor tensed. "What?"

Roo whimpered.

Niall couldn't look at either of them. He'd discovered the pregnancy last night and hoped that Roo and Taylor would think the baby was theirs, conceived after their return.

His mother laughed. "Inventive."

"I'm not lying," Endor said. "I felt the magic in the child yesterday when I held Roo in my arms. You can feel the child too if you try. If you have any love within you, don't hurt either of them."

Niall held his breath and released it with a gasp when the gray tone lifted from Roo's skin, though his mother still held her wrist in an iron grip. Niall edged closer, his head buzzing. *My baby. Our baby.*

"How dare you speak to me of love?" the queen snapped. "You, who never loved me. It was your fault Oisin was born defective. You were tainted by that mortal."

Endor elbowed Niall aside and walked toward her, but she held up her hand. "Keep back."

"What more can you do to me?" he asked. "I'm a shade away from death. Your tarsis has its fingers around my throat."

Her hand dropped.

"Jealousy destroys love. It smothers happiness and steals freedom," Endor said in a whisper. "Come to my home. Let Oisin rule."

"I am queen of this realm."

"You can be queen of my realm." He held out his hand.

"I—"

"You have no choice," he said at her ear. "Show the court your strength now in defeat."

It seemed a long time to Niall before his mother accepted the rout. Roo sagged as the queen released her hold and she collapsed into his and Taylor's arms.

Niall watched his mother straighten. She turned to look at the court and then faced Oisin. "Your Majesty. With permission, it seems there is a wedding to prepare for. Allow me to make arrangements."

Niall didn't trust her. He glanced at Oisin, hoping his brother wasn't taken in.

"No," Endor said. "Come with me now. We're not needed here."

Her shoulders fell. "I should gather my possessions."

"We'll come with you." Aeden beckoned to Daire.

The moment she left the room, the court bowed to Oisin, and Niall joined them, tugging Roo and Taylor into a show of respect. Congratulations rang out as courtiers bustled around his brother and Stephanie. Niall's heart felt so light he thought it might rise from his throat and float away.

"Is that it?" Roo whispered. "She's not going put us all to sleep for a hundred years and wrap the castle in impenetrable vines or turn this into an ice palace?"

"My great-grandma already tried the first two," Niall said.

Roo gaped at him.

Taylor kissed her but glared at Niall.

Niall felt a tug on his arm and turned to see his father smiling at him.

"How did you do that?" Niall asked.

Endor guided him to a quiet corner of the room. "Do what?"

"Put the tarsis on Roo and Taylor. She didn't, you couldn't and I

don't know how, so—" Niall sighed. "Ah Oisin."

"With help from Daire and Aeden," Endor said. "You think I've spent all these years watching this thing cover my body without trying to find an escape? I know it intimately yet can't remove it from myself. I needed to fool the court into believing your mother had put her blood mark on the mortals. Seems fitting that she's outed in a bloodless coup."

Niall laid his fingers over the tarsis on his father's hand. "Will she stop this?"

"She might when she realizes she'll be on her own if she doesn't."

"Now you have to live with her. You've sacrificed your happiness." A lump rose into Niall's throat.

"Happiness is always within reach. And I had my moment in the sun. Her name was Katy Elizabeth Sutton. A very beautiful mortal. Taylor's great-aunt. I was her imaginary playmate as you were to Taylor. But our love was never consummated."

Niall's jaw dropped.

"You think you're the first to find that tear between the worlds? The only difference is that I came from the west, you found it from the east. Katy died just before Oisin was born. I could have protected her from disease, but not a crumbling crag face. I crept to the house and heard the sobs of her parents, of her brother. Your mother was right that a mortal had my heart. If Katy hadn't died, perhaps life would have been very different. Love your mortals well, Niall. They're a precious gift."

"Niall?"

He turned at the sound of Taylor's voice and his fist caught Niall straight in the jaw and knocked him off his feet.

Taylor's heart pounded so hard he could hear it in his head along with two words. *Roo pregnant.* He threw himself on top of Niall and pressed his shoulders into the floor. He felt hands reach to pull him off but then let him go.

"You told her you couldn't get her pregnant."

"I didn't think I could," Niall said with a groan.

Roo yanked at Taylor's arm. "Get off him. I said I was on the Pill."

Taylor growled. "Your come so special it bypassed that?"

"I didn't do it on purpose." Niall pushed Taylor off and sat up.

Taylor sagged on the floor, shoulders down, chest heaving.

Oh damn. Niall pulled him into his arms and kept hold despite Taylor struggling to get free. "I didn't do it on purpose," Niall repeated.

"I'm going to kick you both in a minute," Roo snapped, and Endor laughed. "I've got Harry Potter growing inside me and you two are fighting?"

"I wanted—" Taylor pressed his lips together.

Roo pulled him to his feet. Niall stood at his side.

"There are things I wanted too," she said. "Like not to be told in public that I'm having a baby before I even knew myself. If the time came, I'd planned to buy four of those kits from the chemist and we could have watched them together, and we wouldn't have known whose baby it was until it changed its diaper itself."

Endor roared with laughter. Taylor bit his lip.

Roo squeezed Taylor's fingers. "This is something you couldn't both be first at. But you can be second at."

"It wasn't my—" Niall shut up when Roo glared at him, but he sent Taylor a desperate look.

Taylor got it. Niall hadn't been trying to get Roo pregnant. Taylor smiled at him. Maybe it was better this way, a done deal. And there was one thing Taylor could be first at.

He took Roo's hand in his. "Will you marry me?"

Roo exhaled with a smile. "Even though I'm apparently carrying another man's child?"

"Especially because of that," Taylor said. "And I was thinking..." He glanced at Niall and mouthed, "Ask her."

"After you've married Taylor on the other side, will you marry me here?" Niall asked.

"I get two rings, two dresses, two cakes?" Roo grinned.

Niall laughed.

"You get two of everything," Taylor whispered.

Roo took hold of their hands. "Then the answer is yes."

Epilogue

"OhmyGodohmyGodohmyGod," Roo wailed.

"Breathe," Niall urged.

"You try and breathe when you're fighting to give birth to a bowling ball."

"I'm counting how long the contractions are apart," Taylor said.

"Good for you," Roo said through gritted teeth.

"Anything you want?" Niall asked, clutching her hand.

"An epidural, gas and air?" Roo had already asked for those, several times despite being told they didn't exist on this side. Nor could magic be used to help her give birth. *What was the fucking point of—* "Yooowww," Roo wailed as her body tried to turn inside out.

"Breathe," Niall blurted.

"Pant," Taylor said.

The pain fell away again and Roo relaxed into the bed. The faery midwife had examined her, said she'd be ages yet and then buggered off. Niall and Taylor were making such a fuss that Roo wasn't surprised the woman had left.

She closed her eyes and thought back to her two weddings. How lucky was she? Niall had been Taylor's best man. Taylor had located her mother and sister who still lived in Greece and had asked Roo if she wanted to invite them. Damned if she did and damned if she didn't. Roo didn't want them to refuse and yet felt they had no right to come to her happy day, particularly in case they spoiled it. So she said no to asking them.

The pain came again and Roo groaned as she squeezed the guys' hands. Whose bright idea was it that giving birth had to hurt quite this much? It was a wonder anyone had sex with the risk of this to follow.

Taylor had been Niall's best man when they married on this side. Endor and Vanda had come back for the ceremony, minus the tarsis. Vanda looked different—younger somehow. Maybe it was the smile on her face.

Maybe the best thing of all was that Oisin had married Stephanie and taken her to see her parents at Sutton Hall. Taylor had asked them to come home, not told them why and then explained everything when they arrived. His mother had believed instantly, his father had taken longer but had cried when he realized his daughter still lived.

"Owwwwwww," Roo grunted. "You still timing these? Aren't they close enough yet?"

"You're doing great," Taylor said.

"How do you know? You're not a doctor," Roo snapped. "I want a doctor." The pain faded and she groaned. "Sorry. Can't help it."

Niall wiped her forehead with a wet towel. "Won't be long now."

Roo had lost count of how many times she'd heard that. She wanted to go home. Home was Sutton Hall, now owned by Taylor, and the three of them lived both there and in Faeryland. Taylor had passed on the private detective business, which had never had his heart, to Jonas, who'd insisted on being the baby's godfather.

The pain came again, gripping her body like a monstrous claw, and Roo clenched her teeth. *Please let this baby be all right.* She didn't care if it had magical powers or not so long as it was healthy. Maybe it was slow to come out because it had wings? *Shit. That's going to hurt.*

"Talk to me. Distract me," Roo said. "Oh no, it's okay. It's gone off. Ooh, that's better."

Taylor had set up an internet business called what-you-need.com to supply lists for every occasion—what you need for a wedding, a new baby, to move house, the perfect picnic, what to do in case of vampire attack. Roo had come up with that one. The list was endless, as Taylor liked to say. Advertisers loved it. All three of them worked for the company and they were already on their way to their first million.

"Here it comes again," Roo gasped. She sighed and then hiccupped. "It's going off. Arrgghh. No, I was wrong."

She heard someone telling her she could push, and when she did, the relief was so instant, Roo gulped back a sob. Two more pushes and Roo felt the baby slither out. *No, bad word, not slither but jump into the world.* Niall and Taylor were messing around at the business end, their eyes wide, faces wreathed in smiles.

"Oh my God," Taylor gasped. "You did it."

"Totally beautiful," Niall said with a sigh.

Not at the moment. Oh yes, they mean the baby. Damn.

"What is it?" Roo croaked.

Niall lifted the bundled-up newborn into the air to show her.

"Yes, I know it's a baby, but what is it?" Roo asked.

Taylor leaned down and kissed her. "A velociraptor."

"That isn't funny," Roo said with a moan.

"A girl," Niall said. "She looks just like you."

Roo could guess. Red-faced and bad-tempered.

"Beautiful," Niall and Taylor said in unison.

Yep, her guys holding their child. Roo thought she'd never seen such a beautiful sight.

About the Author

Barbara Elsborg lives in West Yorkshire in the north of England. She always wanted to be a spy, but having confessed to everyone without them even resorting to torture, she decided it was not for her. Vulcanology scorched her feet. A morbid fear of sharks put paid to marine biology. So instead, she spent several years successfully selling cyanide.

After dragging up two rotten, ungrateful children and frustrating her sexy, devoted, wonderful husband (who can now stop twisting her arm) she finally has time to conduct an affair with an electrifying plugged-in male, her laptop.

Her books feature quirky heroines and bad boys, and she hopes they are as much fun to read as they are to write.

Visit at www.barbaraelsborg.com or her blog, barbaraelsborg.blogspot.com.

Stockbroker meets stock breaker. But who's taming whom?

Cowboys Down

© 2012 Barbara Elsborg

London stockbroker Jasper Randolph flies to Jackson Hole with hopes as high as the Grand Tetons. Hope that the getaway will force him to let loose, get dirty, and overcome a deep-seated phobia about horseback riding.

He hadn't counted on an attraction to the dude ranch owner's son, a man with sun-tousled hair, eyes bluer than Wyoming skies...and a father who'd rather eat tofu than accept his only son's sexuality.

The moment Calum lays eyes on the uptight, buttoned-down Brit, he's lost. But with his own saddlebags full of emotional baggage, he knows he should be looking at anything but Jasper's spotless riding boots and tight-fitting jodhpurs. Trouble is, Jasper makes his heart buck like a wild horse trying to break free.

Despite the differences that set them oceans apart, they fall hard and fast. Trouble isn't far behind, and they're in for a rocky romantic ride. Especially since there's growing evidence that someone is willing to do anything—no matter how dangerous—to poison their love.

Warning: Mix one sun-bronzed cowboy with a yummy Brit who'd give Darcy in his wet shirt a run for his money. Mix gently. Try not to drool.

It's all about the story...

Romance

HORROR

www.samhainpublishing.com